To God—

For inviting me to be part of your story

For waterfalls of grace

For words with wings

Acclaim for *The Dandelion Field*

"*The Dandelion Field* is a lovely contemporary romance that's sure to warm your heart. Springer renders a down-on-her-luck heroine and an honorable hero that will have you rooting for love to conquer all. Small town secrets, resonating faith, and a poignant backstory make *The Dandelion Field* an inspiring tale of beautiful beginnings."

— Denise Hunter, bestselling author of *Dancing with Fireflies*

"In this charming novel, Kathryn Springer takes an honest look at life's trials through the lens of imperfection, fear, hope, and redemption. *The Dandelion Field* tackles the hard issues of the heart, then wraps it all up in faith and love. A truly enjoyable read. Don't miss it."

— Rachel Hauck, author of *The Wedding Dress* and *Once Upon A Prince*

"Kathryn Springer's *The Dandelion Field* captured me from the very first page and held my attention until the end. With heart-breaking grittiness and vivid poetic narrative, this story touched my heart and brought out every emotion I've ever felt about being a mother, a wife, and a woman. This is a story of unconditional love and radiant hope. And we all need those two things, right? Treat yourself to a book that will lift you up and make you want to hug your children and hold tight to God's love."

— Lenora Worth, author of *Bayou Sweetheart* and *Forced Alliance*

The Dandelion Field

Kathryn Springer

ZONDERVAN

The Dandelion Field

This title is also available as a Zondervan e-book. Visit www.zondervan.com.

This title is also available as a Zondervan audiobook. Visit www.zondervan.com.

Requests for information should be addressed to:

Zondervan, *Grand Rapids, Michigan 49546*

Springer, Kathryn.
The dandelion field / Kathryn Springer.
pages cm
ISBN 978-0-310-33963-2 (paperback)
1. Single mothers—Fiction. 2. Fire fighters—Fiction. I. Title.
PS3619.P76D36 2015
813'.6—dc23 2014030508

Interior design: Walter Petrie

Printed in the United States of America

14 15 16 17 18 19 20 / RRD / 20 19 18 17 16 15 14 13 12 11 10 9 8 7 6 5 4 3 2 1

Chapter 1

Okay, Ginevieve. What's bugging you?"

Besides being called Ginevieve?

Gin's back teeth snapped together so she wouldn't be tempted to say the words out loud. Even though a side dish of sarcasm accompanied every blue plate special Sue Granger served to her customers, Gin's boss didn't tolerate it from the hired help.

"Nothing." Gin knew she sounded like a surly twelve-year-old, but she couldn't help it. It had been *that* kind of morning.

"Right." The handle of a wooden spoon found a sensitive spot between Gin's shoulder blades and dug in like a cattle prod, herding her toward the back of the diner. "You got ten thumbs today, and none of them are working right."

"Sue—"

"*Sit.*"

Gin sat.

Sue maneuvered her barrel-shaped frame into the booth and shoved a plastic coffee carafe across the table.

"When you hired me, you said you weren't going to be my mother," Gin dared to remind her.

"If I remember correctly, I also told you not to jerk my chain." Sue's top lip peeled back, revealing a row of teeth stained a delicate shade of sepia from years of smoking filterless Camels.

Gin hadn't forgotten. And so far, out of a healthy respect for the woman who signed her weekly paychecks, she hadn't touched her chain either.

The day after her car died in Banister Falls, Gin had spotted a Help Wanted sign in the window of a diner two blocks off Main Street. The building, propped up between Eddie's Bar and an auto parts store, wore a shaggy coat of charcoal-gray paint. The tattered awning, pulled low over the windows like an old tweed cap, shielded its weathered face from the sun.

My Place. Some people might think the diner's name showed a complete lack of imagination. Or a surplus of arrogance. But the moment she'd met Sue Granger, Gin knew it wasn't either one. The hand-painted sign above the door was a victory banner. Through bits and pieces of kitchen gossip, she'd discovered that Sue had broken free from an alcohol addiction and an ex-husband who'd kicked her around instead of the dog.

Gin's own life hadn't exactly been the proverbial bed of roses, but compared to Sue's, she'd given up all whining rights. She wasn't about to claim them now.

"Really. I'm fine. But I better get back to work." Gin strove to keep her voice light. "My boss let a waitress go last week for slacking off."

"Was that the rumor?" Sue snorted. "I can deal with a person slacking off once in a while. It's stupid that gets you fired." She leaned forward, elbows on the table, hands steepled together. "Now. Tell Dr. Susie everything."

Gin couldn't. That's what was driving her crazy. She had no clue what was going on with her daughter.

Ordinarily she wasn't the kind of mother who overreacted. Besides that, she and Raine were close. They didn't keep secrets from each other. The girl left her journal lying around in plain sight. Read parts of it out loud, for goodness' sake.

Maybe she isn't happy here.

Guilt seeped in, adding another layer to the weight that had been pressing down on Gin since she'd left the house that morning.

Banister Falls, Wisconsin—population 8,112—wasn't exactly a hot spot of excitement for an eighteen-year-old girl. Or her thirty-six-year-old mother, if anyone was asking. But it was Raine's senior year, and *she* was the one who'd made Gin promise they would stay put until graduation. Even though the thought of staying in one place for more than a few months left Gin with what Raine liked to call the Turtleneck Sweater Syndrome.

Gin didn't like turtlenecks. They were uncomfortable. Tight. Like someone's hands were wrapped around her throat, cutting off her air.

And Gin needed to breathe.

"One. Two."

Gin's head snapped up and her gaze met Sue's, fascinated and terrified as to what would happen if her boss actually made it to three.

"Raine wasn't feeling good when I left for work," she blurted.

"So?"

"She said it was cramps."

Hormones. A girl's get-out-of-jail-free card.

"But you don't believe her."

"I should." Except Gin had seen the statistics on eating disorders in teenage girls. As she'd hovered outside the bathroom door, it sounded like Raine had been throwing up.

On the way to the diner, Gin had taken an inventory of the food she'd seen Raine eat over the past few days. Tuna melts for supper. A bagel with cream cheese for breakfast—the girl loved carbs—but Raine *had* turned down the slice of lemon meringue pie Gin brought home from work the night before.

Sue snapped her fingers under Gin's nose. "Hello. Still having a conversation here."

"I think she might be bulimic." There. She had said it out loud. But saying the word didn't make her feel better. Now Gin felt as if *she* were going to be sick.

"Bulimic, huh?" Sue fished a pack of Camels from the pocket of her stained apron and struck it against the side of the table in a blatant disregard for the grease-spattered No Smoking sign that divided the salt and pepper shakers.

Gin's fingers twitched. She'd quit years ago, but fear had the power to resurrect a small contingent of nostalgic, nicotine-loving cells. "Raine's always been thin, but she's never obsessed about her weight the way some girls do." She suddenly remembered that Raine hadn't asked for lunch money the day before.

"Morning sickness?"

The question slammed into Gin. Her entire body jerked from the impact. *"Sue!"*

The older woman didn't flinch. "Just a question. My first-grade teacher said there was no such thing as a stupid one."

"Except *that* one." No matter that she was speaking to her boss, Gin wasn't in the mood to be polite. "Raine wouldn't . . . She isn't even dating anyone, for Pete's sake. She has a . . . a friend. They worked together on a school project a few months ago, but that's it."

Sue opened her mouth. Closed it again.

"What?"

"None of my business."

Now it was none of her business? Gin's eyes narrowed. "Do you know something?"

"Yeah." Sue's voice was as dry as an AA meeting. "Teenage girls who claim that a guy is just a friend."

"This one is. Trust me. He's not the type that would get Raine's attention." Or hold it. Gin had met Cody Bennett once, and he could be the poster child for small-town Middle America. Clean-cut, upright, and green as a cornstalk.

"Whatever you say."

"Raine's a great kid," Gin persisted. "She has goals. Dreams."

Sue pursed her lips and blew a plume of gray smoke into the air. Shrugged. "So did we."

CHAPTER 2

Four missed calls.

Dan Moretti frowned as he scrolled through the list of phone numbers. All from Evie Bennett and all within the past few hours.

He was about to press number one on speed dial when Hopper Jones, the youngest member of the crew, poked his head around the partition that separated Dan's sleeping quarters from the rest.

"Evie called while you were gone. Twice." Hopper's teasing smile, all but hidden under the tangle of rusty barbed wire he insisted on calling a mustache, warned Dan that the news had already circulated through the fire station.

Adrenaline spiked, heating the blood that pulsed through Dan's veins as he downloaded the information. "Did she say why?"

"That's a negative, Captain. I told her you were at an all-day training session." The smile slipped a notch. "Do you think everything is okay?"

"I'll give her a call." Dan dodged the question. "I'm heading home now anyway." He peeled off his T-shirt and waited for his friend to leave before he returned Evie's call.

She answered on the first ring. "Danny."

The slight hitch in Evie's voice was as unusual as a call to the fire station when he was on duty. "What's wrong?"

"Cody." Evie said the one name that had the power to send Dan's heart crashing into his rib cage. "The vice principal called and said he left the school grounds without permission right after lunch. She wanted to know if I knew about it. If he had an appointment or got sick and forgot to check in with the nurse."

Her words funneled out in a single breath, and Dan tried to sort through them as he propped his shoulder against the locker and yanked off a boot. "Cody went home sick?"

"That's what I'm trying to tell you. I don't know because he hasn't come home at all." Evie's voice thinned, her usual calm stripped away, leaving the bare wires of her deepest fears exposed. "He missed supper and he's not answering his cell phone. I called Sam and Ben, but they didn't even know Cody had left early."

"How did he get to school this morning?"

"He walked . . . but when I got home, the Jeep was gone. He must have come back for it."

"I'll take a drive through town." Dan reached for his coat as adrenaline burned away the fatigue from a day spent teaching an incident command seminar at the local technical college. "Maybe he drove out to the ridge."

"It's February! The campground is closed for the season. Why would he go there?"

"It's his thinking place."

"But Cody always answers his phone . . ."

Unless.

The unspoken word pulsed in the silence between them.

Dan dragged in a breath. "Cell phone batteries die. And reception is spotty out there, so he might not know you've been trying to reach him. I'm sure he'll be walking through the door any minute."

"Okay." Evie didn't sound too sure.

Dan could picture her standing in front of the window in the living room, spinning her gold wedding band round and round on her finger. A common default whenever she was upset—as if touching a part of Max, however small, would give her courage.

Dan didn't hold it against her. The shield from his best friend's helmet, charred and misshapen from the heat of the flames, was pinned to the visor of his truck. He and Evie both had their touchstones. Their ways of keeping Max's memory alive.

He tried to think of something that would make her smile. "Did you check J. C. Penney?"

Silence followed the question, and Dan hoped she didn't think he was making light of the situation. She'd called him in for reinforcements that time too. Dan had left work and helped her search every aisle of the store. They'd finally found the missing six-year-old in a far corner of the footwear department, lining up a pocketful of plastic action figures on a bunker made from discarded shoe boxes.

"He's eighteen. He's supposed to know better."

Dan heard the shimmer of a smile in her voice and released the breath he'd been holding. "He's still a guy. Sometimes we forget. I'll call you soon—and don't worry."

"I won't."

They both knew she was lying.

Chapter 3

On the way home from work, Gin decided that she and Raine needed to have a little talk. She'd never been the kind of person who chose to let things simmer on the back burner.

She'd forgotten her daughter wasn't that kind of person either. Raine was perched on the edge of the couch, waiting, when Gin walked into the trailer.

Five minutes later, the piece of paper listing the warning signs of an eating disorder had been compressed to a tiny ball in Gin's hand.

"Say something," Raine whispered. "Please."

In her daughter's plea, Gin heard the echo of a conversation that had taken place when she was Raine's age.

"Say something."

"I can't believe you were that stupid."

"Mom—"

"If you keep it, you're on your own. Don't expect any help from me."

"Why would I start now?"

The words had hung in the room like an acrid cloud of smoke. Burning Gin's eyes. Clogging her lungs.

"You want to mess up your life, fine. Go ahead. But your mistake isn't going to mess up mine."

"I'm sorry." Raine buried her face in the lumpy, star-shaped pillow she'd made in freshman home economics, her shoulders heaving as she started to cry.

Sorry. Sorry. Sorry.

The word ricocheted through Gin's head and pulled her away from the shadowy ledge that overlooked her past. The image of her mother's face faded until she and Raine were the only ones in the room.

Gin focused on a stain on the cushion, afraid that if she opened her mouth she would say too much. Or not enough.

"Are you sure?" she finally whispered.

The pillow dropped an inch. A pair of brown eyes, rimmed in red and swollen with fear, blinked up at her.

"I took a test."

Raine began to rock from side to side, something Gin hadn't seen her do since she was a toddler. But the low, keening moan that accompanied it was new and drowned out everything else in Gin's head. The questions. The accusations. The lectures.

The denial.

Gin yanked Raine into her arms and held on tight. Smoothed away the baby-soft wisps of golden hair stuck to her daughter's flushed cheek. Absorbed another round of shock waves as Raine curled against her.

Through a glaze of tears, Gin stared at the coffee table, somehow knowing that ten, thirty, *fifty* years from now she would remember every single item spread out on its scarred surface. An English text and a book of poetry with its ruffled hedge of pink Post-it Notes that marked Raine's favorites. The flecks of silver glitter suspended in a bottle of turquoise nail polish. A journal, covered with stickers from the places they'd lived over the years.

A dozen applications from colleges across the country.

"Mom?"

Gin heard the fear in Raine's ragged whisper and knew she would remember this moment too. She pulled Raine closer. So close she could feel the rapid beat of her daughter's heart.

Your baby's heart is already beating, Miss Lightly. Listen.

"I love you, sweetheart," Gin whispered. "And nothing, *nothing*, is ever going to change that. Whatever you decide, I'm right here with you."

The words she'd wished *her* mother had said.

CHAPTER 4

Dan hung up the phone, his brain already beginning to separate the facts from fear.

It *was* unusual for Cody to skip school, no doubt about it. The kid defied every stereotype about teenage rebellion. Cody had made it to his senior year of high school without taking so much as a step out of line. No back talk. No broken curfews. If the boy had, on occasion, walked too close to the edge, it was only to rescue someone in danger of falling.

Guilt tweaked Dan's conscience. Maybe he should have told Evie where he thought Cody might be—who he might be with—but at this point it was a only a hunch that would have fueled her concern, not extinguished it.

He shrugged on his coat and debated whether he should check in with the rest of the crew before he left. As it turned out, it wasn't necessary. Three heads swiveled in Dan's direction the moment he stepped into the lounge.

"Everything okay with Evie?" Sid asked.

Dan scowled at Hopper, who pretended not to notice while he stirred a kettle of chili on the stove. Two wooden tables separated the kitchen from the recliners that faced the television, but they didn't stop the flow of information.

"She's fine."

Every firefighter at Second Street Station had a vested interest in the Bennetts. Max was no longer with them—hadn't been for a long time—but Evie and her son would always be part of the fire department's extended family.

"I'll see you tomorrow."

"Saw Cody's Jeep about two o'clock." Jerry tried to talk around the piece of cornbread he'd stowed in one cheek. "Looked like he was heading out of town, toward the park."

Dan resisted the urge to ask if Cody had been alone in the vehicle. "Thanks for the update. I'll see you tomorrow."

A chorus of "Night, Cap'n" followed Dan down the hall.

Snow glazed the parking lot, and his foot slipped off the step, leaving a skid mark on the asphalt. Dan began to line up his thoughts one at a time, before panic squeezed in and overrode his internal circuit board.

The chances Cody had been in a car accident were slim. He was a good driver—Dan had made sure of it. He'd been the one sitting in the passenger seat when Cody was learning how to parallel park and make a Y-turn. The one who'd paced the floor of the DMV during Cody's road test.

He was the one who was going to lecture the kid for not coming home on time and making Evie worry.

Making *him* worry.

A car glided past and came to a stop a few yards from Dan's truck. The door opened, and a woman whose scarlet hair matched her wool coat emerged from the leather cocoon of her Cadillac like an exotic butterfly.

"Yoo-hoo! Daniel!" Gertrude Fielding lifted the tail of her cashmere scarf and waved it like a flag. "I stopped at the church to pick up the donation box for the food pantry today and heard Evie talking to the vice principal. Something about Cody getting sick?"

Dan had always suspected that Mrs. Fielding was more interested in picking up gossip than donations, but her heart was in the right place.

"I'm sure Cody is fine." Dan drummed his fingers against the doorframe. "I'm heading over to their house now."

Gertrude Fielding's smile, the one that had won her the title of Miss Wisconsin back when the votes were still being tallied by hand, flashed a smile that lit up the space between them. "You take such good care of them, Danny. Evie is blessed to have a friend like you."

Yep, that's what he was. A friend.

Thanks for reminding me, Gert.

"She sure is." Retired pageant winners weren't the only ones who could manufacture a smile on cue.

Dan turned the key in the ignition and bowed his head as the engine rumbled to life.

Okay, God, you know where Cody is. Lead the way.

He cruised down Main Street and cut through the parking lot behind the bowling alley, a shortcut that led to the park.

At the four-way stop on Crescent Street, a silver Jeep rolled through the intersection. Cody sat behind the wheel.

Dan made a U-turn and followed him all the way to Rosewood Court. In a former life, the subdivision had been twenty acres of cornfields. Tired of being at the mercy of the weather, the farmer who'd owned the land divided it into neat little squares and sold them off piece by piece, like brownies at a bake sale, and retired to Sarasota.

Max Bennett had bought one of the first lots and built a two-story house for Evie with an inheritance he'd received from his grandmother. Max had planted the row of shrubs against the foundation, and Dan kept them trimmed so Evie's lawn remained level with the one next door.

Cody was still in the Jeep when Dan pulled in behind him. The headlights of his truck illuminated the interior. He could make out the cardboard air freshener dangling from the rearview mirror and the dejected slump of the boy's shoulders.

Dan hopped out of the truck and rapped on the window.

Cody's head snapped up, and the raw pain in his blue eyes—Evie's eyes—severed the cable holding Dan's heart in place and sent it plummeting to his feet.

Neither of them said a word as they trudged side by side up the shoveled path to the front door. It opened before Dan's hand closed around the knob, and Evie stood in the doorway.

"Cody?" Her gaze swept over her son from the top of his head to his hiking boots.

It was the same maternal triage Dan's mother had performed on him and his five siblings countless times while they were growing up. A single look that instantly assessed the physical, emotional, and spiritual health of her children.

Evie must not have liked what she saw, because her eyes darkened. She linked her arm through Cody's and tugged him into the foyer. Into the light. "What happened?"

"Mom." The word unfurled with Cody's sigh. "I thought you'd be asleep."

"Asleep?" Evie repeated. "I've been worried sick. Mrs. Wendt called me at the church this afternoon and said you left school grounds without permission. You know that means an automatic detention."

Cody's gaze dropped to the floor. "I skipped PE and a study hall. Big deal."

Evie looked at Dan and he stepped between them, responding to the SOS flashing in her eyes.

"It is kind of a big deal, Cody. What was your mother supposed to think? You knew she would worry when you didn't come home."

Cody's shoulders twisted in a shrug.

"I tried to call you half a dozen times."

Dan could tell Evie was struggling to keep her voice even, but it cracked in the center.

"Why didn't you answer your phone? Where have you been?"

"With Raine."

"Raine." Evie echoed the name like she'd just tasted something sour.

Dan put his hand on her arm and gave it a squeeze, more as a warning than an offer of support. He knew how Evie felt about the girl.

Raine Lightly had moved to Banister Falls at the beginning of the school year and somehow ended up as Cody's partner for a class project. He and Evie had been raking leaves when the girl showed up at the house one Saturday morning. One look at Evie's face and Dan knew she would be praying that Raine and Cody's relationship ended with the assignment.

Cody had a penchant for collecting strays, and Raine Lightly was the human equivalent of a golden retriever pup, from her mane of honey-blond hair to a pair of enormous, liquid brown eyes. She was polite. Quiet. She also had a dove tattooed in the hollow between her shoulder blades, framed between the lace straps of a piece of clothing that even Dan could tell was more suited to a slumber party than a study session.

He wasn't surprised when he'd caught a glimpse of Raine at some of the youth events at Hope Community Church over the next few weeks. Cody's strong faith had earned the respect rather than the ridicule of his fellow classmates over the years, because he reached out to kids regardless of where they happened to be ranked in the high school hierarchy.

What had surprised Dan was Evie's attitude toward the girl. As the full-time Director of Women's Ministries at Hope Community, Evie had a reputation for offering encouragement and compassion to the women who sought her counsel. But even now, Dan could see it took a supreme effort on her part not to let her frustration show.

"Why were you with Raine?" she asked.

Cody walked away, shedding his coat and Evie's question. "She needed to talk."

Evie motioned to Dan as she followed her son into the living room. "And it was so important she couldn't wait until after school? So important you couldn't answer your phone?"

Cody stopped so abruptly that Evie almost ran into him.

"Yes." He hurled the word at her, but Evie didn't back down.

"Tell me what's going on, Cody. Please."

Cody pushed his fingers through his hair, a gesture so reminiscent of Max that Dan suddenly felt a burning sensation behind his eyes.

"Raine . . . she's pregnant."

Evie pulled in a startled breath. "I'm so sorry, Cody. I know you've tried to be a friend to her the past few months, but you have to understand that people make their own choices and sometimes . . . they aren't always good ones."

The subtle undercurrent of disapproval in her voice telegraphed that this was exactly the kind of choice she thought someone like Raine would make.

Cody's throat convulsed. "Raine isn't just a friend. We've been . . . going out."

"Going out." Evie's eyebrows dipped together. "You mean dating?"

Cody's chin jerked in a nod.

"And she went out with someone else?" Evie glanced at Dan. A see-I-was-right-about-her glance. "I know that must hurt, but isn't it better that you found out now what kind of girl Raine is—"

"Mom. *Stop.*" Cody cut her off midsentence. "Just stop. You aren't listening to me. Raine is *pregnant.*"

"I heard you, sweetheart. But Raine . . . she isn't your responsibility."

Evie tried to pull Cody in for a hug, but he stepped away, just beyond her reach.

Dan saw the truth glittering in Cody's eyes before it took the shape of words and—*God give us strength*—he knew what was coming next.

"The baby is mine, Mom," he whispered. "It's mine."

Chapter 5

Raine had switched schools often enough to know what was coming when Miss Peterman, the senior English teacher, walked over and stood in front of her desk on the first day of class last September.

Pleasedon'tpleasedon'tpleasedon't.

"Before we get started, I'd like to take a moment to welcome a new student." Miss Peterman smiled down at her, and Raine's toes curled inside her shoes.

The buzz of conversation died as she braced herself for fifteen seconds of torture.

You can do this.

Short but painful. Kind of like getting her eyebrows waxed.

The teacher fluttered her hands. "Would you like to introduce yourself to the class?"

What Raine would *like* was a normal name. But, seeing as how she hadn't had a choice in the matter, she was forced to give hers.

"Raine Lightly."

Laughter rippled around the room.

Yup. She'd known that would happen too.

Raine didn't hold it against her classmates. It was Joey Meyer's fault that her name sounded like it belonged to a girl wearing a gauze caftan and a crown of daisies around her head. Her bio-dad's "commitment issues" had surfaced when Raine's mom presented him with her first baby picture—a grainy black-and-white from the ultrasound technician. Joey took off a few days later, taking her mom's tip jar and his normal last name with him. Raine was forced to go through life with Ginevieve's maiden name stuck to her like a *Make Love, Not War* sticker on the bumper of a VW van.

She pretended she didn't hear the giggles from the Emilys and Jessicas and Rachels. Pretended she didn't notice the speculative glances from the boys who hoped her name meant she'd been raised in some kind of commune that believed in free love.

Pretended she was invisible.

And that's when she happened to make eye contact with a boy in the next row. No smirks. No snickers. He'd tipped his head sideways and . . . nodded. The way a person did when something made sense. It was the first time in eighteen years that Raine actually *liked* her name.

She looked away, fixed her eyes on the whiteboard, and waited for the attention directed at her to subside. Halfway through class, Raine discovered that if she shifted a little to the left she scored a perfect view of the boy's profile. He was cute too. Tall enough that his knees bumped against the bottom of the desk, but not gangly. Strands of sandy-blond hair dipped over one eye whenever he looked down at the textbook.

When the bell rang, instead of walking out the door, the boy veered off course and headed to the back of the classroom. Three social outcasts—her first day and Raine could pick them out of a crowd—had melted into a corner, trying to avoid the verbal shoves as the rest of the kids funneled into the hall. She watched the trio fall into line behind the boy like a flock of baby ducklings as he led them out the door.

Flying under the radar was a survival skill she had honed herself over the years, but she still felt sorry for the other kids with targets on their backs.

By the end of the day Raine had discovered two things. The boy's name was Cody Bennett—and he was way more intriguing than any of the electives Banister Falls High School offered.

Raine decided to take up a new hobby. Some people watched birds. She was going to watch this boy who moved through the halls, talking to everyone like a goodwill ambassador in a flannel shirt and faded Levi's. Maybe she wouldn't get a grade, but it was a better use of her time than, say, trying out for the cheerleading squad. Or making friends.

Raine knew her limitations.

The first thing she did was try to figure out which clique Cody belonged to. Between classes she would see him laughing with the jocks, and yet he didn't play sports. He talked to the skaters and studied with the nerds. Raine finally came to the conclusion that Cody wasn't *in* one.

Finally she caught a break in PE class when she eavesdropped on a conversation in the locker room. Two girls were talking about bringing banana nut muffins to "Cody's group" on Friday morning. It made sense. Raine had heard a rumor that he was neck and neck with Brian Engles for valedictorian.

On Friday morning, Raine grabbed a bagel and a coffee-to-go from the BP and made it to Room 212 by quarter after seven.

Laughter filtered through the crack underneath the door and Raine paused to read a handmade sign taped to the wall.

Parables of Jesus

Come on in!

Raine kept walking.

Chapter 6

Dan had sentenced himself to a five-mile run after leaving Evie's place the night before, lobbing one-word prayers at the star-studded sky like grenades.

Please. Help. Why?

By the time he looped back to his house and aimed toward the light flickering in the kitchen window, the disappointment and anger that fueled his energy had burned away, leaving behind a smoldering, gaping hole.

A place Dan remembered all too well.

Max's death had sent him hurtling into that deep pit twelve years ago. Dan had held on tight to God's hand as he clawed his way back to the surface, only to discover things didn't look the same. Like an out-of-control brush fire, grief had forever changed the landscape of his soul.

Cody's confession pressed hard against the scar tissue that had formed over the previous wound, making it difficult for Dan to take a deep breath and exhale the pain.

Knowing what Evie and Cody were going through, sleep felt like an indulgence, so Dan brewed a pot of coffee and watched the sun rise instead. Fortunately Will, the younger brother who'd claimed an empty bedroom in Dan's house after his last tour in Iraq, was pulling a double shift at the factory. Dan wasn't ready to face questions he didn't know how to answer.

Ten minutes after he let the dispatcher know he was taking a personal day, the phone rang.

"I just got a call from the school office." Evie didn't waste time on pleasantries.

"Cody didn't show up for class?" Dan kept the phone pressed against one ear while he riffled through the dresser drawer and extracted a clean pair of jeans.

"No. Do you think he's with . . . her?" Evie asked.

That's where I would be.

Dan literally had to bite his tongue to hold the words inside. "Probably," he said instead. "I'm sure Raine is pretty upset too."

"I can't believe this is happening. Cody barely said a word before he left the house this morning." Fear and frustration clashed in Evie's voice, striking a note Dan had never heard before. Making him wonder what had preceded Cody's decision to cut class again.

It was clear that Evie didn't want to see Cody and Raine as a single equation—an equation that added up to a sum of three.

A baby.

Dan closed his eyes and saw Cody racing around the yard in denim overalls and a bright red T-shirt, dousing shrubs with the garden hose. Pretending to be a firefighter.

Praying for wisdom, Dan exercised the same caution he would when the crew responded to a call and he wasn't sure what he would find on the other side of the smoking door.

"Maybe Cody will talk if you include Raine in the discussion."

Evie's silence told Dan what she thought of the idea.

Finally a soft, "You're right. All of us should sit down and talk about this."

That's my girl, Dan said.

But not out loud.

When it came to Evie, there were always two conversations going on. The words that came out of his mouth and the ones that rolled around in his head. Dan continued to hope that the two would eventually merge, but until then he remained stuck in a holding pattern that had become as familiar as the route he drove to the fire station.

"If you want me to, I'll track down Cody and set something up," Dan offered. "What time works for you?"

Evie acquiesced with a sigh. "Are you free after your shift?"

"I took the day off." On standby, just in case another fire started in the Bennett family.

"So did I. It doesn't matter what time. I'll be here."

Dan wished he could tell Evie that everything would be okay, but at the moment he had no idea what okay looked like.

"I'll find him." Dan repeated the promise he'd made the night before.

"Thanks, Danny."

Dan didn't want Evie's gratitude. He'd been a huge part of Cody's life since the boy was six years old, teaching him how to ride a bike, shoot hoops, and change a flat tire. Dan had spent more time with Evie and Cody Bennett than anyone else.

Even Max.

Dan shoved the thought aside, feeling like a traitor.

On his way to the garage he punched in Cody's number, but the call went right to voicemail. Fine. Dan moved to Plan B and called the police department. He knew Raine was in the system because Cody had mentioned helping her fill out a report after her bike was stolen.

"Mornin', Beautiful. I need the address for Miss Raine Lightly."

"Danny Moretti!" Trish McCarthy's gum snapped in his ear. "You know I can't give out that information."

"Sure you can." Dan wasn't above flirting when the situation called for it. The greater good and all that. "The police and fire department are two sides of the same coin, right? Protect and serve?"

"Serving up a load of bologna is more like it," Trish muttered. "Why do you want her address? Are you going to ask her out?"

"No. Raine Lightly happens to be one of Cody's friends."

"Well, why didn't you say so in the first place? I'll take a look and see what I can find."

Dan realized he should have played that card first. Everyone in the public service sector had a soft spot for Max Bennett's son.

"Here we go. Ginevieve and Raine Lightly. Looks like they live on the Avenue . . . number 416."

The Avenue. Terrific.

"Thanks, Trish. I owe you." As soon as the words were out, Dan mentally smacked himself in the forehead.

"Then how about dinner?" she purred. "I'm free this weekend."

"Come to church with me on Sunday. Mom is making lasagna afterward."

They both knew Trish hadn't set foot in church since she'd played Mary in the junior high Christmas program. On the journey up the aisle to Bethlehem, she'd stepped on the back of Joseph's robe and left him standing in front of the congregation wearing nothing but a Superman T-shirt and yellow boxers.

"Don't think I won't call your bluff, Dan Moretti," Trish huffed. "Everyone knows your mom is the best cook in the county."

"I'm not bluffing. I'll save you a seat." Right next to his brother Will, single and always looking. "And Trish? Thanks."

He hung up the phone, his grin fading as he contemplated his next mission. He could call Cody again and extend an invitation to Raine and her family over the phone, but it wouldn't hurt to do a little recon. Depending on what he discovered, he could prepare Evie before she met the girl's parents.

The snow-packed culvert bucked as Dan drove over it and turned onto Fifth Avenue. The irony of the name wasn't lost on anyone in Banister Falls. A creek that lay stagnant most of the year separated a quiet neighborhood of modest homes from an old salvage yard that had been converted into a mobile home park long before Dan was born.

The wind streaked ahead of his pickup, rattling the rusty skeletons of abandoned swing sets and peeking underneath loose shingles. Dan was familiar with the general layout of the place. A winter didn't go by without one of the residents forgetting to shut off a space heater or failing to clean their furnace, and the fire department would get a call. Before the trucks arrived, people stacked up like cordwood to watch the show. Some of the more seasoned spectators pulled out their lawn chairs.

Dan veered to the right and tried to make out the numbers on the mailboxes.

416 on the Avenue. The address could have led Dan to the kind of upscale boutique his twin sisters loved, not a double-wide the color of dried mustard. Two faded stencils flanked the windows where shutters had once hung, and a piece of the gutter jutted from the roof like an arm with a compound fracture.

Dan hopped out of the cab and followed the shoveled path leading up to the door. He put one boot on the metal step and the whole thing tilted.

Two ragged strips of silver duct tape formed an X over the doorbell, the words *Don't Bother* scrawled across the center in Sharpie marker.

Someone had a sense of humor.

The door swung open, catching Dan mid-smile.

The polite greeting he'd been rehearsing died in his throat, his vocal cords paralyzed by a pair of eyes the translucent green of a luna moth. The woman standing in the doorway didn't look old enough to be the mother of a high school senior, but then again, neither did Evie.

A man's flannel shirt grazed the knees of her faded jeans but didn't detract from mile-long legs and a willowy figure. Hair the color and sheen of Grandma Moretti's mahogany table spilled over slender shoulders, framing a face that couldn't be labeled as pretty. Stunning would have been more accurate.

Dan tracked a straight line from the cinnamon-colored freckle stamped on the woman's left cheekbone to a tiny silver scar that traced the curve of her lower lip.

"Can I help you?"

Dan realized he was staring when the silver-tipped toe of a cowboy boot began to tap out a warning beat on the scuffed linoleum.

"I'm not sure I have the right address," he finally said.

The woman parked her hands on her hips. "Tell me who you're looking for and I'll tell you where to go."

Dan didn't doubt that for a minute.

"I'm—" *Come on, you remember.* "Dan Moretti. Cody Bennett is a friend of mine. Is he here?"

"For now." Sparks shot from those light green eyes.

Maybe he should have worn his turnout gear.

"You're Raine's mom?" Dan rubbed his palms together, still chilled from the steering wheel, before he extended one.

"Gin Lightly." She stared down at his hand, and just when Dan thought she was going to ignore it, her palm grazed his. "You may as well come in."

CHAPTER 7

Gin wished she could rewind the last six months to August fifteenth.

If she were given a do-over, she wouldn't ditch the main highway and take the scenic route that meandered from small town to small town like a game of connect the dots. Wouldn't dismiss the blinking red light on the dashboard of Jasmine, her ancient but faithful Impala, warning them of impending doom. Wouldn't let Raine sweet-talk her into staying in Banister Falls until she received her diploma.

Because Gin knew if she had done one thing differently—*just one little thing*—she and Raine would be living somewhere in the Twin Cities, choosing from a list of colleges instead of OB/GYNs.

Cody Bennett, the kid who'd just changed her daughter's future, would be sitting at a desk in his first-hour class, not in her living room. He had appeared on their doorstep at six a.m., red-eyed and rumpled. Gin had been tempted to slam the door in his face. Unfortunately, Cody knew the right password. *Please.*

He'd gone into the bathroom—a room Gin had been banished from earlier—and she could hear the low murmur of a one-sided conversation. Maybe Raine would have contributed if she hadn't been throwing up.

They'd emerged a little while later, Raine as white as the frost etched on the window and leaning on Cody for strength.

Gin made them pancakes because it was better than the alternative—throwing the cast-iron skillet through the window.

And now this Dan Moretti had invaded her territory. Cody's friend. Given the fact he was closer to her age than Cody's, Gin figured there had to be something more to it than that.

"Do you want me to take off my boots?"

Gin had planned on ignoring him, but the question was so unexpected she swung around to face him.

The guy was good-looking, no doubt about it. About six foot two, with hair as dark and glossy as a coffee bean. Although it was the middle of February, the summer sun had permanently cast Dan Moretti's features in bronze, the perfect backdrop to a pair of hazel eyes. The warm palette of greens and browns looked as inviting as a walk in the woods.

Gin preferred the city.

"It's not necessary." He wouldn't be here that long.

Cody rose to his feet and Raine came with him, clinging to him like the stuffed pink bunnies Gin had bought her for Valentine's Day the previous year. The ones bound together by a piece of hidden Velcro on their paws and a heart-shaped tag stamped with the words WE'RE IN THIS TOGETHER.

Together, Gin thought, *just got bigger.*

"Dan." Cody tucked Raine closer, his expression wary. "What are you doing here?"

"Your mom is concerned." Dan shucked off his fleece-lined coat, revealing a pair of broad shoulders and a lean but athletic frame. The room, not very large to begin with, seemed to shrink in size.

Make yourself comfortable, Gin wanted to say. Instead, she aimed a pointed look at the coat draped over his arm. "Would you like a cup of coffee?"

"Sure." His easy smile told Gin that Dan Moretti had a built-in immunity to sarcasm.

"Sit down." She motioned to one of the chairs. "I'll pour you a cup."

"Thanks." He didn't move.

Gin realized Dan was staring at the chair, and she tried to figure out what had caught his attention. Another hole? Ketchup stain?

"Is something wrong?" she finally asked.

"This chair." Dan Moretti's smile returned for an encore, and this time it coaxed a dimple out of hiding. "My mom got rid of one just like it a few months ago. She didn't think anyone would notice, but it was my favorite. Right next to the window in the family room."

It was Gin's favorite too. She'd bought the chair at the secondhand store on Bird Street. The nubby gold fabric reminded her of a teddy bear Raine had dragged around the house when she was a toddler.

Gin twisted the loose tails of her flannel shirt together—also a thrift shop find—and forced herself to look Dan in the eye. "It's probably yours, then." Hopefully her shirt wasn't one of his castoffs too. "Do you want it back? I paid ten, but I'll let it go for fifteen."

Attitude had become Gin's first line of defense against men who invaded her space. She was forced to put up with them at the diner, but it felt different having one here. In her living room.

"I appreciate the offer, but it looks like it found a good home."

Dan settled into the chair's wide lap. The worn cushions shifted beneath his weight, molding to his frame as if he'd left a permanent imprint there.

The thought pushed Gin into the kitchen.

Keeping one eye on Raine, Gin emptied the last two inches of coffee into a clean mug. She didn't know why the man was here, but there was no way she was going to let him bully or lecture her daughter.

"Cream?" Gin asked the question out of habit and instantly regretted it. Not because all she had in the fridge was a quart of skim milk, but because Dan Moretti wasn't a customer. Gin wasn't obligated to make his stay so comfortable he couldn't wait to come back.

Dan twisted around to look at her. "No thanks."

After handing Dan the steaming mug, Gin stationed herself next to Raine, who'd collapsed on the couch next to Cody. The teenagers leaned into each other, finding a delicate balance at the place where their shoulders touched. A human house of cards.

Dan rocked forward and looked directly at Raine. "How are you doing?"

Tears spilled from the corner of Raine's eyes, catching in her lashes before they rolled down her cheeks. "Okay," she croaked.

Dan's eyes closed for a moment and Gin wondered what he was thinking. She was pretty good at reading people. Especially men, whose eyes flashed their intentions like the neon signs in the window of Eddie's Bar. Dan Moretti was already proving to be something of an anomaly. She didn't trust him.

Gin reached for the box of tissues, the second one they'd gone through in twelve hours, and handed it to her daughter.

Raine pulled out two and shared with Cody. Gin hadn't realized his eyes were glistening too.

She looked away because she didn't want to feel sorry for him. Cody Bennett might feel bad, he might feel guilty, but when push came to shove, he could walk out that door and never look back. Men could always walk away. But what Gin never quite understood was how they could so easily *forget* what they'd left behind.

Dan didn't say anything. Just stretched his arm over the coffee table and gripped Cody's knee. Cody flinched.

"I suppose Mom's upset that I skipped class again," he muttered.

The kid obviously didn't know how to do defiant. He couldn't even look Dan in the eye.

"I think she understands a baby takes precedence over senior English."

Dan's quiet statement illuminated the path ahead, and Gin's throat swelled shut. She'd already traveled it, and she wanted something different for her daughter. A road that wasn't rough and uneven. A road that didn't leave callouses on hands and feet and heart.

Raine was everything she hadn't been at this age. Smart. Talented. Beautiful. Gin had done everything in her power to give Raine a bright future, never imagining her daughter would trust it to an eighteen-year-old boy's careless hands.

"We don't know what to do," Cody whispered.

"Neither do I." Dan's admission surprised her. "So how about we take a step forward? Your mom wants you to come over sometime today—all of you—and talk this through."

Gin wasn't sure why the suggestion scraped against her already frayed nerves. Maybe because it meant acknowledging that other people were in their lives. People Gin hadn't invited in.

"I don't know." Raine bit her lip and looked at Cody.

Who looked at Dan. A silent message passed between the two, and the boy nodded.

"All right. Raine isn't feeling good, so maybe we should wait until tonight."

"Six o'clock okay? We'll get together at your house." Dan rose to his feet and peeled his coat off the back of the chair. He turned to Gin. "Does that work for you and your husband?"

Gin lifted her chin. "I'm a single mom."

"So is Evie." Dan's lip softened in a half smile that cleared up any mystery over the role Dan Moretti played in the Bennett family.

Gin started for the door, suddenly anxious to send the man on his way. Dan took the hint and followed her.

"Thanks for the coffee." He shrugged on his coat, and the scent of fresh pine and some tangy masculine soap drifted into the air.

Gin took a step back. It was always dangerous to inhale. "No problem."

Cold air sifted through the foam weather stripping around the door, and Gin hoped he couldn't feel it. When Dan delivered his report to Evie Bennett, she was sure it would include a list of the trailer's flaws.

And hers.

Chapter 8

"Danny."

Evie came off the couch so fast she almost stepped on Diva's feathered tail. The golden retriever, submerged in her morning nap, didn't so much as twitch as Dan walked into the living room.

Even in the midst of a crisis, Evie had taken time to put on makeup and dressed the way she would for work, in a knee-length wool skirt and a silk shirt that matched her eyes. Blue. Max's favorite color. The only evidence of a sleepless night was the faint lavender shadow underneath her eyes.

An image of Ginevieve Lightly flashed in Dan's mind. Oversize flannel shirt and faded jeans, a waterfall of mahogany hair spilling over her shoulders. The clear green eyes had reflected wariness and suspicion whenever she'd glanced his way and pain when they'd lingered on her daughter.

In some ways, the woman had been a surprise. A study in contradictions that Dan was still trying to figure out. She could have slammed the door in his face, yet she'd invited him inside. She had attitude to spare and looked tough as nails, but he'd seen the wrinkled tissue peeking out from the cuff of her flannel shirt, evidence that Raine wasn't the only one who'd cried in the past twenty-four hours.

The inside of the trailer had been a surprise too. The fake pine paneling was riddled with holes from an ever-changing gallery of photographs and pictures tacked up by previous renters, but the furnishings looked clean and comfortable.

But it was the bouquet of flowers on the kitchen windowsill that lingered in Dan's memory. A mixture sold at the checkout of every local convenience store, it provided a splash of color that broke up the flat, snow-covered canvas outside.

He remembered the way Gin had offered to sell his dad's old chair for more than she'd paid for it, and he battled an unexpected urge to smile.

"Did you find Cody?" Evie stopped two feet away. "Did he go back to school?"

Dan wanted to draw her into his arms, but that meant crossing the invisible barrier between them, the one built by Evie's hands, one for every day she'd spent with Max instead of him. The foundation had been laid back in high school the day Evie told him that Max had asked her out.

Dan had pushed down his feelings and faked a smile. Max liked girls and girls liked Max, and although the three of them hung out together all the time, Max had never showed any interest in Evie. Not like that.

But one date had turned into two, and then there was homecoming and prom. Dan got so used to pretending, that when Max dragged him to the jewelry store to help him pick out a ring the week after they graduated, his smile looked as genuine as the diamond Max put on Evie's finger the next day.

When Max asked him to stand up as his best man, Dan had locked his feelings away and chosen to be happy for his two best friends.

"I found him." Dan peeled off his coat and draped it over the back of a chair. "He was at Raine's."

He deliberately sidestepped the second question. Cody and Raine had looked shell-shocked, and Dan knew neither one of them would have been able to concentrate on their classes.

"Raine." Evie's lips pressed together in a thin line at the mention of the girl's name. "I can't believe Cody just accepts the fact this baby is . . . his."

"Cody isn't denying that he and Raine were together, Evie."

Evie flinched and looked away, one hand pressed against her stomach as if the thought made her physically sick. "I thought you talked to him. About *that.*"

"You're blaming me?" Dan struggled to keep his tone even.

Evie's moment of hesitation propelled him toward the kitchen. He needed another shot of caffeine.

"I'm sorry." Evie followed, her sigh settling over Dan as he opened the cupboard and pulled out a clean mug. "It's just . . . Cody has counseled other teenagers to wait until marriage. Abstinence is something he believes in."

Present tense, but Dan didn't correct her. Although there was evidence to the contrary, he prayed Cody still believed in it.

"I know." Dan had covered the same ground during the night.

He and Cody had had dozens of conversations about purity over the years—he'd even taken Cody on a guys' weekend for a Brewers game to celebrate his twelfth birthday. Dan had sprung for a hotel with an indoor water park and carved out some time for The Talk. An outing Cody had laughingly referred to later as "the birds and the bees and baseball."

"Cody and I have a close relationship. He's always been honest with me." Evie's hands curled around the back of one of the wooden chairs circling the kitchen table. "But he never said anything about Raine. You can see what kind of influence she's had on him. Keeping secrets. Sneaking around behind my back. I didn't even know he was in a relationship." Evie put air quotes around the last word. "And now he tells me the girl he's been seeing is pregnant." Her voice frayed around the edges of the word.

Dan wondered if Cody hadn't confided in Evie because he knew his mother didn't approve of Raine. And besides that, there were certain topics a teenage boy didn't feel comfortable discussing with his mother.

"I knew," Dan heard himself say.

Evie stared at him. "What?"

"Not that they were dating—" One look at Evie's face and Dan began to doubt that old adage about confession being good for the soul. "I mean I knew he liked her."

He'd seen them together once, talking on a street corner when he was on his way back to the station after an early morning call. Cody had been looking so intently at Raine, he hadn't even noticed Dan drive past. In a fire truck. Cody had a lot of friends, but something told Dan it was more than that. He kept waiting for a good time to bring it up, but apparently he'd waited too long.

"And you didn't *tell* me?"

"We talked about this, Evie." Guilt nipped at Dan's conscience. "In order to build trust, Cody had to know that what we talked about on the basketball court stayed on the basketball court."

"Unless it was something potentially dangerous. Then you were supposed to let me know."

So she did remember that conversation. "I didn't realize things between them had gotten serious."

An understatement. And the truth was, even if he had known, Dan hadn't expected Cody to stumble. The kid had a stronger commitment to his faith than Dan had had at eighteen. A faith molded and purified by the fire that had taken his father's life when Cody was only six years old.

The day of Max's funeral, Cody had wrapped his arms around Dan's legs and looked up at him.

Daddy's in heaven with Jesus, isn't he?

Grief had gripped Dan by the throat. All he'd been able to manage was a nod.

He's okay then. Cody had said it with such certainty that Dan had repeated it in the eulogy he'd given at Max's funeral.

Death didn't get the victory, Dan believed that. Max was better than okay. It was the people he'd left behind who were forced to figure out a way to go on without him.

"Serious?" Disbelief darkened Evie's eyes, and Dan had to silently rewind the conversation until he remembered what he had just said. "They've only known each other a few months, Danny! How serious can it be? I can't help but think that Raine . . . that she *planned* this."

"You don't know that, Eves. You can't put all the blame on Raine," Dan said quietly. "She wasn't the only one who crossed a line."

Some people thought the burden fell on the girl to say no. Dan had taught Cody it was a man's responsibility not to try something a girl had to say no to in the first place.

"Did Raine's parents agree to meet with us tonight?"

Dan wasn't surprised when Evie rerouted the conversation. Even as a kid, she had always broken things down and dealt with the pieces one by one.

"As far as I know, it's only Raine and her mom."

Evie's breath rattled between her lips. "Did you meet her? What is she like?"

Intriguing was the word that came instantly to mind. From the cinnamon freckle stamped on her cheekbone all the way down to the silver tips on the toes of her battered cowboy boots.

"Gin is shocked. Worried. Just like you." Although the similarities ended there. Dan couldn't imagine two women being more different, not only in looks but in personality.

"Gin," Evie repeated. "Are you kidding? That's her name?"

"That's what she said." Dan thought it fit the woman with the cocked hip and attitude, but not the one with the worried eyes who'd positioned herself in front of her daughter like a mama bear protecting her cub.

"Where did they *come* from?" Evie pressed. "Do they have family in the area?"

I'm a single mom.

Gin had said the words matter-of-factly, but those clear green eyes dared him to judge.

Dan realized Evie was waiting for his response. No impatient toe-tapping from this woman. Evie had always been incredibly *still.* She'd had to be. The slim blond tether that kept Max grounded.

"No family that I know of."

The day Raine had come over to study with Cody, Dan asked her how they'd ended up moving to Banister Falls. Raine's shrug had been telling.

We didn't move here, we just decided to stay for a while.

The statement had struck Dan as odd at the time. He hadn't known there was a difference.

"If this *is* Cody's baby, what about college? His future?"

Tears shimmered in Evie's eyes as the magnitude of the situation began to press down. "I don't know what to do with this, Danny."

It was a variation on what Cody had said, and Dan couldn't be less than honest with her either.

"Neither do I, Eves. But we'll get through it."

She turned away. "I don't *want* to have to get through it."

Dan frowned, troubled by the undercurrent of anger he heard in her voice. "Evie—"

"I'm sorry." She walked over to the fireplace, where a photograph of Max in his turnout gear claimed a permanent spot on the mantel. The rest of the decorations changed with the seasons.

Dan had seen Evie stare at the photo at least a hundred times—he doubted if she even realized she did it—but it had never bothered him. Until now.

He shifted his weight, feeling the sting of being shut out of her thoughts.

Evie glanced over her shoulder. "You'll be here, won't you, Danny?"

"Always." But even as Dan made the promise, a thought chased through his mind.

Who was there for Ginevieve?

Chapter 9

Gin opened the closet door, slowly, so Raine wouldn't hear the telltale squeak.

"Mom?"

Gin almost jumped out of her skin. "Don't sneak up on me like that! Are you *trying* to give me a heart attack?"

"It's time to go. What are you . . ." Raine's gaze shifted over her shoulder, where a small suitcase waited on standby in the closet. She lurched around Gin, and the carpet bunched as she slammed the door shut. "Mom, *no.* Not this time."

"We don't have to stay here and deal with—" *These people.* "This."

Raine's red-rimmed eyes went nuclear. "I'm not leaving Cody, Mom."

"Unless he leaves you first." The words were out before Gin could stop them.

"Cody isn't like that."

It took everything inside of Gin not to point out the obvious. Her daughter was pregnant. She knew exactly what Cody Bennett was like.

"We don't need them, Raine. They're just going to make a complicated situation even more complicated."

"We told Cody we'd come over tonight."

"And what do you think it's going to accomplish?"

Raine swiped the back of her hand against her eyes, leaving a trail of black mascara across her cheekbone. "I don't know. But Mr. Moretti is right. What Cody and I decide about the . . . baby . . . It affects all of us. We have to talk."

"How did his mother react to the news?"

"Cody didn't say."

Which said a lot, Gin thought. "What's she like?"

"Mrs. Bennett? She's okay."

"Then why are your earlobes turning red?" Better than a lie detector, those ears. From the time Raine was a toddler, Gin had found them to be a perfect gauge to discern the truth from a fib.

"I don't know her, that's all," Raine mumbled. "Cody and I didn't hang out at his house."

"Okay." Gin let it go. She wanted to get the meeting over with as soon as possible.

The suitcase would be there when they got home, just in case Raine changed her mind. It was always there. Gin couldn't pinpoint the exact day she'd stashed a suitcase in the closet without unpacking the contents first. All Gin knew was that it made her feel better. She decided when it was time to leave. She decided where she would go.

The moment Gin drove underneath the metal arch anchored between two brick pillars, the name Rosewood Court entwined in a banner of vines and flowers, she scratched the notion that she and Evie Bennett had anything in common.

"We're not in Kansas anymore," Gin muttered under her breath.

"It's that one." Raine pointed to a two-story brick house rising from the center of the cul-de-sac like a miniature castle. "I know what you're thinking."

"What am I thinking?" Gin parked on the street behind a hunter green pickup, the vehicle of choice for roughly 80 percent of the male population in Banister Falls.

"You're thinking Cody's mom is a snob because she lives in a nice house. Which is just as bad as people thinking we're trashy because we live in the trailer park."

"Well, you're wrong, Miss Smarty-pants." She was thinking that Evie Bennett had made out pretty good in the divorce.

Gin linked her arm through Raine's as they walked up the path, guided by solar lights in the shape of snowflakes that led to the front door. She felt Raine's shiver through her wool pea coat and knew she wasn't cold. Gin pulled her closer, wishing she didn't understand everything her daughter was feeling.

Gin stepped onto the porch and triggered a motion sensor, trapping them in a circle of light. The door opened and Cody stood there, sweet and solemn and way too young to be a father.

How did you punish two babies who were about to have a baby? Gin had no idea. It wasn't like she could ground Raine or take away her cell phone. How did you parent a soon-to-be parent? Cody had changed that, too, and Gin resented him even more.

She followed Cody into a spacious foyer with a chandelier that sprinkled tiny lights on the gleaming hardwood floor like a disco ball. Raine kicked off her shoes, but Gin suddenly remembered a hole in the toe of her sock.

"You can leave your boots on."

Gin's heart skipped three beats at the sound of Dan Moretti's voice, but stalled completely when he reached out and untangled her arms from the sleeves of her coat.

"I thought you were the messenger." Gin slid away from Dan as he opened the closet door and found a hanger. "Or are you working overtime as a bouncer tonight?"

Those hazel eyes went wide and then he smiled. "I'm a friend, remember?"

The Bennetts' friend. That's what Gin remembered.

The heels of her cowboy boots clicked against the floor as she followed Dan down the narrow hall and right into the cover of a home decorating magazine. Not the stuffy kind Gin would have instantly dismissed as pretentious. This was the kind of house she'd once dreamed of living in. Inviting and comfortable. There was even a real fire burning in the fireplace.

Raine and Cody had already claimed the sofa, and a golden retriever with a snow-white muzzle padded over to Gin. She dropped to her knees and combed her fingers through the dog's silky ears. Raine had begged for years for a dog or cat, but Gin had discovered that most landlords wouldn't budge when it came to pets.

"Her name is Diva." The retriever's tail thumped the floor when Dan bent down to pet her. He was too close. Too big.

Gin moved back and tipped her head to the side to avoid the swipe of the dog's tongue. "She doesn't look like one."

Dan's eyes crinkled at the corners. "You wouldn't say that if you saw the way she refuses to go outside when it's raining."

It was obvious he had, which in Gin's mind was one more reason to steer clear of the guy.

"Diva . . . don't assume everyone is here to see you." A woman glided into the room, her tone soft as she scolded the dog. The serene smile stopped short of a pair of smoke-blue eyes. "I'm Evie Bennett. Cody's mom."

She could have left out the last part. Gin instantly saw the resemblance between Evie and her son.

Evie Bennett was one of those lucky women with skin so flawless she looked like a porcelain doll. Her ash-blond hair was cut and styled in a way that drew attention to an oval face and delicate features.

Gin rose to her feet. "Gin Lightly." For all her reservations about meeting Evie Bennett, Gin appreciated the fact the woman hadn't gushed or lied and said it was nice to meet her.

Raine and Cody watched the exchange, their eyes moving back and forth like they were seated on the sidelines at Wimbledon.

Gin still wasn't sure where Dan fit in. Coach? Referee?

"Please, sit down." Evie nodded at a rocking chair next to the fireplace. "Would you like something to drink? Coffee? I have tea and hot chocolate too."

"Mom's usually the one who asks that question." Raine spoke up for the first time.

Evie looked confused, and Gin was forced to explain. "I'm a waitress at My Place."

"The diner off Main Street?"

The fact Evie posed it as a question meant she'd never been there. Gin wasn't surprised. Sue didn't advertise in the local newspaper. Too expensive. The majority of her customers included the guys who came off the night shift at the Leiderman Company, a nondescript factory on the outskirts of town that manufactured hardware for farm implements, and the people who lived in the second-floor apartments on Radley Street. The group as a whole tended to be rowdy and a little rough around the edges and thought a 5 percent tip was generous. Evie looked like a Marie's Bistro kind of girl.

Gin wasn't ashamed of what she did for a living. Waiting tables had paid the bills for years, and in spite of what people thought, the job required a unique skill set.

"That's the one." Gin bypassed the rocking chair with its frilly little skirt and stood with her back to the fireplace. The flames didn't chase away the chill in the air. "You should stop by some time. We've got a great early bird special."

Chapter 10

Dan watched Gin's chin tilt toward the ceiling, a gesture he was beginning to recognize as her way of deflecting any kind of censure or judgment.

He'd lived in Banister Falls all his life and had never set foot in My Place. The quintessential greasy spoon, it wasn't exactly the kind of place you met friends for lunch or took a date you wanted to impress. Like any town, Banister Falls had its hot spots where trouble simmered and occasionally boiled over, and the diner was located in the epicenter of the worst one.

Silence thickened the air and Dan drew in a slow breath, feeling the weight of it fill his lungs like smoke. He sent up a silent prayer for strength as Evie perched on the edge of the recliner.

He hadn't planned on acting as the emcee for the evening, but everyone was looking at him. He felt like he was in a room filled with land mines; one careless step and everything would explode.

When you don't know where to start, start at the beginning, his grandpa Moretti used to say.

Dan looked at Cody first and tried to find the boy he'd spent the last twelve years helping Evie raise. A pale but steady-eyed young man stared back, trying to anticipate Dan's next move the way he did on the basketball court.

What are you going to do now, Dan? Offense or defense?

"Your mom and I didn't realize you and Raine were seeing each other," Dan said carefully. "We don't understand why you kept it a secret."

"Dan's right." Evie waded into the conversation, eyes fixed on her son. "It isn't like you to sneak around, Cody. You've always been honest with me."

Gin stiffened at the implication that Raine was somehow responsible for the deceit. Dan doubted that it was Evie's intent to question the girl's character, but he shot her a warning look just the same.

Hurt flashed in Evie's eyes, but Dan knew they wouldn't get anywhere if Gin and Raine walked out. And at this point, he wasn't so sure Cody wouldn't follow them out the door.

"I know this is my fault." Cody's Adam's apple bulged, as if the words got stuck in his throat. "We didn't mean to cross a line. It just . . . happened."

"Maybe it wouldn't have 'just happened' if you hadn't put yourself in a situation where it *could*." Dan tried to prevent his frustration from leaking out. Hadn't they covered the chapter on avoiding temptation? Group dates. Public places. Respect for the girl and yourself?

"I know." Cody glanced at Ginevieve. "And I take full responsibility."

"Full responsibility." Gin began to pace the rug in front of the fireplace, her hands churning the air at her sides. "You're eighteen years old! How are you going to financially support a child? Raine is supposed to go to college next fall. Are you going to change your plans and babysit while she's in class? While she's at the library working on a paper? You'll be long gone, living your life, not caring that you messed up Raine's."

"That's not true." Cody met Ginevieve's anger head-on. "I'm not going to leave her alone."

"We love each other, Mom." Tears spilled down Raine's cheeks.

"How is that even possible?" Evie looked at Raine for the first time, and Dan saw the panic rising in her eyes. "You and Cody barely *know* each other. You haven't graduated from high school yet. There's no way either of you is ready to be a parent."

Raine tucked her chin and sagged against Cody. "She's right."

"We'll get an A this time, Wats." Cody's arms came around her like a shield. "I promise."

Raine smiled up at Cody, and the kiss he pressed against her temple shut the rest of them out.

Us against them.

That was the last thing Dan wanted.

Chapter 11

In her first week at Banister Falls High School Raine had argued with both the school guidance counselor and the principal in her attempt to get out of Family Living Skills. She'd moved a dozen times in ten years, but apparently that didn't count as a skill. So three days after classes officially started, Raine found herself trudging up two flights of stairs to a spacious room that overlooked the football field and smelled like lemon furniture polish.

Pausing in the doorway, she'd hugged her backpack closer and scanned the classroom. Metal tables were arranged in a semicircle around the teacher's desk, and a row of porcelain sinks lined the back wall. A real live chalkboard took up an entire wall, the words *Mrs. Dewey* winding from one end to the other like a vapor trail.

Raine searched for a familiar face. Her gaze stumbled over a boy sitting near the window.

Cody Bennett.

She took a seat on the opposite side of the room. Making a person your hobby was one thing; letting the person know he was your hobby was stupid.

For the first few weeks the class wasn't so bad. Mrs. Dewey reminded Raine of a jovial Mrs. Santa, round and smiling, her cheeks always blushing like little red apples, which probably made it easier to recite the definitions of body parts in such a way that even the freshman boys in the class didn't snicker.

Whenever Mrs. Dewey emphasized a word in a sentence, she would write it on the chalkboard in neat block letters. By the end of the period, it resembled a gigantic Scrabble board.

There were minimal assignments—a short essay due every Friday and an exam that counted as 50 percent of the final grade. Piece of cake.

And every time Raine glanced at the clock above Mrs. Dewey's desk, she saw Cody's profile too. While everyone took notes on how to plan a weekly menu, she compiled more information on Cody Bennett.

He was left-handed. He wore an old-fashioned wristwatch that looked like it belonged to someone's grandpa. One of his shoelaces was always untied. He smiled a lot.

But never at her.

Raine wasn't quite sure why.

In fact, since that first day of class Cody hadn't so much as looked her way.

Raine was frustrated and relieved at the same time. Because if he *did* talk to her, she would get to know him better and doubtless end up being disappointed. Being a disappointment was a trait hardwired into guys, and Raine didn't need Family Living Skills class to prove it.

She sailed through the chapter on nutrition, blissfully unaware there was a reason the class had the word *family* in it until they were ready to start a new unit. That was the day Raine reached the top of the stairs and saw Mrs. Dewey standing outside the door of the classroom, a wide smile on her face and a stack of folders tucked in the crook of her arm.

Behind Raine, a girl groaned. "I feel the flu coming on."

"I was hoping she'd skip chapter four this year," her friend said.

"What's chapter four?" Raine hadn't bothered to read ahead in the textbook.

"You'll find out."

"Table six." Mrs. Dewey handed Raine a folder.

The entire room had been rearranged. Each rickety metal table was covered with a white linen tablecloth like you'd see in a fancy restaurant, and topped with a single red rose in a glass bud vase.

Raine decided it must be some kind of etiquette lesson.

Until Cody Bennett sat down next to her. Next. To. Her.

Mrs. Dewey closed the door with a snap and took her place at the front of the room.

"The seating arrangement will remain this way for the next few weeks. No exchanges or returns." She chuckled at her own joke. "Now I'd like everyone to take a minute and say good morning to your spouse."

Wait a sec . . . *spouse*?

Raine swallowed her gum when Cody turned to look at her.

"Hi." His eyes were even bluer up close, and she could see tiny flecks of silver scattered like glitter around the irises.

"Hi." Raine somehow managed to break a one-syllable word into three separate pieces.

"All the pertinent information is in your folders." Mrs. Dewey wrote PERTINENT on the board. "Your first assignment is to fill out the questionnaire and give it to your spouse to take home today. Consider it a form of speed dating. You'd find these things out during the natural development of a relationship, but unfortunately we only have a month to complete this lesson."

Raine filled out the questionnaire in absolute silence, and each answer was as painful as removing her clothes one piece at a time. At the end, she would be standing in front of Cody Bennett with no secrets between them.

Cody finished ten minutes before her and doodled in the

margin to make it look like he hadn't, which Raine thought was kind of sweet.

She went to bed early that night, tucked the covers around her waist, and propped his questionnaire against Mrs. Freckles, the stuffed giraffe she'd won at a county fair in Illinois. By midnight Raine knew all the "pertinent" details about Cody Bennett and was left with one conclusion.

She wanted to know more.

Mrs. Dewey handed out another sheet of paper to add to their folders the next day.

"This is your Couple Profile," she said. "Left to your own devices, I would end up with a classroom of professional football players and supermodels, so I've taken the liberty of giving you a dose of real life."

Raine scanned the sheet and decided that Mrs. Dewey's version of real life stunk.

Cody worked at a car dealership for minimum wage (boring) and she was a nurse's aide (gross). The first week, they were required to create a budget out of their combined income. Not so bad, although Cody insisted on setting 10 percent of their paycheck aside for a tithe—whatever that was—and Raine wanted to slash the grocery budget to make payments on a convertible.

They decided to go hiking on the weekends because it was free and figured out a way to divide the household chores. Raine chose vacuuming and doing the laundry, and Cody opted to take out the trash and clean the bathroom. Neither of them knew how to cook, so Raine suggested they eat out. Cody skimmed five dollars from the grocery budget and bought a cookbook instead.

Every once in a while Mrs. Dewey would pass around a glass jar filled with slips of paper that corresponded to what she called "life's little ups and downs."

For all her pink-cheeked smiles, the teacher had a dark side.

There were car accidents and layoffs and in-laws who stopped over without calling first.

Everyone started to dread The Jar, because in Mrs. Dewey's world there were a lot more downs than ups.

On Tuesday Cody quit his job and decided to go to college. On Thursday Raine signed up for a credit card behind his back and went on a shopping spree.

By the end of the week each couple was required to hand in a short essay on how they'd solved the conflict. Raine was tempted to ask Mrs. Dewey how to solve a conflict about solving conflict.

The final unit wasn't in the textbook. Apparently Mrs. Dewey had added her own unique twist to things after watching a disturbing episode of *20/20*.

Real Baby.

Raine hadn't known about that, either. She'd walked into the classroom at the end of the second week, and all the silk rose centerpieces had been replaced with infant seats.

She peeked at one as she scooted around a table. Wrapped like a flannel burrito inside the infant seat was a rubber replica of a baby that didn't look like any baby Raine had ever seen before. Years of being squeezed, dropped, and stuffed into lockers had obviously taken its toll.

Real Baby wasn't a doll with a tiny hole in its rosebud mouth that would bleat when you tipped it forward. No, the whole idea behind Real Baby was to terrify teenagers into never having one.

Mrs. Dewey programmed every baby to cry at random intervals. Like every two hours all night long, the girl at the next table whispered to Raine. The crying could last anywhere from five minutes to an hour—unless you were one of the unlucky ones whose baby had the colic chip, and then it could be even longer. According to the couple at the next table, the babies of "parents" involved in sports never had colic.

Another reason Raine should have signed up for volleyball.

She sorted through her folder, wondering how they were going to afford diapers and formula if Cody refused to drop out of college and try to get his old job back at the car dealership.

Raine didn't get a chance to discuss it with him. The second bell rang, and he still hadn't shown up for class. Seriously? He was a no-show the day they had a baby?

She gathered her courage and lifted a corner of the quilt draped over the infant seat. Blue flannel. It figured she'd have a boy.

Raine took a quick glance around the room, wondering if she could switch with someone without Mrs. Dewey noticing. While she contemplated that, Cody slid into the seat next to her, his hair damp from the shower and looking so cute it was impossible to stay mad at him.

"Here." He slid a candy bar across the table. Not Hershey. Something wrapped in gold foil with a name Raine couldn't pronounce.

"What's this for?" Not that it mattered. Chocolate was chocolate, no matter what the occasion.

"Fourteen hours of labor."

She winced. "How do you know?"

"Because I was there, Watson. Holding your hand. Reminding you to breathe."

As always, the nickname warmed Raine like a cup of vanilla cappuccino.

Cody had started calling her Watson the day after she'd handed over the questionnaire, because she had written down Sherlock Holmes as one of her three favorite books of all time. It was probably weird, preferring old books to the ones other kids her age read, but Mrs. Dewey had told them to be honest.

"Why not Jo March?" she asked him when Mrs. Dewey had her back turned. "She was number two on the list."

"Because every time I see you around school, you always look so deep in thought," he whispered back. "You have this cute little frown between your eyebrows, like you're looking for clues."

Raine tucked the word *cute* away for later and didn't admit *he* was the mystery she'd been trying to solve. "So why not Sherlock?"

"Everyone knows Watson was the real brains behind the operation."

Later that day it occurred to Raine that, wonder of wonders, Cody had been watching her too.

"Congratulations to all our new parents!" Mrs. Dewey shuffled into the classroom wearing blue scrubs and a stethoscope draped around her neck like a black rubber boa. "I hope all of you have gotten acquainted with your brand-new babies."

"Oh, please," Raine muttered.

Cody's knee nudged hers underneath the table. It was the first time he'd touched her—ever—and Raine's heart slid off its footings.

He peeled back the quilt and twitched the flannel blanket to one side, something Raine hadn't scraped up the courage to do. What if they'd gotten one of the flat-faced babies?

"You have an advantage, class." Mrs. Dewey was swinging the stethoscope back and forth like a pendulum. "Most parents don't get a set of instructions when their babies arrive."

"Yes, they do," Cody murmured. "It's called the Bible."

Raine was still surprised every time Cody mentioned God. When they'd had to list something that was really important on their questionnaire, he'd written the word *prayer.* From anyone else it would have seemed weird. But when it came to Cody it seemed . . . right.

On the way home from school, Raine found herself looking up at the sky more often, searching for God's face in the clouds. She remembered a nicely dressed couple knocking at the door of their apartment when she was little. Her mom was busy in the kitchen, but the woman had knelt down right on the rug Raine had spilled grape soda on that morning and invited her to church on Sunday.

Raine read the pamphlet they'd left and asked her mom if she believed in God. Her mother said yes, which kind of surprised her, but when Raine showed her the pamphlet and asked if she was a child of God, her mom's expression changed. She'd muttered a word Raine hadn't heard before and walked away. Raine didn't know what a prodigal was, but she figured it had something to do with people who moved around a lot.

"You and your spouse can choose your baby's name and decide how you'll split up the time caring for him or her," Mrs. Dewey droned on. "There's a chip inside each baby that collects data, so it will record feeding times . . . as well as neglect or abuse."

Cody lifted the baby out of the carrier, the only one in the entire class to actually touch the thing until absolutely necessary.

Raine took a peek and breathed a sigh of relief. It had a nice round face.

"It's a boy," Cody whispered.

"I know." Raine didn't bother to hide her disappointment. "It's too late to switch with someone else, though."

"You didn't want a boy?"

"I didn't want anything," Raine said honestly.

Cody frowned and lapsed into silence for thirty seconds. Raine counted. She should have known he'd take this as seriously as he had their budget.

"What should we name him?"

"Sally," Raine said, just to see Cody smile again.

He didn't disappoint her. "We have to fill out this birth certificate before the end of class."

"I don't care. You name him."

"How about Max?"

"Max is a dog's name."

"It was my dad's name."

"Sorry . . . but it still sounds like a dog's name." Raine silently scrolled through the options. "How about Dillon? I kind of like that one."

Cody stared down at the baby. "My dad was a hero."

"Was?" Raine frowned. Had she missed something on the questionnaire?

"He died when I was six." Cody's voice softened to a whisper. "He was a firefighter. Maxwell Bennett."

Raine was jealous. It was sad his dad had died, but at least Cody could tell people he was a hero. What could she say? "My dad was a selfish jerk who abandoned me and my mom"?

"Dillon Maxwell?" she suggested. Because Mrs. Dewey was always preaching about the importance of compromise in a marriage.

"Maxwell Dillon."

"Fine." Raine grabbed a pen to fill out the birth certificate while Mrs. Dewey drifted from table to table, activating babies. Some of them immediately began to cry, and Raine wanted to press her hands against her ears.

"This is a nightmare," she said under her breath. "I'm not going to get any sleep this weekend."

"Come on! Look at him." Cody bumped her shoulder. "He has his mommy's big brown eyes."

"And your nose." Raine dared to tease him back.

Cody smiled down at the rubber baby. Their rubber baby. "Welcome to the world, Maxwell Dillon," he said.

And right then and there, Raine fell head over heels in love with Cody Bennett.

CHAPTER 12

Gin wondered how in the world she'd missed this.

The way Cody and Raine were looking at each other . . . the way they clung together, arms linked, forming a fragile knot even as their future was unraveling.

Why hadn't Raine confided in her? She'd talked about boys before, on occasion even invited one over for pizza or to watch a movie. Gin knew she and Cody had worked on a class project together, but the kid hadn't even registered on Gin's maternal radar as a possible threat.

"Are you sure this isn't a false alarm?" Evie was looking at Raine now.

"I took a test." Raine's cheeks flushed crimson. "Yesterday."

Evie's gaze didn't waver. "Are you dating anyone else?"

"*Mom.*" Cody leaped to his feet.

"It's a fair question," she argued. "If you and Raine were in an exclusive relationship, I would have expected you to invite her over on the weekends. Talk to her on the phone. Sit with her in church."

Gin didn't think it was a fair question at all. Not when the implication was that Raine slept around.

"I wasn't seeing anyone but Cody," Raine said in a low voice, her eyes clinging to Evie Bennett.

Judging from the look on Evie's face, she didn't believe her. In her mind, Cody was an innocent victim.

"I think we should go." Before Gin said something she wouldn't regret.

Evie glanced at her. "I'm sorry, but you have to understand, I . . . I wasn't prepared for this."

"And you think I was?" Gin couldn't believe Cody's mom had such a low opinion of them. Like a teen pregnancy was something she'd seen on Raine's list of goals for the future.

Dan stepped between the fireplace and the sofa, momentarily blocking Evie from view and Gin's path to the door. "Time out. Let's take a minute and regroup."

Gin glared at him. She didn't want to regroup. She wanted to leave—and Dan Moretti was in her way. "It was a waste of time coming here. This feels more like an inquisition than a conversation. Raine isn't the only one who made a mistake."

Dan's gaze didn't waver. "I realize that."

Well, he might, but it was clear Evie Bennett didn't.

"Men take what they want and don't care about the consequences." A picture of Joey Meyer's face uploaded from Gin's memory, overriding her thoughts like a computer virus.

"I know Raine and I messed up . . . but I refuse to call this baby a mistake. You always say God doesn't make mistakes, and He's the one who creates life." Cody took two steps toward Dan that brought them nose to nose. "You also told me that a man should take responsibility for his actions. Or am I only supposed to do that when it lines up with what everyone else wants me to do?"

Dan didn't flinch or back down. "What do you want to do? That's why we're here."

Cody and Raine looked at each other, and a silent message passed between them, so quickly that Gin didn't have time to decipher it.

"College is still an option for both of you if you and Raine consider putting the baby up for adoption." Evie rose to her feet and faced Cody. "There are a lot of couples who can't have a child of their own. It would . . . it would be a loving thing to do, if you think about it."

The kids stared at her, stunned. Gin was stunned too. But what was more surprising was the wave of grief that washed through her, as if she'd just lost something precious.

"Can we go home now, Mom?" Raine disengaged from Cody, and Gin could see the tears pooling in her eyes.

Yes please, Gin thought. She didn't want any witnesses to her meltdown either.

This time Dan didn't try to stop them.

Cody followed her and Raine out of the room and closed the door behind him. "I'll pick you up tomorrow morning, okay?"

"It depends on how I feel," Raine murmured.

Cody frowned. "We have a test first hour."

Raine didn't respond, but Gin sure wanted to. Cody claimed he would be there for Raine, but when it came right down to it, he would be the one sitting in class and Raine would be camped on the bathroom floor next to the toilet.

"I'll give her a ride to school." Gin plucked her coat off the hook.

"Thank you." Cody still looked troubled, but Gin noticed he didn't offer to skip class and hold her daughter's hand again. Not when a grade was on the line.

The sound of a door opening and the soft but steady tread of footsteps coming toward them were signs that Evie's private follow-up meeting with Dan had come to an end. Or else she'd sent him to make sure they weren't trying to steal the paintings off the wall.

"Ready?" She quickly nudged Raine toward the door.

The wind nipped at Gin's face, and she hoped Jasmine would start. The car's chronic respiratory issues were the reason they'd gotten stranded in Banister Falls in the first place.

Raine pushed ahead of her. She didn't like cold weather, and the chill had started twenty minutes ago, in Evie Bennett's living room.

"Hey."

Gin tried not to groan when Dan caught up to them at the end of the sidewalk. "Are you okay?"

It took Gin a moment to realize he was talking to her this time and not Raine. She hiked an eyebrow. "What do you think?"

"I think we all need some time to adjust to this." Dan's sigh frosted the air. "I know it wasn't easy coming over here tonight, but I'm glad you did. The kids need to know they don't have to go through this alone."

"If that's what this was about, I'm not sure you accomplished your goal."

"Neither am I."

Dan's quiet admission shocked Gin down to her frozen toes. She wiggled them to get the circulation going and heard the car rumble to life. Raine must have swiped the keys from her coat pocket.

"I have to go."

"Ginevieve." Dan took a step closer. "Don't be too hard on Evie, okay? She's—"

"Danny?" The door opened, and Cody's mom stood in a pool of light on the front step. The shadows concealed Evie's expression, but Gin heard the question in her tone.

Why are you talking to her?

Gin was wondering the same thing.

CHAPTER 13

"Finished already?" Miss Peterman looked up as Raine approached her desk. "You could have waited until tomorrow to make up the test, you know. You're still looking a little pale."

"I'm okay." Raine tried to compensate for her lack of color—and the fib—with a smile.

Once Raine had gotten over the introduce-yourself-to-the-class humiliation on the first day of school, Miss Peterman had become her favorite teacher. She wore broomstick skirts with high-top Chuck Taylors and kept a stash of chocolates in a jar stamped with the letters PMS. She claimed the company had accidentally scrambled her initials, but the girls knew better. Miss Peterman was also notoriously stingy with As and expected people to take her class as seriously as she did.

That's why, when Raine had shown up for class forty minutes after the bell rang, she wasn't sure Miss Peterman would even let her take a makeup test. Raine had taken her seat, aware that Cody was watching her, and waited until after class to apologize for being late. Miss Peterman took one look at Raine's face and offered her a piece of chocolate and the opportunity to take the test after school.

"I finished grading your last journal entry." Miss Peterman's turquoise nails tapped the folder Raine had turned in the Friday before.

In senior English Miss Peterman replaced the pop quizzes that other teachers favored with essays. Several times a week she wrote a word on the board, and everyone was required to write a short paragraph about it. Based on the groans that erupted around her, Raine was the only one who actually looked forward to the assignment.

She tried not to look at the folder. Had she messed up? Gotten a low grade? Miss Peterman didn't seem to be in any hurry to put Raine out of her misery. She continued to hold the folder hostage.

"Are you planning to go to college, Raine?"

Raine's stomach, which had been behaving most of the afternoon, tilted sideways. She knew exactly how she would have answered the question a few weeks ago. Now what came out was a weak "I think so."

"And what are you interested in studying?"

Raine wondered if Miss Peterman would laugh if she told her. Only her mom—and Cody—knew she wanted to be a writer.

"English . . . or creative writing."

"A difficult career to break into." Another series of taps on the folder. Raine wished she could decipher the cryptic message. "I've noticed a difference in your work lately."

She *had* gotten a bad grade. "I'm sorry."

"Don't be sorry, Raine. I'm saying that as a positive thing. You played it safe in the beginning of the year, and I got the impression you were trying to figure out what I wanted you to say instead of letting the real Raine Lightly shine through. You're a very talented writer.

"I don't know what's changed, but I see a depth—a richness—that wasn't there before. I would like to think it has something to do with my teaching"—Miss Peterman smiled as she slid the folder across the desk—"but I don't think I can take the credit."

Raine knew what had changed. *She* had.

"I'll see you tomorrow." Miss Peterman reached for another folder on the stack. "And Raine? I would be happy to help you put together a portfolio of your best work when you apply for scholarships."

"Thank you." It was a good thing Miss Peterman had those essays as evidence, because Raine was having trouble stringing more than two words together.

Talented. Writer. No one had ever told her that before. Raine didn't know whether to jump up and down or sit on the floor and cry. She forced herself to walk to the door instead.

The moment she was out of sight, she fled to the bathroom. Two girls standing by the sink reared back as Raine charged past them and claimed an empty stall.

"Gross," she heard one of the girls mutter as the restroom door snapped shut behind them.

Raine picked herself up off the floor a few minutes later and stumbled down the flight of stairs to the parking lot. At least she didn't have to face Cody right away. She'd managed to avoid him all day without making it *look* like she was avoiding him, and on Wednesday nights he helped set up for youth group.

What would the guys in Cody's study think when they found out she was pregnant? Would they doubt the baby was his? Evie Bennett assumed she slept around—Raine had seen it in her eyes.

Cody had stuck up for her. And he'd sounded so sure when he told their moms and Dan Moretti that the baby was a gift from God. But Mrs. Bennett said they should think about adoption. Did that mean the gift was meant for someone else?

Bile backed up in Raine's throat. All this was her fault.

Cody hadn't wanted to keep their relationship a secret, but she'd insisted. She'd never had a boyfriend. They moved so often, Raine didn't want to start a relationship that was destined to die a quick and painful death on the inevitable day when she would come home and see cardboard boxes stacked like Jenga blocks in the living room. Not to mention her trust issues, the ones that seemed to be part of the Lightly genetic code.

And Cody Bennett? He was so popular, and as the perpetual "new kid," Raine shied away from attention. She hadn't wanted people talking about them.

Now *everyone* would be talking about them.

Raine dug in her pocket for her keys and didn't see Cody until he pushed off Jasmine's rusty bumper.

"I was beginning to think Miss Peterman gave you an hour of detention instead of a makeup test." Cody reached for her, but Raine backed away.

She wanted to tell him what the teacher had said, but did it matter? Was college even an option anymore?

"I don't feel very well." Avoiding his eyes, Raine opened the door and tossed her backpack onto the passenger seat.

"I'm sorry." Frustration filtered through Cody's sigh. Was he mad at her for being sick? For being pregnant? For messing up his plans to go to college? "Will you be able to come to church tonight?"

Raine started the car and tugged on the door, forcing Cody to back up a step. "I don't know."

All she knew was that she had to get away. Because right now, the weight of three futures was more than she could carry.

CHAPTER 14

"Go ahead. Don't keep me in suspense." Gin didn't look at Sue as she untied her apron and tossed it in a plastic bin. "I've been waiting all day to hear I told you so."

"Didn't we already establish the fact that I'm not your mother?"

"Yes."

"Then you won't hear it from me." Sue leaned against the butcher-block island in the center of the kitchen, her arms folded across her chest. "So what happens now?"

"I don't know." And it was driving Gin crazy. "*They* don't know."

"They?" Sue pounced on the word. "The *friend* is sticking around?"

It was close enough to the I-told-you-so that Gin rolled her eyes. "His name is Cody Bennett and he claims he's not going anywhere."

"And you're thinking Raine isn't either."

It was scary, really, how Sue could read her mind. Everything Raine had worked so hard to achieve was in jeopardy. When Evie had brought up adoption the night before, a solution that would clear the way for Raine's future plans, Gin had had mixed feelings. This was Raine's child.

Her *grandchild.*

The thought that kept running through Gin's mind was what if she'd given Raine up for adoption? Life hadn't been easy, but at least they were together. Raine had been the one bright light in Gin's life. The reason she'd gotten her act together. The reason she put her feet on the floor every morning. What if she'd missed out on all that was Raine? Gin couldn't even imagine eighteen years of regrets and unanswered questions instead of memories.

"Hey." Sue's elbow speared Gin in the side. "You need a few days off?"

"Are you trying to get rid of me?"

"Get rid of you?" Her boss snorted. "I'm surprised you're still here."

"So am I." Gin was too tired to pretend she didn't know what Sue was talking about. The packed suitcase waited on the other side of the closet door, ready to go at a moment's notice.

"But I'm pretty sure Cody's mom would be thrilled if we left town."

"Are you talking about Evie Bennett?"

"You *know* her?"

"Everyone in Banister Falls knows Evie Bennett." Sue flipped a damp towel over her shoulder. "She's Max Bennett's widow."

"A widow?" No one told her anything anymore. "She's my age."

"Evie couldn't have been more than twenty-four or twenty-five when Max died. He was a firefighter. Died in the line of duty when they were called to a house fire." Sue's forehead pleated. "There's a plaque in city hall with his picture on it. I think the whole town turned out for his funeral."

Gin tried to process that information. On the outside, Evie Bennett appeared to have the perfect life. Perfect house in a perfect neighborhood. Perfect hair. Perfect clothes.

Perfect champion.

Don't be too hard on Evie.

The words still rubbed raw. Dan had been in the room that night. Just who had been hard on whom?

"Have you heard of Dan Moretti?" As soon as the words slipped out Gin wanted to take them back, but Sue didn't appear surprised by the question.

"Heard of the family. There have to be at least a dozen Morettis running around town, but they never come in here." Sue sounded matter-of-fact about it rather than offended. "Who is he?"

"A family friend. Theirs, not ours." But even knowing that, Gin couldn't seem to stop thinking about him. The conversation he'd left unfinished.

"Don't make Raine pick sides," Sue warned. "Raine and Cody will form their own team."

"Where do you come up with this stuff?" Gin rolled her eyes, even though she had a hunch her boss was right about that too.

"You didn't know about my psychology degree?" Sue reached for one of the pies cooling on a rack. "Raine likes my apple pie, right?"

"Yes, but I doubt she'll be able to keep it down."

"Then you eat it. You look like you've lost a few pounds too. That's bad for business." Sue slid the pie into a paper sack. "Don't try to pay me. I'll take this out of your tip money."

Gin didn't have to fake a smile this time. "See you tomorrow."

"You won't have to work a double. I'm hiring a new waitress."

"Great." They'd been shorthanded for weeks, but with the cost of doctor bills, prenatal vitamins, and a host of other upcoming expenses, Gin could have used the extra money.

"*You* have to train her, though." Sue's laughter followed her into the oversize storage closet that doubled as a break room.

Gin checked her phone, but there were no messages or missed calls from Raine. In this case, she hoped that no news meant good news. Another bout of morning sickness had had Raine running late that morning, so she'd dropped Gin off at the diner and taken the car to school.

Gin walked outside and scanned the cars parked along the curb, but Jasmine wasn't one of them. She sent a quick text, letting Raine know she'd decided to walk home.

Gin's steps slowed when she was parallel with the fire station on Second Street.

What would that have been like, to lose your husband at that age? Worse than never having one at all? Gin had practically begged Joey to marry her when she found out she was pregnant, but deep inside she knew it wouldn't have worked. He would have been like her dad—only sticking around until something, or someone, better came along. He would have broken her heart twice.

The back door of the fire station opened and a burst of laughter preceded the group of men that spilled out of the building. In spite of temperatures that stubbornly hovered in the twenties, all the firefighters wore a casual uniform of gray T-shirts and black cargo pants.

Gin's heart plummeted when she recognized one of them.

Dan Moretti was a firefighter too. Like Evie's husband.

Had they been friends? Worked together? It would explain the close bond between him and Cody. And him and Evie.

She cast another furtive glance in his direction. Dan wasn't the tallest in the group and he wasn't built like a boulder, either, but his easygoing smile and air of confidence drew people in. Gin could see it in the way the other men had formed a circle around him, hanging on every word he said.

One of the men looked her way, and Gin dipped her chin into the fold of her scarf. She plunged over the curb and took a side street before Dan spotted her.

The front door of the trailer was locked when she got home, which she found unusual. She anchored the pie against a hip and fished in her purse for the key.

The hum of the furnace was the only sound in the house, and

Raine's bedroom door was shut, which meant she was either taking a nap or studying.

"Raine? Sue was in a good mood today." Gin set the pie down on the table and walked down the hall. "Guess what I brought home."

There was no answer, so Gin opened the door and peeked inside.

"Hey, sweetie. Are you sick again?" The shade was pulled down, bathing the room in shadows, but something wasn't right.

Raine wasn't there.

Gin's pulse spiked, rising in direct proportion to the feeling of unease that propelled her to the window. She lifted the shade, saw the empty space behind the trailer where Jasmine should have been parked, and punched in Raine's cell phone.

Her daughter's lilting voice came over the line. "This is Raine . . . leave a message!"

"It's Mom. I just got home from work and I'm wondering where you are. Call me when you get this."

The chicken thawing out in the fridge could wait until Raine returned. Gin sorted through the mail, put away the breakfast dishes, and then jumped in the shower to wash away the smell of Wednesday's cabbage rolls.

Wednesday.

Relief spilled through Gin, diluting the worry that had been making her stomach churn. She'd forgotten that Raine had been going to Cody's church in the middle of the week.

Gin's cell phone chirped from its perch on the ledge of the sink, letting her know she had a new voicemail. She wrapped herself in a towel and tapped in her password to retrieve Raine's excuse.

She heard Cody's voice instead. "Um . . . I'm sorry to bother you, but could you ask Raine to call me? She wasn't feeling good after school, and I just wanted to make sure she's okay."

They weren't together.

Gin tried calling Cody back but there was no answer.

She grabbed her clothes out of the hamper again, pulled a hat over her wet hair, and ran out the door.

Chapter 15

Hope Community Church was like a second home to Dan. His parents were married in the stained glass sanctuary at twenty and dedicated every one of their six children to the Lord. At fifteen, Dan helped the youth group build the addition on the back of the church. At eighteen, he joined the men's Wednesday night Bible study. A few years later the leader answered a call to the mission field and somehow Dan had become his replacement, although he didn't always feel qualified for the job.

Six guys met in a room at the end of the hallway, the one with the faulty vent system that didn't pump enough cold air in the summer or heat during the winter months. It was a graveyard for mismatched tables, stacks of outdated Sunday school materials, and wobbly chairs deemed a hazard by the head usher.

The Landfill, some of the wives called it. For some reason the room had been bypassed during two major renovation projects and was the only place off-limits during Vacation Bible School because it contained hazardous materials—a coffeepot and an ancient microwave as large as a piece of Samsonite luggage.

The group voted on a book of the Bible to study, and this year it was Proverbs. Dan had an edge, because he and Cody had studied the book together when Cody started his freshman year of high school.

The book of wisdom.

Something Dan thought Cody had a little of—until a few days ago.

"What about you?"

Dan's chin snapped up, and he realized everyone's attention was trained on him. "Me?"

"Any prayer requests?" Mort Swanson was the only one who actually wrote them down. Some guys kept a black book filled with the phone numbers of attractive women. Mort kept a black book filled with the trials and tribulations of the men who gathered around a pockmarked table, stained with ink that no professional-grade cleaner could remove.

Dan hesitated. There were no secrets here, but he was reluctant to throw open the door to Evie's personal life.

"Dealing with some changes." It was careful. It was safe.

It was so far from the truth that Dan felt guilty the moment the words were documented in Mort's notebook.

Dan bowed his head, eyes open, as the group cast out their prayers one at a time, hoping to catch some grace.

The men filed out after the study ended, but Dan tossed a few empty cups into the wastebasket and rinsed out the coffeepot. Yeah, he was stalling, but he felt like a total hypocrite. Two weeks ago he had challenged the guys to be real with each other, and here he was, waiting for them to leave the building so he didn't have to smile and pretend everything was okay.

He should have waited a little longer. The minute he stepped into the hallway he was ambushed by one of the men he'd been trying to avoid. His youngest brother.

"You okay, Danny?"

"Why wouldn't I be?" Dan knew he sounded testy, but everyone knew the bond between siblings had a bit more give than other relationships.

"I don't know." Will cocked his head. "You seemed a little distracted tonight."

If Will had noticed, chances were good that Mort had too, and had added a special addendum to Dan's generic prayer request.

Dan slapped his brother on the shoulder hard enough to make him wince. "It's nice to know you care."

"I do." Will looked serious. "I . . . ran into Evie a little while ago. She seemed kind of distracted too."

"Really?" Dan must have not hidden his expression fast enough, because Will's eyes narrowed.

"Did you two have a disagreement?"

"No." It wasn't a lie. The word didn't quite describe what they'd had after Ginevieve and Raine left the house the night before.

Dan's stomach pitched at the memory. When he'd gone back inside, Cody had already retreated to his room and Evie was in the kitchen making a pot of tea.

"I think that went well," were the first words out of her mouth.

"You're kidding, right?" had come out of Dan's.

The conversation had gone south from there.

Dan still couldn't believe Evie had brought up adoption. It was an option, yes, but he questioned her timing. The shattered expressions on Raine's and Cody's faces told him they were still trying to come to grips with the results of the pregnancy test.

He knew Evie was upset, but if Raine and Ginevieve would have been sitting in her office at church instead of her living room, Dan had a feeling she would have responded with a little more compassion.

"If you say so." Will looked skeptical. "How are things going with Cody? You guys weren't at the gym last night."

"I didn't realize I had to check in with you whenever my plans changed."

"Well, you do." Will's easy grin finally surfaced. "I can't be passing bad intel to Mom."

Dan would have laughed, but his brother was only half joking. Angela Moretti liked to know what was going on in her children's lives, but he wasn't ready to tell his family about the pregnancy. Mom and Dad considered Evie and Cody part of the family. As a teenager Evie had spent more time in Angela Moretti's kitchen than her own, and the two had grown even closer after Max died.

Dan knew his parents would be upset by the news, but Evie had asked him not to say anything until she and Cody met with Pastor Keith.

They'd had a discussion about that too. Dan was concerned that Evie only saw how the situation affected Cody.

Men take what they want . . .

Ginevieve's accusation ricocheted through Dan's head.

Take, not get. A choice of words that continued to chew at the edges of his thoughts.

What was her story? She couldn't have been more than eighteen or nineteen when Raine was born. Had Raine's father abandoned them? Or stuck around and made their lives miserable?

"Earth to Dan." Will slugged him in the arm as they reached the end of the hallway. "This is what I'm talking about. You aren't even pretending to listen to me."

"Sorry—" Dan pulled up short as an auburn-haired woman in cowboy boots charged past them.

"Wow." Will's eyes bugged out. "Who is that?"

Dan shoved his Bible and notebook into his brother's hands. "I'll be right back."

The double doors were already swinging shut as he reached them.

Dan glanced over his shoulder, tracking Ginevieve's flight in reverse, searching for whatever had upset her.

Evie stood next to the welcome center, her cheeks a shade lighter than usual. She was still rooted to the floor when Dan reached her side a few seconds later.

"What happened? Why was Ginevieve here?"

"She just showed up out of the blue, wanting to talk to Cody. I said he was busy, and she asked if I'd seen Raine here tonight."

"Why was she looking for Cody?" Dan had caught a glimpse of Ginevieve's expression. She'd looked panicked, not angry, and Gin struck him as the kind of person who didn't scare easily.

"Who's looking for me?" Cody had come up behind Evie. "Is Raine here?"

"Her mom was," Dan said tightly. "Did you and Raine have an argument or something?"

"No." Cody's eyes locked with Dan's. "We didn't even get a chance to talk today. I saw her after school but she wanted to go home. She said she wasn't feeling well."

Dan turned to Evie. "Did Gin say anything else?"

"Something about Raine not being there when she got home from work."

Cody made a lunge toward the exit, but Dan grabbed his arm. "I'll talk to Ginevieve and find out what's going on."

Evie's expression clouded. "Danny . . ."

Dan could count the number of times he'd ignored a plea from Evie on one hand, but he turned to Cody. "If you hear from Raine, let me know."

Dan pushed through the double doors that led to the parking lot. He caught a glimpse of Gin, zigzagging between the cars, her head bent against the wind. Had she *walked* from Fifth Avenue to the church? It was at least a quarter of a mile and she wasn't exactly dressed for the weather.

Dan jumped into his pickup. At the rate she was moving, he'd catch up to her faster with four wheels than on two feet.

At the corner he pulled alongside her and rolled down the window.

"Get in."

Chapter 16

Where had Dan Moretti come from?

Gin stumbled forward on the icy sidewalk and suddenly there he was, reaching out to steady her. Blocking her path.

"Evie said you were looking for Raine. What's going on?"

"I'm not sure." Gin knew she wouldn't be able to shake the man loose until she told him the truth. "I got home from work tonight and Raine was gone. She's not answering her phone and I have no idea where she is. Satisfied?"

"Not until we find her."

We.

For a split second Gin held onto the word.

"I don't need your help." She pivoted away from Dan, but he snagged her elbow. Heat shot up Gin's arm and she spun around, ready to give it to him with both barrels, but the genuine concern in Dan's eyes doused her anger.

"Come on, Ginevieve." He let go, but his eyes held her in place. "I'll take you to the police department."

"They won't get involved. Raine is considered an adult."

Dan opened the passenger side door. "One of my friends is on duty. Just talk to him. He'll want to help."

Because doing something—anything—was better than giving

in to the fear that bit deeper than the wind, Gin reluctantly climbed into the cab of his pickup.

The interior smelled like freshly laundered cotton and . . . Dan. A badge of some sort was pinned to the visor, but she didn't get a chance to look at it too closely because the light on the dashboard faded away when Dan closed the door.

Most of the businesses had closed for the day, and another cold snap had driven people inside the snug cocoons of their homes. In spite of the warm air blowing from the vents, Gin imagined Raine in some cold, shadowy place and couldn't suppress another shiver.

Where are you, Raine?

"It'll be okay."

Gin didn't acknowledge Dan's words. It wasn't the first time a man had made a promise he couldn't keep.

Banister Falls' Police Department shared space with the Parks and Recreation department in an old brick building on Main Street. Dan parked in the back and hammered on the door until it opened.

"Moretti." A uniformed police officer who looked like he could have been a lineman for the NFL greeted them with a wide smile. "What are you doing here?"

Dan nodded at Gin. "Ryan, this is Ginevieve Lightly. Ginevieve, Ryan Tate."

"Officer Tate to you." He gave Dan's shoulder a good-natured shove, but when his gaze cut to Gin, the smile faded. "Is there something I can do for you, ma'am?"

Gin didn't know what it was. Lack of sleep or the worry gnawing holes in her self-control, but tears burned the back of her eyes. "My daughter. Raine. She . . . I don't know where she is."

"Let's talk in my office." The officer ushered them through the dispatch area to a large room sectioned off into cubicles. "Have a seat, please." He rolled an extra chair toward her.

Gin sat down and Dan pulled up another chair, positioning

himself behind her shoulder. He hadn't asked if he could sit in on the meeting, just settled in and made himself comfortable, the way he had when he'd shown up at her place to talk to Cody. The scent of that masculine soap stirred the air, and Gin tried her best to ignore it. To ignore *him.*

"How old is your daughter, Mrs. Lightly?"

"It's Miss," Gin murmured. "And Raine is eighteen."

"When was the last time you saw her?"

"This morning. She dropped me off at work on her way to school."

"Did she attend classes?"

"The office never called and reported her as absent, so I assume she was there all day. We usually call or text during her lunch break, but I knew Raine had a test to make up, so I assumed she was busy."

Gin watched the officer jot something down.

"Are you sure she isn't with one of her friends?"

"We haven't lived in Banister Falls very long. Raine doesn't really have any friends." Gin realized how that sounded when Officer Tate frowned.

"What about family?"

"No." Gin shook her head even as a faded image of Sara's face flashed through her mind. Her younger half sister had never approved of what she referred to as Gin's "gypsy lifestyle."

Gin's mom had had a brief fling with the son of a wealthy banker, who'd denied paternity—no surprise there—and walked out on her. Ginevieve was eight and Sara three when the man's mother found out about the affair and swooped in to rescue Sara. A sizeable deposit in Ginevieve's mother's bank account was made on the same day she signed a document terminating her parental rights.

Gin had watched the block-long car pull away with Sara inside and wondered when the tall woman with the silver hair and pretty clothes was going to come back for her.

A private detective Sara had hired knocked on Gin's door when Raine was six years old. Her half sister wanted to have a relationship, but the thread that connected them was so fragile, the weight of their differences put a strain on it from the beginning. For Sara, life had been ballet lessons, shopping trips to New York City, and private schools. For Gin it had been trying to graduate from high school and keep her mom sober.

Gin hadn't discouraged Sara from keeping in touch with Raine over the years, but she lived in Maine, not exactly close enough for a person to pop in and say hello.

"Did you and your daughter have an argument recently?"

"No." It was no mystery where this line of questioning was going. In the officer's eyes, Raine was probably one more kid trying to escape a bad home life. Every question he asked gouged another hole in Gin's heart.

She shouldn't have let Dan talk her into coming here. Gin was an outsider. A stranger. People whose roots tunneled deep into the soil of their hometown wouldn't understand why she preferred to see what was over the next horizon.

And things had been fine until they'd landed in Banister Falls.

Now Gin was stranded here and Raine was gone and Gin had no idea where to start looking for her. Places, not people, filled the pages of the photo album on their coffee table. Gin had taken pride in that. Until now. Now she wished she knew there was someone out there watching over her daughter.

"Has Raine . . . left home . . . before?"

"No. She doesn't break curfew or drink or do drugs, either."

The officer didn't appear ruffled by Gin's terse statement. "So this isn't typical behavior?"

"Would I be here if it was? Raine is a great kid. An A student. She doesn't do things like this. I—"

I'm the one who leaves.

The thought stripped the breath from Gin's lungs.

Suddenly Dan's hand settled on her shoulder, a steady pressure that should have felt suffocating instead of comforting.

"Are you concerned that Raine might be a danger to herself or others?"

"No . . . of course not." Gin couldn't bring herself to tell the officer that Raine was pregnant, and she hoped Dan wouldn't say anything. Officer Tate would judge Raine—the way Gin had been judged.

She twitched her shoulder and Dan's hand dropped away, but she felt the imprint of every blunt fingertip through two layers of clothing, all the way down to her bare skin.

"I'm afraid there isn't much I can do at this point." The officer's eyes narrowed. On Dan. "Based on my experience with teenagers, your daughter will show up in a few hours and wonder what all the fuss was about."

"She has the car." Dan didn't look too happy. "Can you at least ask the guys on the next shift to keep an eye out for it?"

"That I can do." Ryan's gaze swung back to Ginevieve. "I'll need a description of the vehicle and the license plate number."

Gin gave him the information and pushed to her feet. Based on *her* experience, she doubted he'd follow up on it. "Thank you."

"I can't make any promises, but I'll let you know if someone spots her or the car." The officer turned to Dan. "I'll see you Sunday."

"Thanks, man." Dan gripped his friend's hand. "I appreciate this."

Gin didn't stick around to watch the male bonding ritual. She was anxious to get home and see if Raine had come back. If not, she would leave a message on her voicemail—again. Before Gin reached the door, Dan maneuvered around her and opened it.

"I can—"

"We're not going to have this argument again. I won the first time, remember?" He opened the passenger side of the truck and waited until she was inside before he shut the door.

Dan turned up the heat, and this time Gin couldn't help but lean into the warm air blowing from the vent.

"Better?" His husky voice rolled over her, and Gin wanted to lean into that too.

What is wrong with you?

This was Dan Moretti. Cody Bennett's role model. Evie Bennett's . . . whatever he was. Not that that always mattered. Gin had worked as a waitress long enough to notice a wedding ring on a guy's hand when she handed him a menu and a bare finger when she returned to take his order. Somewhere between that first cup of coffee and dessert, he would make it clear he was interested in something that wasn't listed with the rest of the daily specials.

For all his steady-eyed calm and heart-stopping good looks, Dan Moretti was probably hoping the rumors about single moms who changed boyfriends as often as some women changed the color of their nail polish were true.

He turned onto Fifth Avenue, and the Jamesons' pit bull dove out of the shadows and streaked toward the road, its forward momentum stopped only by the heavy chain wrapped around the leg of their porch.

And the stereotypes just kept piling up.

Dan pulled up in front of the trailer—the dark trailer—and was there to open the door before Gin's foot even touched the ground.

"Watch your step," he murmured.

Always, Gin thought. She fumbled for her key, ready to put an end to what had been a very long day.

"Ginevieve . . . wait."

Gin wasn't surprised by Dan's husky command. What did surprise her was the disappointment that burned a path down her throat. He was just like all the other guys who hit on her. Churchgoer, upstanding citizen, firefighter . . . it didn't matter.

Dan's fingers folded over hers, holding her captive. "God—"

You're so beautiful? Sexy?

Gin's mind raced ahead to fill in the blank even as the touch of Dan's hand made her heart buckle.

"Ginevieve is worried about Raine—we all are," Dan continued in a low voice. "We don't know where she is, but You do. Watch over her, keep her safe, and please bring her home."

Gin tried to follow the unfamiliar script.

Was Dan really talking to . . . God? Praying for Raine?

For *her*?

Dan didn't look offended when Gin jerked her hand free. "What are you doing?"

"Asking a friend for help."

A friend.

An unexpected surge of longing crashed through Gin even as she shook her head. "You think God listens?"

"I *know* He does."

Maybe God did listen to the perfect Evie Bennetts and Dan Morettis in the world. But Gin was pretty sure He had never so much as glanced her way.

Chapter 17

Are you listening, God?

Raine waited for a response, but all she heard was the thump of Jasmine's tires against the road.

The headlights pierced the darkness, illuminating a narrow corridor between the walls of trees. By now her mom would be wondering where she was. Raine knew she should turn the car around, but the farther she got from Banister Falls, the harder it was to go back.

She saw a gas station up ahead and pulled in. The place looked kind of sketchy, but the car had been running on fumes the past half hour. While the tank filled, Raine searched her purse for the lunch money she hadn't spent the last few days.

The skinny guy at the register checked her out when she came inside to pay.

Raine changed her mind about using the restroom and grabbed a couple of things to tide her over. An apple, a package of peanut butter crackers, and a bottle of ginger ale she hoped would settle her stomach.

"How are you doing today?"

"I'm fine." Raine mumbled the correct response as she set the things down on the counter.

His eyes raked over her again and he grinned. "Can't argue with that."

She pushed a wrinkled five-dollar bill across the counter. There were times she wished she was more like her mom. Her mom could put a jerky guy in his place with one look.

He picked up the apple and studied it like he'd never seen one before. No way she was going to eat it now.

"It's a nice night for a drive."

"I guess."

Her mom had always claimed an open road cleared her head, but Raine had driven almost a hundred miles and it still hadn't happened. If anything she was even more confused.

"Where you headed?"

Raine figured the guy was making polite conversation, but she couldn't suppress a shiver when he tipped the change into her hand and his thumb slid across her wrist.

"Thanks." Raine pretended she hadn't heard him and stuffed the bills back in her purse.

She felt him watching her as she walked away and stopped by a display of brochures near the door to check her phone. He didn't have to know its battery was dead.

When he stepped out from behind the counter, Raine grabbed a brochure from the display and pushed a shoulder against the door.

Tears burned her eyes as she got into the car.

What should I do, God?

She couldn't keep driving—but she wasn't ready to go back, either.

She started to stuff the brochure into the outside pocket of her purse, but the logo at the top caught her attention. Whisper Lake Camp.

Raine recognized the name. Cody had mentioned it at youth group one night. The guys in his Bible study had rented a cabin for a week over summer vacation, and Cody said the owners had invited them to come back anytime.

Underneath a photograph of the sun rising over a sapphire blue lake was a verse Raine recognized too. *Let the morning bring me word of your unfailing love, for I have put my trust in you.*

She flipped the brochure over and looked at the map on the back. A red star was half an inch away from a town she'd driven through a few minutes ago.

A smile worked its way to the surface. Cody said there were no such things as coincidences . . .

I do trust You, God.

A tap on her window startled Raine. The skinny clerk stood next to the car, staring down at her. She rolled the window down a cautious inch.

"Do you need directions or something?"

The look in his eyes told Raine he was hoping she'd pick the something. The guy probably made more money selling weed than gasoline.

"No, thanks. I know where I'm going." Raine set the brochure down and rolled the window up.

At the end of the parking lot, she whispered a thank-you. And turned left instead of right.

It was almost ten o'clock when Gin's phone rang. She snatched it up, saw Raine's name on the screen, and collapsed against the sofa pillows in relief. "Where are you? Are you all right?"

"I'm okay, Mom." The phone crackled in Gin's ear. "I didn't mean to worry you."

"Then you should have called a long time ago!"

"I couldn't . . . my cell phone died."

Gin bit down on the inside of her cheek to avoid stating the obvious. If Raine had been home where she belonged, she could have *charged* her cell phone. "I was worried sick. You could have left a note letting me know where you were."

"I didn't plan to be gone so long. I just got in the car and kept driving." A pause. "I figured you'd understand."

Raine hadn't meant the words to hurt, but Gin felt the sting. She understood all too well. How many times had she gotten behind the wheel just so she could watch everything disappear in her rearview mirror? But . . .

"I take you with me."

"I know," Raine whispered. "I had to think."

Gin understood that too. "Is this because of what happened last night? At Cody's house?"

"Everyone's talking about the future like we don't have one anymore."

Gin closed her eyes. "You have one, sweetheart." But Raine was just beginning to grasp how much it had changed. "We can talk about it when you come home."

Silence stretched between them, and Gin felt a stab of fear. "You are on your way home, right?"

"Not yet."

"Where *are* you?" Gin had a sudden, terrifying image of Raine driving a temperamental Jasmine halfway across the country to see Sara.

"I'm staying at a camp about three hours north of Banister Falls. Cody talked about it, and the Russells are really nice. They don't have any cabins open right now but they're letting me stay in their house."

A camp . . . Their *house*? What kind of people invited a stranger into their home?

"You don't know anything about them!" Gin didn't know anything about them.

"It's called Whisper Lake and it's a Bible camp. If it makes you feel any better, the people who own it are related to Dan Moretti."

Gin didn't know if that made her feel better or not. She reached for her ancient laptop to google it. "What about school?"

"I'll catch up. I won't be gone long, Mom. I promise. I need some time to figure things out. To . . . to pray."

To pray.

As if it were happening all over again, Gin felt Dan's hand fold around hers. Heard the quiet confidence in his voice when he'd prayed for Raine.

Do you think God listens?

I know He does.

Gin released a slow breath. "All right. But you have to check in with me too."

Dan had driven around town for an hour looking for a ten-year-old burgundy Impala. Trying to shake the memory of Ginevieve's reaction when he'd taken her hand.

The split second before he'd closed his eyes to pray for her, Dan had seen something in hers.

Resignation.

The thought made him physically sick. Not because he'd done anything wrong, but because Gin had been waiting—no, *expecting*—him to come on to her.

Dan hadn't planned to pray out loud. He'd acted on impulse—something he thought he had been trained out of over the years—but he didn't regret it. What he regretted was Gin's assumption that she had to go through this alone.

His cell phone broke the silence, and Dan's heart jumped in

time with the opening beat of the ringtone when a familiar number flashed on the screen. "Hello?"

"It's Ryan. I figured you'd still be up."

"I'm surprised you are." Dan pushed himself onto one elbow and checked the time. "I thought your shift ended at ten."

"I decided to put in a little overtime." Ryan hesitated. "Drove out to Maple Ridge."

"You found Raine's car?"

"Not Raine's. A silver Jeep. License number KX567. Recognize it?"

Dan should. He was the one who'd put it on. "Cody's there?"

On a school night. Which meant Evie assumed he was asleep in his room.

"He's not in the vehicle. Do you want me to take a look around?"

"Yes . . ." Dan smeared his hand across his jaw. "No."

"If it's multiple choice, does that mean I get to pick one?"

"I'm sure Cody is okay." More okay than Dan would be if Evie found out he knew that Cody had snuck out of the house and hadn't told her. "He knows his way around the park."

And the fact he'd gone there meant he wanted to be alone.

"Your call, buddy. No one's reported *him* missing."

Dan didn't bite. "I appreciate it, Rye. I'll check in with Cody in a little while."

"So." Ryan drew out the word. "What's the story with you and Ginevieve Lightly?"

"Story?"

"You two friends?"

Dan's lips twisted in a wry smile. "I guess that depends on which one of us you ask."

Chapter 18

From a corner of the couch in Wade and Kimberly Russell's living room, Raine could see Mrs. Russell in the kitchen, ladling chicken soup into a bowl.

If the couple had been shocked to find a stranger on their doorstep at night, they hadn't shown it. Raine had asked about renting a cabin, but when they found out she was a friend of Cody's, Kimberly insisted she take a spare room in the main lodge. Their *home*.

Raine had almost burst into tears right there. She still couldn't believe her mom had agreed to let her stay at the camp for a few days. Although she'd probably already brought up the website on her computer.

"There are fresh towels in the bathroom off the guest room." Kimberly set the bowl of soup down on the coffee table. "And a new toothbrush with your name on it."

Tears again. "Thank you."

"You called your mom?"

"Uh huh." Her mom had taken it way better than Raine expected.

But now she had to call Cody.

"Good." Kimberly gave her a quick smile. "Make yourself at home, and we'll see you in the morning."

Raine waited until Kimberly left before she reached for her phone again. Seven new voicemail messages, but she hadn't had the courage to listen to them. She took a deep breath and called him. Just like her mom, Cody didn't bother with a hello.

"Are you kidding me, Wats? Why aren't you answering your phone? I've been trying to get ahold of you all night."

Raine had never heard Cody sound this upset. Not even the day she'd told him she was pregnant. "I went for a drive."

"I would have gone with you."

That was *why* she hadn't told him. "It was a spur-of-the-moment thing. And you had Bible study."

"I was worried about you. When your mom came over to the church—"

"What?" Her mom hadn't mentioned that. "Why?"

"I called her when you didn't answer your phone. She was worried too."

"I'm sorry." Raine had been saying that a lot.

"It's okay. How about I pick you up tomorrow morning? You can look through the notes I took on the documentary we watched in Mrs. Dewey's class."

Raine plucked at a corner of the afghan. "I'm not home, Cody."

"Not home," he repeated slowly.

"I need some time to figure things out."

"I thought we were going to figure things out together."

The sudden tension in Cody's voice pulled at Raine, weakening her resolve.

"Where are you? How long are you planning to be gone?"

"Not long." Raine hoped he wouldn't realize she'd dodged the first question.

"What about school?"

"That's what my mom said."

"Your mom knows about this? And she doesn't mind?"

"She did at first. But I told her . . . I told her I needed time to pray."

Cody was silent for a moment. And then, "We can do that together too."

"I know." Raine was glad he couldn't see the tears sliding down her face.

"Don't shut me out, Wats."

The weight was pressing down on her again. "I'm not."

"And I'm not going to walk out on you the way your dad did."

Raine pulled her knees protectively against her chest but it didn't matter. She'd given Cody her heart—and along with it, access to her deepest fears. "We aren't even applying to the same colleges, Cody! How are you going to help out with the baby? How are we going to make it work?"

A rattling sound muffled his response, and Raine pressed the phone closer to her ear. "What's that noise?"

"The wind."

The wind?

"Where are you?"

"I'm at the tree house."

"Cody." It was thirty degrees outside. "What are you doing there?"

"Waiting for you."

"Wait for me."

Raine's shoes had slipped on the frost-covered ground as she struggled to keep up with Cody. They'd taken the Family Living Skills unit exam the first week of November, and Raine was pretty sure when they moved back to their original seats it would mean the end of their relationship.

But he'd shown up at her door the next Saturday morning with a steaming cup of cappuccino and a question. "Ready?"

Raine nodded and grabbed her coat, ready for anything if it

involved spending time with Cody. He drove past a park on the outskirts of town while she tried to guess their destination.

"I know! You're going to show me the waterfall."

Cody burst out laughing.

"What?" Raine pretended to be offended. "The town is called Banister Falls, right? There has to be one around here somewhere."

"Only after a heavy rain in the summer." Cody turned onto a narrow dirt road. "The rest of the time, it's a rock wall."

"False advertising," Raine grumbled.

"Vision." Cody had winked at her and made her forget all about the waterfall.

The sun shook free of the clouds and sprinkled glitter on everything. Raine picked up the pace, following the pattern of Cody's footprints like she was playing a game of hopscotch.

Cody glanced over his shoulder. "Okay?"

She was better than okay. Even though her nose was running, her muscles ached, and her Hello Kitty socks had bunched up in the toes of her boots.

The trees began to thin out, and Raine spotted a barbed wire fence.

"Hold on a second." She balked, knowing her mom would put her on house arrest if she got into trouble. "Is this private property?"

"Of course not. It belongs to the county." Cody lifted up the bottom strand of wire so she could get through. "There's a campground and picnic area about a mile away, but that part is closed this time of year."

"A mile?" Raine squeaked.

"Where we're going isn't that far."

Cody's idea of "not far" turned into another ten minutes. Raine felt the first blister forming on her little toe when he veered toward a small stand of trees.

"Here we are."

She looked around. "There were trees just like this when we got out of the car."

Cody grinned. "Look up."

Raine tipped her head back. Someone had stuck a wooden box in the branches. "What is that?"

"It's an old tree stand. For hunting."

She studied the bowed walls and scabs of moss that darkened the shingles. "How old?"

"I found it when I was eleven."

"Eleven." Raine silently did the math. "Are you sure it's safe?"

"Nope."

Sometimes Raine wished Cody wasn't so honest. "It's great. Can we go back now?"

"Don't you want to see it?"

Raine nibbled on her lower lip. "It looks like a good place for critters to hide."

"Critters hibernate this time of year."

"Yeah . . . in *trees.* Don't you watch *Animal Planet*?"

"I won't let you fall." Cody beckoned her over. "Come on."

"If I break something, you're the one who's going to have to tell my mom."

The warning would have terrified anyone else, but Cody simply nodded and boosted her onto the first branch.

"The ladder rotted away, but there are still chunks of wood nailed to the trunk. Put your feet on those," he instructed.

"Because *those* chunks of wood wouldn't be rotten."

"That's what I like about you, Wats." Cody grinned up at her. "Always looking on the bright side."

What I like about you.

Raine held on tighter to the words than she did the next branch. Cody followed, the only barrier between her and the ground.

Whenever she glanced down at the ground, his face was in the way, his smile urging her on.

The stand was larger than it looked from the ground. Raine pushed aside the piece of canvas that doubled as a door and scanned the interior for hibernating creatures. "What do you do up here?"

"Think." Cody stretched out on the floor and folded his hands behind his head.

Raine sat down next to him and pulled her knees up to her chest. Studied the ice that mortared the cracks between the walls. "If this is what you do for fun, I'll bet you can't wait to go to college."

"Not really."

"What?" Raine's mouth dropped open. He had to be kidding. "Mr. 4.0 Valedictorian? You'll probably get a free ride."

He didn't say anything, and Raine tried to crack the code of silence. "You *want* to go to college, don't you?"

Cody stared at her.

"What?"

"No one has ever asked me that before."

"Well, I'm asking you now." Raine propped her chin on her knees and waited.

"I don't want to leave Banister Falls." His voice barely broke above a whisper, as if he were afraid someone was listening in on their conversation.

"Ever?"

"No. I like it here. But my mom, she wants me to go to college and get a degree in business."

"You can't wait to own that car dealership, huh?"

Cody laughed, warm and low. "A noble profession, but I don't think it's right for me."

"What is right for you, then?"

Cody fixed his eyes on the rafters in the ceiling. "Did you know this tree stand is the same height as a two-story building?"

Raine knew he was changing the subject, but she decided to humor him. "You could have told me that sooner." She poked him in the ribs. "Like when we were on the ground. I'm not a fan of heights."

"Neither am I. It took me a whole summer to get the courage to climb up here."

"Why didn't you just build one on the ground?"

"You have to be able to climb a ladder this high when you're a firefighter."

Raine realized that Cody hadn't been trying to change the subject.

"You want to be a firefighter?" He hadn't put that on Mrs. Dewey's questionnaire. Raine would have remembered.

"It's all I've ever wanted to be."

"Wow." Raine's stomach tightened at the thought of Cody running into a burning building. "Does your mom know?"

"No." The word rolled out in Cody's sigh. "She thinks it's too dangerous, and I can't really argue with that, can I? I mean, my dad died fighting a fire. He wasn't that much older than me."

"Your mom wants you to be happy, doesn't she?"

"Mom wants me to be safe . . . but I don't think that's at the top of God's list."

Raine wasn't surprised when Cody brought God into the conversation. He did that a lot. She'd gone to youth group with him a few times and bought a little red New Testament at the secondhand store on Bird Street. She hadn't told Cody, just started reading Matthew. By the time she finished the gospel of John, getting to know God wasn't just a way of getting to know Cody better. Raine wanted to know God better too.

"You think God has a list?"

"I know He has a plan for my life . . . but what if His plan and Mom's plan don't match? She's been through a lot. I don't want to upset her."

Raine could relate. It wasn't a coincidence that every college her mom talked about was smack-dab in the middle of a big city. There were more opportunities, more things to see and do.

I want the best for you.

Raine couldn't count the number of times she'd heard those words. Cody was right. How could a person argue with that?

"My mom sounds like your mom." Raine sighed into her knees. "She had a hard time saying yes when I asked if we could stick around here until graduation. She thinks small equals stunted."

"Mom grew up in Banister Falls, but for some reason she wants me to move away." Cody shook his head. "We toured some of the state colleges last summer, and I couldn't wait to get back here and shoot hoops with Dan and the guys on his crew."

"Maybe Dan would talk to your mom." Raine knew how much time the guys spent together.

"He doesn't know either," Cody admitted, shocking Raine all the way down to her frostbitten toes. "I haven't told anyone."

Anyone but her.

Raine looked away, afraid Cody would be able to read her thoughts. Would see how much she liked him. Cody had never given any indication that he thought of her as more than a friend, and Raine didn't want to make a fool of herself.

"If I go to college and get some nine-to-five job in an office, I know I'll feel like I'm living someone else's life," Cody whispered. "What am I supposed to do?"

He was asking *her* for advice?

"Before I start writing a story, I see this blank page and it stresses me out." Raine's heart picked up speed, but she measured the words out one at a time. "What if I write the wrong thing? What if I mess it up? But when I finally write down that first word . . . the rest of it flows out, and everything that follows makes sense."

Cody didn't say anything, and that made Raine wish she hadn't. She held her breath, afraid he would laugh at her. But she should have known better.

"One word," he repeated. "It sounds easy."

"It isn't." Raine had to be honest. "But maybe . . . maybe God will give you that one word, and then you'll know what you're supposed to do."

"I feel like I was born to be a firefighter. But . . . I don't know. Maybe I'm not brave enough."

"If it's on God's list, won't He help you be that too?"

Cody rolled toward her and propped himself up on one elbow. "I'm glad you talked your mom into staying . . . even if you're only using Banister Falls as a setting for your first novel."

"Names will be changed to protect the innocent." Raine held up one hand. "I promise I won't mention your secret hideout."

"It's not so secret anymore." Cody smiled. "I suppose I could post a *No Girls Allowed* sign on the door."

"Hey!" Raine rocked back on her heels. "What am I?"

The teasing light faded from Cody's eyes. "You're the exception, Wats."

A log in the fireplace snapped, sending up a spray of sparks, and Raine realized both of them had lapsed into silence on their phones. "Do you remember the first time you took me there? What we talked about?"

"Yes." The smile in Cody's voice opened space for Raine to breathe again.

"That's why I left. I'm asking God for a word. I can't make any decisions about the future until I know what He wants me to do about the baby."

"*Our* baby, Wats."

"I know," Raine whispered. "That's why I want you to ask Him too."

Chapter 19

Breakfast at Marie's, Captain?" Hopper wiped the soot from his face with the back of his hand. "I'd say we earned it."

Sid cuffed the back of the kid's head. "Earned it? You were doing the job you got paid for."

The good-natured jibes flew back and forth as Dan stowed the rest of his gear into the compartment of the fire truck. They'd responded to a call in the middle of the night, but fortunately the fire had been contained to the chimney. All they'd had to do was drop in a dry chem bomb, calm the panicked young couple who owned the house, and deliver a short lecture on the importance of annual maintenance checks for creosote buildup.

"We don't have to go out. I'll make pancakes and sausage for everyone," Jerry offered.

A chorus of groans rose toward the sky. Everyone knew the guy couldn't cook, so it was a threat more than a bribe.

Dan peeled off his turnout coat. "How about breakfast at My Place?"

"You're going to cook for us, Captain?"

"It's the name of a diner," Dan said brusquely.

"My Place." Jerry frowned. "Isn't that the dive on Radley Street?"

"Yeah." Sid grinned. "If you don't catch something from the food, you probably will from the waitresses."

Anger flared, quick and hot, inside of Dan. "Never mind."

"Why do you want to go there, Captain?" Hopper pressed.

Dan suddenly realized he was surrounded. Everyone was staring at him, waiting for an answer.

"No reason." He closed the door a little harder than necessary. "I thought it would be nice to change things up a little, that's all." And he wanted to check on Gin. Find out if she'd heard anything from Raine since he'd dropped her off the night before.

His men passed a glance around the circle.

"We can give it a try." Sid shrugged. "You can't screw up eggs and toast, right?"

No one else looked as confident.

Dan's confidence faded a little too, when Ginevieve breezed through the swinging doors that separated the kitchen from the dining area. Translucent green eyes flashed with something even a thick-headed male could identify as irritation, and Dan realized his mistake. There were four firefighters who'd been out on an early morning call, and from the looks of it, one waitress to handle the regulars.

Ginevieve grabbed two pots of coffee from the warmers and fell in behind Dan's crew as they shuffled to the back of the diner. Two men in flannel shirts raised their coffee mugs in salute as they filed past.

"Moretti." One of the guys stretched his leg into the aisle, and Dan found his path blocked by a steel-toed boot. "Haven't seen you in a while."

"Cozie." He and Craig Cozielle had never traveled in the same social circles, hadn't since Craig got busted for underage drinking at the eighth grade dance, but Dan decided it wouldn't be polite to point that out.

"Save another basement this morning?" Cozie slapped his hand on the table, and the sound of his laughter carried around the dining room.

Dan didn't bother with a comeback as he stepped around the guy's leg. "Excuse me."

Gin didn't even ask who wanted coffee. She flipped over the chipped ceramic mugs and started pouring while his crew—who'd regressed to junior high blushes and averted eyes—remained mute.

There was nothing provocative about the way Gin was dressed. Faded jeans dipped low on her hips but covered everything they needed to cover, and her long-sleeved T-shirt was on the boxy side. The flowing mahogany hair had been woven into a neat braid that trailed between her shoulder blades.

A stack of silver bracelets jingled on her slender wrist, and you would have thought someone had jumped up on the table and started belting out the national anthem, based on the way everyone gave that their full attention too.

"Don't forget about us, baby." Cozie's gaze tracked Gin's every movement as she took a lap around Dan's table with the coffeepot.

"Yeah," his friend chimed in. "We were here first."

Dan recognized Paul Hanson, disguised by a heavy beard, by his whine—he'd heard it often enough when they'd played on opposing teams during summer baseball league.

"I'll be with you in a minute." Gin turned to Hopper. "What can I get you?"

"Don't you have an order pad or something?" Hopper stammered.

"I have something." Gin folded her arms. "It's called my memory. So what will it be?"

A tide of red washed over Hopper's jaw and continued to rise like the liquid in a thermometer all the way up to his hairline. Dan almost felt sorry for the guy.

"Ham and cheese omelet? Wheat toast?"

One mahogany brow lifted. "Are you telling me or asking me?"

Hopper's eyes bulged. "B-both?"

Gin's lips curved in a genuine smile, and Dan could have sworn every man pulled in a breath at the same time, depleting the oxygen from the room. He was feeling a little light-headed himself.

Sid snapped his menu shut. "Steak and eggs, but only if you can guarantee it's a decent cut of beef."

"Sorry. I can't even guarantee it *is* beef." Gin retreated to the kitchen, only to be summoned a few minutes later by Craig Cozielle.

"My shift starts in fifteen minutes, Gin!" he bellowed. "What's the holdup?"

Dan was about to shoot him a glare, but Jerry beat him to it.

The half doors parted and Gin strode out, a steaming plate balanced in each hand. Cozie and his buddy, Hanson, had moved closer to the window, forcing Gin to lean over the table to set their order down.

"Anything else I can get for you?"

"How about some sugar?" Craig's fingers twitched, his hand hovering a millimeter above the curve of her hip.

"You touch me, Cozie, and I swear I'll stick a fork in the closest body part."

Gin's smile didn't falter, but Dan's self-control did. The feet of his chair scraped the floor as he rose to his feet.

Chapter 20

Gin stepped out of Cozie's reach and almost collided with Dan Moretti. The grim look on his face told Gin that he'd heard what Cozie said.

Gin shifted her weight, blocking Cozie's smirk from view. "Is there something I can get for you?" She forced herself to meet Dan's eyes, aware they had an audience. Every one of his crew had stopped talking to watch the exchange, their expressions ranging from confusion to outright disbelief.

"No." Dan shot Cozie a hard look and eased back into his chair. "I'm good."

"Good." Gin pivoted toward table four, scraped a handful of change into her apron pocket, and ducked into the kitchen with the handful of slips. "Table five."

"I heard." Sue stood at the grill waving a wooden spoon and barking orders at Wendell, the diner's jack-of-all-trades. The poor man couldn't obey fast enough, stacking cords of bacon and sausage links on plates with Sue directing his every move like the conductor of a symphony.

Gin ladled maple syrup into plastic cups and tried to tune out the bursts of masculine laughter in the dining room. She didn't have any problem isolating Dan's from the rest of the crowd. It was an audio-enhanced version of his smile, rich and smooth as a piece of French silk pie.

Sue caught Gin's eye as she reached for a potholder. "The fire department," her boss mused. "Kind of funny, them showing up for breakfast this morning. Did you ask if it was Marie's that burned down?"

Gin held back a smile. Her boss was smart enough to know the diner hadn't been written up in the local newspaper as the newest place to experience fine cuisine.

"It wasn't the bistro. I heard one of them say something about a chimney fire." Gin lifted the lid on the Crock-Pot and gave the contents a quick stir. Sue's sausage gravy was the color and consistency of wet concrete, but if a person could get past the appearance it actually tasted pretty good.

"Isn't one of the Moretti boys a firefighter?" Sue wasn't done with her investigation.

While Gin was considering the question from all angles and wondering which answer wouldn't open the door to a whole new set of questions, her coworker hijacked the conversation.

"Dan. Dan Moretti." Wendell grabbed a chunk of ham and began to hack it into pieces with a chef's knife. "He put out a grass fire at my mom's house a few years ago. She said he stopped over on his day off and helped her with the cleanup."

"A real upstanding guy." Sue was looking at her, not Wendell. "Isn't he the one you asked about?"

Gin gave a curt nod, mentally kicking herself for giving in to her curiosity and asking about Dan. *"Yes."*

"Huh."

Gin hadn't known a single grunt could say so much. "He's a friend of Evie Bennett's, remember?"

"I remember." Sue aimed the wooden spoon straight at Gin's heart. "Just making sure *you* do."

Gin had no idea how to respond to a crazy statement like that, so she chose silence. A timer beeped, and Sue jerked her chin at the microwave.

"Biscuits. I had to take them out of the freezer."

Not that thawing out Sue's biscuits would change their overall texture, but Gin tore one open anyway and examined the center before dumping them onto a plate.

"Hold on, Gin." Wendell leaped in front of her and decorated Dan's pancakes with a sprig of wilted parsley.

"What is that?"

"A garnish." The dishwasher glowered at her. "I saw it on one of those cooking shows when I lived in the barracks."

Whenever Wendell talked about "the barracks," Gin knew it was a veiled reference to his two-year stay at the Waupun prison for check forgery. He'd stopped at the diner one morning to inquire about a job, and Sue had hired him on the spot because the current dishwasher hadn't shown up for work. Gin hoped it was a coincidence.

She stacked plates up her arm and carried the order to table five, careful not to make eye contact with Dan.

"Smells good," one of the firefighters ventured.

"I'll be sure to tell the cook." Gin picked up the ketchup bottle and gave it a shake. "Leaving out the shocked look on your face, of course."

The man's mouth dropped open.

"Yeah, that's the one." Out of the corner of her eye, Gin caught the young redheaded firefighter grinning at her. She aimed a look at his plate. "Do you need that slice of ham cut up, sweetie, or can you manage on your own?"

He grabbed the closest knife and started sawing.

"Good." Gin scanned the table, making sure she got everyone's orders right before checking on the groggy couple at table two. The woman tended bar at Eddie's, and every time she sauntered into the diner she was clinging to the arm of a different guy, showing him off like a new handbag.

"Hey, Tina." Gin felt the guy's bloodshot eyes slide over her and hoped this one didn't last very long. "More coffee?"

"Just hook it up to an IV." The bartender tucked a lank strand of platinum blond hair behind her ear. "Eddie's shorthanded if you're looking for a few more hours. Tips are better."

"Quit trying to steal my waitresses, Tina!" Sue yelled.

"Then start paying them more so they won't be tempted!"

Shouting matches between the kitchen and dining room at My Place weren't unusual, but from the reaction at table five, Gin could only assume they didn't occur at Marie's Bistro.

Gin took advantage of the momentary distraction to slip her cell phone from her apron pocket and check to see if Raine had sent her a message. Nothing. Gin tapped in a quick LOVE YOU and hit send.

"Order up!" Sue slapped a plate on the pass-through, pointed a warning finger at Tina, and then retreated to her lair.

Gin felt Dan's eyes on her as she delivered a poached egg to Agnes Bardowski. The elderly woman showed up several times a week and made her way to a table in the back of the diner, where she alternated each turn of the dog-eared page of a romance novel with a sip of coffee. When the cup was empty, Agnes toddled up to the register and paid for her breakfast with shiny dimes she doled out to Gin one at a time from a tiny sequined purse that looked like a rose.

"Here you go." Ginevieve set the plate down and nudged the saltshaker closer to avoid another condiment mishap. Last week Agnes's poached egg had ended up being sugared instead of salted.

"Are there going to be firefighters here every day?" the woman whispered.

Not if Gin had anything to say about it. "I don't think so, Mrs. B."

Disappointment flickered briefly in Agnes's eyes, and she went back to reading her novel.

Gin started a fresh pot of coffee brewing and was wiping down the counter when Cozie sidled up to the cash register.

"Hopping little place this morning," he drawled. "Guess I'll have to stop by later when you're not so busy. If I want some *personal* attention." Craig added an eyebrow wiggle just in case Gin hadn't gotten the hint.

She counted out change for a ten and slid it across to him. "Have a nice day, Cozie."

He settled one hip against the lip of the counter and leaned closer. The pungent scent of tobacco and cologne that reminded Gin of the citrus spray Wendell used to clean the bathrooms assaulted her nose. "I'd rather have a nice night, if you know what I mean."

Gin had originally pegged Cozie as a guy who liked to present himself as a player in front of his friends, but the predatory look in his eyes was a little unnerving.

Dan walked up to the counter, and Gin tamped down a sigh. The guy's timing couldn't have been worse. Or—Gin noticed the tight line of Dan's jaw—had it been deliberate?

Cozie shot a glare over his shoulder and refused to budge. "Wait your turn, Moretti."

"Looks to me like you're done here." Dan shot a pointed look at the loose sheaf of bills in Cozie's hand.

Cozie's fingers closed in a fist around them and his lips flattened. "I'm done when I'm done."

Gin ignored him and looked at Dan. "Are you ready for your check?"

He nodded, his hazel eyes searching her face. "Please put everything on one slip and I'll take care of it."

He's just another customer, Gin. Treat him like one.

She pinned on a smile. "Sure."

"Please," Cozie mocked softly. "Guess I'll have to use the magic word next time."

"Come on, Craig." Hanson, Cozie's wingman, sidled up, his expression uncomfortable. "We'll get written up again if we don't punch in on time."

Cozie continued to stare at her, and Gin suppressed a shudder. This was one of the reasons why she wouldn't let Raine work at the diner on the weekends. There was no way she would subject her bright, beautiful daughter to guys like this.

Dan took a step closer to the counter. Cozie backed off, but his eyes held onto Gin a moment longer.

"See you later." He stalked toward the entrance, Hanson trailing at his heels. The door snapped shut behind them.

"Be careful around him," Dan murmured.

"Is that an order, *Captain*?"

"A suggestion."

Gin tallied up the numbers and handed him the final bill. "I'm used to guys like Cozie."

It was Dan Moretti she didn't know what to do with.

Chapter 21

I'm used to guys like Cozie.

That explained a lot, but it sure didn't make Dan feel any better.

He pulled a worn leather wallet from his back pocket and kept one eye on Cozie. He and Hanson stood in a huddle next to the curb, their backs pressed against the wind while they lit cigarettes.

"Gin!" The cook poked her head through the pass-through. "The delivery truck is parked in the alley. Can you give Wendell a hand unloading it?"

"I'll be right there."

Dan thumbed through the contents of his wallet and took his time extracting the right amount of change. "Raine?"

For a moment he thought Gin was going to ignore the question. "She called last night."

Called. "She didn't come home?"

"She asked for a few days. She's thinking through some things."

Dan could only imagine. "Did she tell you where she was?" Gin's eyes narrowed. A warning he was getting close to the none-of-your-business line. He stepped over it anyway. "I remember you told Ryan that you don't have family around here."

"Apparently she's staying with yours."

"What?" Dan couldn't have heard her right.

"Whisper Lake. Cody told Raine about it, and she ended up there."

With Kimberly and Wade Russell, his aunt and uncle.

Thank you, God.

Raine hadn't shown the best judgment taking off like she did, but in Dan's opinion she'd made up for it by choosing the camp as a temporary refuge.

Dan found his voice again. "Raine couldn't have ended up with better people, Ginevieve. Safer people."

Is there such a thing?

Gin didn't have to say it out loud. Dan saw the doubt chase through her eyes, and he wanted to erase all the situations—and people—in her past that had put it there.

"Gin!" The shout was followed by a blast of cold air that swept in from the kitchen.

"Coming." She handed Dan his change and pivoted toward the half doors.

A thought suddenly occurred to Dan, and he stepped in front of her. "What about your car?"

"I'm planning to buy another one this weekend, but I still can't decide between the Lexus and the Corvette."

In spite of his mounting concern, Dan felt a smile coming on. Ginevieve didn't miss a beat.

"Breakfast *and* stand-up comedy," he murmured. "I wonder if Marie realizes what she's up against."

Ginevieve's lips tipped up at the corners, and Dan felt his pulse stutter.

"I don't mind the walk, okay?"

No, it wasn't okay. Not when Craig Cozielle looked at Gin like she was an item on the menu.

"Ready, Captain?" Jerry suddenly materialized at his side. "I think we'll hit the gym and shoot a few hoops before we go home."

"Sounds good. I'll meet you outside."

"Okay, Captain."

Dan turned back to Ginevieve just in time to see the doors swing shut behind her. His crew trooped out, and he walked back to the table to leave a tip. Cozie and Hanson had scattered a handful of change, mostly pennies and nickels, in the center of their table along with a pile of wrinkled napkins and toast crumbs.

How could Ginevieve make a decent living at a place like this?

Dan replaced the five-dollar bill with a ten and tucked it underneath the saltshaker, the way his dad always did when they ate at a restaurant.

"She's a nice young woman."

Dan followed the thin thread of a voice and found it attached to an elderly woman sitting at a table in the back of the diner.

"I'm Agnes Bardowski." She pointed at the ceiling. "I live in 3B upstairs."

"It's nice to meet you, Mrs. Bardowski. I'm Dan." His curiosity got the best of him. "You know Ginevieve?"

"I know she's like Savannah." Frowning, the woman waved a paperback novel at him. "But don't let her scare you off. A woman needs a man who will defend her when the pirates show up."

Okaaay. Dan hid a smile. "Pirates?"

Agnes lifted her cup and took a dainty sip. "They don't all have an eye patch and a wooden leg, you know. Sneaky things, pirates. Always creeping around, looking for a way in. A woman can't let her guard down—not for a second."

Dan caught a glimpse of Ginevieve in the kitchen, her arms clamped around a cardboard box. The guy at the next table, the one sitting next to the thin blonde with bloodshot eyes, was watching her too.

"Thanks." Dan's smile faded. "I'll keep that in mind."

CHAPTER 22

Raine sat on the Russells' bathroom floor, her bare feet tucked underneath her as she waited for the nausea to subside.

Who'd named this morning sickness, anyway? It came and went throughout the day, triggered by a variety of mysterious things. The glass dish of potpourri on the kitchen windowsill. Buttered popcorn. The Russells' overweight goldfish.

Raine's cell phone vibrated against the ceramic tile. She closed her eyes but it was too late. She'd seen Cody's name pop up on the screen. It was the first time she'd heard from him since she'd told him that she needed a few days, and she missed him so much she wondered if that was making her stomach hurt too.

She rubbed at a smudge on the back of the phone. Ignore it? Read it? Raine wanted to respond just to remind Cody he was supposed to be talking to God, not texting her.

The phone vibrated again.

What if something had happened? Something she should know about?

Raine peeked at the subject line.

DO NOT DELETE THIS MESSAGE. THIS IS A PUBLIC SERVICE ANNOUNCEMENT.

Cody.

Raine pressed her knuckles against her mouth to stifle a laugh.

MISS PETERMAN'S NEWEST ESSAY QUESTION (BECAUSE I KNOW YOU DON'T WANT TO GET BEHIND) MY BEST DAY AND MY WORST DAY. EVER. IN FIFTY WORDS OR LESS.

Raine didn't need that many; she only needed three.

The same day . . .

Muffled laughter had followed Raine into the hall, but she'd kept her head down, tried to tune it out. What she couldn't tune out was the ugly word in black marker on the door of her gym locker, now scrawled indelibly inside her head—a fitting finale to the whole rotten day. At least PE was seventh hour, so she could go home and lick her wounds in private.

Halfway down the block, her cell phone began to ring. "Hello?" She injected the greeting with what she hoped was the correct amount of cheerfulness.

"Hey. Where are you?" The soft timbre of Cody's voice bumped against the fresh bruise on Raine's heart and caused it to wobble.

"On my way home."

"I thought we were going to hang out after school."

"I can't." Raine picked up speed, just in case Cody was trying to catch up to her. "Mom wants me to stop at the diner."

"What about after?"

"I've got a paper to write for Peterson's class."

"You sound funny. Is everything okay?"

"Tired."

"What about youth group tonight?"

"I'm not going."

"Okay . . ." Cody waited for her to tell him why. When she didn't, he said, "I'll see you tomorrow."

But Cody showed up at her door a few hours later. Raine had been curled up on the sofa with Mrs. Freckles and what was left of a pint of Ben and Jerry's Chunky Monkey.

"What are you doing here? Aren't you supposed to be at church?"

"I asked Eric to lead the study tonight." Cody cupped his hands together and blew a stream of air into the narrow opening between his thumbs. "Can I come in?"

"You better not." Raine curled her toes into the rug to hold her ground. "Mom's closing tonight. I don't want to ruin your reputation."

She regretted the words the moment they slipped out of her mouth. She'd told herself she wasn't going to tell Cody what had happened, and already she'd said too much.

"Come on, Wats." Cody's knee bumped the door. "Let me in."

"Fine." Raine shrugged as if it didn't matter and stepped to the side. "But you can't stay long. I have that paper to write, remember?"

Cody stripped off his jacket and spotted the empty cardboard container on the table. "You had ice cream for supper?"

"I *wanted* ice cream," Raine snapped. "It's not like that's all we had in the house to eat."

"I know that." But Cody was looking at her like he didn't know who she was.

At the moment, Raine didn't either. She dumped the spoon in the sink and the container in the wastebasket and took a lap around the kitchen table. Cody stepped in front of her, a five foot ten, blue-eyed obstacle that prevented her from starting a second. He grabbed her hand and led her to the sofa. Instead of sitting on Mrs. Freckles or sweeping her off to one side, Cody picked up the giraffe, straightened the frayed satin bow around her floppy neck, and set her in Raine's lap.

Tears washed over her eyes, and Raine tried to blink them away before Cody noticed.

"What's wrong?"

He'd noticed.

"Just because I ate ice cream for supper, you think something is wrong?" Raine countered.

"No, I think something is wrong because you won't look me in the eye."

Raine tried. She really did. But where other guys looked at her, Cody had this uncanny way of looking *inside* her. One more reason why she shouldn't have let him in the house.

"Raine?"

Her head came up, only because Cody never called her by her name anymore. It was always Wats or Watson. She loved the nicknames because they reflected the teasing sparkle in his blue eyes. The sparkle was missing now, and Raine knew he wouldn't budge until she'd told him the truth.

She folded her arms around Mrs. Freckles, but the stuffed animal provided a flimsy shield. "You know Bradley Renquist, right?"

He nodded once, and Raine took that as her cue to continue.

"He and I are lab partners, and we were studying for the biology quiz this Friday." Raine had been happy when the teacher paired them up. Bradley was an honor student like Cody, played the drums for pep band, and didn't come up with ways to brush up against her when they worked together on an experiment.

"Anyway, Bradley thought it would be funny if we made up acronyms to help us remember the vocabulary words. I came up with one, and he burst out laughing." In her mind's eye, Raine saw the entire class turn and stare at them. "Apparently Bradley's girlfriend's best friend is in the class too. And she told Vanessa that I was flirting with him."

"Vanessa can be a drama queen." A small wrinkle appeared between Cody's eyebrows. "Did she get in your face about it?"

"Not in my face. In my gym locker."

"She left you a note?"

"Actually . . . it was only one word." Raine tried on a smile and felt it slip sideways.

Cody's expression changed. Hardened. "What word?"

Raine hesitated, afraid if she said it out loud it would cut that much deeper. "It doesn't matter."

"It matters if it upset you."

She told him, and it was the first time she'd ever seen Cody get angry. He reached for her hand and threaded his fingers through hers.

"Don't let it bother you. It's not true."

Raine wrestled free from his grip. "It doesn't matter what's true. It matters what they *think* is true. I have a weird name and a tattoo, so it means I'm automatically out to steal their boyfriends."

Cody tipped his head. "You have a tattoo?"

"A dove," Raine muttered. An eighteenth birthday present to herself because her mom refused to give her permission or the money to pay for it. "Don't tell me you didn't see it the day I came over to your house to study."

"Nope. Didn't see it."

Evie Bennett had. Raine had thrown on her sweatshirt jacket, but the damage was done. From that moment on, Cody's mom had looked at Raine the way a person looked at a stain on their favorite sweater.

Maybe her mom was right about big cities being better than small towns. You didn't stand out in the crowd. For a moment, Raine thought about the suitcase in her mom's closet. The one she never unpacked. If Raine told her mom she'd changed her mind—that she didn't want to stay in Banister Falls until graduation—the suitcase would come out of hiding and they'd be on the road by lunchtime tomorrow . . .

"That's not all, is it?"

Raine wished Cody didn't see so much. Weren't guys supposed to be clueless when it came to stuff like this? He should have been reaching for the remote control right now, eager to ditch the conversation for a few hours of whatever sport was in season.

"Isn't that enough?"

"Whenever I ask a question you don't want to answer, you hide behind another question. Did Vanessa say something to you?"

"Maybe . . . but it was something I already knew." Raine tried to slam the lid over the memory of Bradley's girlfriend trapping her by the sink in the bathroom after lunch, where she'd proceeded to insult everything from the brand of Raine's jeans to the place where she lived. But it was her parting shot that had inflicted more damage than the ugly word scrawled in Raine's locker.

"I've seen you staring at Cody Bennett too. He's never going to be interested in someone like you."

"What did you know?" Cody pressed.

"That I'm not good enough for you, okay?" Raine unhooked her leg from underneath her and tried to rise to her feet, but Cody was faster. His hands came down on her shoulders and he gently pushed her back down. Raine sank into the hollow between the lumpy sofa cushions and couldn't move. She might as well have been stuck in a bowl of tapioca pudding.

"What," Cody said softly, "are you talking about?"

The genuine confusion on his face made her angry.

"I wasn't born and raised here. My dad wasn't a hero. I don't live in Rosewood Court." Raine began to go down the list. "I-I'm that quirky character in the book that disappears before the end of the story."

Cody smiled. "Not my story."

"See!" Without thinking, Raine fired Mrs. Freckles at him. "You even say the perfect thing because you're *perfect*. I'm just . . . different."

"I'm not perfect—and I like your different."

"You're just saying that to be nice."

"I'm saying that because I love you."

Raine's heart skipped a beat. And then another three when Cody leaned closer.

"I love you, Raine," he murmured against her lips.

Cody had kissed her before . . . but not like this.

Feelings began to swirl around her and inside of her and Raine felt like she was drowning in the newness of it all. She broke away and set her palms against Cody's chest. Felt the rapid thump of his heart beating underneath her fingertips.

"You should go," she whispered.

Cody reached for her again. Kissed her again. "I should."

But he didn't . . .

The next day at school Raine couldn't look at Cody because he wouldn't look at her. Their desks were a yard apart in Miss Peterman's class, but it might as well have been a mile, with Cody near enough to touch but somehow beyond her reach. Why did people claim that sex brought two people closer?

Raine went to the tree house after school to be alone. So did Cody—and the first thing Raine noticed was his bloodshot eyes.

Guilt sent her lurching toward the door, but Cody blocked her escape.

"I'm so sorry." He didn't sound like Cody at all. "You told me to leave and I didn't listen. I wrecked everything, didn't I?"

Cody thought *he'd* wrecked everything? She was the one who hadn't stopped him. Hadn't said no.

"You wouldn't even l-look at me today." Raine was trying not to break down, so the words came out in starts and stops. "I was the one who didn't want anyone to know about us, and look what happened. God probably h-hates me now."

Cody groaned and wrapped his arms around her. "We made a

mistake, that's what happened. And God doesn't hate either of us. We just . . . we have to make sure it doesn't happen again."

"You think we should break up?"

Panic flared in Cody's eyes. "Do you?"

"I don't want to," she whispered.

"Neither do I." Cody rested his forehead against hers. "I meant what I said last night. I love you, Wats. I want to do things the right way."

"But what if—" Raine stopped, afraid to say it out loud.

"We won't. We'll meet at the library from now on. Ms. Davenport will be a great chaperone."

Raine traced Cody's lopsided smile with her fingertip and didn't tell him what she'd been about to say. It was one time. *One time.* She couldn't be pregnant . . .

"But you're here, aren't you?" Raine whispered. "And we're going to do what's best for you."

She shut off her phone and set it down on the Russells' bathroom floor and asked God to tell her, please, what that was.

Chapter 23

I told you I already hired a new waitress. Now quit pestering me or I'll be hiring someone to take *your* place too."

Gin set her back against the door of the walk-in refrigerator and blocked Sue's exit. "She said she has some experience."

Sue had the disbelieving snort down to an art form. "She's trouble. I can see that from a mile away."

"You hired Wendell." Gin felt a stab of guilt for pointing that out, but there was no getting around the fact the guy was an ex-con.

"Wendell doesn't have three rug rats that are going to get the chicken pox or the flu or head lice. All of which will give her a reason not to show up for work and leave us shorthanded in the dining room the next time the fire department comes in for breakfast."

Gin decided to ignore the last part of Sue's rant. "Just look over the application. Maybe you can give her a few hours a week and see how she does."

The girl—she couldn't have been more than four or five years older than Raine—had wandered in with three small children in tow after the supper crowd had shifted loyalties and drifted into Eddie's for the remainder of the night.

Gin had assumed the girl was the babysitter until she heard one of the kids call her Mom. The girl didn't even open the menu, just asked for the cheeseburger plate. When Gin brought it out, she cut the burger into four pieces and divided up the fries, a sign that her bank account was as thin as her winter jacket.

Sue narrowed her eyes. "Is she a friend of yours?"

"I've never seen her before."

It was mostly the truth. Gin didn't know the girl but she recognized her. Recognized the stubborn tilt of her chin. The desperate look in her eyes. The hunch of her shoulders, weighted down by the knowledge that someone was depending on her. In this case, three little someones.

The second time Gin returned to the table to check on the family, the girl had asked if she could fill out an application, and Gin was sucked back in time.

"I'm not hiring right now."

Ginevieve followed the cook right into his kitchen. "The sign in the window says Help Wanted."

"Okay . . . I don't want help from runaways."

"I'm not a runaway."

"What kind of experience do you have?"

At that point Gin almost gave up. If she lied and said she'd been a waitress before, something told her the gruff old geezer would know it.

"None. But it's not rocket science—I'll figure it out."

"I'll tell you what." The cook tossed an apron at her. "You work a shift right now and then we'll have a little chat."

By the end of the day Ginevieve's feet throbbed, her back ached, and her self-esteem was black-and-blue from the hammer of constant criticism, but she'd made enough in tips to cover her prenatal vitamins.

"Rocket science?" The cook found her sprawled on the floor in the backroom, checking one of her feet for blisters.

"Easier." Gin pressed on her big toe and winced. "Way easier. I have no idea why people think it's such a big deal."

The cook's entire face flexed in a smile. "I'll put you on the schedule. Be here at six a.m. tomorrow."

Gin had worked there the next two years, until the restaurant changed hands. The new manager immediately fired the cook and then systematically began to replace the waitstaff with members of her extended family. By that time Gin knew her way around a dining room and had no trouble getting hired at a pizza place in the next town. Because someone had given her a chance.

Gin pushed a little harder even though she knew Sue would push back. "She can shadow me until you decide if she'll work out."

"So you're going to split your tips with her."

It wasn't a question, but Gin didn't back down. "That would be the fair thing to do."

"Fine," Sue growled. "I'll take a look at the application. Now get out of my way before I turn into an ice sculpture."

"That might drum up more business." Gin dared a smile. "I don't think Marie has one of those." She slipped out before Sue could retaliate.

The girl was still bent over the application, a chubby-cheeked toddler teetering on the sharp ledge of her hip. The other two children, a boy and a girl who looked like they could have been born in the same calendar year, were punching buttons on the jukebox.

She didn't look up when Gin refilled her water glass. "I'm almost done."

"No rush." Gin smiled at the toddler and received a shy grin in return before she buried her face against her mother's shoulder. She reminded Gin of Raine at that age. A baby bird, mostly eyes and tummy and a single tuft of golden hair.

The girl approached Gin at the cash register a few minutes later, sliding the application across the counter with the trembling hands and furtive eyes of a person about to rob a bank.

Skimming through the first few lines, Gin silently matched

details to the girl in front of her. Nicole Chapman. She'd written down her birth date, but there looked to be a lot more years than twenty-three stacked up behind the charcoal-lined eyes.

She stopped at a blank square. "You didn't fill in your address, Nicole."

"It's Nicki. And I'm staying with my sister for a few days." The girl's gaze flitted from the cash register to the container of toothpicks to the dish of peppermints, looking for any place to light other than Gin. "We're . . . kind of between places right now."

Which probably meant she'd been evicted from her apartment.

"Phone number?"

Nicki remained mute.

"Okay. Not a problem." Except that Sue was going to kill her. "My boss just hired a waitress but sometimes it doesn't work out. Stop in on Monday morning and we'll let you know if something opened up."

"Thanks." Nicki worked at the buttons on the toddler's coat with her free hand. "We have to go now, guys."

Her other children scampered over to the counter and peered up at Gin. The older girl's light brown bangs were notched across her forehead, clearly the work of a pair of kitchen scissors, but her clothes were clean and fit well.

Nicki lingered another fifteen minutes, fussing with zippers and snaps and shoelaces until Gin got suspicious. The moment the children's attention was focused on something else, Gin pulled her aside.

"When you said you had a place to stay, you weren't lying to me, were you?"

Nicki's eyes went wide but she didn't look away this time. "No."

"Just not a place you're in a hurry to go back to?" Gin guessed.

Nicki's reluctance to answer was an answer in and of itself, but Gin waited her out.

"It's temporary," she finally said. The whispered comment sounded like she was trying to reassure herself more than Gin.

Wendell clumped past, head bobbing to a melody no one else could hear. Nicki's children pressed together like a flock of baby chicks and streaked to their mother's side. The dishwasher, with his tattoos, pasty white skin, and fondness for dressing all in black, tended to have that effect on people.

"You might as well take this with you." Gin crowded as many leftover biscuits as she could into a takeout box, along with a Styrofoam container of lukewarm chili.

Pride lifted Nicki's chin, but Gin took it down a peg with a warning look. "Don't even try. You and I both know you've got three reasons to take it."

Nicki grabbed the box and mumbled a thank-you as she herded her brood into the night.

Gin wasn't sure she'd ever see them again.

"I'm not running a soup kitchen, Gin," Sue snarled when she walked into the kitchen to help clean up.

She should have known she'd get caught.

Wendell muttered something under his breath and stabbed the mop into a five-gallon pail, spraying droplets of gray water on the wall.

Sue's scowl expanded to include him. "Did you say something, Wendell?"

"Yeah." He didn't look up. "I said someone should."

Chapter 24

No matter how hard he'd tried, Dan couldn't shake the memory of those jerks ogling Gin at the diner. The crude comments Cozie and Hanson had slung back and forth when Gin disappeared into the kitchen. The thought of her dealing with that kind of disrespect on a regular basis made Dan feel sick. If anyone treated his sisters that way, he would have invited them outside for a private conversation.

A muttered comment Sid had made told Dan the other men had noticed—and felt the same way.

"Cozie is always looking for trouble, and if he can't find any he stirs some up," his friend had said.

Dan had braced himself for the speculation and good-natured teasing the guys on the crew liked to dish out, but his men had been unusually quiet on the way to the gym. There were a dozen questions in their eyes, but Dan doubted he would have been able to answer a single one.

Still, Sid's comment had clung to Dan like a burr the rest of the day. Ginevieve's sharp tongue and sassy attitude would keep most men at arm's length, but there were some who might see them as a challenge. Dan didn't like the way Cozie had made "see you later" sound more like a threat than a casual statement.

Dan put the truck in gear and pulled onto the road, debating what to do next. He contemplated stopping by Evie's house, but she'd told him that she was taking Cody out for pizza to try to get his mind off Raine. As if it would be that easy to distract him . . . Cody was eighteen, not eight, and worried about the woman he loved. Whether or not Evie approved of Raine, Dan thought she should be a little more in tune with what Cody was going through.

At the four-way stop Dan saw a group of teenage boys loitering underneath a streetlight. One of them flicked the glowing butt of a cigarette into the gutter when he drove past.

The smirk on the kid's face reminded Dan of Cozie.

On impulse, he drove to the Avenue and slowed down when he came up alongside Gin's trailer. Other than the porch light, there was no sign that anyone was home. Feeling a little like a stalker, Dan took another turn around Main Street. He'd learned to trust his instincts over the years, and right now they were on high alert.

Ginevieve doesn't want you hanging around, Moretti. Get that through your thick head.

But she didn't have a vehicle, and the diner wasn't located in the best part of town.

Dan cut through the alley to Radley Street. Sal's Auto Parts was closed up tight for the day, but music rattled the windows of Eddie's Bar. Through the tinted glass Dan could see a hedge of people lined up at the bar. It occurred to him that Ginevieve might be in there, but he shook the thought away.

He'd overheard the blond woman at the table in the corner tell Gin she should apply at Eddie's. The older woman framed in the pass-through had had plenty to say about that, but Dan hadn't caught Gin's response. He had, however, caught the way she'd kept her distance from the blond's companion.

Dan glanced at the clock on the dashboard as he put his truck in park. The Open sign still hung in the window of the diner, but unlike Eddie's, the place looked deserted. The door of the bar opened, and a burst of laughter sprayed over Dan like buckshot as he crossed the street.

The bell over the door gave a half-hearted jingle as Dan walked into the diner. A stick-thin guy with ink black hair was mopping the floor, each movement synchronized in a jerky choreograph to the Beach Boys' "Little Deuce Coupe" blasting from the jukebox. The song choice didn't seem to fit with the baggy jeans and the tattoo of a cobra winding around his right bicep.

Dan lifted his hand. The guy bobbed his head and pointed to a table by the window. There was no sign of Ginevieve—no sign of a waitress at all.

The cook who'd yelled at Gin about the delivery truck that morning shoved her head through the pass-through and spotted him. She scowled and disappeared, but Dan heard her shout something above the rumble of the furnace. Whatever she said was followed by the sound of glass shattering.

Dan winced.

A minute later Ginevieve was standing in front of his table. "We're closing in five minutes."

"Great." Dan leaned back and felt a button pop in the booth's worn vinyl coat. "I made it just in time." He could have sworn he heard a snicker from the guy pushing the mop.

Gin glared down at him. Her mahogany braid was draped over one shoulder, the tip twitching like the tail of an angry cat. "Don't you ever go home?"

"Don't you?" The words slipped out before Dan could stop them.

"Not that it's any of your business, but one of the waitresses called in sick. I offered to cover for her."

And because she hadn't wanted to face the emptiness waiting for her at home. Dan could see it in her eyes. He remembered feeling the same way about familiar places after Max died, but he knew Ginevieve Lightly would never admit it.

"What can I get for you?"

Dan glanced down at her feet. Yup. Toe tapping an impatient beat. Call him crazy, but he was starting to find the rhythm soothing.

"A piece of pie—any kind—and a cup of coffee."

"To go?"

"No."

"Then you have four minutes to finish it."

"You can drop the act," Dan said mildly. "I'm not buying it."

Ginevieve's eyes narrowed. "What act?"

"The customer-is-always-annoying act."

"Not 'the customer.' *You.*" Gin whirled around, the heels of her boots clicking as she headed back to the kitchen.

Her body language, the sarcasm and pointed looks were all staged, but Dan sensed the real stuff was right there, hidden behind the attitude. He used the only weapon he had to draw her out.

"Could you warm it up, please?" he called after her. "I'll subtract fifteen seconds."

The plate Ginevieve set down in front of him a minute later displayed a perfect wedge of warm apple pie. He could tell it was apple because the filling was bubbling around the fork impaled through its center.

Dan couldn't help it. He laughed.

"Nice touch."

Gin's guard slipped a notch, and a smile chased through her eyes. As fleeting as it was, Dan felt a sense of accomplishment. He didn't understand why he felt so comfortable teasing her. Or why their encounters made him feel so . . . alive.

With Evie, he had to think before he spoke. Weigh out his words, careful not to cross a line or offend. They were childhood friends who had been able to tell each other everything, until Evie had given everything to Max.

Gin held up the coffeepot. "I suppose you want a refill."

"Is it regular or decaf?"

"What do you want it to be?" Her lips lifted in a smile as artificial as the packets of sweetener on the table.

"That answers my question." Dan covered the top of the cup with his hand. "I'm good, thanks."

Ten minutes later, with a belly full of pie he didn't need and a cup of coffee that would probably keep him awake until Sunday, he waited for Ginevieve to return so he could offer her a ride home.

But it was the tattooed cleaning guy who emerged from the kitchen and waved a white slip of paper at the register. "I'll take care of this when you're ready."

"Where's Ginevieve?"

The guy raised a scraggly eyebrow with enough metal piercings to set off every alarm in an airport security system. "She's gone."

"Gone?" Dan glanced at the front door, not sure whether he should believe him.

"Back door leads to the alley." He jerked a thumb toward the kitchen and shot Dan a pitying look. "*Dude.* Don't you know anything about women?"

"Not this one," Dan said under his breath. He dug his wallet from his back pocket, thumbed through what was left of his last paycheck, and pulled out a ten dollar bill. "Keep the rest."

Snow spit from the back tires as Dan pulled out onto the street and turned down the alley. He caught up with Gin at the end of the block and reached across the seat to open the passenger door.

"Ginevieve."

She ignored him—of course—and stumbled forward, the heels of her cowboy boots providing no traction whatsoever on the frost-coated ground.

"It's cold and you shouldn't be walking home alone," Dan heard himself say. He winced. "I know, I know. I sound like your mother."

"Not even close." Gin kept on walking. "My mother wouldn't have realized I hadn't come home until at least noon the next day."

Dan filed that away to think about later.

"Just get in. Please."

"I'm good, thanks," Gin said, echoing the words Dan had said in the diner.

"Good gravy." Dan felt the front tire scrape the curb and adjusted the steering wheel. "Will you stop being so stubborn?"

She stopped. "Did you just say *good gravy*?"

"One of Grandma Moretti's favorite sayings. She would be thrilled to know I borrowed it."

Gin veered toward the pickup and Dan stomped on the brake.

He couldn't help but feel a little triumphant—until she slammed the door shut and sealed him inside the cab.

Fine.

He followed her for another block, the headlights of the truck lighting the way. At the next stop sign, Ginevieve stalked toward him. Dan braced himself for round two, but this time she climbed into the truck.

"What do you want?" A slender finger speared his coat sleeve. Her beautiful green eyes wary.

A woman can't let her guard down. Not for a minute.

Strangely enough, it was Agnes—the gray-haired sage from the diner—whose words chased through Dan's mind. He could have made a joke. Told Ginevieve it was a cold night and he was simply playing the Good Samaritan. But an inner nudge told Dan to tell her the truth instead.

"I don't want you to be alone."

Chapter 25

Gin's frustration drained away and she sank against the seat. "I like being alone." She *wanted* to be alone. It was so much easier than being disappointed.

But she couldn't seem to shake the guy. It was bad enough Dan and his entire crew had shown up for breakfast, but she hadn't been expecting him to waltz in five minutes before the diner closed.

"He's here. Again." Sue had notched her voice above the hiss of the griddle.

It took a second for the words to register. When they did, the glass Gin had been washing slipped between her hands and shattered on the tile.

She didn't have to ask who "he" was. It was the "why" that made her heart race.

"I'm definitely going to have to hire that girl if business picks up." Sue didn't even glance at the mess on the floor. "First, it's the fire department. Next thing I know, the Banister Falls Police Department will be having their Christmas party here."

Gin grabbed a broom and began to sweep up the shards of glass. "Dan Moretti isn't here for me."

He was here for Evie. Dan's loyalty lay with the Bennett camp, and as Sue had so eloquently said, she'd better not forget it.

"Uh huh." Sue kicked a shard of glass toward her. "Then why has the man shown up twice in the last twelve hours? He's here more than Cozie."

Gin, who usually lumped all men in the same category, didn't like the two men's names linked together in the same sentence. But then, she hadn't liked the totally unexpected flutter of butterflies in her stomach when she'd charged out of the kitchen and seen Dan sitting at a table by the window either.

"Pretend I'm not here." Dan put the truck into gear and hit the gas.

"Right."

"You do a pretty good job of ignoring people." Dan fiddled with the heat and adjusted the vent so it was blowing directly on Gin's feet. "It shouldn't be too difficult."

It shouldn't be . . . but it was.

Dan Moretti was pretty hard to ignore, and not just because he was sitting less than two feet away.

She didn't want to deal with him. Didn't want to *like* him.

They drove the rest of the way to the Avenue in silence.

Dan pulled up in front of her trailer and Gin saw one light in the window, the one she had left on for Raine. The thought of the empty rooms, the silence, settled over her like a wool blanket and made it difficult to breathe.

"Thanks for the ride." She reached for the handle to open the door, but for some reason, she couldn't get her feet to move.

"Ginevieve?" The way Dan drew out her name, syllable by syllable, had a strange effect on her pulse.

"It's *Gin.*" She scowled at him. "You can't just . . . change my name."

"Isn't your name Ginevieve?"

"Yes."

"Then I didn't change it." His teeth flashed, a light in the shadows.

Dan Moretti made his living putting out fires, but the guy could inflict serious damage of his own with that smile.

Gin yanked on the handle, ready to make her escape. The squeak of the door coincided with the muffled chirp of a cell phone. Her phone. She yanked it out of her coat pocket and peered down at the screen.

A text message from Raine.

It didn't even occur to Gin to wait until she was inside the trailer—alone—to read it. Her fingers shook as she squinted down at the screen. STILL FINE. DON'T WORRY. LOVE YOU TOO.

Relief and frustration poured through Gin and distilled into a ragged sigh.

"Raine?" Dan cut the engine and turned toward her, his expression so full of relief that it didn't cross Gin's mind to remind him that it was none of his business.

She nodded, held up one finger, and immediately tried to call her daughter back. The phone went right to voicemail.

"Raine!" Gin folded in half and pounded her forehead against her knees.

"They have no idea, do they?" Dan said quietly. "They think they're independent. That their cart isn't hitched to anyone else's."

A strange way to put it, but it made sense.

Gin's eyes met Dan's, and she realized he understood. He described himself as a family friend, but he sounded like a dad. And he was right. No one warned you that parenting was a roller-coaster ride. You were strapped in with your children, experiencing every high and low, every twist and turn.

As a single mom, Gin had never had anyone to talk to while Raine was growing up. She'd tried to figure everything out herself, usually based on a simple formula: what Gin wished *her* mother would have done.

"When is she coming home?" Dan's question hung in the silence.

"I have no idea. This is all I got." Gin brought up the text message and read it again. Out loud.

"Straight and to the point." Dan gave her a wry smile. "Wonder where she got that."

Gin didn't want Raine to be like her. She'd spent the last eighteen years doing everything in her power to make sure it didn't happen. To give her daughter the opportunities Gin had never had.

She pressed the phone between her palms, not willing to let it too far out of her sight. Those three, choppy little sentences connected her to Raine.

"I talked to Cody this afternoon," Dan said after a moment. "Raine won't tell him where she is."

Gin tried not to let Dan see how surprised she was by that little piece of information. Raine must have been afraid that Cody would drive up to the camp. Not that Gin hadn't considered it. "It's probably better that way."

"Do you mind if I tell him about the text?" Dan asked.

"Go ahead." Gin slipped the phone into her pocket. "That's why you're here, isn't it?"

Dan stiffened. "What do you mean?"

"Isn't it your job to gather information and report back to the Bennett camp?"

"I'm sorry that's what you think I'm doing." His voice was soft.

Gin attempted a shrug and felt a corresponding pinch in the vicinity of her heart. "It's the only reason I can think of for all this attention."

"The only reason?" Dan released a slow breath. "Because last night you thought I was going to make a pass at you."

A blush came out of nowhere. Gin felt it wash over her collar and flood her cheeks. "It wouldn't be the first time."

"I'm sorry about that too."

Dan's gaze didn't waver, and that's when it hit her. Gin had tried to figure out the difference between Craig Cozielle and Dan Moretti at the diner that morning. Standing side by side, the two men were roughly the same height and build, although Cozie's waist was already beginning to thicken from his frequent stops at Eddie's after shift change.

The difference was in their eyes. Cozie's were flat, absorbing everything around him and giving nothing back. But Dan's were clear, lit by a source Gin couldn't identify, and filled with gifts she was afraid to accept.

She pushed the door open and bailed out of the truck.

The engine continued to idle for several more minutes after she was inside, long enough to make her curious. She peeked between the curtains covering the door. The moon lit up the cab, and she could see Dan still sitting in the driver's seat, his dark head bowed over the steering wheel. Lips moving even though Gin could see he wasn't on the phone.

Gin pressed her cheek against the frosted window glass and closed her eyes. "What he says, okay?" she whispered.

Chapter 26

Dan drove straight to Evie's house. A neighbor walking a white powder puff of a dog waved a greeting and Dan waved back. No pit bulls battling their chains in Rosewood Court.

The front door opened as Dan's foot touched the top step.

Diva snuck past Evie and lumbered up, her tail wagging.

"Hey." He reached down to give the dog's ears a scratch. "It's not too late, is it?"

"Of course not." Evie motioned him inside. "We just got back a few minutes ago."

"How did it go?"

"Not well." Evie took his coat and hung it up in the closet. "Cody has been pacing around the house like a caged animal since he got home from school. I can't get him to concentrate on his homework, and he barely touched the pizza tonight."

"I'll talk to him."

"It's worth a try." Evie mustered a smile. "Nothing I've done has made any difference."

Dan resisted the urge to say that maybe it was what she *hadn't* done that was the problem.

Cody was lying stretched out on the couch staring up at the ceiling when Dan walked into the living room.

"Hey, bud."

Cody shifted to make room but didn't look at him. "Hey."

The lackluster response was so out of character that Dan understood Evie's concern. He decided to put Cody out of his misery as quickly as possible. "Raine sent a text to her mom."

Cody jackknifed to a sitting position. "When?"

"A little while ago." Dan put his hand on Cody's knee, holding him steady.

"What did she say? Is she on her way home?"

"She told her mom that she loved her . . . and that she's fine."

Cody's mouth fell open. "That's it?"

Dan couldn't suppress a smile. "That's the same reaction her mom had."

"I'm going to check my phone. Maybe she sent one to me too." Cody vaulted to his feet and was out of the room before Dan could stop him.

Evie wasn't watching her son's abrupt exit. She was staring at Dan. "When did you see Gin Lightly?"

Oh boy. "I gave her a ride home."

"From where?"

"My Place."

The color drained out of Evie's face. "What?"

"Not *my place.*" Dan smiled in an attempt to get her to see the humor in the misunderstanding. "The diner where she works. I stopped in for a few minutes."

Evie tried to smile back but it was strained, hindered by the next question Dan saw rising in her eyes.

"Why?"

Because he hadn't trusted the look in Craig Cozielle's eyes, that's why. But Dan couldn't tell Evie that. It would mean explaining he'd been there that morning too.

"Ginevieve is worried about her daughter, Evie." It was the truth. "The same way you're worried about Cody."

Evie started to walk away, but Dan knew exactly where she was going and beat her to the mantel, blocking her view of Max's photograph. "You asked me to get involved. What's wrong?"

"I don't understand why you felt the need to talk to her again, that's all."

"And I don't understand why you won't." Dan tried to smooth the rough edges from his voice, but judging from the way Evie flinched, he hadn't done a very good job.

"You were here the other night, Danny. That woman doesn't want to have anything to do with me."

"That has never stopped you before," Dan pointed out. "When someone is hurting, you're the first one to show up at their door with a basket of homemade blueberry muffins and a thermos of coffee."

"She'd slam it in my face."

"Then you knock again." Dan was still haunted by the look on Ginevieve's face right before she'd bailed from his truck. "I would think you'd want to talk to someone who understands. Someone who's going through the same thing you are."

"Want?" Evie whispered. "None of this is what I *want,* Danny. I want Cody to go to college and fall in love with a girl who shares his faith. I want my grandchildren to be born *after* he gets married. I want him to experience the bright future God has planned for him. And now this girl has *ruined* it—"

"Mom."

Cody stood in the doorway, and in the space between them Dan saw the tears glistening in his eyes.

Evie started toward him, her arms lifting, but Cody grasped her hands before she could pull him into an embrace, and held her at arm's length.

"Raine *is* a believer, Mom, and this isn't her fault. If you're going to blame someone, blame me. I knew it was wrong, and I shouldn't have let things get out of control. But all we can do now is go forward."

"Forward." Evie's voice came out in a raw whisper. "That's what I'm talking about. You've got your whole future ahead of you. I don't want you to look back at your life someday and have regrets."

"You had me when you were nineteen." Cody's voice shook with emotion as he let go of Evie's hands. "Do you regret that?"

Chapter 27

"One more!"

"One more!"

Samantha and Mei, Kimberly Russell's youngest daughters, bounded into the living room and bounced onto the sofa next to Raine, who rescued her journal a split second before it slid off her lap.

"One more what?" she teased, even though she'd heard the words a hundred times over the past few days.

"One more story!" The two girls, cheeks flushed from sleep and their hair in a tangle, wriggled closer.

Kimberly walked in from the kitchen and sent Raine an apologetic look. "Girls, Raine has to leave in a little while. No time for stories this morning."

"I don't mind." Raine hooked an arm around Mei's shoulders. "There's always time for stories," she whispered in the four-year-old's ear.

Mei giggled.

The front door opened and a gust of wind preceded Wade's entrance. "I filled up your car and checked the oil. You shouldn't have to stop on your way back."

"Thank you." Raine was still amazed by the Russells' kindness. She wished her mom could meet them. Ginevieve assumed everyone had a hidden agenda, but Raine couldn't help but think her mom might have found someone who proved that theory wrong if they'd stayed in one place a little longer.

"I've got the hot water on for tea, Raine." Kimberly wagged a finger at her daughters. "One story and then breakfast."

"Okay!" The girls curled into Raine, their bare toes poking out from the hems of matching flannel nightgowns.

"You can read this one." Six-year-old Samantha patted Raine's journal.

Raine thought about her last entry and tucked the journal underneath the pillow. "I'll let you pick one out."

By the time Kimberly announced that breakfast was ready, the "one more" book had turned into half a dozen. Raine didn't mind. She'd fallen in love with Samantha and Mei when they'd scrambled onto her bed the morning after she arrived. She had woken up from a sound sleep and seen two little faces smiling down at her.

The girl with a shiny cap of coal black hair had pushed closer until her nose was almost touching Raine's. "You have a funny name!" she'd announced.

"Mei!" The other girl's eyes had gone wide. "That's not nice!"

"I know it's funny." Raine lowered her voice like she was going to tell them a secret. "My mom named me after someone in a book she liked when she was little like you."

Their faces had lit up. "We like books!" They'd returned with an armload a few minutes later.

The Russells had six children, ranging in age from five to fourteen. Samantha and Mei were the youngest in the family, and both of them were adopted. Growing up as an only child, Raine had no idea that families could be so . . . loud. Her mom never talked about Aunt Sara, but Raine wondered if they had run around the house and giggled together.

"Don't you want pancakes?" Mei tugged on Raine's arm.

"You go ahead. I'm not hungry." Raine glanced at the grandfather clock in the corner. Fifteen minutes and she had to be on the road.

Her stomach contracted, and this time Raine couldn't blame the scent of food. Cody hadn't tried to call her since she'd left. She'd asked him not to, but still. She had no idea what to expect when she saw him again. Had he heard an answer to his prayers? What if it wasn't the same as hers?

"The girls are sure going to miss you." Kimberly returned with a steaming cup of tea, and Raine wondered if she'd guessed why she couldn't eat breakfast in the morning.

"I'm going to miss them too."

"If you needed time to think, I'm not sure you came to the right place." Kimberly chuckled. "You haven't had more than five minutes to yourself."

Raine took a sip of tea, and it warmed her like the truth that had begun to seep in over the past couple of days.

She'd watched Kimberly teach their older children algebra at the kitchen table. She'd watched Wade wrestle with the boys on the rug in front of the fireplace at night. She'd heard temper tantrums and squeals of laughter and a comforting silence that spread through the house when the last light went out.

Raine thought God had led her to the camp because she'd needed a place to be alone. But now she realized that "alone" wasn't what she'd needed at all.

"Thank you . . . for everything." Raine rose to her feet.

Kimberly reeled her in for a quick hug. "Tell Dan hello for us. We don't get to see the family as often as we'd like."

"I will." Raine unzipped her backpack and stashed the journal inside.

"Let us know you made it home all right." Wade strode in and traded Raine's coat, draped over his arm, for her backpack. "The roads are good, but your car is a little moody."

"And Wade is a little protective," Kimberly said in a mock whisper.

The older kids grabbed their coats and trooped outside to see her off while Mei and Samantha perched in the window, their noses pressed against the glass.

Raine blinked back the tears and waved good-bye. In the rear-view mirror she could see Mei blowing kisses. For a split second, Raine was tempted to stay one more day. She texted Cody instead.

MEET ME AT THE LIBRARY. TEN O'CLOCK.

Chapter 28

Gin woke to the sound of her cell phone ringing.

She almost rolled off the couch as she snatched it from the coffee table. Her vision was too blurry to read the name on the screen so she didn't even try, just rasped out a groggy hello.

"Hi . . ." The greeting tapered into silence, but Gin recognized the voice.

"Cody?" She stifled a groan and glanced at the clock above the breakfast counter. Seven a.m.

"I'm sorry to call you so early."

Gin was sorry she'd answered the phone.

"I haven't heard from her, Cody." Gin rolled onto her back and stared at a large yellow watermark shaped like the state of Texas on the ceiling tile.

"I have."

"What?" Gin sat upright and swung her legs over the side of the couch, her toes automatically curling under as they connected with the cold floor. "When did you talk to her?"

"She texted me a few minutes ago."

Gin tried not to let it bother her that Raine had contacted Cody first. What did it matter, as long as she was on her way home.

"Did she say what time she'd be here?" Gin grabbed the bowl

of popcorn seeds and a lukewarm can of ginger ale, debris left over from a night spent watching Masterpiece Theatre—Raine's influence—until she couldn't keep her eyes open any longer.

"In an hour or so." Cody hesitated. "She said she had something she wanted to talk to me about first."

"She's stopping at your house?" Gin couldn't believe it. Her daughter had been gone for three days and she was going to the Bennetts' house first. Okay—Gin was big enough to admit it—that bothered her.

"She'll be home soon," Cody promised. "She's anxious to see you too."

It was weird, but the kid's honesty, delivered in a calm, steady voice, reminded her of Dan. He hadn't come into the diner again, leaving Gin to wonder if her accusation about his gathering information for Evie had been accurate.

She pushed thoughts of Dan aside as she straightened up the living room, took a quick shower, and got dressed.

The minutes ticked by. Every glance at the clock, every crunch of tires rolling past, drew Gin to the window. Finally she couldn't take it anymore. She yanked on her boots, grabbed her coat off the hook, and started walking until she passed under the hallowed archway of Rosewood Court.

Gin felt like a stalker, lurking next to the hedge that divided Evie Bennett's yard from her neighbors. If Cody and Raine didn't show up soon, someone would notice her and dial 911 . . .

"Good morning."

Gin jumped at the sound of a voice behind her.

Evie Bennett stood a few feet away, her hands tucked in the pockets of a turquoise wool jacket. She'd even taken the time to wind a stylish scarf around her neck. Gin would have felt completely underdressed if Evie hadn't been wearing a pair of ratty felt bedroom slippers that looked older than she was.

"I'm just . . ." Gin fumbled for an explanation that would make sense and decided on the truth. "Waiting."

"So am I." Evie hunched into the scarf until only her eyes peeked over the top.

"They're not here?" Now she felt like a stalker *and* an idiot.

"Cody left about half an hour ago." Concern etched a line between Evie's perfectly arched brows. "He didn't tell me where he was going."

Cody disappeared for thirty minutes and Evie looked worried. Raine had been gone for three days.

"Did you walk here?" Now Evie's gaze dropped to Gin's snow-encrusted cowboy boots.

"It's not that far." At least not by city blocks. Annual income was another measuring stick altogether.

The silence linking them together was broken by Evie's sigh. "Why don't you come inside until they get back?"

Gin could think of a lot of reasons, but none of them outweighed the fact that she could no longer feel her toes.

"Thanks."

She followed Evie down a narrow path to the back of the house—the servants' entrance, perhaps?—and into a tiled laundry room.

Gin propped one arm against the washing machine to tug off her cowboy boot but almost lost her balance when Evie slipped out of her coat. Underneath the fitted wool jacket was a shocking pink T-shirt decorated with a lopsided heart made from multicolored rhinestones.

"A Christmas gift from Cody." Evie caught Gin staring and plucked at the hem of her shirt. "I'm not sure if he has no clue or a wicked sense of humor."

Cody spent a lot of time with Dan. If Gin had to pick one, she'd guess the wicked sense of humor.

Gin would have been fine at the kitchen table—or standing on the back porch—but Evie walked into the living room. Following her, Gin had a feeling of déjà vu. The last time they'd been here, things hadn't gone so well.

Neither of them sat down. Evie walked over to the window and stared out at the street, but Gin couldn't stay still very long. She wandered over to the fireplace and spread out her fingers, letting the heat sift between them.

Everything in Evie Bennett's house was warm—except the woman herself. Not that Gin expected anything more. Their paths wouldn't have crossed if it hadn't been for Cody and Raine.

A tidy row of silver photo frames stretched across the mantel. Snapshots of Evie Bennett's life. There was one of a handsome young firefighter with white-blond hair and a mischievous gleam in his eyes. Gin saw traces of Cody in the sculpted cheekbones and the razor-straight line of his jaw. Evie's husband. One half of a golden couple.

Gin lingered in front of the next photograph. A smiling teenage version of Evie Bennett in a pair of jean shorts and a tank top sat on a stone wall, flanked by two boys. The one on the left Gin recognized as her husband and the other one . . . Dan. His hair was shaggier and his frame on the lanky side, but there was no mistaking the warm hazel eyes and appealing smile.

Gin felt a tightening in her chest. The three of them couldn't have been more than sixteen or seventeen years old when the photograph was taken.

Not wanting to get caught staring at Evie's personal belongings, Gin shifted her attention to the painting above the fireplace. The entire surface had been painted a pale shade of green, a subdued background to the bright yellow daubs scattered all over it.

"My one and only attempt at watercolor." To Gin's astonishment, Evie walked across the room and stood beside her. "Max, my husband, insisted I hang it here."

"It's good." Gin tried to step away from what had to be a sensitive topic, but Evie continued to stare at the painting.

"No. It isn't." A small smile tugged at the corners of Evie's lips. "But the memory is."

From the look in her eyes, Gin could tell that Evie had a lot of good memories. An idyllic childhood. A storybook wedding. A man who'd obviously adored her . . .

Gin looked back at the photograph of Evie sitting on the wall.

Or had it been *two* men? Because while Max Bennett was smiling at the photographer . . . Dan was smiling at Evie.

What would that feel like? To have someone who knew you better than you knew yourself? Who was there for you, no matter what? Memories began to rise, threatened to pull her under, leaving Gin no choice but to scramble for safer ground.

"Why dandelions?"

Evie was silent for so long, Gin wasn't sure she'd even heard her. She was debating how to end the awkward moment when Evie reached out and straightened a picture frame Gin hadn't noticed was crooked.

"When Cody was little, he'd run all over the yard and pick bouquets of dandelions for me. We would put them in a juice glass in the center of the table and they'd be wilted the next morning—you know how fragile dandelions are."

Gin knew. Raine had picked bouquets for her too.

"I picked Cody up from preschool one morning and when he got out of the car, he burst into tears. Max had mowed the lawn before he left for work, and the dandelions were gone." Evie's gaze lingered on the photograph of her husband, and her lips lifted in a smile. "He battled those dandelions constantly. He thought they ruined the look of the yard. He didn't say much when I told him how Cody had reacted, but when Max picked him up from school the next day they didn't come inside right away. I looked out the window and there they were, in the yard, blowing dandelion seeds everywhere."

Gin smiled at the picture.

"I went outside and Cody told me they were planting a dandelion field. I teased Max about it later, when Cody was taking his nap. Why would the man who constantly waged war against dandelions plant them on purpose?"

Evie stopped, as if that were the end of the story.

"What did he say?" Gin couldn't contain her curiosity.

"Max said, 'You do whatever you have to do so they know you love them.'"

"He sounds like a really great guy."

"He was. We got married a month after graduation and Cody was born eleven months later." Evie spun the gold band on her left hand, slow and careful, the way someone would if they were searching for the combination on a safe. Unlocking more memories that made her smile.

Her husband had died over ten years ago, and Evie hadn't taken off her wedding ring. It was obvious she'd done everything right. Lining up the events like the photographs on the mantel, in the order they were supposed to go. Marriage. A baby. Gin had jumbled it all up.

"I'm sorry you lost him," Gin murmured.

"I didn't lose Max." Evie folded her hands together, shielding the ring from view. "I know exactly where he is . . . and someday I'll see him again. But that doesn't mean I don't miss him every single day *here*."

Gin knew Evie was talking about heaven, but she didn't know how to respond. God was up there, and Gin doubted He would recognize her. If He did, she knew what He would say.

You messed up, sweetheart. You're on your own.

Gin had heard the words from her mom and Joey Meyers and a couple of stepfathers in between.

"Do you hear that sound?" Evie's smile vanished as she pivoted toward the window.

Gin recognized Jasmine's throaty purr and was already halfway there.

Her heart bottomed out when she saw Raine sitting in the driver's seat. Neither of the kids got out of the vehicle, and Gin's toes itched in her socks. She wanted to fly out the door and hug Raine. And then ground her until graduation.

"Should we . . ." Evie's question trailed off when Cody hopped out of the car. Gin noticed he came around to Raine's side and opened the door, the way Dan did for her.

Neither of them so much as glanced at the house as they stopped on the sidewalk. Cody's hands were stirring the air, and whatever he'd said stirred up Raine. She whirled around, her arms folded in a woman's universal code for "back off" as she walked away from him.

Gin held her breath, expecting to see them part company, Raine storming back to the car and Cody to the house. But he scooped up a handful of snow, pressed it into a ball, and lobbed it at Raine. It splattered against the back of her coat.

Evie sucked in a breath.

Yeah, that's your son—Gin clapped her hand over her mouth as Raine plowed her bare hands through the snow and retaliated.

Gin and Evie watched as the teens chased each other around the yard like puppies, throwing snowballs and dodging for cover behind the shrubs. Cody trapped Raine behind the mailbox, a flimsy barrier against the snowball he tossed up in the air and caught again. The street had been plowed and Raine had run out of ammunition.

"I can't believe this," Evie breathed.

Neither could Gin.

Cody bent down to make another one of the frozen bombs, and Raine made a break for it. He caught up to her in two strides and held her captive with one hand, sifting snow onto her head with the other while she laughed and squealed for mercy.

Evie must have decided it was time to put a stop to their nonsense, because she reached up to knock on the window. It was a little unsettling for Gin to acknowledge that her own hand was clenched at her side, a heartbeat away from doing the same thing.

Evie's hand never connected with the glass.

She and Evie watched the scene change, separated from their children by a thin piece of glass and things Gin couldn't even begin to name.

Cody had dropped the snowball and pulled Raine against him, his hand cupping the back of her head. Gin could see her daughter was no longer laughing. She sagged against Cody, limp as a ragdoll, and leaned into him as the tears began to roll down her face.

"What do we do?" Evie whispered.

Gin watched Cody and Raine rocking back and forth, their arms forming a cradle for a tiny human being none of them could see.

She had no words of her own so she borrowed someone else's.

"Whatever we have to."

CHAPTER 29

Raine pressed her cheek against Cody's chest and felt the rapid thump of his heart. "Okay." She breathed the word. "You win. We'll tell them together. Just let me call my mom and let her know you'll be with me."

"You don't have to," Cody murmured. "She's already here."

Raine pushed away from him and spun toward the house. Her mom and Evie Bennett were standing in the window.

"Come on." Cody took her hand, and Raine wobbled along next to him up the sidewalk.

It was her mom who opened the door.

Raine let go of Cody and threw her arms around her mom's neck, aware that Evie Bennett stood a few feet away. "What are you doing here?"

"Waiting." Her mom brushed a strand of hair from Raine's cheek. "I figured I could shave off a few minutes if I came here."

"That's good," Raine choked. "Because we wanted to talk to you . . . together."

"It's warmer in the living room." Cody's mom didn't smile, but she didn't look angry either.

Raine pulled in a breath. God had been with her up until now—He hadn't stayed out in the car until this part was over.

Cody flopped down on the sofa and Raine sat down next to him. The same spot she'd claimed the last time she was here.

The touch of his hand gave her strength.

"I'm sorry I left without saying anything." Raine glanced at her mom. "But I'm not sorry I left. I needed—Cody and I both needed—some space. Some time to figure things out. I thought I'd stay in a little cabin at a camp Cody told me about and have all this time by myself, but it didn't work out that way. I was never alone." Raine thought about Samantha and Mei and smiled. "But it was okay. Because I'd been praying about what to do . . . and the Russells—they were my answer."

"I had no idea where Raine was. She wouldn't tell me." Cody squeezed her hand. "But I was praying too."

Cody had done more than that. He'd written the answer down, and when they met at the library he showed it to her.

Maxwell Dillon.

Raine couldn't believe it. Her nose had started to run and she got all leaky again and Cody had led her behind the wall of periodicals.

"Why are you crying? What did you write?"

"The same thing."

Fresh tears sprang up now, and Raine lifted the tail of her shirt to wipe them away, aware that Evie and her mom were waiting.

"Both of us want what's best for the baby." Raine focused on her mom, tried to read her expression. It wasn't hard. The love in her mom's eyes—the love Raine had felt even before she was old enough to know what it was—gave her the courage to go on. "I know Cody and I are pretty young to be parents . . . but we'll be good ones."

"You're keeping the baby?" Evie leaned forward.

Her expression wasn't as easy to read. But how could Raine

explain to Cody's mom that as she'd watched Kimberly and Wade and their children, the answer had become as clear as Whisper Lake. This baby wasn't an obstacle, blocking the way to Raine's future. He—or she—had already become part of it.

Chapter 30

On Wednesday nights Hope Community sounded more like a football stadium than a church.

Dan tucked a tower of disposable cups under his elbow and grabbed a stack of napkins from the welcome center, a safe zone that separated him from the herd of children thundering to their classrooms.

A gnarled hand gripped Dan's shoulder. "I've been praying for you. The Lord keeps bringing your name to mind."

Mort.

"Thanks." Dan shoved a handful of creamers into his coat pocket. "I appreciate that."

"Read the lesson tonight." Mort shuffled alongside Dan as they walked down the hall. "Good stuff."

Dan tried to round up the key verse they'd be discussing tonight, but it ducked behind an image of Cody and Raine sitting in church together on Sunday morning.

He'd worked a forty-eight hour shift over the weekend, insulated from the fallout of Raine's return by the brick walls of the fire station and the duties he was obligated to perform. Evie had left a voicemail on his cell with a brief update that didn't begin to fill in the blanks. Dan didn't get an opportunity to talk to her after the service because she had a women's ministry meeting, and Cody and Raine had left right away.

It wasn't in Dan's nature to worry or dwell on a situation, but the restlessness that clung to him like smoke over the past few days had finally started to permeate his mood.

"You ate my piece of chocolate cake." Will caught up to him and Mort at the door.

Dan felt a stab of guilt. He'd heard the shower running when he got home but hadn't asked his brother if he wanted to ride along with him to church. It was the second time in less than a week that Dan had avoided a member of his family. Keeping secrets from them was like trying to hide an injury.

"That wasn't a piece . . . it was half a cake and I brought it with me. To share," Dan added as he flipped the lights on.

"A generous man will prosper." Mort rapped his knuckles against the worn leather cover of his King James Bible.

Will flipped a chair away from the table and straddled it. "I haven't memorized that one yet." He looked past Dan's shoulder and grinned. "Are you lost, kid?"

Dan turned around, surprised to see Cody framed in the doorway. "What's up?"

"Nothing." Cody wandered in, hands tucked in the front pockets of his jeans as he looked around the room.

A chorus of grunts rose from the men milling around the coffeepot. Cody lingered by the bulletin board, a marquee that hadn't been updated for several years.

"Did you want to talk to me?" Dan said in a low voice. "I can meet with you after we're done."

"I thought I'd sit in on your group tonight."

Dan squashed his first impulse—to tell Cody he wasn't old enough—and his second—to ask why—and motioned to an empty chair next to Will. If anyone wondered why Cody wasn't leading the teen study in the youth wing, no one—not even his brother—said anything.

Dan opened in prayer and then sifted through the Old Testament until he found the passage in Proverbs they would be studying. Cody volunteered to read a few verses and contributed to the discussion in a way that had Mort bobbing his head in approval.

At the end of the hour, the men straightened in the folding metal chairs, an unlikely, mismatched group of soldiers coming to attention in the presence of their commanding officer. Mort fished the little black book from his pocket.

"I heard Leiderman is going to cut another fifty people from the floor." Jamie Reed spoke up first. "I been there almost twenty years but if it's true, ain't no way I'm going to dodge the ax this time."

Dan had heard that rumor too. "I'm sorry, Jamie."

A murmur of agreement followed. These were strong men. A nod of the head, a twitch of the eyebrows stood in for the things they didn't know how to say.

"Does anyone else have a prayer request to share?" Dan scanned the faces around the table.

Mort's pen started to descend. The soft tap of the metal clip against the table had become a familiar benediction.

"I do."

All eyes swung to Cody.

"My girlfriend . . . Raine . . . she's pregnant. We would really appreciate your prayers."

Mort's pen clattered to the floor as Cody bowed his head.

Will's foot connected with Dan's ankle under the table, jump-starting a flow of words Dan wouldn't remember by the time the final amen was said.

Even Mort remained silent as the men collected their Bibles and filed out the door. Cody didn't seem to realize the pack was exhibiting unusual behavior.

Dan snagged Cody's elbow as he fell into line behind them. "Can you stick around a few minutes and help me clean up?"

"Sure."

Dan sent a silent message to his brother, who grabbed Cody and put him in a friendly headlock before backing out the door. "See you later."

"Yup." Cody began to guide empty cups from the table into the wastebasket with the plane of his hand.

It was a task one person could have finished in less than a minute, but Dan joined in anyway. "You could have given me a heads-up that you'd be joining my group tonight."

"Sorry." Cody didn't look at him. "I didn't know until an hour ago."

Dan frowned. "I thought you were leading a study on James for the guys in the youth group. What happened?"

One of the cups tipped over and sent a river of cold coffee flowing into the seam where the two tables had been pushed together. "Eric has everything under control."

Everything.

The word jumped out at Dan as he studied Cody's profile. "You stepped down."

"Pastor Keith and I talked this afternoon and I think it's best . . . for now."

"Okay." Dan expelled a long breath, but it didn't ease the pressure on his chest. He didn't want to think about Evie's response to Cody's decision—or what had prompted it.

Once word about Raine's pregnancy got out, Dan knew there would be people quick to judge and others who would just as quickly forgive, and some whose reaction fell somewhere in between. But Cody wasn't just a role model at Hope Community. He was practically the Proverbs 22:6 prototype. *Train a child in the way he should go, and when he is old he will not turn from it.*

Did Cody feel the pressure of people's expectations—or had he placed certain expectations on himself?

"What did Raine say? About you taking a break from youth council?"

"She doesn't know yet. She's behind in her homework so she stayed home tonight to catch up." Cody glanced at his wristwatch, an ancient gold Timex with a face the size of a compass that he'd inherited from Evie's father. "I'm going to ask Mom to drop me off at Raine's so we can go over the notes for the test in world history."

"I'll take you over there."

Cody didn't look nearly as surprised by the offer as Dan was for making it.

You must be a glutton for punishment.

Dan hadn't seen Ginevieve since she'd accused him of spying. It had cut deep, knowing Gin viewed his motives with the same level of suspicion she did Craig Cozielle's. Now that Raine was back, Ginevieve didn't need a ride home from work and Dan couldn't come up with a reasonable excuse to stop by the diner. Other than the fact that he wanted to see her, of course.

Somehow he doubted Ginevieve would think that fell into the category of reasonable. And for that matter, neither would Evie.

He unplugged the coffeepot and flipped off the lights.

There was no sign of Will lurking in the hallway, but Dan knew his brother would be slouched in the recliner waiting for an explanation when he got home. Good. It would give Dan a little time to come up with one.

At the end of the hall he spotted one of the men from his group standing in a triangle with his wife and oldest daughter.

Dan saw Cody smile at the girl, but her mother intercepted it with a cool look that made Dan's fists clench at his sides. Fortunately, Cody was too preoccupied with seeing Raine to notice.

Dan riffled through the coats on the rack until he found the right one. "How about we shoot some hoops tomorrow after school?"

"Can't. Raine has a doctor's appointment and I want to go with her."

Four doctors shared the clinic in Banister Falls. It was split down the middle, identical square blocks hinged together by a common waiting room. Dan could picture the row of chairs lined up tight against the window, the only divider a rickety magazine rack.

The physicians were bound to confidentiality by HIPAA laws, but the patients waiting for an examination room weren't as restricted. Trying to match doctors to patients and their possible ailments was more entertaining for some than watching the school of Nemo look-alikes in the waiting room's aquarium.

The clinic had always been a fruitful shoot of the local grapevine. By the weekend, Dan had no doubt the news of Raine's pregnancy would be all over town.

"Is Ginevieve going?" Dan lowered his voice as a woman collected her children's coats and a diaper bag from a nearby shelf.

"She's driving Raine to the clinic."

"What about your mom?"

Cody's face clouded. "I didn't ask her."

"Why—" Dan saw Evie approaching and exchanged the rest of the sentence for a smile. "Hi."

"Hi." Evie's smile didn't quite make it all the way to her eyes. She slipped the lanyard with its pale blue name badge, the one that labeled her the Women's Ministry Director, over her head. "Pastor Keith wants to meet with me for a few minutes, Cody. Do you want to call Raine and let her know you're going to be a few minutes late?"

"That's okay." Cody waved to a group of junior high boys as they charged toward the double doors. "Dan offered to give me a ride over there."

Evie's smile disappeared altogether. "I won't be more than ten or fifteen minutes. Can't you wait that long?"

"It's already eight o'clock, Mom. Raine gets pretty tired by the end of the day, so the sooner I get over there, the better."

"I don't mind, Eves." Dan didn't understand why she was so reluctant to let him give Cody a ride. The Avenue wasn't that far out of his way.

"There you are, Evie!" Pastor Keith jogged up to them. "Sorry, I got tied up for a few minutes there. The head usher had a question about a change in the order of service."

He clapped a hand on Dan's shoulder. "How are you doing?"

For some reason, the ordinary—some might even say trite—question rankled. Maybe because it forced Dan to respond with an ordinary—if not entirely truthful—response. "Good."

"Great. *Great.*" Keith had a habit of repeating words both in his everyday conversations and in the sermons he preached, putting an emphasis on the echo with a close-fisted victory jab to the air.

That rankled too.

Dan decided it was time to leave. "Ready, Cody?"

"Hold on." Evie caught Cody's sleeve a split second before he sprang at the door. "What time will you be home?"

"Ten."

"Do you want me to pick you up?"

"I'll walk." Cody wriggled free. "Bye, Mom."

"All right." Evie didn't look happy, but she let Pastor Keith lead her away, guiding her toward his office with a benign smile and the five-pound leather study Bible in his hand.

Dan waited a moment, but she didn't look back.

CHAPTER 31

"Cody's here!"

Raine vaulted from the sofa, and a tower of textbooks on the coffee table toppled over, causing a pileup of colored pencils and spiral notebooks. A glass of orange juice would also have been at risk if Gin hadn't been close enough to make a grab for it.

She moved the glass to a safe zone and peered through the blackened door of the oven to check the pizza. Raine's morning sickness had subsided while she was away, unleashing a healthy appetite that Gin hoped wouldn't outpace the weekly grocery budget. She had made spaghetti and meatballs for supper, but when Raine stopped memorizing algebraic equations and started foraging through the cupboards, Gin took a pizza out of the freezer.

The front door opened and cold air snapped at Gin's heels, signaling Cody's arrival. She tossed a hello over her shoulder without turning around.

"Hi." Cody's cheerful greeting was intertwined with another deeper masculine voice. One that raised every hair on the back of Gin's neck. She spun around so fast one of the vertebrae in her spine crackled in protest.

Dan filled the doorway, wearing a button-down plaid shirt in colors that matched the warm palette of his eyes, faded jeans, and a smile that threatened to make Gin forget everything she'd learned about men in the last thirty-six years.

"Hi." All the moisture in her mouth evaporated and somehow ended up on her palms.

For almost a week she'd tried to scrub Dan Moretti from her thoughts with a determination that rivaled Wendell's when he was trying to remove dried egg yolk from the bottom of a plate.

"I told Cody I'd drop him off on my way home from Wednesday night group." Dan didn't move from the square of carpet in front of the door, but he'd brought the scent of fresh air and snow inside with him, one that Gin had a feeling would linger in the air long after he was gone.

She scraped her palms against the front of her jeans and nodded even though she had no idea what went on at Wednesday night group.

"Do you mind if Cody and I use the computer in your room, Mom?" Raine asked. "We have to do an Internet search for an assignment."

Gin glanced at the teenagers. Cody had shed his coat and they were already fused at the hip, two magnets that seemed to increase in strength when they were together. Gin had already decided it would be wiser to treat them as a single unit than attempt to pry them apart, especially after their announcement on Saturday.

"I suppose." Gin rushed ahead of them to make sure she hadn't left her clothes lying around.

By the time she returned, Dan was gone. No, not gone. In her kitchen, taking the pizza out of the oven. A gray cloud rolled out and the smoke detector bleated a warning.

"It's burned, isn't it?" Gin stalked into the kitchen and waved her hands in the air to dispel the smoke. "I think this oven was the first one ever invented."

"Have you asked your landlord to replace it?" Dan handed her the pepperoni-shaped pizza cutter.

"No." She wouldn't be in Banister Falls long enough to bother. "Look at the crust." Gin began to saw at the blackened edge.

"Don't throw that away," Dan protested. "It's the best part."

"It's all yours." Gin shaved off another piece and handed it to him before she thought it through. Which would have been a good idea, because feeding a man didn't appear in the top five list of ways to get rid of him.

Dan popped the whole thing into his mouth and his eyes went wide. He reached for the glass of ice water on the counter and downed it.

Her ice water.

Gin arched a brow. "Hot?"

"Firefighter." Dan winked at her. "It's what we do."

What *Gin* did was put men who flirted with her firmly in their place. And she would have—if she could only form a complete sentence. She opted for Plan B. Ignore him.

That didn't work, either.

He took her glass over to the sink and filled it with water, poured two more for Cody and Raine, and refilled the ice cube tray while Gin finished cutting the pizza into even slices.

She wasn't used to having a man underfoot, but now that Dan had invaded her kitchen, he didn't appear to be in any hurry to leave. When he thought she wasn't looking he snagged another piece of the crust she'd discarded.

Gin rolled her eyes. "You can have a whole piece, you know. There's plenty."

"To go or dine in?"

The fact Dan had asked—and that the teasing sparkle Gin would have expected to accompany the words was curiously absent from his eyes—made her say, "I don't care."

She planned to keep telling herself that until it was true.

Gin delivered half the pizza to Raine and Cody and ended up

clearing a space on the desk so they wouldn't use the computer mousepad as a coaster, all the while listening for the telltale squeak of the front door. Dan had either made a quiet getaway . . . or he'd decided to stay.

Both possibilities terrified Gin for completely different reasons.

"Everything okay, Mom?"

Raine and Cody were both looking at her.

"Fine." Gin backed out of the room. "Don't spill anything on my keyboard."

She hopscotched down the narrow hall, dodging loose floorboards under the rumpled carpet so they wouldn't creak and give away her position. She peeked around the corner. The kitchen counter had been wiped clean of crumbs, and Dan was carrying the pizza and a pitcher of water into the living room.

"I think I've got everything." He tipped his head toward the coffee table. "I didn't want to move Raine's stuff, so I hope this is okay."

This wasn't okay, *she* wasn't okay, but Gin sat down on the sofa anyway and curled her feet underneath her.

Dan paused to give the arm of the nubby chair the affectionate squeeze due an old friend and sat down—next to her.

The couch was what Raine referred to as a "three seater," so there was an empty space between her and Dan. An empty space that completely disappeared when he turned to look at her.

"So . . . she's home."

Gin managed a nod. Dan barely knew Raine. How was it possible the relief in his eyes could be such a close match to what Gin had felt on Saturday, when she looked outside and saw Raine sitting in the car in front of Evie's house?

A burst of laughter erupted from the bedroom, where Raine and Cody were camped in front of the computer.

"Homework!"

She and Dan shouted the word at the same time. Which of course resulted in more laughter.

Gin couldn't help it. She joined in.

Dan started to choke.

"This is what I used to tell Raine." She handed him the glass of water. "Chew. Swallow. Talk."

Chapter 32

Breathe.

Dan silently added another command as his hand brushed against Ginevieve's.

His sister, Liz, made a dessert for special occasions that she called Speechless. A 2,000-calorie concoction made of chocolate and butter and whipping cream so rich and gooey it lived up to its name, because it was impossible to say a word until you'd finished it.

That was Ginevieve's laugh.

Dan actually licked his lips. To catch the water dribbling down his chin.

Fortunately, Gin didn't notice when he grabbed a napkin from the stack and mopped it up.

"It would be easier to treat her like an adult if she didn't wear Hello Kitty pajamas and watch cartoons on Saturday morning. Or"—Gin tossed a scowl in the direction of the bedroom even though it was wasted on Raine—"take off without letting me know where she was right away."

"If I know my aunt and uncle, it didn't throw them for a loop at all, having Raine show up at the door."

"Raine said they have six children. *Six.*" Gin sank back against the cushion and closed her eyes. "Most of the time I don't know what to do with the one I've got."

"You're doing great." Dan smiled. "Raine is young, but she's smart and capable. A lot like you were at that age, I'm guessing."

Gin stiffened. "You'd be guessing wrong. I was a mess when I was her age."

Dan knew he was treading on dangerous ground, but he asked anyway. "Raine's dad?"

"He left. Too young to handle the responsibility."

Gin was letting the guy off way too easy. "What were you? Eighteen?"

"Seventeen and a half." Gin tipped her head back and stared at the ceiling. "Eighteen when Raine was born."

"Evie was barely nineteen," Dan murmured.

"Apples and oranges."

Dan frowned. "What makes you say that?"

"Cody's dad probably didn't start throwing things when Evie told him she was pregnant."

The furnace shuddered to life, and in the series of thumps coming through the thin walls of the trailer, Dan recalled the sound of feet pounding against a glossy hardwood floor.

"Meet me at the gym."

Max had hung up the phone before Dan could say a word. When he'd arrived, Max was running ladders on the court. He looked so distraught Dan could only assume something terrible had happened. He'd practically had to wrench the basketball from Max's hands to get him to stop.

"What's going on?"

"Evie—" Max folded in half, hands on his knees as he gasped for air.

Dan grabbed a handful of T-shirt and jerked him upright. "What about her?"

"She thinks she's pregnant."

Dan had made it through the wedding. Sent Max and Evie off with a smile when they left on their honeymoon. But it took ten Mississippi's to wrestle down the jealousy before he could smile.

"That's great."

"Great? We've only been married a few months!" Max staggered to the wall and slumped against it, leaving a trail of sweat on the concrete blocks as he slid to the floor. "I'm not ready for this, man."

"I'm not sure anyone ever is." Dan dropped down next to him.

"But a kid." Max groaned. "You know what that means. Cold food. Sleepless nights."

"Think of it as practice." Dan jabbed an elbow in Max's ribs. "By the time the baby is born, we'll be firefighters. You'll have an edge."

They'd enrolled in the training program at the same time and, based on future retirements, planned to slide into the two available openings before the ink was dry on their certificates.

"I don't know." Max didn't rally at the thought of being part of the crew at Second Street Station. He looked so glum that Dan felt a stirring of unease. And resentment.

"What's not to know?" he demanded. "A wife. Children. It's all part of the package."

"I wanted Evie to myself for a while," Max muttered. "Is that so bad? I know she wants kids, but I was hoping it wouldn't be for a long time."

Or had he been hoping Evie would change her mind?

Dan didn't voice the thought aloud because another one suddenly occurred to him. "You acted excited when Evie told you, though, right?"

"I don't know. I guess so." Max shrugged. "I probably looked shocked. She had to leave for work so we didn't get a chance to talk about it. Then I called you."

Dan almost wished he hadn't. Because right now he wanted to thump his friend's head against the wall. Evie would be devastated if she suspected Max was anything less than ecstatic about the baby.

Max groaned. "I don't have brothers and sisters coming out of the walls like you do. I have no idea what to do."

"I know." Dan wasn't going to start lying to him now. "But you're still going to be a great dad."

"What makes you think so?" Max's staggering confidence had evaporated, leaving behind an uncertainty Dan hadn't seen since they were ten years old and had accepted a dare to walk the roofline of his grandparents' garage.

"Because you're great at everything," Dan reminded him. "At least that's what you're always telling me. Why would this be any different?"

"You're right." The familiar grin began to work its way to the surface.

"So, you're going to buy Evie a big bouquet of flowers—daisies, not roses—and take her out for dinner tonight."

"I am?"

Dan nodded. "And you're going to tell her that you can't wait to have an addition to our team in a few years."

The flicker of interest in Max's eyes was a good sign that he was coming around. "I never thought of that."

"Sure. You can pass on your skills."

"If it's a boy."

Now Dan did thump Max's head against the wall.

"Hey!" Max winced. "What was that for?"

"My sisters who won the state championship last year."

"Jerk."

"Takes one to know one." Dan grabbed Max's wrist and yanked him to his feet. "One on one. I've got just enough time to make you cry before I have to go to work."

Max scooped up the basketball. "You'll be the one crying, Danny boy."

Dan started walking toward the center of the court, but Max grabbed his arm and spun him around.

"You're supposed to wait until we get to the line," Dan told him.

"I just—" Max's grip tightened. "Thanks, buddy."

"That's what friends are for." Dan made a grab for the ball and Max spun away, laughing.

Cody Maxwell Bennett came into the world eight months later.

Chapter 33

Dan had disappeared.

Oh, he was still sitting beside her on the couch, smelling better than the deluxe pizza on the coffee table, but Elvis had definitely left the building.

Gin didn't mind. Maybe when Dan snapped out of his temporary coma, he would have forgotten what—or rather who—they'd been talking about.

She couldn't believe he had actually compared her to Evie Bennett. She and Evie might have been close in age when their children were born, but judging from the photographs on Evie's mantel, that was all they had in common. Evie had had the support of her husband and her family. And her husband's best friend. Gin had been on her own, trying to figure out how she was going to make ends meet.

Things would be different for Raine. Gin would make sure of it.

"Mom?" Raine poked her head around the corner. "What was the name of that restaurant in St. Louis? The one with the bars on the windows?"

"The Attic."

"That's right! Thanks."

"You aren't planning to go there anytime soon, are you?"

"Very funny." Raine made a face and ducked out of sight.

"Who said I was kidding," Gin muttered. She made the mistake of glancing at Dan and ran right into his smile.

"I hope the bars on the windows were for decorative purposes only."

"They were. It was all part of the ambiance." Gin rounded up the crumbs on the table and swept them onto a napkin. The simple task gave her something to focus on besides the shifting golds and greens in Dan's eyes, as fascinating as the play of sunlight through the trees. "The owners leased the top floor of an old warehouse and put in a brick oven. There were hardly any windows and the ductwork in the ceiling was exposed, but the suit-and-tie crowd assumed they left it that way on purpose."

"They couldn't afford the renovations," Dan guessed.

"Exactly. They were smart enough to go with it, but it didn't really matter. The food was phenomenal."

"It sounds like you know a lot about the place. Did you work there?"

"At a place down the street, but I talked to the manager a few times. It takes vision to turn trashed into trendy."

"I don't think your boss has caught that vision yet."

Another laugh bubbled to the surface. "Sue has her own way of running the diner, and whether you believe it or not, she planned it that way."

"Have you thought about working at Marie's?"

She had—for about ten seconds. Gin had stopped in for a cup of coffee a few days after she and Raine got stranded in Banister Falls. The manager's lips had snapped together as tight as Agnes Bardowski's little red coin purse when Gin asked for an application.

"White linen tablecloths. Low lighting. Real china." Gin listed the bistro's qualities. "Marie's caters to people who want to forget who they are for a little while. The people who come to the diner want to kick back and be themselves."

"If you worked at the bistro you wouldn't have to put up with guys like Craig Cozielle."

"Guys like Cozie are everywhere, and besides that, Marie only hires people whose names are on her Christmas card list." Gin saw the confused look on Dan's face. "People she's known since birth or who are related to her."

"I could put in a good word for you."

"I'm happy where I am. Sue's a decent boss."

"All bark and no bite?"

"Oh, she bites. I talked her into hiring a new waitress, and if she doesn't work out I'll probably lose my job too."

"That doesn't seem right."

"It's not—but that doesn't mean it won't happen. Sue likes to make an example of people once in a while. She believes that a healthy fear keeps the employees in line."

Dan lifted a brow. "I can't imagine you being afraid of anyone."

I'm afraid of you.

"So . . ." Dan stretched his legs under the coffee table. They were so long they poked out the other side. "No dreams of owning a restaurant of your own some day?"

And here was a perfect example of why Gin was afraid of Dan Moretti. No one had ever asked her that before. She was a good waitress, and that's what people saw when they looked at her.

It's what she wanted them to see—but for some reason, Dan always saw more.

"The business side fascinates me." Gin didn't know why she was telling him the truth, but once she started, she couldn't seem to stop. "But I never went to college. Everything I've learned came from paying attention, but there's nowhere to put that on a résumé."

"Why don't you take some classes?"

"Raine's dreams are more important. I've been saving for years to send her to college."

"You could go together." He wasn't joking.

"I'll be babysitting."

Dan stiffened. "She's keeping the baby?"

Gin was surprised no one had told him. "She and Cody told us the day she came home from that camp . . . you're *glad*."

She saw tears glittering in Dan's eyes, and her breath caught in her throat. Gin had felt the same way when Raine told her, but she didn't expect anyone else would understand.

Dan's cell began to ring. He unclipped it from the holder on his belt and glanced at the screen, already rising to his feet as he took the call.

"Hi . . . I came inside for a few minutes." Dan raked his hand through his hair. "No, don't apologize. I'm on my way."

Gin began to build a pyramid on the cardboard circle with the dishes they'd used. She couldn't hear the other person on the line but she had a good idea who it was.

Evie.

Dan hung up the phone and turned to her. "I'm sorry—"

"No problem." Gin wrestled Dan's coat off the back of the chair and released the scent of his cologne in the air. It took every ounce of her self-control not to bury her face in the fabric.

He slipped it on—slowly—almost as if he didn't want to leave. "Thanks for the pizza—and the company."

The door closed behind him, and the silence Gin had grown accustomed to grew louder—a lot louder—than it had ever been before.

CHAPTER 34

The clinic smelled like vanilla potpourri and the science lab on dissection day.

Raine located the women's restroom—just in case—as she followed her mom into the waiting room. The woman behind the glass window smiled at Ginevieve.

"Miss Lightly? We have several forms for new patients to fill out." She handed a clipboard to Ginevieve, who handed it to Raine. "Please have a seat and the doctor will be with you shortly."

The only other person in the waiting room was a gray-haired man watching the flat-screen TV mounted to the wall. Her mom picked a chair by the aquarium, and Raine sat down next to her with the clipboard, feeling as fidgety as she had the day she'd taken the ACT.

"Doing okay?" her mom murmured.

"Uh huh." Raine glanced at the receptionist and wrote down *checkup* as the reason for her visit. Because technically, that's what it was.

The door opened and Raine glanced up, expecting to see Cody. A slim, dark-haired girl limped into the waiting room, clutching her dad's arm, and Raine slid lower in the chair.

Great. Just great. Alicia Vandenkleat was in two of Raine's classes. Why hadn't she made her first OB/GYN appointment in another town? Raine dipped her head and let her hair swing forward to hide her face . . .

"Raine?" Alicia collapsed in the chair next to her.

"Hey, Alicia." Raine turned the clipboard over on her lap.

"I did something to my ankle in track practice." Alicia shifted in the chair and winced. "Dad!" She waved at the man talking to the receptionist. "I need an ice pack like right now!"

"I hope it's not too bad."

"So do I. We have our first meet next month. Dr. Kellan is the best for sports medicine, though, so Coach sent me over here." Alicia glanced at Raine's ankles. "What are you seeing him for?"

Um. Nothing that Dr. Kellan could help her with.

Raine felt her mom's nudge. "You can give the forms to the receptionist if you're done with them, sweetheart."

Oh, she was done. Raine vaulted to her feet just as Cody walked in. Their eyes met and she telegraphed a silent message.

Alicia Alert. Head cheerleader. Editor of the yearbook.

Cody didn't look like he cared about Alicia, so Raine scooted around him with the clipboard, handed it to the receptionist, and pressed the pump on the bottle of hand sanitizer once. Twice. Three times.

And almost bumped into Cody when she turned around. "Mom and I had a miscommunication about the car, so I had to wait at the church until she could drop me off."

"Mmmm." *Alicia. Alicia.*

"Raine Lightly?" The nurse practically shouted her name.

The gray-haired man turned toward the window and frowned. Alicia snickered.

That's when Cody noticed her. "Hi, Alicia."

Alicia's gaze fell on his backpack and she brightened. "Hey, do you have your calc homework with you? I'm stuck on one of the problems."

"I'm—"

"Raine?" the nurse called again.

"Mom? Are you coming?" Raine couldn't look at Cody. She wanted the caption under his yearbook picture to say Most Likely to Succeed, not Most Likely to Get a Girl Pregnant. Cody might not care about his reputation, but she did.

He took a step forward, as if he were going to follow her, and Raine glanced at Alicia. This time Cody must have seen the panic in her eyes.

He sat down.

The nurse led them to a room, asked a bunch of questions, and took Raine's blood pressure. Dr. Lewis came in a few minutes later and spent a few minutes reviewing her chart and then asked more questions.

"Well, it looks like you're almost ten weeks along." Dr. Lewis didn't smile. Maybe doctors didn't smile when you were eighteen and not married. "It's a little early, but let's see if we can hear baby's heartbeat."

"Okay." Raine heard *her* heart, pounding in her ears.

"I'll be back in just a minute to set things up."

The paper crinkled underneath Raine as she lay back on the table. "Did you hear my heartbeat this early, Mom?"

It took her mom so long to answer, Raine thought she hadn't been paying attention.

"Not this early, no."

It occurred to Raine that her mom had been pretty quiet since the nurse had ushered them into the tiny room. "I'm glad you're here."

"Where else would I be?"

That sounded more like her mom. It sounded like Cody too.

The nurse rolled a metal table closer, and Raine pushed herself onto her elbows. "Mom—" The rest of the words got stuck in her throat as her mom rose to her feet.

"I'll get him."

Ginevieve returned a few minutes later with Cody. And his mom. Raine resisted the urge to tug her shirt down.

Evie stayed right by the door, but Cody was at Raine's side in an instant, reaching for her hand.

"Wats." He squeezed it. A silent thank-you.

"This is going to feel cold." Dr. Lewis put some gel on Raine's belly and slowly began to move the Doppler. Raine felt Cody's grip on her hand tighten as a few more seconds passed.

And then a few more.

"I don't hear anything." Cody said what everyone was thinking.

"Raine's next appoint—" A sound interrupted the doctor, and her hand stilled. "Here you are." Dr. Lewis was smiling now. "Someone was just being a little shy."

Someone. A real someone with a real heartbeat.

Raine sank back, overwhelmed as she listened to the steady thump chase away the silence in the room.

She felt a touch on her shoulder and looked up. Found herself looking straight into a pair of blue eyes, sparkling with tears.

Evie Bennett's eyes.

Chapter 35

You should come with us, Ms. Lightly."

Gin cringed inside whenever Cody called her that. For one thing, it made her feel a hundred years old. And for another, she expected to see her mother's reflection when she looked in the mirror. "Thanks for the invitation, but I've got a few things to do this afternoon."

Cody and Raine glanced at each other, and Gin knew she was about to be tag-teamed. Sure enough, they moved into place like pieces on a chessboard. Cody stationed himself on one side of the coffee table while Raine plopped down on the sofa and sat on the corner of the cookbook Gin had been paging through.

"Like what?"

Like cleaning out the refrigerator. Dusting the light fixtures. Anything but attending an annual event called the Chilly Bowl at Hope Community Church.

"I have to do the taxes."

Raine doubled over laughing—that was a little insulting—and even Cody smiled.

"What?" Gin glowered at her daughter. "You think I have my personal accountant handle it?"

"I think you can put it off for a few hours on a Saturday afternoon." Raine grinned. "Come on, Mom. It'll be fun."

Gin had the strangest feeling she and her daughter had switched roles. They definitely had different definitions of the word *fun*. "I thought you said it was a football game."

"Flag football," Cody said, as if that made a difference.

"It's forty degrees outside and there's still snow on the ground."

"That's kind of the point, Mom." Raine poked her toe into Gin's thigh. "People get cabin fever this time of year, so the church came up with something fun to get them out of the house for a while. There's a bonfire and chili supper after the game."

The word *fire* conjured up an image of Dan's face. Gin had no doubt he would be there—with Evie. For once she wished Sue would have scheduled her for a Saturday shift and taken the decision out of her hands.

"I told Sue I would cover a shift at the diner this afternoon if she needs me. I better stick close to home in case she calls." Gin waited for Raine to remind her that cell phones made it possible for people to leave home *and* stay in touch with people, but she did something even worse. She sighed.

"All right." Raine pushed to her feet, her big brown eyes filled with disappointment.

"If you change your mind, we'll be there." Cody's smile heaped another layer on the mother's guilt that was already weighing Gin down. "The game starts at three o'clock."

"I'll keep that in mind. You two have a good time."

They grabbed their coats and shuffled outside. Leaving Gin, the pin that had punctured their happy balloon, alone.

By two thirty she had cleaned out the fridge and was actually contemplating retrieving the manila envelope stuffed with a year's worth of receipts from the top shelf of the closet when she tossed the rag into the sink.

Why was it so important to Raine that she attend this particular event?

Why are you avoiding it even though you know it's important to her?

Gin tried to drown out that little inner voice with a low growl, but her conscience refused to back down. It occurred to her that Raine was dealing with her own set of insecurities.

She remembered the sideways glances and whispered comments from people who'd heard about her "situation." Gin had made a promise to herself that she'd always be there when Raine needed her.

She abandoned the receipts and grabbed her coat.

Cars and pickup trucks packed the church parking lot, and the overflow lined the street for two blocks. Cody hadn't been kidding when he'd said there was always a good turnout.

Gin almost turned around. Twice.

She wedged her car into a narrow valley between two pickup trucks and turned off the engine. The theme from *Rocky* blasted from a set of speakers mounted on a pole, and Gin followed the sound to the field. Working her way through the perimeter of lawn chairs, she searched for a glimpse of Raine and Cody. A group of men formed a loose circle around a tower of wooden pallets, but thankfully, Dan wasn't among them.

A whistle pierced the air and people began to stream onto the field.

Gin spotted Evie walking with a trio of women, and in about thirty seconds their paths would intersect. She changed directions, which put her face-to-face with a teenage boy who shoved a bucket under her nose.

"Pick a color."

Gin reared back. "What?"

"Don't be shy!" The kid shook the bucket under her nose. "Pick one!"

What was this? Some kind of special drawing? Gin dipped her hand into the bucket and pulled out something that looked like a belt with two tattered strips of canvas trailing from each side.

"Looks like you're green. Good luck." He jogged backwards onto the field.

The football field.

"Wait a second!" Gin started after him, but a woman with a perky blond ponytail grabbed the sleeve of her jacket and towed Gin toward the center of the field.

"I'm glad you picked a green flag! We need all the help we can get."

Gin didn't have time to explain she hadn't *picked* anything—she'd been tricked—because another woman waved her into the huddle. Before she knew it, Gin was absorbed into a group of men and women of all ages, shapes, and sizes.

"Welcome to the Mean Green Machine!" One of the women greeted Gin with a friendly wink. "I'm Hannah."

"Gin."

It was a little, Gin thought, like watching a power outage.

One by one the bright, welcoming smiles disappeared.

Heat pricked the back of Gin's eyes and she blinked it away. What was wrong with her? She wasn't back in middle school, being judged by the kids who'd seen her snitch a pair of gym shorts and matching T-shirt from the lost-and-found box because her mom had forgotten—for the third time—to send money to the office so she could buy the required uniform.

The whistle blew again and a short, stocky man pointed to a line spray-painted on the field. "Time to line up, Green!"

This was *such* a bad idea.

"You're over there—by Charlie." Hannah nudged Gin toward a guy in his early thirties. "He's the quarterback."

Gin didn't know much about football, but she was pretty sure the quarterback was the player the other team wanted to put out of commission. At least it was flag football, right? No tackling involved.

She squatted down on the line and closed her eyes, wishing she'd stayed home. Wishing she'd worn tennis shoes instead of her cowboy boots . . .

"Hey."

Her chin snapped up and swung six inches to the right.

Now she knew why she hadn't seen Dan by the bonfire. He was the quarterback for the blue team.

"Hi." It sounded more like a gasp than a word.

"I'm surprised to see you here." A smile lurked at the corners of Dan's lips.

"Yeah, well, I'm kind of surprised to be here."

The smile turned into a full-blown grin, and Gin had to shift her weight when the hinges on her knees suddenly went weak.

Green's quarterback—Charlie?—shot her a stern no-fraternizing-with-the-enemy look.

After that, Gin might as well have been invisible.

Fifteen minutes of being jostled and bumped and stepped on—mostly by her own teammates—and she'd had enough. She fell back as another play began.

"Mom!"

Gin heard Raine's voice lift above the cheering crowd. So much for a quick getaway. She spotted Cody and Raine on the sidelines, their arms raised toward the sky.

"Go, Ms. Lightly!" Cody bellowed.

That was exactly what Gin planned to do. She took another step toward the parking lot.

Raine cupped her hands around her mouth. "Behind you, Mom!"

Gin spun around just in time to see Dan wind back and throw the ball.

A dozen thoughts funneled into one as Gin watched it rocketing straight toward her, but only one made it through.

His aim wasn't off. He'd done it on purpose.

CHAPTER 36

Ginevieve. Here. And this time, she wasn't fleeing toward the nearest exit.

Dan couldn't stop smiling while he watched the pastor's youngest son flip a coin to see who got the football. Until he overheard the whispered conversation between two of his teammates.

"Did you see those cowboy boots?"

"I know. Seriously? It's a football game, not a rodeo."

A ripple of laughter told him the comments had drifted beyond the ears they were intended for.

Dan's fingers curled at his sides until his knuckles turned white. "Are we playing football or what?"

Looks of surprise changed to speculation but Dan didn't care. The Chilly Bowl was supposed to be what Pastor Keith called a "community outreach event." Which, in Dan's opinion, kind of meant reaching out to the community.

He understood that people weren't quite sure what to do with Gin. They would be caught between loyalty toward Evie and Cody and a natural, but completely unfounded, suspicion of Ginevieve and Raine, two people they thought had the potential to hurt them.

So why did Gin look like the one who'd been hurt?

Out of the corner of his eyes Dan tracked her movements on

the field. Several times she was wide open, but no one so much as glanced her way, let alone threw her the ball.

"Take it easy." Dan jabbed his elbow into his friend's ribs after he'd bumped Gin out of the way to get to the green team's quarterback. "This is supposed to be for fun, remember?"

Buck shrugged him off with a grin. "Who said I'm not having fun?"

Frustration surged through Dan as he took his place on the line. Where was the sassy grit Gin had displayed when she'd dealt with Cozie and Hanson at the diner?

He slid a glance at her, and the air emptied from his lungs. Were those tears in her eyes?

The whistle blew and Dan heard the sound of Velcro tearing. Both flags fluttered to the ground as he got "sacked" by a green player.

"Off your game today, huh, Moretti?" Arnie Aimes broke into a country line dance to rub it in.

Two of Dan's teammates yanked him to his feet and set him in position.

"Come on, Moretti." One of them clapped him on the shoulder. "Don't lose your focus."

Oh, Dan wasn't losing it. He felt like it was being fine-tuned instead.

He jogged backward, searching for someone who was open. His gaze locked on Ginevieve standing alone near the end zone. She wasn't playing the game. She wasn't even watching the game. She was looking at the parking lot.

Dan knew without a doubt she was about to quit. Not only that, she would never darken the door of Hope Community again.

He heard Cody and Raine shouting something. Saw Gin glance over her shoulder. Following an instinct that started in his gut and raced up his arm all the way to his fingertips, Dan released the ball.

It sailed in a wide arc over the players, following a preset course to the slender woman in the denim jacket and cowboy boots.

Come on, Ginevieve.

At the last possible second, she lifted her hands. Dan didn't know if it was an instinctive gesture meant to protect herself from being hit or a deliberate attempt to catch it. But he heard a smack as it connected with Gin's palms and stayed there.

"Run, Mom! Run!" Cody and Raine's chorus rose above the commotion on the field.

Gin must have realized that a large group of people wearing blue flags was charging toward her, because she took a few hesitant steps down the field.

Dan didn't waste time tearing flags off belts. He knocked down everyone in his path, blue and green, until he was right behind her.

Gin cast a panicked glance over her shoulder.

"Keep going." He growled the words.

She lurched forward—probably to get away from him—and ran a crooked path toward the touchdown line. Dan remained glued to her shoulder, creating a solid barrier between Gin and anyone who tried to get to her.

He heard heavy footsteps closing in and whirled around. Buck's eyes met his and he fell back, hands raised in surrender as he dropped to the ground.

Gin was panting, her feet were sliding all over, and at the two-yard line the football almost shot from her hands like a bar of soap.

"Almost there," Dan told her.

She surged forward and pitched over the line for a touchdown.

Dan grabbed her around the waist before she fell and spun a celebratory circle. For one heart-stopping moment, he felt Gin lean into him.

The world began to expand and Dan was aware of two things.

His arms were still around Ginevieve—and it was the first time in Chilly Bowl history that no one was cheering after a touchdown.

A piercing whistle joined forces with the referee's, and Dan knew it was Cody.

The toe of Gin's cowboy boot connected with his ankle—Dan wasn't sure if it was an accident or not—and he set her down in a puddle of melted snow. She didn't seem to notice.

"What are you doing?" Gin's finger poked him in the chest, and gold sparks flew from her eyes. Dan was so relieved to see those instead of tears that he smiled. "You're not even on my side!"

Dan became aware of his teammates—the ones he'd mowed down on his quest to get to Gin—picking themselves up from the grass. On the sidelines, the entire Moretti clan had gathered in a tight huddle of their own. His mother had a bead on Gin, not him.

Dan stifled a groan. *Wonderful.* Nothing got past Angela Moretti. She would show up at his door within twenty-four hours and wring an explanation from him with a batch of double fudge brownies.

Gin whirled away from him, and her foot slipped on the wet grass. Dan saw her bite her lip. Not in frustration, in pain.

"Are you okay?"

Gin seared him with a look as she hobbled off the field. "Leave me alone."

"Let me see your foot."

"Be a little creative, Moretti," she tossed over her shoulder. "I've heard that one before."

In spite of the fact that his team looked ready to lynch their former quarterback, Dan couldn't stifle a grin. "I'm a first responder."

"Respond to someone else."

Cody and Raine rushed up, and Raine threw her arms around her mom. "You and Dan scored the first touchdown!"

Cody grinned. "And he isn't even on her team."

Over Ginevieve's shoulder, Dan saw Evie watching them from the sidelines. He had a sinking suspicion she was thinking the same thing.

Chapter 37

Gin refused to feel sorry for Dan as his teammates descended upon him. Using her wet feet as an excuse, she managed to extricate herself from Raine's enthusiastic hug and made her way inside the church, the closest building with a ladies' room.

Most of the people were standing in line for a bowl of chili, so Gin hoped that meant she would have a brief reprieve from her sudden and unexpected moment in the spotlight.

Her breath hissed between her teeth as she fumbled with the light switch. The powder room looked like a photo in a home decorating magazine. Pale pink walls and yellow accents, as sweet and feminine as a bouquet of spring flowers.

Gin felt as out of place in its very *pinkness* as she had the first and only time she'd wandered into Marie's Bistro.

She slid to the floor, where a metal vent, painted to match the raspberry pink trim, pumped warm air against her face. Gin turned into it and closed her eyes. Her fingers were numb, her foot was throbbing, and thanks to Dan, her heart was pumping an irregular beat.

What was he *thinking*?

She'd seen the football hurtling toward her, seen Dan sprinting in her direction, pushing everyone—blue and green—down along the way.

Gin barely had time to process the field of human debris left in his wake before he was at her side, commanding her to keep going. Not a problem. Gin wanted to get as far away from Dan Moretti as possible. It just so happened the end zone was in her way.

Her feet had barely crossed the touchdown line when her ankle folded over on itself. She felt a streak of pain and knew she was going down, but at the last moment Dan had swept her against him. Spun her around. In front of everyone.

Had he realized she was getting the cold shoulder from her teammates? Somehow known she'd been a split second away from walking off the field?

She didn't need Dan and his hero complex. The man was hard-wired to protect people. He would have done the same thing for anyone. It wasn't personal. Gin knew that.

But for a moment it had felt . . . good. She pressed her forehead to her knees and groaned.

The door opened and a middle-aged woman strode into the powder room. She reminded Gin of a raven-haired Katharine Hepburn. Tall and slim, her features striking rather than pretty.

She zeroed in on Gin. "You sprained your ankle."

"I think it's a blister." Gin mentally kicked herself. Why hadn't she taken refuge in one of the stalls?

"Let's see who's right." Katharine Hepburn knelt down on the tiled floor. One freckled hand braced against Gin's knee, the other grasped the heel of her cowboy boot.

"You don't have—" Gin clamped off the sentence with a gasp as the dull ache in her foot bloomed into a fiery ball of pain that traveled all the way up her leg.

"Sorry about that." The woman looked like she meant it. "Let's have a look."

Before Gin could form a protest, off came her sock.

"Not too bad . . . and no, I'm not a nurse." A smile spilled into the creases fanning out from a pair of fern green eyes. "But I raised six children, four boys and a set of twin girls. Separating sprains from breaks is part of my skill set."

Gin hoped she was right. Her ankle looked puffy and her skin matched the walls, but when she tried to wiggle her toes all ten seemed to be in working order.

"There you are!" The door swung open again and two women who looked to be in their mid-to-late twenties waltzed in.

Gin blinked, wondering if the pain was causing her to see double. No. Identical twins. Shining sable hair, cocoa brown eyes, and matching smiles. They weren't dressed alike—Twin One looked like a model for an outdoor magazine in jeans and a long-sleeved thermal shirt while Twin Two wore a bright green tunic over leggings, suede boots, and a trendy scarf.

Except for the color of their eyes, Gin could see a marked resemblance among the three women in both face and figure.

Katharine Hepburn rocked back on her heels and shot them a look Gin couldn't quite interpret. "I told you I would be right back."

"We wanted to see if you needed anything, Mom." The matching smiles disappeared when they noticed Gin's foot.

"Ouch." Twin One winced in sympathy.

"It looks worse than it feels." Gin tried to push to her feet and almost twisted the other ankle in a futile attempt to avoid the six hands that reached out to steady her.

"Independent I admire," the woman said. "Stubborn—"

"Will get you a week of kitchen duty," her daughters chimed in.

It wasn't difficult to scrape up a smile. Gin stepped gingerly into her cowboy boot and tried not to wince. "I'll be fine."

"That was a nice touchdown, by the way." Twin Two smiled at Gin. "People are still talking about it."

"I'm sure they are," Gin muttered.

To her amazement, their mother folded her hand around Gin's

and gave it a squeeze. Tears poked Gin's eyes and she blinked them away. A delayed reaction to the pain . . .

"Are you sure you don't want a cup of coffee or something to eat?" The twins flanked Gin as she shuffled to the door. "There's always plenty."

"I'm sure." Really sure. Gin took another tentative step toward freedom, sucked in a breath, and wished she'd parked closer to the building.

"You girls can save me a spot at the table, and I'll make sure Ginevieve gets to her car." The younger women were dismissed with a wave of a freckled hand.

Gin couldn't remember telling the woman her name. Which meant people had been talking about her. No surprise there. Gin had seen the reaction from her teammates when she'd introduced herself. It didn't matter they'd all been wearing green flags. Every one of them was on Team Bennett.

"Take a left. There's less traffic this way."

Gin was guided down a narrow corridor lined with colorful bulletin boards to a door that opened onto a large brick patio. Fortunately, there was no sign of Dan.

"I can make it the rest of the way on my own."

"Of course you can." The woman patted Gin's arm. "But isn't it nice to know there are times you don't have to?"

Gin had no idea what to say to that.

They worked their way slowly through the maze of parked cars in silence. Gin was never so happy to slide into Jasmine's lumpy seat, but the woman's forehead pleated as she watched Gin wrestle with the seat belt.

"I can find my son and ask him to give you a ride home."

"It's my left foot—and like you said, it's only a sprain."

Gin worked the key into the ignition but couldn't leave. Not without shutting the woman's hand in the door.

"If you won't stay and have something to eat, maybe you'd like to join my family for dinner after church next Sunday?"

Gin gaped at her, half expecting the woman to burst out laughing and say "Got you!" When she realized it was a genuine invitation, Gin was forced to come up with a genuine response.

And that response was "Why?"

A smile danced in the fern green eyes. "I like feeding people."

It was the last thing Gin expected her to say, but the only thing that had the power to dispel any lingering suspicions about her motives. Gin believed her because she liked feeding people too.

"All right." The swelling must have gone to her brain. Gin had no doubt she would regret the decision when Sunday came around.

"Wonderful. I suppose I should introduce myself, shouldn't I?" The woman laughed and held out her hand. "I'm Angela Moretti."

Angela Moretti. Dan's mother.

Never mind regretting it on Sunday. Gin was regretting it now.

CHAPTER 38

Raine aimed the airplane she'd made from a piece of notebook paper at Cody's textbook. It overshot and hit his shirt pocket.

"I'm studying."

"You haven't turned the page for twenty minutes." Raine had counted.

Cody didn't look up. "Would you believe I'm memorizing it?"

"If it wasn't a photograph of lightning striking a golf course, maybe I would."

Cody rocked back on his chair. "Sorry. I'm a little distracted."

"Was your mom mad you didn't stay home tonight?" Raine knew the text messages had been flying back and forth between Cody and his mom after she picked him up.

"She didn't act like it. Dan was probably coming over anyway."

"Like a date?" Raine said slowly. Cody had never said anything about his mom and Dan being more than friends.

"Kind of." Cody closed his textbook. "Are you ready to go?"

"Sure." Raine tried to hide her confusion. Going to the library had been Cody's idea, but he'd hardly said a dozen words to her all evening. Had she done something wrong? Had someone made a comment about her or the baby?

Ms. Davenport glanced up as they walked to the door. She was a petite woman who practically disappeared behind the circulation desk, and Cody said she had worked at the public library so long he wouldn't have been surprised to find out she'd invented the Dewey decimal system.

Raine liked her though. Lately, Ms. Davenport was one of the few people who didn't stare at Raine's stomach when they saw her.

"How's your mom doing, Cody?" Ms. Davenport flagged him down with a wrinkled copy of the *Chicago Tribune*. "She's been on my mind today."

"Thank you." Cody, Mr. Social, didn't stop and talk to the librarian like he usually did.

"Please let her know I'm thinking about her."

"I will." Cody picked up speed, and Raine practically chased him out the door and into the parking lot.

"What was that about? Why was she asking about your mom?"

Cody opened Jasmine's door on the driver's side, and rust sprinkled down like confetti. "She's known Mom for years."

Raine had a minute to replay the conversation while Cody walked around the hood and got into the car. "But Ms. Davenport said your mom was on her mind *today*."

"Looking for clues, Wats?"

"I'll settle for a straight answer."

Cody sighed. "Today is the anniversary of my dad's death."

"Cody." Raine felt awful for pushing him. "I'm sorry."

Silence.

"You don't want to talk about it?"

"See, that's the problem. I don't know what to talk about." Cody tipped his head back against the seat. "It's an annual tradition. Every year on this day, we make the kind of pizza my dad liked and Mom and Dan tell stories about him. I have a whole whopping two of them."

"What are they?"

"I remember him taking me to the fire department and I slid down the pole."

"I thought you were afraid of heights."

"I was . . . but Dad was at the top and Dan was waiting for me at the bottom."

"That's a good memory," Raine said softly.

"I look at the photo albums and there are dozens of pictures of my dad holding me after I was born. Christmases and birthday parties. I feel guilty I don't remember more."

"You were just a little kid when he died."

"I remember the funeral. There were fire trucks lined up all the way down the street, and the firefighters knelt down and shook my hand. I couldn't figure out why they were all crying."

"That's a good memory too."

Cody smiled. "I realize you're trying to cheer me up, but that's a stretch."

"No, it isn't. It means that people loved your dad. You've got Dan and the Morettis and a whole town that knows who you are and cares about you." Raine tried to keep the envy from sneaking into her voice, but Cody's mood hadn't affected his ability to read her mind.

"Did you ever meet your dad?"

"Mom won't talk about him. When I was younger, I'd imagine he was in the witness protection program or a spy who had to keep his identity a secret. Why else would a dad leave, right?"

Cody reached for her hand. He always knew when to do that too.

"Mom says that just because a man can father a child doesn't mean he'll be a good one."

Cody's hand slipped from hers, and Raine's heart went with it when he drew back and turned to look out the window. She shouldn't have said that.

"Are you afraid you won't be a good dad because you didn't have one?" she ventured.

The question brought Cody's head around. "I had Dan."

"Did you ever wonder why Dan and your mom didn't get married? I mean, you said he's been around since you were a kid."

"I remember asking Mom once why Dan didn't live with us. I even told her that he could sleep in my room."

"What did she say?"

"One of those typical mom things." Cody's laugh was low and soft. "She said she loved me so much, I took up all the room in her heart and no one else would fit."

Raine would have laughed, too, except something told her that Evie Bennett hadn't been joking. If she lost Cody, she would feel the same way. Raine pressed a palm just below her belly button, where she'd felt a delicate little flutter, the graze of a butterfly wing, that morning.

Evie kind of intimidated Raine, but for the first time, it made sense why she was so protective of Cody.

And why she didn't want him to be a firefighter.

Chapter 39

Dan didn't know which he hated more—pretending this particular Friday was just like any other at the fire station or pretending it wasn't.

He got into his truck and pulled the door shut, creating a buffer between him and the sympathetic glances he'd been receiving from the guys on his crew. He reached up and straightened Max's shield on the visor, his thumb tracing the eagle's head in the center of the emblem.

"There's a lot going on here, buddy," Dan murmured. "You're going to be a grandpa. Crazy, isn't it? A lot of guys our age are still having kids. But you'd be proud of the way Cody is handling it. He's fearless, just like you . . ."

His cell phone began to ring, interrupting Dan's one-sided conversation. He intended to ignore it until he saw Evie's name flash across the screen.

Relief poured through Dan. He and Evie hadn't spoken since the Chilly Bowl on Saturday, when he'd single-handedly broken every rule governing flag football and probably a few others that had nothing to do with sports.

"Hey." Dan didn't ask Evie how she was. He already knew. "It's good to hear your voice."

"Hi." A short pause. "Do you have plans for tonight?"

The fact that she had to ask made Dan regret that he hadn't called her first. "What are you thinking?"

"I'm making homemade pizza and you haven't been over for a while . . ." The sentence trailed off, leaving room for Dan to fill in the blank. To decide.

"That sounds great. What time?"

"Six o'clock? Same as always?" There was something in Evie's voice Dan couldn't quite identify.

"Sure. I'll be over in a little while." He drove home and intercepted Will at the bottom of the stairs, dressed for Friday night in sweats and a T-shirt.

"Mom's car is making a funny noise, so I'm going to take a look at it. I thought I'd grab a burger on the way home if you want to come along."

"Sorry—I already made plans."

"You're ditching me again, big brother?" Will veered toward the fridge, looking for something to hold him over for an hour. "I'm going to start taking it personally."

"I'm going over to Evie's house to have supper with her and Cody."

Understanding dawned in Will's eyes. Dan looked away before it turned to sympathy, but years of sharing a bedroom with his three younger brothers left very little room for secrets.

Will gave him a shove—his own unique version of a hug. "You can't avoid Mom forever, you know."

"I'm not avoiding anyone."

"You skipped Sunday dinner last weekend."

Dan shrugged off his guilt. "Mort needed help moving a pile of wood."

"Uh huh."

"Tell Mom I'll be there this Sunday for sure."

Will wasn't finished. "We all care about Evie and Cody, you know. We want to know what we can do to help."

His brother was right. There were going to be people in the community who judged Evie for Cody's mistake, but Dan knew his family would rally around her and offer support.

He grabbed his gym bag in case Cody wanted to shoot some hoops and drove to Rosewood Court.

"Hello." Dan knocked as he opened the door. Garlic and the aroma of baking bread scented the foyer as he bent down to greet Diva.

"In the kitchen."

Evie stood at the sink. In faded jeans with the hems rolled up and a sky blue T-shirt, she didn't look much older than Cody. He wasn't used to seeing her dressed so casually. Even on weekends, Evie leaned toward khaki pants and crisp, button-down shirts.

She glanced over her shoulder. "I hope you're hungry."

"Starving." Dan reached for a carrot stick and popped it into his mouth. "I stopped at the video store and picked up a movie." Dan leaned against the counter. "I saw the poster in the window and remembered Cody wanted to see it."

"Cody isn't here."

Dan glanced at the table and noticed it was set for two. "I thought he was having dinner with us."

"Raine picked him up a little while ago. They made other plans." Evie opened the oven door and peeked inside. "Two more minutes. Can you put together a salad?"

"Sure." Dan opened the fridge and grabbed a head of lettuce. He'd played sous chef so many times, he knew the layout of Evie's kitchen better than his own.

She began to arrange warm breadsticks in a wicker basket. "If you'd rather stretch out your legs, we can put the movie in and eat in the living room."

"I don't mind waiting until Cody gets back before we start it."

"He told me not to wait up for him."

Dan frowned. "We could have had dinner together another night. You didn't have to go to all this trouble just for me."

"It isn't any trouble, Danny." Evie opened the oven door and slid the pizza onto a baking sheet. "We used to do this all the time."

That was true, but why wouldn't she look him in the eye?

"I think it's done." Evie studied the pizza. She always took it out a few minutes before the timer went off, just to make sure the crust didn't turn a shade darker than golden brown.

Dan could see Ginevieve in his mind, sawing the burned crust away.

"Why are you smiling?" Evie was studying him now.

He *was* smiling. Dan scrubbed it off with the back of his hand. "Just thinking."

"I put extra pepperoni on the pizza." Evie padded past him, her slippers slapping against the floor.

Dan recognized them immediately. "I can't believe you haven't thrown those away."

"What?"

"Those slippers." Dan pointed at her feet. "I'm surprised the bottoms haven't completely disintegrated by now."

"They have." She lifted up her foot and showed him the sole, reinforced with silver tape.

"I should have known."

Evie wiggled her toes. "They're comfortable."

And Max had bought them for her for Christmas the first year they were married. Dan had been there when he'd picked them out. He'd bought a pair in another color for his sister Lisa, but he was pretty sure she'd replaced them at some point over the last nineteen years.

Evie wasn't holding onto an old pair of slippers because they were comfortable, she was holding onto a piece of Max.

Oh, Eves. Aren't you ever going to move forward?

The question changed shape as it circled back to Dan and hit him square in the chest.

Are you?

They transported everything to the living room, and while Evie divided up the pizza, Dan went to add another log to the fire.

The radio on his belt crackled to life and he heard one of the police officers on duty check out at Eddie's Bar. Dan recognized the code for a fight in progress, and a knot formed in his chest.

Was Ginevieve working? If Raine had picked up Cody, that left her mother without a car. He glanced at the grandfather clock in the corner.

Evie noticed. "Do you have to be somewhere?"

"Nope." He forced a smile.

"Good." Evie kicked off her slippers and sat on the sofa, tucking one bare foot underneath her. "Will you pray?"

Dan bowed his head and thanked God for the food, a prayer for Ginevieve a silent addition to Evie's murmured amen.

"How are things going with Cody?"

"He got another letter from the dean at Carroll College."

"What did it say?"

"I have no idea. It's still sitting on the desk."

"Evie—"

"Do you mind if we talk about something else?" She nudged his arm. "Just for tonight?"

"Like what?"

"Like the plot of this predictable movie you picked out."

"You don't know it's predictable!"

"Let me guess. The guy is running away from something or

someone, there are sports cars so he can get to wherever he's going faster, and things blow up in order to slow down the people who are after him."

"How did you know?"

"Because I know you, Danny." Evie grinned. "We used to take turns picking out movies, remember?"

"I remember you made me watch *The Princess Bride*."

"You liked it."

"I *pretended* to like it."

"Then why did Lisa and Liz tell me you said it was a good movie?" she demanded.

"You know the answer to that. Causing trouble is considered a sport when it comes to my twin sisters."

"How about we watch the movie you brought—and then I get to pick one out? That would be the fair thing to do."

It would also prevent him from stopping by the diner to see if Ginevieve needed a ride home. Not that Dan planned to give her a choice.

"Did you pick up an extra shift tomorrow?" Evie pressed.

"No." *Don't look at the clock again.* "I can stay."

The dispatcher broke into the conversation, relaying some details about the people involved in the altercation.

"You should turn off your radio, Captain," she teased. "The guys will call you if they need you."

Dan didn't tell Evie he'd been listening to the police officers, not the crew at the station.

They cleaned up the kitchen between movies, and Dan took Diva outside while Evie picked out a DVD. He tuned into the police frequency again but the chatter had died down.

He thought about texting Cody and suggesting he and Raine give Ginevieve a ride home from the diner, but he'd made a promise to Evie. And tonight wasn't a good night to leave her alone.

Dan slid the radio into his coat pocket and walked back into the living room.

"*Pride and Prejudice* or *Sleepless in Seattle*?"

"Neither." Dan stashed the remote control under the sofa pillow.

"That is so not going to work. We agreed I could pick out the next movie." To his astonishment, Evie reached behind him and made a playful grab for it.

"Hand it over."

Laughing, Dan held it above her head. "Nice try." He'd expected her to give up, but Evie jumped up and tried to wrestle it away from him. Her sleek blond hair went every which way and her breath came out in short bursts as they battled for control.

"You couldn't get the best of me in sixth grade, and it's not going to happen now," Dan told her.

"But I know your weakness, Danny Moretti." Evie's fingers dug into his ribs.

She was *tickling* him.

Dan let go of the remote—but Evie didn't let go of him. Her hand stayed on his side, her fingertips traced the ridge of muscles on his abdomen.

Dan felt his chest cave in. "What's going on, Eves?" he said softly.

She moistened her lower lip but her gaze didn't waver. "I don't know what you mean."

Dan moved a fraction of an inch and her hand fell away. "If I didn't know better, I'd think—"

"Think what?"

"That you were flirting with me, okay?" He tried to laugh, but it got caught in his throat this time. The whole situation felt strange. Surreal. As if he'd been sucked into one of the romantic comedies Evie had wanted him to watch.

"Maybe I am," she stunned him by saying. "I'm a little out of practice, though."

"Out of practice?" Dan repeated. "You've *never* flirted or played games."

"I'm not playing games." Evie leaned forward until Dan could see his reflection in the clear blue depths of her eyes.

Her hands cupped his face, holding him in place. Dan saw a blush wash through her cheeks. Read the shy invitation in her eyes.

He'd waited for this moment. Dreamed of it. A month ago, he would have pulled Evie into his arms and never let go. But now he folded his hands over Evie's and pressed them against his heart. "What is this about?"

"Does it have to be about anything?" She tried to tug free but this time, Dan was the one who held on. "I thought . . . I thought this was what you wanted."

What he wanted.

The air emptied out of Dan's lungs. He'd always assumed Evie didn't know how he felt about her. That love for Max had clouded her vision, her perspective. Her ability to see *him.*

But if she'd known all along, what had changed? And when?

"What do *you* want, Evie?"

"I want things to be the way they were," she choked out.

Before Max died? Before Cody had made a life-altering decision? Dan held back the words and gently squeezed her hands. "I'm here for you, Eves, but I can't push the rewind button. I can't change things."

"Are you here for me?" Tears welled up. "Because sometimes it doesn't feel like it."

Sometimes.

In his mind's eye Dan saw an image of Evie's expression after Gin scored the touchdown. "Is this about Ginevieve?"

Evie ducked her head, but not before Dan saw the truth in her eyes. "You made it pretty clear whose side you're on."

"I'm not taking sides!" Dan fought to keep his frustration under control. "Evie, you know how I feel about you."

"How? How do you feel about me?"

Dan stared at her. The words were right there, part of a script he'd rehearsed over and over in his mind, but he couldn't say them. *Why* couldn't he say them?

Evie stood up and wrapped her arms around her middle. "I think you should go, Danny."

"Evie—"

"Please." She wouldn't look at him. "Just go."

Chapter 40

She hates me. I should just quit before she fires me."

Nicki, the new waitress, was shivering in the corner of the walk-in cooler when Gin found her.

"Don't flatter yourself. Sue hates everyone." Gin dragged the girl into the kitchen and parked her in front of the griddle to thaw out.

"I screwed up three orders tonight." Nicki lowered her voice in case Sue was lurking nearby. "Three strikes and you're out, right?"

"That's baseball." Gin smiled. "At My Place, you only get two."

She'd been teasing, but the anguished look on Nicki's thin face triggered Gin's maternal instincts. Probably because the girl wasn't a whole lot older than Raine.

"I really need this job, Gin." Nicki scraped at a tiny pink flamingo glued to her thumbnail.

Sue had agreed to a one-week trial because Eddie had already stolen the waitress who was supposed to start over the weekend.

"Your mom won't let you move back in?"

"My stepdad said no. He claims the kids give him migraines, and Mom thinks I should stay with Victor until I figure things out."

Nicki's mom was thinking about herself. Gin had seen the purple smudge of a bruise, roughly the size and shape of a man's thumbprint, in the shadow of Nicki's jaw when she'd come into work.

"What about your sister?"

"She's watching them now, but she has to work the night shift tonight." Nicki's lower lip rolled under. "At least I hope she's watching them. Last time Cheryl fell asleep and left Lily in charge. Lily is responsible and everything, but my three can be a handful."

Nicki's niece might be responsible, but if Gin remembered correctly, she was also ten years old.

Gin silently balanced the number of customers in the dining room against the clock. "Why don't you leave a few minutes early tonight?"

Nicki's face brightened. "Really?"

"It's getting close to eight, and Eddie's is drawing a bigger crowd tonight than we are." Gin hadn't even realized a fight had broken out in the bar until it spilled through the door onto Radley Street. "Just make sure you sneak out the back door before Sue sees you."

Nicki tried to smile, but it turned into a grimace instead. The bruise on her cheek, barely disguised by a layer of foundation, must have been fresh. She'd gone to so much trouble to cover it up, Gin knew not to ask. Not yet anyway. Nicki waved and slipped out the door into the alley.

"She's a terrible waitress." Sue had sneaked up behind her.

"She'll get better."

"Who runs this place? You or me?"

"You."

"Just making sure you remembered." Sue's eyes narrowed. "The chairman of the fire department auxiliary called yesterday and ordered half a dozen pies for some fund-raiser next month. Do you know anything about that?"

"Why would I?" Gin plunged her hands into the sink even though she ran the risk of starting a turf war with Wendell.

"You're the one with a firefighter."

"I don't *have* a firefighter." Hopefully Sue would think the steam rising from the dishwater had put the color in her cheeks. "Have you seen one around here lately?"

"Miss him?"

Yes.

Gin could hardly admit it to herself, let alone her boss. This was why she didn't stay in one place very long. When you stayed in one place, you got to know people. And the more you got to know them, the more space they took up in your head . . . and your heart. If—no, *when*—they walked away, you lost another piece of yourself. After Raine's father had taken off, Gin didn't have a whole lot left . . . and certainly nothing to give a man like Dan.

He deserved someone who didn't have a ton of baggage—or a suitcase on standby in the closet. He deserved someone like Evie Bennett.

"Let's call it a night." Sue emptied the last of the coffeepot, a trickle of black water thickened with grounds, into her cup. "Eddie won."

Gin glanced at the clock and realized it had stopped, the hands frozen on the two and the six. "I can close up."

"Sounds good to me." Sue rubbed the back of her neck. "I feel a migraine coming on. Must be new-waitress related."

"Nicki will catch on."

"Take one of those apple pies when you leave," Sue commanded. "I knew I made too many."

Gin smiled. Her boss also knew that apple was Raine's favorite.

She dimmed the lights and made sure Wendell had cleaned up the kitchen before he left. Shrugging on her coat, Gin took a pie from the dessert case and let herself out through the back door. High-pitched laughter and the lyrics of a bad country song rolled over her as she walked past Eddie's.

Just beyond the dumpsters, a man stepped out of the shadows and flicked a burning cigarette into Gin's path.

"Where's your bodyguard?"

Gin pulled up short as Craig Cozielle loomed in front of her. "I don't need a bodyguard."

Cozie swayed closer, his eyes raking a slow path from Gin's face to the pie she held in her hands. "I call this perfect timing. I've had a craving for something sweet."

"Maybe you should google a new pickup line." Gin tried to step past him, but Cozie's hand snapped around her arm.

"Or maybe I should drive a fire truck, huh?" Jealousy burned in the bloodshot eyes, and Gin smelled whiskey on his breath. Hard liquor and natural mean made for a dangerous combination, and for the first time Gin sensed she wasn't going to escape the situation using her usual set of tools.

"Get out of my way." Gin heard a faint hitch in her words, and the grin that split Cozie's face told Gin he had too.

He shifted his weight, backing Gin up against the brick wall. The pie slipped out of her hands and landed in a puddle of melted snow.

"Oops." Cozie kicked it out of the way before Gin could move and locked his arms against the wall, one on each side of her, creating a cage she couldn't escape.

"Come on, Gini."

Someone else's voice. Someone else's hands holding her in place.

"You know what people say. There's no such thing as a free lunch, right? If you want to get away from your mom, you have to give me something in return."

Gin peered over the muscled rise of Cozie's shoulder. Radley Street seemed farther away than usual and there was no sign of . . . anyone. Cozie's breathing was the only sound she could hear.

You're not going to help me, are You?

The words shot out of her heart a moment before Gin realized who they were meant for. Her first prayer and she was *yelling* at God. If He was here—the way Dan claimed—He would probably turn His back on her and walk away . . .

Light washed over them, and Gin realized a car had turned into the alley. When it stopped, Cozie swore under his breath and stepped even closer, blocking her from view. Whoever it was would assume they were a couple of Eddie's regulars, sharing a private moment in the alley.

The driver's side door opened, and in the pale shaft of light Gin saw the silhouette of a man large enough to hold his own against Cozie.

"Everything okay here?"

Gin's knees turned to liquid as she recognized the voice.

Cozie must have too, because his hand tightened like a vise around her arm.

"Everything's fine," he called back. "The lady and I are just having a little chat."

Gin opened her mouth to yell, but Cozie swooped in and kissed her. His aim was off, but Gin's stomach turned inside out as his lips mashed against her chin.

A car door closed.

She was alone . . .

"Ginevieve?" The beam of the flashlight swept over them.

Gin pushed a shoulder against Cozie's chest, leaving him with no choice but to release her. She stumbled toward Ryan Tate on legs she wasn't sure would hold her up.

Gin didn't know what the police officer saw in her eyes, but Ryan turned on Cozie with a snarl that made Gin glad he was one of the good guys. "Get out of here."

"Whatever you say, Officer, sir." With a mock salute, Cozie sauntered away.

"Thank you." Gin shoved her hands in her pockets before Ryan could see they were shaking.

His eyes skimmed over her, looking for damage, and lingered on the chunks of apple pie scattered at her feet. "I would recommend pepper spray if you're going to be walking through the alley this time of night. All cinnamon is going to do is make guys like Cozie drool more than usual."

The dry comment, meant to distract, wrung out a laugh. "I'll remember that."

Ryan jerked his head toward the squad car. "Come on. I'll give you a ride home."

It didn't cross Gin's mind to argue. Or turn him down.

Ryan opened the passenger side door and waited until she was buckled in before he closed her inside.

"Just so you know—" Gin braided her fingers together in her lap as Ryan guided the squad car onto the street. "I didn't encourage him."

"I know."

"How?" Gin cast a cautious glance in the officer's direction. "I was sure you'd think I was with Cozie by choice."

"I saw how it was between you and Dan."

The matter-of-fact statement shocked her. "There's nothing between me and Dan."

"If you say so."

"I'm surprised you recognized me." Gin began to replay the scene in her mind.

"I didn't . . . not until I was about three feet away."

"Then why did you stop?" Gin twisted in the seat to look at him.

"I got a tip."

It wasn't what Gin had expected him to say. "Someone called you?"

"You could say that." Ryan was smiling now. "I just got back from a two-day training seminar in Madison and I was about to drop the squad car off at the station. I was almost there and . . ." He filled in the blank with a shrug.

"And what?"

"I felt a nudge. Decided to take a little detour."

Radley Street wasn't a detour. It was several blocks off the beaten path and nowhere near the police department.

"A nudge," Gin repeated.

"Even when I recognized Craig, I figured you were one of his girlfriends." Ryan shook his head. "Believe it or not, the guy is quite the ladies' man—and none of them seem to care he doesn't treat them like ladies. I was about to get back in the car but I had this feeling I should walk over there . . . just to be sure. You've got someone looking out for you, no doubt about it."

Someone looking out for her.

Someone who'd heard her call when dark memories had flash-frozen her in place.

Warmth spread through Gin. She couldn't explain it. Had never experienced it before. But somehow—and Gin couldn't explain that, either—it made the sensation even more real.

"Thank you," Gin murmured.

Ryan glanced at her, amusement in his eyes. "You already said that."

Gin didn't tell the officer she'd been talking to someone else this time.

Ryan drove past the fire station and Gin saw Dan's pickup parked in the shadows. Lights blazed from the windows of the building next door.

"The gym." The officer didn't miss a thing. "Dan had a hard day. He must be running off some steam on the court."

Gin saw a blur of movement in the window. "You've been out of town . . . how do you know Dan had a hard day?"

"I just know." The squad car slowed down to a low purr as Ryan pulled up even with the curb. "Is this your stop?"

Gin wanted to laugh and tell him no, she'd had enough of men for the evening. But Dan wasn't men. Dan was . . . Dan.

Ryan's foot touched the accelerator, and the car began to creep forward again.

"Wait." Gin reached for the handle and then panic set in. "If Dan had a hard day, is he going to want company?"

"Does it matter?"

Gin thought about that. Smiled. "Absolutely not."

Chapter 41

Dan went in for a lay-up and caught a glimpse of a squad car through the window. Ryan was at the wheel, checking up on him. Everyone was checking up on him.

In the last few hours there had been half a dozen text messages from his siblings, an invitation to watch the latest Disney princess movie with his nieces, and an Instagram of the cake his sister-in-law had baked for Sunday dinner at his parents' house. German chocolate, homemade coconut frosting.

Dan knew they meant well.

He should have gone home—except that Will would be back by now. Would ask how things went with Evie.

How did things go with Evie, Dan?

He could still feel her hands framing his face, the confusion in her eyes when he hadn't kissed her.

Dan still wasn't sure *why* he hadn't kissed her. Spending the anniversary of Max's death together had become a tradition every year, but Evie had never turned to him before . . . not like that.

Taking her into his arms, kissing her, would have changed things between them.

But wasn't that what he wanted?

Dan took out his frustration on the basketball and launched it at the net like a grenade. It went wide, ricocheted off the wall, and rolled toward the door.

He chased the ball down the court, where it bumped into a pair of pink-and-white tennis shoes. His gaze traveled up. Faded jeans. Denim jacket. Light green eyes.

"Ginevieve." What was she doing here?

She picked up the ball and tossed it back to him. "I saw your truck parked outside."

"You're wearing tennis shoes." Dan's gaze dropped to her feet. "Pink tennis shoes."

"They're Raine's." She glowered down at them.

She was too appealing. He was feeling too unstable. Dan stumbled away and took a slow charge at the basket. When the ball swished through the net, he caught it on the rebound. Gin was still there when he turned around.

Their eyes met and her chin lifted.

After a day of sympathetic glances and somber eyes, the challenge in that chin was a welcome change and stirred a similar reaction in Dan. He tucked the ball against his hip.

"Do you need a ride home?" Dan tossed the question at her, knowing she'd turn him down.

"Yes."

Well, wasn't everyone just full of surprises tonight?

"Let's go." Dan stuffed the basketball in a nylon bag and grabbed his T-shirt off the bench. Out of the corner of his eye he saw Gin look away a split second before he yanked it over his head. He grabbed his coat and keys and followed her to the truck. The fact that she actually stepped aside so he could open her door raised his suspicions.

"Did Ryan tell you to check up on me?"

Ginevieve looked surprised by the question. "He was by the diner when I got off work and . . . he offered me a ride home."

Dan felt a stab of guilt. Eddie's Friday night crowd could get rowdy. He should have stopped in to check on her, but after he'd left Evie's house he was too keyed up. Not fit company for anyone. The gym hadn't provided the refuge he'd needed, though. He and Max had spent hours there, shooting hoops. All it did was bring back memories Dan had tried to hold at bay all day.

The truck rattled over the culvert as he turned onto Fifth Avenue. Melting snow had flooded the road, and water sprayed from the tires as Dan maneuvered through the potholes.

The trailer was dark when he pulled up next to it.

The last time Dan had given Ginevieve a ride home, she'd bailed out so fast he had to make sure she hadn't left her boots behind. Now she didn't move.

"Cody and Raine won't be back until eleven. Come inside. I'll make you a cup of hot chocolate."

If she'd phrased it as a question rather than a command, Dan might have refused. As it was, the adrenalin was draining away, leaving a bone-chilling numbness behind.

He put the truck in park and turned off the ignition.

Music blared from the trailer next door, and Dan saw teenage faces pressed to the window as he followed Gin up the steps.

The slight chill in the air felt good after a punishing workout. Dan stopped just inside the door and let it settle over him.

"Daniel." He flinched at the sound of Gin's voice, the touch of her hand when it cradled his elbow. She guided him into the living room. "Sit down."

The joints in the legs of the nubby chair creaked as she nudged him into its lap. "I'll be right back."

A bouquet of fresh flowers covered a water stain on the coffee table. Dan reached out and adjusted a bright pink carnation.

Gin returned and set two cups down. "You probably should rehydrate with water, but the marshmallows wouldn't taste as good."

There were a lot of those, bobbing on the surface of the hot chocolate. Dan took a cautious sip to test the temperature. "Thanks."

Gin sat forward, forearms resting on her knees, and watched him.

Dan smeared away the marshmallow mustache clinging to his upper lip. "Aren't you going to drink yours?"

"I'll wait."

"Wait?"

"Until you tell me what happened today."

Dan assumed Ryan had told her. Otherwise, why would Ginevieve have invited him inside?

"Not today." Dan pushed the cup away. "Thirteen years ago."

Gin waited, a question in her eyes.

"My best friend died."

Chapter 42

Dan's throat convulsed, the pain in his eyes so fresh Gin would have thought the tragedy could be counted in weeks, not years.

"I'm sorry." Gin said the words even though she knew they wouldn't scratch the surface of his grief. Now she understood Ryan Tate's cryptic statement. The people closest to Dan knew how difficult this day was for him.

She remembered the photograph on Evie's mantel. How young Dan and Max had looked. "You were friends a long time."

"We went through training together, but Max got hired first. I was glad."

Gin could see he meant it.

"He and Evie had gotten married, and Max needed a full-time job. A spot opened up at the station about five months later and I took it. According to the rumor, Max had pestered one of the guys into early retirement. He was something else. Our moms used to complain that what one of us didn't come up with, the other one would, but that wasn't quite true. Max came up with an idea, and I was the one who figured out how to increase our chances of making it out alive."

Guilt mixed with the grief, and the weight pushed Dan back in the chair. "It always worked when we were kids, anyway."

A knot swelled in Gin's throat. Did Evie know Dan blamed himself for Max's death? Did anyone? Or had Dan simply accepted that burden and made it his own?

"What happened? The day of the fire?"

Dan didn't move, but Gin saw him retreat. "You can ask anyone in Banister Falls."

"I'm asking you."

A sigh rattled in Dan's lungs. A sign Gin took as a *no* until he started talking.

"The fire started in one of the older houses by the railroad tracks. The call came in around ten in the morning, and you could see the smoke three blocks away. There was a woman standing in the front yard screaming when we got there. A neighbor told us that her four-year-old grandson was still inside the residence. She couldn't find him and had to get out because the place was filling up with smoke. In a house that age, it's like setting a match to kindling.

"Kids get scared when there's a fire, and their first instinct is to hide. Closets. Under beds. Max and I went inside the house and split up." The shadows that slashed across Dan's face accumulated in his eyes. "There's a protocol we follow, of course, but Max and I had to find that little boy. Things were exploding and the walls were starting to come down, but all I could think of was what if it was Cody, terrified and alone? Max and I were talking to each other through the headsets and neither of us could find him."

Dan lapsed into silence, and Gin waited until the memories subsided enough for him to wade back in.

"An alarm sounds before our tanks run out of air, and I heard it go off, so I told Max we had to get out." Dan tipped his head back and stared at the ceiling. "I asked where he was, but Max didn't answer. He must have let go of the hose to check a crawl space under the stairs and then gotten disoriented when his oxygen ran low. Couldn't find his way back.

"Sid came on the radio and told us to get clear of the house. One of the next-door neighbors had just found the little boy. We found out later that his grandma had fallen asleep on the couch so he snuck outside to play in the sandbox. When he saw the smoke he hid in their garage. I'd just made it out when a section of the house collapsed. I looked for Max . . . but he was still inside."

Dan stopped, and Gin knew she'd been given the abridged version. The one that had made the front page of the local newspaper.

"You couldn't get back in, could you?" Gin whispered.

"I tried." Dan's voice faltered. "They wouldn't let me. Ryan and one of the other officers wrestled me down on the grass and held me there. I heard Max's voice come over my headset and he kept saying the word *no,* over and over.

"The guys on the crew thought he was saying that because he didn't want to die, but I knew Max was talking to *me.* He knew I would be doing everything I could to get inside that house. But all I could do was watch it collapse, and then Max . . . I couldn't hear him anymore."

Gin couldn't imagine what he'd gone through in that moment.

"Jerk." A drop of liquid dripped off Dan's chin and his quiet laugh shook Gin more than the tear. "He was always telling me what to do."

A fragile silence settled between them.

"I never told Evie," Dan said softly. "Not that."

"Why not?"

"It wouldn't have helped her."

It might have helped you, Gin thought.

"The chief and I drove over to Evie's house, and she was standing in front of the window. When she saw us get out of the car, she knew. Her face . . . it was like a mask. She didn't cry. She didn't say anything."

Gin knew why. Evie Bennett had prepared herself for that

moment. The mischievous gleam Gin had seen in Max's eyes as a teenager had hinted at the man he'd become. A man who took risks, who made up his own rules.

"I shouldn't have left without him," Dan murmured. "I should have known Max was in trouble."

"It wasn't your fault. You didn't know the roof was going to collapse." Gin had to make him see that. "Your oxygen would have run out. You would have died too."

"I should have. Evie and Cody . . . they needed Max." Dan closed his eyes. "I was the expendable one."

Gin wanted to tell Dan he was wrong, but the words stuck in her throat. Instead she threw caution to the wind along with a whole lot of other self-inflicted rules and reached for Dan's hand.

His fingers closed around hers.

Two months ago, she hadn't known Dan Moretti existed . . . but now Gin couldn't imagine a world without him.

But she couldn't tell him that, either.

Chapter 43

I invited Ginevieve and Raine Lightly over for dinner."

"You what?" And just when he thought nothing could shock him more than walking into the sanctuary before the Sunday morning service started and spotting Ginevieve sitting next to Raine.

"Invited them for dinner." Angela tucked the silk scarf his dad had bought her for Christmas into the front of her blazer. "I didn't realize you'd have a problem with that."

More than one, Dan thought.

"When did you talk to her?" He followed his mother up the center aisle.

"After the football game. She twisted her ankle, you know, so I popped into the ladies' room to check on her."

No, Dan hadn't known, but it explained the tennis shoes Ginevieve had been wearing on Friday night. His thoughts wanted to stray in that direction, but he kept them in line.

"Why would you invite her over?" Sunday dinner always had the potential to be a circus, and Dan didn't want Ginevieve in the center ring.

Angela gave him a stern look. "I'm surprised you have to ask, Daniel. I always invite newcomers over for Sunday dinner. I'm not doing anything I haven't done a hundred times before."

That was true, but Dan couldn't help but feel there was more to it than that. Ginevieve hadn't said a word about meeting his mother—or about accepting an invitation to Sunday dinner—the last time they'd spoken.

You weren't exactly making light conversation though, were you, buddy?

Dan still couldn't believe he'd unloaded on Gin like that. He'd never told anyone about Max's last words. On the way home he'd expected to feel the weight of regret settle in. But all he'd felt was the touch of Ginevieve's hand covering his.

"Don't give Ginevieve the third degree." Dan trailed his mother out the front doors of the church to the parking lot. "She's a private person and you have to respect that."

His mother snorted. "I haven't seen you practicing what you preach, son."

Dan felt his cheeks get hot. "She hasn't lived in Banister Falls very long. She doesn't know anyone else in town."

"I think it's time we changed that, don't you?" Angela's smile and the snap of the car door severed the rest of the conversation.

Dan took a shortcut and beat his mom and dad home. Lisa and Liz were already in the kitchen, arguing over whether to use Mom's regular dishes or Chinet.

"I can't believe you're actually debating this." Dan grabbed a pickle spear from the relish tray. "You know what Mom is going to say. The—"

"Currier and Ives." Angela swept into the kitchen and made a beeline for the stove, where a kettle of marinara sauce had been simmering on the back burner. "I saw a robin in the yard. We're celebrating spring."

In the Moretti family, breaking out Grandma Moretti's china after the first robin sighting was a tradition as old as gathering around the table for Sunday dinner.

Dan walked over to the window and peeked outside to see if

Ginevieve had arrived. One look at the number of cars parked along the curb and she'd probably drive right past.

"Uncle Danny!" Amanda barreled into the kitchen and plowed into him. "Look what I got!" She tipped her head back and pushed her tongue against her front tooth. "Iths really looth."

Dan knelt down in front of his niece. "You'll be able to squirt water at your sister without opening your mouth."

"Thank you, Uncle Instigator." Carissa, Stephen's wife, walked into the kitchen and clipped him with her purse.

"Uncle *Danny,* Mama." Amanda grinned, her front tooth hanging like a door with a broken hinge.

Dan tweaked one of his niece's golden pigtails. "Two days tops," he whispered. "When I see the tooth fairy, I'll put in a good word for you."

Amanda's cocoa brown eyes lit up and she hugged his leg.

"I got one too, Unca Danny." Emily scampered up and bared her pearly whites at him.

"So competitive." Dan winked at Carissa. "They must be spending too much time with their aunts."

Liz crossed her eyes and stuck out her tongue. Lisa imitated her and added a head bobble.

"I rest my case." Dan went for another pickle, but his mother slapped the back of his hand.

"Don't spoil your dinner," Angela ordered.

"Hi, Mom." Stephen came in, nose tilted toward the ceiling like a timber wolf as he made his way over to the stove. "Something smells great."

"I made ziti and a kettle of cioppino." Angela pursed her lips and blew a kiss at Dan's brother. "Lisa, please set the table."

"How many?"

"Let's see. Your family, Trent and Jennifer and Bree. Dan's friend—"

"Dan has a friend?" Will wandered in and went straight for the relish dish. The baby and self-proclaimed favorite of the Moretti clan, *Will* didn't get a hand slap from their mother. "Who did you pay this time?"

"Ginevieve." Angela scooped up Emily, settled her on one hip, and handed her the wooden spoon.

"Raine Lightly's mom?" Lisa and Liz looked at each other. "The one we met at the Chilly Bowl?"

Dan's gaze swung to his twin sisters. "You met her too?"

Lisa nodded. "In the ladies' room."

"She hurt her ankle after you helped her make that touchdown." Liz opened the pantry and grabbed one of the aprons hanging on a hook inside the door.

Was he the only one who didn't know Ginevieve had gotten hurt?

"What about Evie?" Carissa ventured. "Aren't things a little . . . awkward . . . between her and Ginevieve Lightly?"

Carissa attended Evie's weekly Bible study, which made Dan wonder what people were saying.

"Maybe, but Evie isn't coming over today so you don't have to worry," Angela said briskly. "I need someone to put together a salad and someone to slice the bread. Everyone else—except my adorable granddaughters, of course—out of the kitchen."

"When the doorbell rings, I'll answer it," Dan said.

Angela rolled her eyes. "Your brother feels the need to warn Ginevieve before she meets our family. I have no idea why."

"She's already here." Will opened the refrigerator and looked inside, scoping out the contents even though they were about to eat a dinner large enough to feed the entire county.

Dan grabbed his brother's arm and spun him around. "What do you mean she's here?"

"I heard her talking to Dad when I came in. I think they're in the den."

Chapter 44

Ginevieve turned down Cedar Street and passed a line of cars parked in front of a row of cookie cutter, two-story houses. Unlike Evie Bennett's neighborhood, this one was older but still well maintained. She found the Morettis' address but had to keep going until she found an opening.

Angela Moretti's invitation had shocked her, and the woman had taken her silence as assent. When Raine had backed out at the last minute, claiming she had an essay due on Monday, Gin wanted an excuse to bow out too.

Maybe it wasn't too late. She pulled over to the side and contemplated her next move.

A giant of a man who looked like a modern day Paul Bunyan in buffalo plaid flannel and denim was ambling toward her. Two fluffy white dogs the size of bath poufs danced at his heels, and Gin smiled at the incongruous sight.

Instead of walking past, he cut in front of Gin's car and came around to the driver's side. Gin had no choice but to roll down the window.

"I'm not lost," she said by way of greeting. "I'm just not sure I'm in the right place."

"Are you Ginevieve?" Deep-set eyes the color of Sue's coffee settled on her.

"Yes."

"Then you're in the right place." The man opened the door, and one of the dogs tried to jump into her lap. "Down, Skittles. These aren't mine, by the way. I'm only seen in public with them because I love my wife."

Gin was charmed by the gruff admission. "I guess that's a good reason."

The man stuck out his hand when she got out of the car. "John Moretti. I'm Daniel's father."

"It's nice to meet you." Gin felt the scrape of callouses as John's huge hand wrapped around hers. "Raine won't be able to make it today. She has homework."

"No worries. We do this every Sunday."

Every Sunday.

Gin tried to imagine what that would be like.

As they got closer to the house, Gin heard a ripple of laughter from inside. Why was she doing this? How did Dan feel about her crashing his family's weekly dinner?

She didn't realize she'd stopped in the center of the sidewalk until John patted her arm.

"I can sneak you in the back door."

She didn't care if he was teasing or not. "That would be great."

Dan's father bypassed the enclosed front porch and led her around the back of the house. A waist-high stone wall separated the Morettis' yard from the neighbors', but it appeared to be more for decoration than privacy.

"Neil and I built that fence to corral the kids years ago," John said with a shake of his head. "Our only mistake was not making it ten feet taller."

Gin nodded even though she had no idea who Neil was.

They entered through the back door, and the two dogs scampered toward a ceramic dish on the tiled floor. John reached for a canister and shook a few bacon-scented treats into the dish.

"That'll keep them busy for a few minutes." He turned to Gin and caught the panicked look on her face. "You like flowers, don't you?"

Was this a trick question? "Yes."

John smiled. "Come with me."

Bemused and grateful that she could prolong the inevitable, Gin followed Dan's father down the hall. He opened a door and ushered her into a small room.

"My girls call this the man cave."

"It looks more like a greenhouse," Gin said without thinking.

John chuckled. "That's what my Angela says, but I think it's plain old jealousy. The woman can't keep a cactus alive."

He pointed to a three-tiered wooden shelf positioned in front of the window. "I have six different kinds of orchids. Everyone claims they're touchy little things, but I never have a problem getting mine to bloom."

Pets and plants—Gin's life wasn't a nurturing environment for either one. She drifted closer and stopped to admire an orchid with glossy pink flowers tipped in white. Each petal so perfect, it could have been fashioned out of wax.

"That's my favorite." John looked pleased.

"It's beautiful." Gin was still trying to make sense of a man built like a forklift who liked to putter with flowers. At least no one would be brave enough to tease him about his hobby.

John pointed at a terra-cotta pot on the far end of the shelf. "This yellow orchid was a Father's Day gift from my kids."

Gin didn't see anything yellow. She saw two twiggy brown sticks she probably would have tossed out long ago.

"It's only playing dead." John read her mind. An ability he'd obviously passed on to his son. "Give her a few months and she'll be in full bloom again. Once a week I put a few ice cubes in each pot. Can't rush anything, not even watering them. Orchids take patience."

Which was why Gin would never be able to keep one alive.

On the wall next to the plants, a mishmash of family photographs caught Gin's attention. It was obvious the Moretti clan weren't world travelers; other than a staged photograph with Mickey Mouse in front of Cinderella's Castle, most of the pictures had been taken in and around Banister Falls.

Gin recognized the stone wall in the Morettis' backyard, but it took a second longer to place the three children sitting in a line on top of it.

"Dan, Max, and Evie." John's voice rumbled close to her ear. "The Three Musketeers, I called them. Max lived in the house next door and Evie across the street. From the time they were kids, you couldn't pry them apart."

In this photograph Dan sat in the middle, one arm draped around Max and the other around Evie. The center link, holding them together. Protecting them, even then.

If Dan had been the one who'd died in that fire, Gin couldn't help but wonder if Max and Evie would have fallen apart.

"I didn't realize you were here."

Dan burst into the room and aimed an accusing look at his dad—which gave Gin a moment to reset her pulse.

"I smuggled your friend in through the back door." John smiled at her. "Wanted to show off my orchids."

"Well, dinner is ready and Mom wants to show off her grandchildren, so you better make an appearance."

"Tell my angel I'll be there in a minute." John gave one of the pots a half turn. "I've got one little thing to take care of first."

Gin followed Dan down the carpeted hallway, but he stopped before they reached the end of it.

"I have to warn you about my—" The rest of the sentence was lost as Gin was cut off from Dan by a human stampede and swept into a formal dining room overlooking the backyard.

An oak table stretched the length of the room. Picture frames decorated the walls, and centered above the antique buffet was an oil painting of a basket of bread.

"You didn't change your mind. Good." Angela Moretti grasped Gin's shoulders and gave them a quick squeeze. Her refreshing honesty reminding Gin why she hadn't. "Did Raine come with you?"

"She had homework this afternoon. I'm sorry."

Angela dismissed Gin's apology with a firm shake of her head. "Next time, then." She sounded as certain there would be a next time as her husband had been.

Angela began the introductions, and Gin tried to commit the names and faces to memory. Carissa and Stephen, one of Dan's three brothers, married with two adorable little girls, Amanda and Emily. Trent and his wife, Jennifer, and a rosy-cheeked toddler named Bree. Dan's youngest brother, Will, and the twins, Liz and Lisa, who had come into the powder room after the football game.

"Your daughter is in her first trimester, isn't she?" Carissa's question was an unsettling reminder that the news about Raine's pregnancy had become common knowledge. Gin wondered what else they'd heard. "She's probably catching a nap. I was exhausted those first three months."

Trent looked at Stephen. "Here we go."

Out of the corner of her eye she saw Dan mouth the words, *I tried to warn you.*

"I remember it well." Jennifer ruffled Bree's sunny curls. "Some days I was so tired I could barely get out of bed in the morning."

"I had to lure her out with a bowl of chocolate-covered pretzels," Trent said.

"One of those weird cravings." Jennifer patted her abdomen. "Hopefully next time it will be broccoli."

"Next time?" Angela grinned.

Trent's eyes crinkled at the corners, another appealing trait the Moretti men shared. "Not for a while, Mom, so don't start knitting another Christmas stocking."

"But don't put the high chair away yet," Jennifer whispered.

"Here's your father." Angela smiled at John as he trudged into the dining room. "Everyone sit down before the food gets cold."

Ginevieve felt like she'd crash-landed on the set of *The Waltons.* The good-natured teasing. The laughter. Even the blue-and-white dishes on the table featured a sweet pastoral scene.

Dan tried to herd Gin toward a chair at the opposite end of the table from his siblings. Any farther down and she'd be sitting in the kitchen.

"Stop tailgating, Moretti," Gin muttered.

The buzz of conversation halted and all heads swiveled in their direction.

"Fine." Dan raised his palms. "I'll get off your . . . bumper."

"Does my son always hover like this, Ginevieve?" Angela asked.

"Sometimes he's worse."

"I can't get too close." Dan pulled out a chair and took a large step back while she sat down. "Ginevieve has a built-in force field."

"We have a field too," Amanda chimed in. "It's behind our house."

"That's our yard, sweetheart." Red tinted Stephen's jaw.

The little girl frowned. "But Mommy calls it a hayfield."

"I think your grandpa should say the blessing before anyone else ends up in trouble." Angela winked at Gin.

Prompted by some unspoken cue, everyone reached for the hand of the person sitting next to them. On Gin's left, Lisa didn't hesitate to take her hand. But Dan did. Not long enough for anyone but Gin to notice.

Was he thinking about Friday night too? That moment of connection between them? At least the prayer gave Gin a moment to compose herself.

"Lord, we thank You for the people gathered around this table." John's rich baritone lifted above the silence in the room. "For Your love and mercy and provision. Thank You for the beautiful hands that prepared this food. Use it to strengthen and nourish us, so we in turn can strengthen and nourish others. Amen."

Chapter 45

Dan felt a tiny tug and realized he hadn't let go of Ginevieve's hand. He looked around to see if anyone had noticed, but his nieces had stolen the spotlight, showing off their loose teeth in a pre-dinner show.

"Start the bread basket, Ginevieve. Will, take some salad and pass it down." As always, his mother supervised the flow of dishes with the calm efficiency of a traffic guard.

"I see Neil and Betty's house is up for sale again." Will snagged two breadsticks as the basket changed hands. "Isn't this the third time now?"

Dan had noticed the sign too.

Max's parents had sold the house and moved away six months after he died. There were fresh flowers delivered to his grave every Memorial Day, but as far as Dan knew, the Bennetts had never returned to Banister Falls.

"The fourth." Trent's attention to detail made him a successful attorney in the community. "I wonder who you'll get as neighbors this time."

Jennifer chuckled. "Hopefully whoever it is won't dig up the yard and try to plant a garden this time. Nothing grows back there. The soil is like concrete."

Angela and John exchanged a quick glance.

"What?" Lisa noticed and pounced. "You already know someone who's interested in buying it?"

"Actually . . ." His dad paused to refill Amanda's glass with chocolate milk. "Your mother and I are."

"You?" Trent leaned forward, his eyebrows pulling together in what everyone in the family referred to as his badgering-the-witness face. "Why would you want to do that?"

"Your dad is getting close to retirement." Angela patted his dad's arm. "We've talked about buying a house and fixing it up on the weekends."

"You have?" Liz looked confused.

"It would give us something to do together."

"And after you fix it up, you plan on selling it?" Carissa asked.

"We're thinking about renting it out."

"I'd think twice about that." Stephen joined the conversation. "It would be a headache, dealing with renters. You never know what kind of people you're going to get."

"That's not true!" Together, Lisa's and Liz's lilting sopranos had the power to shatter every teacup in their mother's china cabinet.

Trent must have realized how that came across, because the tips of his ears turned red. "There are some good, responsible people out there, sure, but being a landlord means being on call twenty-four seven."

Dad gave him a level look. "Which is why it would be convenient to live right next door."

His mom bobbed her head. "The house is sound, but according to a show I watched last week, the color scheme is out of date."

Liz bent closer to Lisa. "Says the woman who refuses to paint over the bunnies she stenciled along the ceiling of our bedroom when we were seven," she whispered.

"It took me three days to get those fluffy little tails right!"

Angela scowled. "Your dad said it looked like those bunnies left something behind in the grass."

Dan groaned and turned to Ginevieve. "I apologize for my family. Again."

"Just keeping it real, big brother." Lisa grinned.

"Do you have brothers and sisters, Ginevieve?" Jennifer asked.

Dan wanted to shut down the inquisition, but a warning look from his mom stopped him. No other guest would have been exempt from this line of questioning. It wasn't like his family was acting out of character . . . and Dan realized he really wanted to know the answer.

"A half sister," Gin said after a moment. "Sara. But we haven't seen each other for a while."

Judging from her tone, Dan guessed the time they'd been apart could be counted in years, not months.

Lisa tipped her head. "Where does she live?"

Another short silence. "Maine."

"That's a long way away." Carissa's expression softened. "What does she do there?"

"She owns a restaurant in Bar Harbor." Gin looked down, her expression veiled by a fringe of russet lashes.

"I'm surprised you don't work for her." Carissa reached across the table and blotted a smear of marinara sauce from Emily's cheek with her napkin. "It sounds like you have a lot of restaurant experience too."

Ginevieve's shoulders twitched. "Not in the kitchen. I'm a waitress."

"Hard work." His mother smiled. "I couldn't cut it. My first summer job was working at Quigley's root beer stand, and I got fired after three days. My boss complained I was too slow."

"Maybe we could rent it." Lisa looked at Liz. "Our apartment is pretty small."

"And right next door is too close. No offense, Mom and Dad," Liz added quickly.

"Offense?" Mom's eyes twinkled. "We totally agree. I love you all dearly, but that doesn't mean I want you wandering in when your Dad and I are having a romantic candlelight dinner."

"Okay, change of topic!" Trent announced. "Who's ready for dessert? Jennifer made a German chocolate cake."

Angela looked at Gin. "We're closing on the house next month. If you're looking for something with a little more space, maybe you'd be interested in renting it from us."

The breadstick Dan swallowed took a detour into his windpipe.

The Moretti men were in charge of cleanup after Sunday dinner.

As much as Dan wanted to be dismissed from his duty, protesting would be futile. His brothers wouldn't risk cutting short the interrogation going on in the living room.

"Ginevieve is fine." Trent nudged him away from the sink. "Bree is the only one who bites, and she isn't teething at the moment."

"Were you not sitting at the table fifteen minutes ago?" Dan asked. "I wouldn't describe that as fine. The only thing missing was duct tape and a rope."

"Lighten up, bro." Will dropped the silverware into the water, and Dan heard an ominous clink underneath the layer of bubbles. "Ginevieve looks like a woman who can take care of herself."

"She put you in your place." Stephen chuckled.

His siblings had enjoyed every minute of it too. Gin had held her own, though. Even when his mom had suggested she consider renting the house next door.

"Earth to Dan!" A dish towel snapped an inch from his nose.

"Did you say something?"

"Yeah. Three times." Stephen pushed him toward the door. "Get out of here! If you're not helping, you're in the way."

Dan didn't wait around for his brothers to change their minds. He peeked into the family room. His nieces were curled up on the sofa with their blankets, singing along with the Disney princess on the television screen, and the rest of the women sat in a loose circle on the floor. Minus the woman Dan was looking for.

"Where's Ginevieve?"

Liz looked up. "Raine called, so I think she went outside to talk to her."

Dan found Ginevieve in the backyard. She wasn't talking on the phone. She was walking on the stone wall, her arms stretched out for balance.

Hadn't she hurt her ankle a week ago?

He waited at the end of the wall, ready to help her down, but she jumped off the side. Dan wasn't sure what had happened in the short time they'd been apart, but he was looking at two walls. One between the two yards and another, higher one, between him and Ginevieve.

The woman who'd taken his hand Friday night, comforted him, had disappeared.

"How many projects do your parents usually take on?" she asked.

Dan glanced at the house next door. "This would be a first." In spite of the doubts his siblings had expressed, Dan thought their parents had a good idea, buying an investment property.

Gin met his gaze straight on. "I wasn't talking about the house."

It took Dan a second to realize what she *was* talking about. "You aren't a project."

"Right."

"Mom and Dad care about people. They like to help. If there's any ulterior motive, it's to bring about world peace one bowl of pasta at a time."

A smile shimmered briefly in Gin's eyes before she looked away. "I have to go."

"You *want* to go."

"I should check on Raine." She was already moving away from him.

"Hang on, Ginevieve." His dad had emerged from the house with a cardboard box cradled in his hands.

Great timing, Dad. Break out the leftovers while I'm trying to convince the woman she isn't a charity case.

To Dan's amazement, Ginevieve actually stopped. "Thank you again for dinner, Mr. Moretti."

"It's John, remember? I thought you might like this."

Dan peered over Ginevieve's shoulder and saw a pink orchid shrouded in plastic. His heart sank, not for Ginevieve, but for his dad.

John Moretti fussed over and coddled those plants like the head nurse of a maternity ward, and as far as Dan knew, he *never* gave them away.

Ginevieve stared down at the orchid, both hands clenched at her sides. Dan wanted to step in. To rescue. He didn't want his dad to feel snubbed. He didn't want Ginevieve to feel trapped. An inner nudge told him to keep his mouth shut.

"Ice cubes?" she finally said.

"That's right. Three of them, once a week."

"What if I kill it?"

"You won't. Trust me."

Two little words guaranteed to send Ginevieve running . . .

"All right."

His dad held out the box, and Ginevieve's hands opened to his smile.

Chapter 46

Silence greeted Dan when he walked into the living room. His siblings and their offspring had mysteriously vanished, and even the television was on mute. He found his mother in the kitchen, wiping away smudges and crumbs invisible to the male eye.

"I don't even know what that *was*, Mom." Dan took a restless lap around the butcher-block island. "Offering Ginevieve the house next door?"

"Is that what's got you so stirred up?"

"It's on the list," Dan muttered.

"We need a good renter." His mother glided around him. "Don't read too much into it, Daniel."

Dan stopped so fast the sole of his shoe left a skid mark on the linoleum. "You make me crazy, you know that, right?"

"I'm not sure I can take all the credit."

"What's that supposed to mean?"

"It means I've never seen you act this way."

"What way?"

"Out of sorts. Ruffled."

Firefighters didn't get *ruffled*. "Sorry."

"Don't apologize." His mother smiled. "I'd say it's about time."

"You're going to have to speak English, Mom."

"You like her."

Now he understood. "I'm not having this conversation with you."

"You started it." Angela poured two cups of coffee, Dan's signal to sit down. "You're thirty-six years old, Daniel. I watched you grow up outside this kitchen window . . . I watched Evie grow up too. She's like a daughter to me."

Dan tensed, waiting for his mother to remind him that Evie was hurting. That she needed Dan more than ever now that she'd found out her eighteen-year-old son was going to be a father.

"I love Evie," she continued. "But I never thought she was the right person for you . . . or that you were the right person for her."

"What?" Dan gripped the edge of the counter. It was the only thing that kept him upright.

"You didn't fight for her."

"What was I supposed to do?" Dan's knuckles turned white. "Evie fell in love with my best friend, Mom. Was I supposed to get in the way of that?"

"Max did."

The simple statement rocked Dan to the core. "He didn't know how I felt about her."

"Didn't he?" A shadow passed through his mother's eyes. "I would like to think that was true, but you know Max had a competitive streak. He was always looking for a challenge."

Dan couldn't deny it. And he'd never been able to compete with his friend on any level. Max was always a little smarter. A little stronger. A little more everything.

"You wore your heart on your sleeve, Daniel. I can pinpoint the minute you stopped seeing Evie through the eyes of a friend."

So could Dan.

The summer between their freshman and sophomore years of high school, Evie had volunteered to work in the kitchen at a Bible camp in Minnesota, leaving him and Max to their own devices.

Dan had been shooting hoops when the Rolands' minivan pulled into the driveway, but the girl who emerged from the backseat was a stranger. Dan had always thought Evie was cute, but some mysterious metamorphosis had taken place. She'd left with braces and a shy smile and returned eight weeks later with golden skin, a curve in her hips, and a quiet confidence Dan hadn't seen before.

Max, who'd spent their vacation flirting with Trish McCarthy in between mowing her parents' yard and trimming their hedges, hadn't noticed.

"Do you think Evie looks . . . different?" He and Max were playing HORSE the next day and Evie was across the street, helping her dad wash the car.

"Different how?" Max thumped the basketball against the pavement three times, irritated because he was behind.

"I don't know." It was a lie. Dan totally knew. "She got her braces off."

"Oh, yeah." Max eyed the basket. "I saw her chewing gum yesterday."

Dan was amazed—and a little relieved—that was all Max had noticed. His gaze strayed across the street. Evie was watching them and she held up two fingers, part of a secret code they'd developed in third grade to pinpoint their next meeting place. One was Max's garage. Two was the picnic table in Dan's backyard. Three was the willow tree outside Evie's bedroom window.

For some reason, Dan felt an unexpected surge of triumph that Evie had chosen his house.

Max made the basket and punched the air. "It's a tie."

"Let's quit for a while," Dan suggested. "Evie's coming over."

Max glanced over, saw her watching, and twirled the ball on the tip of his finger. "She does look different."

A part of Dan was sorry he'd opened his big mouth, but the other part wanted Max to know what he'd discovered. He chose Door Number Two.

"Evie has sunflowers in her eyes."

"I think *you* need to get out of the sun." Max tossed the ball at him.

A week later, while Dan was gathering the courage to ask Evie out for ice cream, she'd raced across the street, grabbed his hands, and spun circles in the grass until they were both breathless and laughing. Dan didn't want to let go. He'd never known Evie smelled so good. *Felt* so good.

She dragged him over to the wall. "Guess what Max did."

He started with the obvious—Max had gotten grounded again—and ran down the list. Evie giggled through each one until he finally gave up.

"Okay . . . what did Max do?"

Evie pressed closer, until her breath feathered against his ear. "He asked me out."

"He—What?" Dan sat down hard on the wall and felt the jagged edge of a stone pierce his hip.

"Asked me out." Evie plopped down next to him. "Is that insane or what? He came over last night."

"Last night?" Last night he and Max had been playing video games, Evie babysitting for a neighbor down the street. Max had told Dan he had to be home early. "Are you going?"

Evie's cheeks flushed pink. "I think so. Is that too weird? I mean, me and Max. Can you imagine?"

No. No, he couldn't. But Dan knew Evie well enough to know that in the past twenty-four hours, *she* had.

"You know how Max is, Eves." Dan tried to keep his expression neutral. "He goes out with a lot of girls. He gets bored easily." It was the closest thing to criticism Dan had ever said about his best friend.

"I know." Evie dragged her foot against the wall. "But he said the sweetest thing. It didn't sound like Max at all. Maybe he's . . . changing."

"What did he say?"

"He said I have sunflowers in my eyes."

Dan shut down the memory.

"It was a long time ago, Mom. Evie fell in love with Max. Everyone loved Max."

His mom gave him a knowing look. "You and I both know Max Bennett was not perfect. When he died, Evie put him on a pedestal." His mom paused, weighing out her words. "And Daniel . . . you put her on a pedestal too. You treat Evie as if she's made of glass, and I don't know that that's been good for either one of you."

"What if I said her feelings have changed?"

Angela was silent for a moment. "I would ask why . . . after all this time."

Dan had been asking that too. Evie hadn't returned any of his calls since Friday night. He'd looked for her at church that morning, but Cody had come to the service alone.

"Evie's heart is locked up tight, but that lock is on the inside. No matter how hard you try to find a way in, she's the only person who can open it up."

"You just accused me of not fighting for her."

"There's a difference between fighting for someone and trying to wait them out. Both of them work—but not necessarily on the same woman. We're all different, you know."

"Ginevieve sure is." Dan realized he'd said it out loud when his mother chuckled.

"Just in case you were wondering, she likes you too."

Dan shook his head. "Ginevieve doesn't trust me."

"I think Ginevieve doesn't want to lean on anyone—which usually means someone she cared about wasn't there when she needed him."

Dan couldn't shake the feeling it was more than one someone.

"Thanks, Mom." Dan rose to his feet and summoned a halfhearted smile, his head and heart too full to continue the conversation.

"I'm praying for her—and for you."

Dan walked to the truck, thoughts and prayers swirling inside his head. *God, Ginevieve has so many walls up. I don't know if I can get through them.*

Dan didn't always expect to hear what people referred to as that still, small voice, but this time the response wasn't still or small.

I can.

Chapter 47

Gin could tell it was Monday. The phone woke her up an hour earlier than her alarm. Sue bypassed the usual pleasantries, told Gin that she wasn't feeling well and needed someone to open the diner. Gin could only assume that someone was her.

"Who's going to cook?" She squinted at the clock. Five a.m.

"The person who unlocks the door," her boss snapped.

"Sue." Gin flopped onto her back. "I can't cook."

"You *won't* cook. There's a difference."

"What about Denise?"

"Denise can't boil water. That leaves you."

Gin couldn't argue with that—only because Sue had hung up on her.

She swung her legs over the side of the bed and winced when her bare feet touched the floor. The meteorologist predicted a warming trend over the next few days, but in this part of the state, that meant the thermometer grudgingly inched its way to forty-five degrees.

Without closing her eyes, Gin's imagination drew a two-story house, its welcoming front porch curved like a smile from shutter to shutter. There was a stone fence instead of one made from white pickets, but that was okay.

For one moment she'd been tempted, oh so tempted, to accept

Angela Moretti's offer. If the floor plan of the house next door was similar to Dan's parents' home, she would have a huge kitchen, a fireplace to chase away the chill on a winter night, and built-in bookshelves to stock.

And Dan's family as her next-door neighbors.

"Raine?" Gin rapped on her daughter's bedroom door. "Can I come in?"

"Sure." Raine sat up and scooped a handful of hair out of her eyes. "What are you doing up so early?"

"Sue just called. She wants me to open." And cook. "I might be a little late coming home."

"That's okay. There's a concert at the school tonight, and Cody asked me if I wanted to go."

"Do I detect some hesitation?"

Raine rested her chin on her knees. "It's not a big deal."

Gin sat down on the edge of the bed. "Kids are talking about you, aren't they?"

"The guidance counselor wants to meet with me during lunch today." Raine sighed. "Like I don't know what that's about."

"If you don't want to be alone, I can meet you there."

"I won't be alone." Raine stifled a yawn with the back of her hand.

"Cody's going with you?"

"I didn't tell him about it—but it'll be fine. God's got my back."

"Don't forget to take your vitamins." Gin planted a kiss on the top of Raine's head and tasted strawberry shampoo. "I'll call you later."

Raine blinked. "That's it? No skeptical look? No cynical lift of the eyebrow?"

Is that what she'd been doing?

"Not this time." Not after Cozie's ambush and Ryan's mysterious nudge. She didn't understand it, but she couldn't explain it away either.

"Does this mean you'll go to the Mother-Daughter Tea at Hope Community with me on Saturday? They have one every year for the girls who are graduating."

A tea. At church. With the women who'd given a whole new meaning to the word *chilly* in the Chilly Bowl. The ones who thought she and Raine had swept into town with the sole purpose of ruining the reputation of their beloved hometown hero's family. But there were women like Angela Moretti and Dan's sisters too . . .

"Are they going to play football?"

Raine grinned. "Does it matter?"

There was no way Gin could snuff the hopeful look in her daughter's eyes. "Absolutely not."

Raine rolled out of bed and trailed her to the kitchen. "Where did that flower on the table come from?"

"It's an orchid. Mr. Moretti—Dan's dad—gave it to me."

Raine cocked her head. "What about the no houseplants rule?"

Yes, Ginevieve? What about that rule? And the one about keeping your distance from Dan Moretti?

She'd broken both of them in one day.

Nicki was huddled by the door when Gin arrived at the diner. Wrinkled clothes, her hair in a tangle, and her lips the pale blue of the bruise underneath her eye.

"You're opening this morning?" Nicki's relief was palpable. "Where's Sue?"

"Sick." The door stuck and Gin gave it a kick, wishing it were Nicki's hopefully now ex-boyfriend. "I'll make some phone calls and try to get some help with the breakfast crowd. You might be on your own for lunch though."

Nicki caved in on herself. "I was going to ask if I could leave a few hours early. The kids spent the night at my mom's, but now she doesn't want to watch them all day."

"We'll work it out." Gin flipped on the lights and started warming up the griddle while Nicki headed straight for the bathroom. She emerged a few minutes later, whatever had happened the night before covered by a fake smile and a half inch of foundation.

"Turn on the lights and start the coffee," Gin instructed.

"Okay." Nicki started to yawn and it turned into a wince. "Walked into a door yesterday," she mumbled.

"I know." Gin looked straight into her eyes. "Those things come out of nowhere."

Nicki ducked her head and fled.

Gin ran her finger down the piece of paper taped next to the phone and started dialing numbers. It didn't take long because there weren't very many of them. The waitresses kept defecting to Eddie's. As a boss, he was more laid-back than Sue, and Tina was right about the tips being better.

Wendell was on the schedule for six to bus tables, but Gin already planned on stationing him behind the cash register.

"No one is picking up," Gin told Nicki when the girl ventured into the kitchen a few minutes later. "It looks like we're on our own."

"Maybe there won't be a lot of customers this morning."

The bell over the door jingled, but it wasn't a customer. It was Nicki's mother. She marched up to Nicki, a small child clamped in each hand.

"I'll keep the baby for a few hours, but I can't watch these two," she said. "Carl has a terrible headache this morning."

Gin understood that language. Carl had a hangover.

"I'm working, Mom!" Nicki hissed. "You can't leave them here."

"Call Cheryl."

"She worked a double . . . she has to sleep."

The little girl started to whimper and Gin, who had a rule about not getting involved in people's personal business, broke that one too.

"They can play in the break room until I can get another waitress to come in."

The woman released the children, but she continued to stare at Nicki's face. "What did you do this time? Guys like Victor aren't easy to find—"

"Did you want to order something?" Gin interrupted.

The woman snorted. "No thanks."

"Then you have a nice day." Gin shooed Nicki and the children toward the kitchen and waited until she was sure the girl's mom had left before she left the cash register unattended.

"I'm really sorry, Gin." The slump of Nicki's thin shoulders told Gin there were bruises on the inside too. "I'll make sure Luke and Ava don't cause any trouble."

Gin wasn't sure how Nicki planned to do that while taking orders and waiting tables, but they didn't have much of a choice. "We'll manage." She started the bacon frying for the regulars who worked the night shift at Leiderman and dumped a container of sausage gravy into the Crock-Pot.

"Order up." Nicki slapped a piece of paper on the counter and disappeared again.

The bell kept jingling.

Gin was mixing up a new batch of pancake batter when she heard a commotion in the dining room. Framed in the pass-through, she watched a group of men stake a claim at table five. They weren't in uniform today, but Gin recognized their leader.

No. Not today.

She flattened against the wall before Dan spotted her.

Nicki's face popped up in the window, her eyes wide with panic. "I can't keep up. What am I supposed to do?"

"Take their order," Gin said, more curtly than she intended.

"Right." Nicki disappeared.

Of all the days for Sue to be sick. Wendell hadn't shown up for work either, leaving Gin without a busboy and dishwasher.

"Order up." She set two plates piled high with scrambled eggs and hash browns on the pass-through and spotted Nicki huddled in a corner, talking to someone on her cell phone.

But that wasn't what sent Gin's pulse soaring.

It was Dan, working his way from table to table, a coffeepot in each hand.

Chapter 48

"What are you doing?"

Gin charged through the half doors into the dining room and intercepted Dan on his way to Agnes Bardowski's table.

He'd figured their paths would cross sooner or later.

"Refilling coffee cups." Dan lifted the carafes above his head and skirted around her.

Ginevieve followed. "That isn't your job."

"Oh, leave him be," Tina purred. "It was a long night, and this guy is easy on the eyes."

Dan hadn't blushed since junior high, but he felt one coming on.

"Hey, Gin!" A bald guy sitting by the window lifted his empty plate. "The sign says all you can eat."

"Coming right up, Mac."

"Are you the only one working?" Dan poured Agnes's coffee, matching the level against the brown ring on the inside of her cup.

"Sue isn't feeling well and Nicki is a new hire," Gin said under her breath. "If you're in a hurry, there's always Marie's."

"No rush." Dan tamped down a smile. "I'm off today. The crew gets together once or twice a week to shoot hoops, and they wanted breakfast afterward."

"Wasting away here, Gin!" Mac lifted his plate again.

"Excuse me." Gin jogged back to the kitchen, the tails of her apron streaming behind her.

"Oh, waiter!" Sid snickered as he lifted his coffee cup.

"Are you going to sit down, Captain?" Hopper asked.

"Later." Dan stopped at the Leiderman table. "Patience, guys. We're a little shorthanded today. How about a piece of pie while you're waiting? Free of charge."

Behind the swinging doors, Dan heard a muffled growl.

The waitress had hung up the phone and ducked behind the cash register to ring up a bill. Dan spotted two plates under the warmer.

Gin didn't say anything when he grabbed them. He wasn't sure she even noticed. She stood at the griddle, pouring circles of pancake batter while the sizzle of bacon played in the background. Through a doorway behind her, Dan caught a glimpse of two wide-eyed children. A boy and girl, pint-sized replicas of the waiflike blonde behind the counter.

Gin came out of the kitchen with an order of pancakes for the Leiderman guys, and Dan took advantage of the opportunity. When she returned, he'd taken over the griddle.

"Out."

Dan glanced at the slip. "Veggie omelet, no cheese, Ginevieve. Where's the broccoli?"

"Is that even on the menu?" She stalked over to the fridge and looked inside.

"It is now. Someone just ordered one." Dan smiled at the kids and they ducked back into their hidey-hole. "Cute kids."

"Luke and Ava. Nicki's mom dropped them off." Gin picked up the chef's knife and beheaded a stalk of broccoli. "Have you ever worked in a kitchen?"

"I grew up in a family of eight with a mother who believed a boy should graduate from high school knowing how to feed himself."

"I'll take that as a yes." Ginevieve dumped a pile of vegetables in a skillet. "I better check the walk-in. We're getting low on butter."

Dan heard a furtive movement behind him. He glanced over his shoulder and saw the little boy—Luke—watching him. "Did you have breakfast yet?"

"Cereal." The boy rubbed his tummy. "But it's gone now."

"That happens." Dan poured some pancake batter on the griddle. "You and your sister have a seat at that little table back there and we'll see what we can do to fill it up again, okay?"

"Okay." He rewarded Dan with a gap-toothed grin.

Forget the caffeine. Dan could run on one of those all day.

Chapter 49

Gin stepped back into the kitchen, only to find that Dan had abandoned his post.

She followed a string of giggles to the break room. Luke and Ava sat at the table devouring a stack of buttermilk pancakes that practically came up to their chins while they watched Dan juggle three red potatoes he'd swiped from the bin.

Emotion clogged Gin's throat. She'd never met a man like Dan Moretti. The perfect blend of strong and sweet, charming and stubborn. He was standing less than six feet away but Gin felt the gap between them widen.

"Gin?" Nicki sidled up behind her. "Are they being good?"

"Dan made them breakfast."

Dan noticed them watching from the doorway and smiled at Nicki. "I hope you don't mind."

"Mind?" Her voice cracked on the word. "I should have asked if they'd eaten yet."

Tears filled Nicki's eyes, and Dan was at her side in an instant. He chucked her under the chin as if she were Ava's age. "Hey, don't melt on me now. Wendell isn't here to clean up the mess."

Nicki giggled.

Dan's crew left after breakfast, but he stayed through the next shift. Gin didn't know what she would have done without him. Cody and Raine came over and spent their lunch period entertaining Nicki's children before they had to go back to class.

Denise came in at one o'clock, just as the lunch crowd had dwindled down. Wendell shuffled in with a message from Sue at four. Close the diner early and call it a day.

"You talked to her? Is she feeling better?"

"I drove her to the hospital."

"The hospital?" Gin echoed. "Sue never said anything about a hospital."

"I talked her into it. You can't cure a heart attack with a couple of ibuprofen."

"She had a *heart* attack?"

"Not sure yet. Test results aren't back but they let her go. That's a good sign." Wendell was frowning at the dirty dishes stacked on the counter. "I'll take care of these."

Gin realized a small crowd had gathered around them. "You can go, Nic. Luke and Ava look like they're ready for a nap." They all were. "Are you staying at your sister's house?"

Nicki shrugged. "She was complaining she couldn't afford the extra groceries. Until I get my first paycheck, I can't help out. Victor is trying to convince me to come back."

By knocking her around? Gin didn't like the guy's method of persuasion. "Nicki—"

"I know, I know. Guys like Victor are hard to find."

"That's not what I was going to say." Gin's stomach rolled. "Stay with Cheryl. I'll talk to Sue and ask if she can front you a week's pay." She knew Nicki's pride would get in the way if Gin offered her a loan.

"Why?" A wary look crept over Nicki's face.

"Someone did that for me," Gin said simply.

"You can try." Nicki's listless shrug told Gin she wasn't going to get her hopes up.

"I think these two need their batteries recharged." Dan walked out of the kitchen with Luke and Ava clinging to his back like baby koalas.

Gin followed the trio to the door and watched them shuffle away. When she turned around, Dan was watching her.

"At the moment, Nicki is doing the best she can with what she has," she heard herself say.

"I know." Dan tipped his head. "But she could use a little more."

"Nicki won't accept any help from us." Gin wasn't sure why the "us" popped out, but Dan didn't seem to notice.

"Uh huh. But what if she didn't *know* it was us?"

Gin crossed her arms. "I'm listening."

"Have you ever heard of a blessing burglary?"

"No."

"Put the Closed sign in the window and grab your coat."

"Where are we going?"

Dan smiled. "My house."

Gin couldn't explain why, ten minutes later, she was riding in Dan's pickup. Again.

"Will your mom mind if we just drop by?"

"I doubt it." Dan turned off Main Street. "She isn't there."

"I thought you lived with your parents."

"Ouch." He winced. "I'm thirty-six years old."

"That doesn't mean anything. A lot of guys live in their parents' basement."

"Not me." Dan looked so disgruntled that Gin pressed her lips together to seal off a smile. "And for the record, I happen to have a whole house. My grandmother left it to me when she died."

His grandparents had lived in Banister Falls too. Gin couldn't imagine an entire family tree whose branches didn't stretch beyond the city limits.

"I sleep at the station when I'm on duty, so I'm not home much.

Will, you met him at Mom and Dad's yesterday, claimed a bedroom when he got out of the service. Right now he's head of security at Leiderman."

Dan made a right at a stop sign and drove into the kind of neighborhood where people didn't lock their front doors.

His house was charcoal gray with white trim and shutters. The front yard faced north and, in spite of the rising temperatures, a large oak tree still wore a pristine white apron of snow. Gin followed Dan up the steps and onto the open porch. She was right; he didn't bother with a key.

The shoes in the tiled foyer were lined up in a neat row. The living room looked just as tidy, with no sign of the bachelor clutter Gin expected to find.

"What?"

"I didn't say anything."

Dan smiled. "Not out loud."

Gin couldn't help but smile back even while she was terrified he could read her so easily. "It's just . . . clean. Really clean."

"Habit. We have to be organized at the station. Every second counts when a call comes in, so our equipment has to be in the same place. I'm a lost cause—can't seem to shut it off."

"Your spices aren't alphabetized, are they?"

"I don't have any spices."

"Then you aren't a lost cause."

Another smile.

Being in Dan's home . . . it felt too real. Too right.

Gin glanced at the door. Why had she agreed to this?

"Make yourself comfortable." Dan gestured to the oversize leather sofa. "I'll check the freezer in the basement and see what Mom stashed there when I wasn't looking. The women in our family have made me and Will their pet project."

On the drive over he'd explained how a blessing burglary worked.

Basically, you went to someone's house under cover of darkness, dropped off groceries, and ran before someone saw you.

If Nicki's sister was worried about the grocery budget, it was the perfect solution.

Instead of sitting down, Gin wandered around the living room. Angela must have passed on her love for capturing Kodak moments to her sons, because the wall above the fireplace was a patchwork quilt of frames, each square a different member of the Moretti family. His sisters' graduation photos. One of Will in dress uniform. A yellowed photo of a couple Gin guessed were Dan's grandparents, posing in front of Hope Community Church on their wedding day. A crew of firefighters. Gin instantly picked Dan and Max from the lineup. It was a casual photograph, their arms slung around each other's shoulders.

The tread of footsteps on the stairs pulled Gin's attention away from the photographs. Dan appeared a moment later, weighted down with plastic freezer containers, his expression hovering somewhere between amazement and irritation.

"That's it. I'm locking the door when I leave the house from now on." He bypassed the kitchen and dumped the containers in front of her. An avalanche of freezer snow drifted onto the coffee table. "There are enough Swedish meatballs here to go around the equator. Twice."

Gin started to relocate another picture frame into a frost-free zone when the preschool boy in the photograph caught her eye.

"Is this Cody?"

Dan nodded as he continued to stack containers like building blocks. "He was four."

Gin stared down at the photo. Cody was barefoot in the grass, his dimpled hands clutching a bouquet of dandelions that had gone to seed. Eyes closed, lips pursed, the sun turning his hair to gold, a perfect moment in a perfect childhood.

"You took this?"

"Uh huh." Dan peeled back the corner on one of the containers and peered at the contents. "Cody loved to pick bouquets of dandelions for Evie. Max came into the station and said Cody had had a meltdown. Apparently while Cody was at preschool, Max had mowed the grass and cut all the dandelions down. He didn't get why Cody was so upset. Dandelions are weeds, right?"

"Right," Gin echoed, memories of another conversation stirring in the background.

"Max got frustrated because Cody refused to talk to him the rest of the day, and he asked me if he should take his basketball away." Dan chuckled. "I told him instead of disciplining Cody, he had to figure out a way to fix it.

"The next day Max collected a shoe box full of dandelions that had gone to seed and told Cody they would plant a whole field so he'd never run out of bouquets again. Cody ran around the yard, blowing dandelion fluff everywhere.

"Max couldn't stand dandelions in the yard." Dan ran his thumb down the edge of the oak frame, tracing the contours of the memory. "But you do whatever you have to, you know?"

Gin knew.

"Evie had bouquets for the rest of the summer," Dan went on. "She took one of the photographs of the yard and duplicated it for a watercolor class." Dan went on. "It's hanging above the fireplace."

"I saw it."

Gin tried to picture Dan standing at the perimeter of his friends' lives. Giving Max parenting tips from the sidelines, being a friend to Evie, cheering Cody on.

Gin wanted to smack him. And hug him.

Mostly hug him.

Her hand rolled into a fist around the handle of an invisible suitcase. Her walls held up against guys like Cozie, but every moment she spent with Dan chipped another piece away. It was only a matter of time before her heart was fully exposed and Dan would see how damaged it was.

"What are you thinking? You look worried."

"Nicki." Gin rerouted her thoughts as she sank down on the couch. "She's in a bad situation."

"I saw the bruise." Dan's eyes iced over. "Husband?"

"Ex-boyfriend," Ginevieve said. "But apparently he didn't get the memo."

"Hopefully the next one will come with a restraining order."

"She's staying with her sister right now, but it isn't working out. I'm afraid she's going to go back to him."

"That doesn't make any sense."

"I'm not defending her, I'm just telling you how it is. For some women . . . what you know, even if it's bad, is better than being alone. They think if they just hang in there, the guy will change."

"What do you think?"

"I think it's better to be alone—because then you won't be disappointed when he doesn't."

Chapter 50

Gin absently touched the tiny silver scar that followed the curve of her bottom lip, and Dan's heart slammed against his rib cage.

"Is that what happened to you? Raine's"—Dan hated to say the word—"dad. He hit you?"

"Boyfriend Number Four. My mom's, not mine," Gin added. "Billy wore a big ugly ring on his pinkie. Whiskey usually slowed him down, but one day he caught me before I could get to my room and lock the door."

Dan couldn't take his eyes off that scar. He couldn't fathom growing up in a home where dodging her mother's drunk boyfriends was a common occurrence in a little girl's day.

"You're staring." Gin's chin lifted.

Before Dan could stop himself, he reached out and traced the scar with the pad of his thumb. "I'm sorry."

"For wha—"

Gin's breath rushed out. Dan felt it against his cheek when he lowered his head and pressed his lips against the corner of her mouth. From there, it was only a short distance to the cinnamon freckle on her cheekbone.

He saw his reflection in Gin's beautiful green eyes before they drifted closed.

Dan's fingers skimmed the contours of her jaw and lodged in her hair, the journey hampered by the elastic band around Gin's ponytail. He hooked a finger through it and tugged. A waterfall of mahogany hair spilled over his hands as he captured her lips.

Gin sank against him, and Dan felt the rapid beat of her heart as she returned the kiss. Her palms drew restless patterns on his back as he drew her deeper into the circle of his arms.

One by one his senses shut down until he couldn't think straight, all the circuits overloaded from the emotions rushing through him. Dan heard the alarm go off in his head, the one that warned him to back away before he reached the point of no return.

They jerked apart at the sound of the front door opening and closing.

Will.

He'd forgotten he had a brother. Who lived with him.

"Danny?"

But it wasn't Will who walked into the living room.

"Evie." Dan rose to his feet.

The smile slipped from her face when she spotted Ginevieve on the couch. "I . . . I didn't realize you had company."

"No, it's all right. Ginevieve and I were—" Dan stopped as the "were" weakened his knees all over again.

"Planning a blessing burglary," Gin said.

"Really? For who?" Evie actually looked interested.

It was as if they'd all made a silent agreement to pretend this didn't rank first on the list of Life's Ten Most Awkward Moments.

"One of the waitresses at the diner." Gin twisted her hair in a loose rope, and the enormity of his mistake hit Dan between the eyes.

"I can contribute chocolate chip cookies." Evie held up a plastic container.

A homemade apology. Dan felt even worse. He'd left another message on Evie's voicemail on his way to the diner, asking if they could talk. Dan hadn't expected her to take him up on the invitation so quickly.

"Remember the blessing burglary we pulled on the Karlson family?" Evie didn't wait for an invitation to sit down. "We almost didn't survive that one."

"We?" Dan echoed. "You made it over the fence. I was the one who had to convince their German shepherd that I was a friend."

"I came back for you, didn't I?"

"An hour later." Dan glanced at Gin, but he couldn't tell what she was thinking. Now that she wasn't in his arms, the magnitude of what he'd done was starting to settle in.

He'd kissed her—and even though it was the most amazing kiss—a nine point nine nine on the kissing Richter scale—would Ginevieve assume that had been his intention all along? She'd been slow to trust him and now, just when Dan had sensed a softening in her attitude, he'd given her a reason not to. He was no different from the guys like Craig Cozielle who tried to take advantage of her. Ask Agnes Bardowski—Dan was a *pirate.*

Except . . . Ginevieve had kissed him back.

Chapter 51

Only the fact that every bone in Gin's body had turned to mush prevented her from bolting toward the door.

She'd been in Dan's arms for a minute and then Evie walked into his house without knocking first, reminding Gin who belonged and who didn't. The fire in her cheeks had begun to subside and her pulse was almost back to normal, but the only thing holding her together at the moment was the knowledge that Evie hadn't witnessed the kiss.

Evie picked up one of the containers and scratched at the layer of ice crystals covering the label. "Do you and Ginevieve need a lookout?"

Dan sat down again, so hard the cushion underneath Gin lifted a quarter inch. "You want to come with us?"

"Why not?"

Why not? Because Gin couldn't imagine spending the evening as a third wheel to Dan and Evie. Now that she thought of it, after the way she'd enthusiastically returned Dan's kiss, she couldn't imagine spending the evening alone with him, either.

Dan's pager broke the silence.

"I'm sorry . . . I have to go." He was sprinting toward the door before Gin realized what was happening. It snapped shut behind him, leaving her and Evie alone in the room.

Gin stumbled to her feet, because sitting didn't seem appropriate at the moment. "Why did Dan go in? Doesn't the crew on duty respond to the fire?"

"It's possible they're assisting the volunteer department out in the country," Evie said. "Or the fire might be too big for one crew to handle."

Didn't "big" translate into more dangerous?

Gin hurried over to the window, just in time to see Dan's pickup disappear around the corner. Sirens wailed in the distance, and she imagined Dan in a burning building. On purpose.

"It's never easy." Evie came up behind her. "But it's their job. They know the risks."

Gin's throat tightened. She'd seen the fire trucks go out on calls, but even though she knew people were in danger, none of them had had a face. None of them had had *Dan's* face.

"You don't have to come with me to Nicki's house." Gin decided to let Evie off the hook. "You probably have plans for this evening."

"Had plans." Evie corrected her. "Now it looks like I'm free."

Plans with Dan. Gin couldn't believe she'd forgotten.

"Angela stocks the guys' freezer with enough food to feed an army. I'll bet we can rustle up more than meatballs." Evie walked into the kitchen and set to work, pulling containers from the freezer, stacking some of them on the counter, putting others back inside. In what looked to Gin to be alphabetical order.

She watched Evie open cupboard doors and collect what they needed with an ease that told Gin she'd been there a hundred times.

Half an hour later they had two grocery bags filled with meatballs, vegetable soup, homemade rolls, and the chocolate chip cookies. Evie grabbed a bunch of ripe bananas from a bowl, a bright yellow garnish on top.

"Where did you park your car?"

"Raine took it to school today. I rode over with Dan from the diner." Now Evie would ask why Dan had been at the diner.

"Good. I was going to suggest we take mine anyway." Evie fished her keys from her pocket. "Your friend won't recognize it."

"You *are* good at this."

"You sound surprised."

"Let's just say you don't look like the sneaky type."

"What do I look like?" There was a hint of a challenge in Evie's eyes.

Dan's type. That's what she looked like. So it was safer not to say anything at all.

Gin grabbed her coat and followed Evie out the door. The sun had set, making it impossible to separate smoke from the blanket of gray clouds in the sky. Of course the interior of Evie's vehicle smelled like lavender, and the beverage holders in the console between the seats weren't stuffed with junk mail and candy wrappers.

"What's the address?"

"Brewster Street. Nicki's sister lives on the lower level of the house." Gin had looked up the address she'd written on the application.

The neighborhood underwent a subtle change as they continued down the street; the older but well-kept houses on Dan's block sprouted into a row of Victorian homes that looked as tired and faded as the women who came off the night shift at the factory.

"When we were kids, we loved riding our bikes down this street," Evie told her. "We nicknamed it the Gingerbread Street. The houses were in better shape back then." She parked just beyond the reach of the streetlight. "Most of them were converted into apartments."

The Three Musketeers, John Moretti had called them. Gin wondered if the memories ever closed in on Evie and made it difficult to breathe. How did a person sift through the memories, letting the bad ones fall through and holding the good ones close to your heart?

Dogs began to bark as they made their way down the alley, and

Gin remembered what Dan had said about the German shepherd. Maybe this wasn't such a good idea. If anything happened to Evie, Dan would never forgive her.

"It's that one." Gin pointed to a house in the middle of the block.

"It's got an open porch. That's good," Evie whispered.

Gin decided to take her word for it.

Evie ducked behind a hedge that split the two yards. "The television is on. Are you sure no one is home?"

"I was until you noticed the television was on."

They fell silent, gauging the amount of risk. Gin pointed to a dumpster filled with shingles. "The oak tree to the dumpster to the porch." She traced an imaginary line in the air.

Evie nudged her. "You're a natural."

But unlike Evie, Gin's skills hadn't been honed by dropping off care packages to families in need. "Hey."

Gin's head snapped up. Evie was already a few steps ahead of her. Her heel slipped in something Gin thought it best not to stop and examine as she worked her way along the hedge. The breeze carried a hint of cigarette smoke, a sign that someone was close by.

She caught Evie's arm. "I can take it the rest of the way."

"I'm going with you."

They crept forward, keeping their heads low. Three steps leading up to the porch. Gin set the bags of groceries next to the door and gave Evie a thumbs-up sign, ready for a quick getaway.

The six-foot tall obstacle standing at the bottom of the steps made that impossible. The porch light illuminated the man's dark blond hair and lean, chiseled features.

And glinted off the metal baseball bat resting in the crook of his arm.

Gin swung a hip into Evie and knocked her off the step, hoping she'd have enough sense to head straight for the hedge. Instead, she leaped right back onto the porch and stood next to Gin. Gin shifted her weight, trying to nudge Evie off the step again, but Evie nudged back.

The man's pewter gray eyes flicked to Evie and lingered a moment on her face before sliding back to Gin.

He had home court advantage, so Gin had no choice but to play offense.

"Who are you?" she snapped, as if she had every right to be lurking around in the shadows, and he was the one trespassing.

"The babysitter." The stranger shifted his weight, his tone and stance deceptively casual. "Who are you?"

Gin had no idea why, but she believed him. "Two people taking a shortcut to a friend's house. Do you have a problem with that?"

"I do when it involves this particular shortcut." His gaze dropped to the paper sack Evie hugged against her chest. "No one here is interested in what you've got in that bag, so take your party somewhere else."

Evie's mouth dropped open. "This isn't beer!"

"Right."

"It's soup."

"Soup." Evie had his full attention now.

"I'll show you." She jumped off the step and landed right in front of the guy before Gin could stop her. "Why would we have alcohol? It's a week night."

"I don't think the day of the week is a prerequisite."

He talked like a college professor and looked like the leader of a biker gang. Baseball bat notwithstanding, Gin saw something in the man's demeanor that reminded her of Dan. A quiet strength that made him look less like a thug and more like a guardian angel.

"We wanted to surprise a friend." Gin took a chance.

"Does your friend have a name?"

"Nicki—she's staying here with her sister, Cheryl."

The guy reached out, with the hand not holding the bat, and plucked the container of cookies from the bag, ignoring Evie's indignant gasp. Gin waited for him to riffle through the contents and hand it back to Evie.

She glared at him. "Now that it's passed inspection, can we leave?"

Evie Bennett could do sarcastic. Who knew?

"I'll make sure it gets to the right people." He looked at Gin. "If you do this again, don't show up before ten."

Gin waited until they were back in the alley before she said what was on her mind. "Did you not see the aluminum *bat* in his hands? Baseball is not exactly a nighttime sport."

"You weren't afraid of him, so I thought I didn't have to be either."

Great. Evie had followed her lead, and Gin's lead was bluffing, pure and simple.

Evie pressed a button on her key fob, and the loud chirp that accompanied the click of the car doors unlocking drew the attention of several teenage boys standing on the corner.

"I wonder what they're doing out so late on a school night." Evie slid into the driver's seat.

"Drugs," Gin said without thinking. "Drinking."

"We don't have that kind of problem in Banister Falls."

Evie said it with such conviction that Gin believed her. For a second. "It happens in small cities too."

Evie's cell began to ring. She glanced at the number on the screen. "I should take this."

Gin nodded and focused on the passing scenery, granting Evie the illusion of privacy.

"Hi, Mary . . . I'm driving home right now. Yes." Evie drew out the word. "I was with Dan when he got the call."

Gin's stomach tightened.

"I recognize the name. Did everyone make it out okay?"

Gin twisted toward Evie. She couldn't even pretend she wasn't listening.

"Thanks for letting me know. I'll call Janine when I get home." Evie hung up and tossed the phone into her purse. "I'm on the church prayer chain."

"The what?"

"The prayer chain. When we get a request, we pray and then call the next person on the list."

"The person who called . . . was it about the fire?"

"A farmhouse about two miles from town. Fully engulfed, and one of the outbuildings caught on fire too."

Fully engulfed. Gin didn't have to ask what it meant. Those two words were pretty straightforward. She would rather face a guy with a baseball bat than the image of Dan battling a blaze that size.

"You're worried about Danny, aren't you?"

"Aren't you?" The question burst out of Gin before she could stop it. "You know . . ." She bit down on her lip to hold the rest of the words inside.

"What can happen." Evie finished them.

"I'm sorry. I didn't mean to remind you . . ." *Stop. You're doing it again!*

"Don't be sorry. Everything reminds me." Evie touched her wedding band, an unconscious gesture Gin had seen before. "Max is forever twenty-five, and I'm getting older without him. I'm going to be a grandma in the fall, but it feels like I haven't finished raising my son."

The wry note in Evie's voice surprised Gin—and made her smile. "Mothers are never finished—not that I would tell Raine that."

"They'll figure it out soon enough."

We're. They'll. The words became fragile threads, weaving their lives together. But Dan was also bound to Evie—by loyalty and memories and a whole lot of other things Gin couldn't begin to compete with. He might have lost his head for a moment, but his heart belonged to the woman sitting next to Gin.

Evie turned onto Fifth Avenue and stopped right outside Gin's trailer. She'd either hired a private investigator or Cody had told her where they lived.

"Thanks for the ride home, and for helping with the burglary." Gin opened the door a crack, and the scent of smoke mixed in with the breeze sent her pulse into a slow skid. "Does Dan usually call you? When he's . . . safe?"

"Every time."

"That's good." Gin meant it. She reached for the handle, but Evie's hand came down on her arm, holding her in place. Gin looked at her, a question in her eyes, but Evie had one of her own.

"He kissed you, didn't he?"

Gin's blush gave her away. "You saw us."

"Not the kiss." How could Evie appear so calm? "Yours and Dan's expressions when I walked in."

"But . . ." Gin stopped as her thoughts backed up. "Then why didn't you ask if I kissed *him*?"

"Because you looked terrified. And Dan looked . . ."

"Guilty?"

"No." Memories softened Evie's smile. "The way Max used to look at me."

CHAPTER 52

Dan felt the ground shudder under his feet when the barn collapsed.

A few yards away, the farmer's wife and three children formed a single shadow, soldered together by grief.

"Two horses didn't make it out, and one is having a difficult time breathing." Hopper appeared at his side. "The vet's on her way."

Dan steeled himself when Art Lawrence staggered toward them.

"Captain." Unshed tears and smoke scraped Art's voice raw. "Can I go inside the house? Just for a few minutes? Nancy . . . she left her wedding ring on the sink when she was washing up the supper dishes."

Hopper opened his mouth to say something, but Dan silenced him with a look. There was no use pointing out that Art didn't have a house to go back to. Only a gaping, smoldering hole.

"It isn't safe right now, Art," Dan said quietly. "The fire inspector is on his way . . . I promise I'll look for Nancy's ring the first chance I get."

Cars began to line up behind the county squad car parked on the road, and Dan recognized the church van at the front of the procession. News of the fire must have been relayed to the prayer chain at Hope Community.

"Cap'n?" Sid materialized at Dan's side, his face almost unrecognizable beneath a layer of soot. "One of the EMTs wants to talk to you."

"Sure." Dan patted Art's broad shoulder, and the man's muscles, corded from years of hard labor, seemed to dissolve under his hand.

"Hopper, Pastor Keith is here. Can you take Art and his family over to the van?" It was no use trying to get the family to leave. Not yet anyway. He followed Sid, who veered away from the fire truck and strode toward the ambulance.

"Did someone get hurt?" A spike of adrenalin quickened Dan's pace. Art's family had been in the barn doing their evening chores when the house started on fire. By the time the flames had skipped to the outbuildings, both the volunteer fire department and the city crew were on the scene, and Dan had been told that other than the animals, there had been no injuries.

"Yeah." Sid nudged Dan toward a young woman standing by the back doors of the ambulance. "You."

Dan shot him an impatient look. A falling timber had grazed his arm when he was coaxing a mare from her stall, but Dan didn't think anyone had noticed.

"Let me look at that arm." Claire, the only female EMT on the night shift, reached for him.

"It's fine." Dan flexed his wrist to prove it, and pain rattled all the way to his elbow. Okay, maybe not so fine. But not worth fussing over either.

"Sit down, tough guy." The top of Claire's head was even with Dan's shoulder, but what she lacked in height she more than made up for with sass.

"I'm not having it X-rayed." Dan shrugged off his turnout coat.

"Someone's cranky." Claire grinned at him. "You must be in love."

Dan knew the teasing comment was a coping skill meant to lighten the moment, so he tried to answer in kind. "Cranky? That proof wouldn't hold up in court."

"This would." Claire snapped the bright yellow elastic band on his wrist. "Not exactly your color, Moretti."

Dan recognized it instantly. He'd removed that stretchy little obstacle when he'd kissed Ginevieve—yes, he'd *kissed* Ginevieve—but how had it ended up on his wrist?

God, I messed up big time. Ginevieve is never going to trust me again. I'm never going to trust me either.

Because all Dan could think about was how perfectly she had fit in his arms.

"Mild sprain," Claire announced. "Ice it when you get home and pop a couple of ibuprofen. You'll be as good as new."

Dan wished he could tell Art Lawrence and his family the same thing.

"Fire inspector is on his way, Captain." Jerry waved at a vehicle driving around the barricade.

Dan forgot about the injury and rose to his feet. He could shower off the soot, but the heaviness would cling to his soul for days. Art's family had been farming for fifty years, and now he would have to begin the painstaking process of starting over.

As he crossed the driveway to talk to the inspector, Dan saw Pastor Keith's wife, Chrissy, wrapping blankets around Art's children as her husband prayed with them. By morning, Dan knew members of the congregation would be forming a plan to help Art rebuild.

"Ginevieve doesn't want to lean on anyone—which usually means someone she cared about wasn't there when she needed him."

"One day he caught me before I could get into my room and lock the door . . ."

Fragments of two conversations collided in Dan's head and he dug his fingers in his eyes.

Focus, Moretti. You have a job to do.

Two hours later the inspector finished his initial report and the last of the hot spots had been subdued. Art and his family left with Pastor Keith while some of the family's neighbors checked the animals and secured them for the night.

Dan tossed the keys to Sid and climbed into the passenger side of the truck. When they reached the four-way stop at the edge of the city limits, Sid turned to look at him.

"Hospital, Captain?"

"Station."

Disapproval closed in from every side, but Dan ignored it. All he wanted to do was go home, take a shower, and fall into bed.

The aroma of fresh-baked bread greeted Dan as he walked into the station. Next to the coffeepot he spotted a platter of cinnamon rolls and gigantic doughnuts dusted with sugar. "Aww, you baked for us."

"Not me." Jason, one of the firefighters who'd stayed behind to cover the city, pointed to a cardboard box on the table. "Someone left it outside the door a little while ago."

Someone. Dan smiled. It appeared Evie had pulled off a blessing burglary of her own.

The rush of adrenaline began to dissipate as Dan stripped off his turnout gear and checked the equipment. The crew on duty claimed the bunks, so Dan drove home to catch a few hours of sleep.

The house was dark when he got home, but Will had left a note on the breakfast bar.

Saw you on the ten o'clock news. Always trying to make the rest of us look bad.

Dan tried to laugh, but it turned into a weak cough instead. He hit the shower, yanked on a pair of flannel lounge pants, and stretched out on top of the comforter. Almost midnight. Should he or shouldn't he?

He reached for his cell phone.

"It's about time." Evie sounded wide awake. "How are Art and Nancy doing?"

"The barn and house are a total loss, but the family made it out. I called to say thank you."

"You're welcome. Our mission was successful, by the way. Maybe I'll get a chance to meet Nicki and her kids—"

"Hold on." Dan levered onto one elbow. "You went with Ginevieve?"

"I told you I'd go along."

"I know, but I didn't think—" *You'd do it? Ginevieve would agree?* "Never mind. I actually called to thank you for the care package you dropped off at the station. The guys descended on those cinnamon rolls like a cloud of locusts. I was lucky to get one."

Silence.

"Eves?"

"It wasn't me."

"Then who . . ." Dan pressed his thumbs against his temples to hold off the exhaustion creeping in.

"I don't know." A smile flickered in Evie's voice. "Someone else who cares?"

CHAPTER 53

No one had bothered to tell Gin that the Mother-Daughter Tea at Hope Community Church wasn't just an annual tradition—it was the social event of the year. Or that the mothers of the senior girls treated the occasion as an excuse to buy a new dress in a slightly more grown-up version of the one they'd worn for their junior prom.

Gin discovered these things when she followed Raine into what was called the Fellowship Room. A room that had been transformed into a summer garden. Lights twinkled in a canopy of white netting that covered the ceiling. A waterfall had been set up in the corner, spilling into a tiny pond stocked with real live goldfish. Ivy topiaries as tall as Gin flanked the buffet that stretched the length of the wall, and bouquets of fresh-cut flowers on the linen-covered tables released a delicate perfume into the air.

Evie stood next to a wooden podium, looking like one of the daffodils in a yellow sheath dress and matching peep-toe heels. She was deep in conversation with a woman whose hands were moving in rapid sync with her lips.

"Come on, Mom." Raine tugged her forward.

Gin didn't want to go forward. She wanted to go home and change clothes. "Why didn't you tell me everyone was going to be dressed like Cinderella?" she hissed.

"You look great, Mom."

A simple black dress without a sequin or speck of glitter did not fall into the category of "great." Not even close. "I look like one of the caterers."

"No you don't. They're wearing aprons."

Gin gave her a mock scowl and added a nudge for good measure. "Brat."

"Welcome to the Mother-Daughter Tea!"

The woman must have been hiding behind a potted plant, because Gin had no idea where she came from. But the telltale frown between her penciled-in eyebrows hinted that she'd been close enough to hear this mother call her daughter a brat.

"I'm Melanie Gibson." She held out her hand. "Otherwise known as Taylor's mom."

"Ginevieve Lightly . . . Raine's mom."

"I thought you looked familiar. I remember you from the football game."

Forget about going home to change her clothes. Gin just wanted to go home.

"Mom scored a touchdown," Raine said helpfully.

Across the room, Ginevieve saw Evie looking their way.

Smile and wave.

Gin managed the second one.

"Would you like a glass of punch?" Melanie's gaze dropped to Raine's belly button and lingered there a moment.

Why were they here again?

"Punch sounds good." Raine scooted toward the buffet table, and a slender brunette at the end of the line greeted her with a bright smile.

"How are you doing, Raine?"

"Good."

The woman turned to Gin. "I'm Chrissy Anderson, Pastor Keith's wife, and you must be Raine's mom. We're so glad you're here today!"

Gin murmured the appropriate response and felt a surge of relief when the line began to move again. The refreshments looked as beautiful as the centerpieces on the tables. Mosaics of fresh fruit and vegetables arranged on crystal platters, miniature quiches, and sandwiches cut into tiny, elegant slivers. Gin recognized Marie from the bistro presiding over the dessert table and realized she was the one who'd catered the event.

Her thoughts drifted back to a conversation she'd had with Sue earlier in the week. Her boss had stomped into the diner after a follow-up appointment with her physician, furious because he'd told her to quit smoking. Which, in Sue's mind, was worse than finding out she needed two stents in her heart.

"You'll have to run the diner," Sue had said, opening drawers and cupboards in the kitchen on a search-and-destroy mission to locate any stray cigarettes that would wage war against her self-control.

"I don't know how long I'll be in Banister Falls, Sue. You might want to find someone else."

"I'm not going to look. You're the only one I trust."

The words had struck fear in Gin's heart. "Sue—"

"You're here until Raine graduates, right? I'll even let you play with the menu while I'm gone."

Gin didn't know if it was a last-ditch effort to get her to agree or a brilliant strategy on her boss's part, but it didn't matter, because in the end Sue got her way.

"Can't decide?"

Gin's head snapped up. How long had she been staring down at the dessert table? She smiled at Marie, grabbed a lemon tart, and almost smacked into Evie.

"Hi."

"Hi."

This conversation was proving to be shorter but no less uncomfortable than the one she and Evie had had the night of the fire. The night Dan had kissed her. The night Evie had hinted that he had feelings for her.

Gin's cheeks began to glow again. Evie might have mistaken simple chemistry for something deeper, but Gin knew the difference. A man like Dan could never love someone like her, because Gin didn't know how to love a man. You had to trust them first, right? She'd tried that once and had the mangled heart to prove it. Dan deserved better. He deserved . . . someone like Evie.

"I saw Raine's name on the sign-up sheet," Evie said. "I saved you both seats at my table."

They'd moved past uncomfortable and were heading straight into scary. Especially since the table Evie pointed out was in the front of the room, right next to the podium.

"There are some empty chairs at that one too." Gin pointed out another option, right next to the door.

"I already put my things at a table near the front so I can be close to the microphone."

"You have to introduce the speaker?" Raine had mentioned that Evie worked at Hope Community.

A smile slipped into Evie's eyes. "I am the speaker."

No one had told Gin that, either.

Chapter 54

Raine knew she shouldn't have eaten that shrimp puff.

Her morning sickness had all but disappeared over the past few weeks, but there were certain foods that tipped her stomach sideways. Now she could add seafood to the list.

She inched the chair away from the table and silently willed her stomach to hang in there a few more minutes. The hum of conversation and the clink of dessert forks against dishes meant she'd have time to sneak into the ladies' room and splash some cold water on her face.

"Are you all right?"

Her mom's mysterious internal radar—Raine wondered when during her pregnancy she was going to get fitted for one of those—had honed in on her.

"Great." *Great.* Now everyone at the table was looking at her. "I'll be right back."

Her mom and Evie frowned—nope, not fooling either one of them—but neither of them said anything. Raine listened to her stomach and took measured steps to keep it steady until she reached the hallway. The door swung shut behind her, sealing the laughter inside.

So far, so good.

The banner the Sunday school kids had made for Easter hung

on the wall, yards of metallic gold ribbon erupting from a black felt tomb, proclaiming that Jesus had risen.

Raine smiled.

Surprised them, didn't You?

Even Jesus's friends, who'd been told He would rise from the dead, hadn't believed Him. They'd hidden in a room, afraid of the future.

Raine felt the same way sometimes. Everyone at school and church knew she was pregnant now. Knew Cody was the father. Blamed her for ruining his life.

After the Chilly Bowl, Raine told Cody she wasn't going to church anymore. People were talking about them—about her—and even though the high school janitor had painted over the word written on her locker door, Raine saw it in some of the girls' eyes when she walked down the hall.

Cody hadn't said anything right away—he never did, which was one of the things Raine loved about him.

"I get it. I felt that way too," he'd finally said. "But then I remembered there isn't anyone who can stand before God and tell Him they did everything right. If I curl up in a ball and stay on the ground when I fall down, it's like saying I don't believe God has the power to lift me back up."

Raine had gone to church the next Sunday, and it felt like God smiled at her that morning, because her mom went with her too.

For months Raine had prayed for her mom, left sticky notes with Bible verses on the bathroom mirror, and tuned Jasmine's radio to a station that played contemporary worship songs. Her mom hadn't said a thing, but that didn't stop Raine from talking to God about it.

It helped to know her aunt Sara was praying too. Raine hadn't told her mom that she'd called Sara after she got back from Whisper Lake and told her about the baby. Her mom thought Sara didn't approve of the way they lived, but Raine sensed there was more to it than that.

Sara had sent a letter a few days ago, and Raine had put it in the top drawer of her dresser, waiting for the Right Moment.

Maybe today, God.

She slipped inside the ladies' room and dampened a paper towel with cold water. She pressed it against her forehead and closed her eyes.

The door opened and Raine's eyes met Mrs. Anderson's in the mirror. The pastor's wife had always been nice to her, but lately she'd seemed even more attentive, making a point to single out Raine after the Sunday morning worship service.

"Raine! Aren't you feeling well, honey?" Mrs. Anderson bustled into the ladies' room.

"My stomach is a little upset. No big deal." To prove it, she wadded up the paper towel and tossed it at the wastebasket. It bounced off the rim and would have stuck to one of the little bows on Mrs. Anderson's shoe if she hadn't jumped out of the way.

"Are you sure? You look a little pale, sweetheart." The pastor's wife guided Raine to a white wicker chair in the corner. "I had a touchy stomach too, my first trimester."

The shrimp puff in Raine's stomach doubled in size.

"I've been praying for you," Mrs. Anderson continued. "Cody and my husband have met several times, and I know how difficult this must be on you and your families."

Cody hadn't said anything about meeting with Pastor Keith, but Raine found herself nodding.

"Keith said you were taking things one day a time, but you're both so young . . . I know you and Cody want to go to college, but even with the scholarship it will be challenging to raise a child."

"Scholarship?" Raine choked.

"The Mansfield Merit." Mrs. Anderson looked confused. "Cody found out a few weeks ago."

Raine wildly searched her face, searching for some clue that Mrs. Anderson had somehow misunderstood. Cody hadn't even told her he'd been nominated for the Mansfield Merit, a scholarship that covered tuition and room and board for all four years at a college of the recipient's choice.

"Excuse me." Raine stumbled toward the door.

"Raine, wait!" Mrs. Anderson sounded genuinely distressed. "I'm sorry if I said something that upset you."

Raine kept going even though it wasn't something Mrs. Anderson had said. It was what Cody hadn't.

Chapter 55

Raine should have been back by now.

Gin tapped her fork against her empty plate and caught the look that passed between the two women across the table from her.

She'd been getting a lot of those. The other women had tried to include her in the conversation, but it inevitably drifted to things that only the inner circle would know. So-and-so whose grandmother donated a handmade quilt for a youth fund-raiser. An upcoming concert by a band Gin had never heard of. The Sunday school camping trip in July.

"Ladies! If I could have your attention for a moment!" A woman wearing a sparkly green dress had taken control of the microphone. "We'd like to do a fun little icebreaker so you can get to know each other better." She waved a pink envelope. "Look for one of these on your table and answer the question inside! You'll have ten minutes and then Evie Bennett will be giving a special message to our senior girls."

Everyone looked at the envelope propped against the centerpiece.

"I'll go first." Melanie Gibson pulled out a piece of paper—pink, of course, to match the envelope—and read it out loud: "What is something you are looking forward to in the next six months?" She smiled at her daughter, Taylor. "That's an easy one! Taylor and I are going to Chicago for a weekend in June to shop for her dorm room. We're going to eat out every night and stay in a hotel with a pool."

Taylor wrinkled her nose. "Thanks, Mom," she teased. "You just stole my answer."

"Oops." Melanie handed her the paper. "You'll have to think of something else."

"Okay . . . I'm looking forward to living in a dorm!"

Everyone laughed, and the piece of paper was transferred to the next woman in the circle.

"I'm looking forward to visiting our son in Oregon. He's going to take us on a whale watch."

"Those are so much fun!" Melanie said. "My husband and I went on one of those for our twentieth anniversary last year."

The woman handed Gin the piece of paper but didn't meet her eyes. Was she thinking that Gin, with a pregnant teenage daughter, couldn't possibly have anything to look forward to?

Staring down at the words, Gin's heart picked up speed, and suddenly she heard the sound of another heartbeat. A tempo that drowned out the "should haves" and "what ifs" with a joyful "this is!"

"I'm looking forward to being a grandma." Gin didn't say it to shock the women—she said it because it was the truth. The circumstances, the timing, none of it was perfect, but Gin couldn't wish this baby away any more than she could have wished Raine away the day she'd stumbled into the free clinic, alone and without an appointment . . .

You weren't alone.

The three words were as clear as if someone else had joined Gin at the table. And they cut right through the walls she'd spent a lifetime building.

Her eyes met Evie's across the table.

"Excuse me. I have to—" Go. She had to go. The chair almost

tipped over as Gin stumbled to her feet. She heard Evie say her name, but she forged through the maze of topiaries and tables until she made it to the hallway.

Do You really see me? Do You really care?

Gin pushed through the doors of the sanctuary in case Evie tried to follow her, and stumbled right into the answer.

Dozens of white lilies filled the room. This was no careful display like the flowers in the fellowship room. The lilies were in full bloom and they were everywhere. Lining the aisles. Marching up the steps to the altar. Perched on the ledges of the stained glass windows. Crowded on top of the piano.

It was overwhelming and extravagant. And it was for her.

Gin folded over on herself and wished she hadn't forgotten how to cry. Tears backed up in her throat and threatened to choke her. Every time her suitcase came out of the closet, Gin had reveled in that initial burst of freedom. The anticipation of a new city. A new start. It always faded, though, because no matter where Gin went, she dragged her past with her. The scenery changed, but nothing changed *her.*

But maybe someone could. Someone who knew she loved flowers.

What are you looking for?

There it was again. That warmth, spreading through her, filling the cracks and broken places. Healing. Changing.

You, Gin's heart whispered back. *I'm looking for You.*

This time Gin didn't run away. She closed her eyes and sank into it as the tears washed her clean.

When Gin finally opened her eyes, a flicker of movement caught her attention. She blinked until the movement turned into a blurry lump that turned into a person.

Raine, curled into a tight ball in the corner of a pew.

CHAPTER 56

Dan had fallen asleep on the couch watching MacGyver try to deactivate a bomb with a pair of tweezers and a piece of wire—which was probably why Dan's entire body levitated off the couch when his cell phone rang.

He squinted at the clock. Eleven o'clock. If this was Will asking him to preheat the oven for wings, he was going to kill him.

"You woke me up," he barked into the phone.

"Sorry to bother you at home, Captain."

Every nerve in Dan's body went on red alert at the sound of Jason's voice. "What's up?"

"Can you come down to the station?"

"Right now?" Dan scrubbed the sleep from his eyes. "Is there a problem?"

Jason's ragged exhale didn't do anything to put Dan's mind at ease. "I'd have to say yes to both, Captain."

Dan didn't bother to change out of his sweats; he just tossed a fleece jacket over his T-shirt and grabbed his keys.

Jason was waiting for him at the back door when Dan pulled into the parking lot. He didn't say anything, just pointed to the building next door.

Dan walked into the gym just in time to see Cody charge at the basket. He was a wreck. His shirt was stained with sweat, his hair as wild as the look in his eyes. No wonder Jason had called him.

"Hey, Code." Dan approached him cautiously.

Cody sank the shot and caught it on the rebound.

"You should have called." Dan scooped up one of the basketballs and bounced it against the floor. "I would have met you down here."

Cody took another shot and followed the ball to the net. He hung on the rim a moment before dropping back to earth.

Okay, buddy. We'll do it your way.

Dan stripped off his jacket and tossed it in a corner. He got in Cody's way and messed up his next shot. The next thing Dan knew, Cody's fists were knotted in the front of Dan's shirt and he was being propelled backward. Fortunately, the concrete wall prevented Dan from ending up in the street.

He did it again. So did Cody.

This time, Dan twisted at the last second so that only one shoulder, rather than his entire body, absorbed the impact. They met at the center line, toe to toe, with Cody in possession of the ball.

"Want to talk about it?" Sweat broke out on Dan's forehead as Cody feinted to one side and went around him instead of through him.

Dan considered that progress.

"No." The ball smacked against the backboard, and Cody's growl of frustration echoed through the gym. He launched the ball at Dan, who caught it a millisecond before it broke through his sternum.

"Here's what we're going to do." Dan held the ball above his head while Cody tried his best to take it away. "I score a three-pointer in the next five minutes and you have to tell me what's going on. Deal?" It was either that or a heart attack at the ripe old age of thirty-six.

Cody transferred the sweat from his palms to the front of his gym shorts. His narrowed eyes flashed a message.

Deal.

Dan should have made it three minutes. The way Cody kept

coming at him, he'd end up with a heart attack anyway. Dan's lungs were about to burst and his muscles were screaming for relief when he bumped Cody aside and hurled the ball at the net. The flight wasn't smooth and it wasn't pretty, but it made it into the net.

Cody dropped to his knees, shoulders heaving, and Dan joined him on the floor.

"Let's hear it."

Tears burned hot in Cody's eyes, mingling with the sweat running down his face. "Raine broke up with me."

Chapter 57

Gin walked over to the window just as Dan's truck glided to a stop in front of the trailer.

This was getting crazy. How had she known he would show up?

Because you wanted to see him too.

Dan didn't knock or wait for her to open the door. He must have guessed she would still be awake. "Is Raine here?" He looked exhausted.

"She fell asleep about an hour ago." In Gin's arms. "What about Cody?"

"On his way home. He took his frustrations out on the basketball court." Dan rubbed his shoulder. "And me."

"Coffee?"

"It's midnight."

"Are you going to sleep tonight?"

"Good point." Dan raked his hand through his hair and winced.

"I'll be right back." Gin motioned to the chair—it was her favorite now too—and went into the kitchen. She filled an oversize mug with what was left in the coffeepot and grabbed a package of green beans from the freezer. She set the mug down on the coffee table and the package of beans on Dan's shoulder. His hiss of relief made Gin glad that Raine didn't play basketball.

Memories of the last time she and Dan were alone together began to fill the space between them. He hadn't stopped at the diner since the night of the fire—the night he'd kissed her—so Gin could only assume he regretted it.

She pulled her thoughts back in line. This was about Raine and Cody, not her and Dan.

Dan finally broke the silence. "Cody said Raine called and told him that it would be easier if they weren't together anymore. Did something happen at the Mother-Daughter Tea? Did someone say something to her?"

"I don't think so." Gin had already gone over that in her mind. "After we ate, Raine went to the restroom—I don't think she was feeling very well—and then I found her in the sanctuary. All she said was that Cody had kept something important from her."

"That's more than she told Cody when she broke up with him." Dan blew out a sigh. "I reminded him that he and Raine are under a lot of stress, but he said this is different. He doesn't think she'll change her mind."

Gin didn't either. Raine hadn't said a word on the way home. She hadn't cried either, but the glint of determination in her eyes worried Gin more than the lack of tears.

"I have to do the right thing" was the only thing she had said before she retreated to her bedroom.

"Cody told me something else." Dan's eyes darkened.

Gin wanted to reach for him and make that pain go away too. She drew one of the lumpy throw pillows into her lap and smoothed away the creases in the fabric instead. Waited for Dan to continue.

"He isn't going to college in the fall. He's going to stay in Banister Falls and take classes at the Tech to become a firefighter."

Gin wasn't shocked by the news, but she could tell Dan was. "I take it you weren't expecting that?"

"When Cody was about five, I remember Max bringing him

down to the station one day. He looked at me and he said 'I'm going to blow out fires when I'm big too.'"

Gin held back a smile. She could see how a little boy whose only experience with fire was blowing out candles on a birthday cake would describe it that way.

"But then Max died a year later and Cody never mentioned it again." Dan smeared his hand across his jaw. "I had no idea he was even considering it. Until tonight."

"Does Evie know?"

"Not yet." Dan's low groan was an indication of how he expected that conversation to go.

"Are *you* going to support Cody's decision?"

"What else can I do?"

The response was so *Dan* that this time Gin did smile. "Well, you could always try to talk him out of it."

The bag of frozen beans slid off Dan's shoulder as he lurched to his feet. "How can I fault Cody for wanting to follow in Max's footsteps?"

How could a man as intelligent as Dan miss something so obvious? Gin rose to her feet too.

"Cody isn't following in Max's footsteps, Dan. He's following in yours."

Dan looked so stunned Gin wanted to reach across the coffee table, grab those broad shoulders, and shake some sense into him. The only thing that stopped her was knowing she wouldn't be able to let go.

"Cody was six years old when Max died. *Six. Years. Old.* He barely remembers his father. But you . . . you've been there all his life. Teaching him things. Listening to him. Being there when he needed you. Do you really think Cody turned out the way he did because Max Bennett passed on some kind of amazing DNA? Cody is the way he is because he's been watching *you.* You're his hero."

Dan flinched, turned away from her. "I told you what happened the night of the fire."

There'd been an error in judgment the night of the fire, but Gin knew it hadn't been Dan's. She looked up at the ceiling.

What can I say to make him believe me?

Gin heard a creak in the hallway and whirled around. Raine, in her flannel pajamas, stood a few yards away, clutching the afghan she kept at the foot of her bed.

"Dan?" Raine took a wobbly step forward, and Dan turned around.

His expression changed, softened, when he looked at her. Gin grabbed onto the arm of the chair for support. She didn't have to convince Dan he was a hero. Raine did, when she dashed past Gin, fell into Dan's open arms, and burst into tears.

Gin had tried to be everything to Raine for eighteen years, but she hadn't been able to give her this. A strong shoulder. Hands large enough, steady enough, to hold a person together when everything around them was coming apart.

Gin had never let a man get close enough.

But somehow, in spite of all her best efforts, Dan had gotten past her defenses. With his kindness. His patience. His honesty. His stubborn refusal to ignore what Gin said she wanted because he knew what she needed.

Gin's brand-new heart had barely begun to beat, but she knew what this feeling was.

Love. She'd fallen in love with Dan.

Their eyes met over Raine's head and Gin looked away, afraid he would see the truth in her eyes. Just because you recognized something didn't mean you knew what to do with it.

Once the tears began to subside, Dan straightened the afghan around Raine's shoulders and guided her back to the couch. Gin sat down beside her daughter and pushed the box of tissues closer. Tucked a damp strand of blond hair behind Raine's ear.

"I'll get you a glass of water." Dan retreated to the kitchen.

Not just water—a moment for Raine to compose herself.

Gin fell a little bit deeper.

She and Raine leaned into each other, the silence broken occasionally by a tremor that vibrated through Raine and turned into a ragged breath. Dan returned with two glasses of water. He pressed one into Raine's hands and gave the other one to her.

Gin couldn't hear the words, but she knew Dan was praying. Would he believe her if she told him that she was too?

Raine's cell phone began to ring and she ignored it. Two minutes later, it started up again. She pulled it out of the pocket of her lounge pants and looked at the screen. Handed the phone to Dan.

"It's for you."

Dan took a step away and held the phone up to his ear. "Hello?"

"Cody?" Gin murmured.

Raine shook her head. "His mom."

How could Gin have forgotten about Evie? Forgotten that she would always have a prior claim on Dan? Loving him didn't change that. It didn't change the fact that Cody and Evie would always come first. They should.

Dan was handing the phone back to Raine.

"Cody . . . he's okay, isn't he?" Tear-filled brown eyes locked on Dan.

"He will be. Cody is—" Dan hesitated. "Strong."

Because of you. Gin didn't say it out loud, but the frown that creased Dan's brow told Gin he'd heard it anyway. Good.

Maybe it was finally starting to sink in.

"You should go back there and make sure." Raine leaned against Gin's shoulder.

Gin saw the indecision in Dan's eyes. "Raine is right." Gin made it two against one. "It's getting late and we should probably get some sleep. Raine wants to go to the sunrise service in the morning."

"Easter," Dan muttered. "Right."

He glanced back as he reached the door. "I'll see you tomorrow."

The door closed behind him.

"Cody is staying in Banister Falls," Gin said softly. "He told Dan he wants to be a firefighter."

Raine knotted her hands together. "That's what he says . . . but he has to take the scholarship."

"Scholarship?"

"To the college of his choice. All four years." Pride burned away the tears in Raine's eyes. "I can't take that away from him. We'll be friends. We'll work something out after the baby comes, but I don't want Cody to make any decisions based on . . . on me."

Is that what Cody had kept from her? It didn't seem like such a huge thing, especially if a college degree was Evie's dream, not her son's.

"What if Cody doesn't leave?"

"He will—if I'm not here."

Raine's statement shouldn't have come as a shock to Gin's system. Especially given the fact that a few short months ago she would have been reaching for her suitcase. But now there was Sue, facing surgery that would prevent her from running the diner for a few weeks. And Nicki, the young mom who needed some mothering of her own.

And Dan.

No, not Dan. Gin couldn't let her heart go there.

"Have you decided on a college?"

Raine's cheeks turned pink and she rolled to her feet. "Promise you'll keep an open mind, Mom?"

Gin was glad she didn't wait for a response. Raine returned a few minutes later with an envelope. Gin recognized her half sister's handwriting immediately, and her mouth went dry. "What is this?"

Raine set the envelope in her lap. "An invitation."

Chapter 58

"I see I'm going to have to give you a refresher course in the kitchen."

Dan's mom plucked the spatula from his hand and began to flip golden slices of French toast on the griddle. Easter breakfast after the special sunrise service was an annual tradition, and the Moretti clan had helped in the kitchen for as long as Dan could remember.

Now all he could remember was the day he'd helped Ginevieve in the diner. They'd met less than three months ago, but Dan couldn't stop thinking about her. Ginevieve wasn't afraid to get in his face when she thought he needed it, but Dan wanted more than that. He wanted her in his arms again. He wanted her to trust him, but if that never happened, Dan wanted her to trust God.

His conversation with Evie after he'd left Ginevieve's house the night before had shaken his confidence. According to Evie, Ginevieve had left before the tea ended, but she didn't know why. Evie claimed she hadn't noticed anyone being unkind to Ginevieve or Raine, but something must have happened. Raine had broken up with Cody, and Ginevieve . . . who knew what she was thinking? Or what she would do.

You have to trust Me too.

Dan pulled in a breath. *Right, Lord. Sorry.*

"Just hand Danny a fire extinguisher, Mom." Will sauntered past with a platter of sausage. "He knows what to do with one of those."

"Next shift is coming on duty!" A group of people swept into the kitchen to take over. Freeing Dan to look for Ginevieve and Raine.

The women's ministry team had left up the decorations from the Mother-Daughter Tea, one of the reasons the events were scheduled over Easter weekend, so Dan took up surveillance behind a potted plant. Ginevieve had mentioned attending the sunrise service, but it was possible she and Raine would skip out on the breakfast.

"Table behind the waterfall." Dan's feet almost left the ground as Mort came up behind him. "You're looking for your family, right?"

Dan didn't want to lie outright, so he conjured a smile instead. "Thanks."

He wound through the tables and spotted Cody standing with a group of teenagers near the stage.

He's following in your footsteps.

Dan had been blown away by Ginevieve's statement. He'd loved Cody from the moment Evie and Max had brought him home from the hospital. And after Max died, Dan had just gone on loving him. It didn't mean he was a hero. Didn't mean he was anything special. But Ginevieve . . . for her, Dan wanted to be both.

"Over here, Daniel!" A hand flagged the air behind a centerpiece.

The Moretttis took up three tables. Amanda and Emily looked like part of the décor in frilly pastel dresses and lace-trimmed hats. Bree usually held court from a high chair, but this morning it was empty. Because his niece was sitting in Raine's lap.

Dan's gaze bounced from head to head until it landed on a sleek mahogany braid. Ginevieve, tucked between his mother and father.

It hadn't occurred to Dan that while he was looking for Ginevieve, his family might have found her first.

Gin felt Dan's presence before she saw him.

She'd tried to dodge his family but there were just too many of them. Carissa, Stephen's wife, had waylaid them in the hallway after the service and asked if they were staying for breakfast.

Raine didn't give Gin an opportunity to say no, the allure of pancakes and bacon obviously too tempting to pass up. They'd been caught up in a wave of Morettis and swept into the large room where the tea had been held the day before.

John smiled at someone over Gin's shoulder. "He is risen!"

"He is risen indeed."

Gin had heard people greet each other with those words at least a dozen times since John Moretti had pulled out a chair for her, and every time they rose like a song in her heart.

The last twenty-four hours had been a blur—except for that moment of clarity when Gin had heard His voice. Even after everything that had happened, it continued to linger in her thoughts like the aroma of the lilies on the altar.

"Ginevieve." Dan took a chair on the opposite side of the table. In a white dress shirt and charcoal gray slacks that accentuated his lean, athletic build, and his dark hair still gleaming from a recent shower, Dan looked better than the strawberries and whipped cream on top of Amanda's French toast.

"Hi." Gin could feel Dan's entire family tuned into their conversation. She and Raine shouldn't have let Carissa talk them into staying for breakfast. If Dan's family knew Raine had broken up with Cody, she doubted they would have made room for them at the table.

"How are you?" There were a dozen other questions in Dan's eyes, but Gin found she couldn't even answer the first.

"She's hungry. Leave her alone." Angela set a plate of Danish down in front of Gin. Winked at her.

Gin mustered a smile even as she felt another interior wall crumble. She hadn't just fallen in love with Dan Moretti; she'd fallen in love with his entire family.

"I'm hun'ry too." Reaching for one of the pastries, Emily bumped a glass of juice. Her mother's quick reaction saved Gin from being showered with orange liquid, but at the moment she would have welcomed an opportunity to escape.

"Did you lose that tooth yet, Manda Panda?" Dan bent down to rub noses with his brown-eyed niece.

"Shtill sthuck." Amanda showed him.

"It'll happen. Don't force it."

Dan drew Emily onto his lap, and she burrowed against him. "You smell good, Unca Danny."

Gin had to agree.

Had to get out of here.

John waved at someone behind her. "Come on over!" he boomed. "We've got plenty of room."

Gin saw Raine draw Bree against her like a shield and knew who John was inviting to join them.

Chairs shifted to make room for Evie and Cody. Dan's siblings all started talking at once, as if a barrage of words would break down the tension in the air. The trouble was, their aim was off; they assumed the tension was between Gin and Evie.

"I suppose you're starting to plan Cody's graduation party." Carissa, who'd been dividing her scrambled eggs up between Amanda and Emily, turned to Evie with a smile. "Did you decide on a date?"

"Memorial Day. Cody wants to have a cookout in the pavilion at Maple Ridge."

"Sounds like fun." Jennifer reclaimed a fussy Bree from Raine's lap. "Let me know if I can bring anything."

Lisa smiled at Raine. "When is your party?"

Raine glanced at Cody, and with a flash of mother's intuition, Gin knew why she'd agreed to stay for breakfast.

Don't say it, Raine.

"I'm not going to have one. Mom and I are going to Maine on Monday."

A bubble of silence descended over the three tables. Even Bree stopped banging her spoon on the table.

Cody half rose from his chair. "Maine?"

Dan's parents exchanged a look, no doubt wondering why Cody was just hearing about this now.

Raine bobbed her head, her smile too bright. "We're going to visit my aunt Sara."

"She owns a restaurant, doesn't she?" Angela had a good memory.

"Right on the ocean."

"How long will you be gone?" Liz twisted in her chair to look at Gin.

"I'm not sure." Gin could barely wrap her mind around Sara's unexpected invitation.

When she'd opened the envelope, Gin had expected Sara's letter would be a thinly disguised criticism of Gin's parenting skills—especially after Sara discovered Raine was going to be a parent too. But instead, her half sister had told Gin she'd been praying—*praying*—they would be able to put the past behind them and get to know each other.

"Driving out?" Dan spoke up for the first time, his husky voice tangling Gin's thoughts.

"Flying." Sara had offered to pay for their tickets too.

"Sara's condo is only a block from the ocean." Raine closed her eyes and took a deep breath of invisible, saline-scented air.

There's plenty of room for you and Raine and the baby, if you decide to stay. Jenna, my hostess, is leaving in the middle of June, and I'm hoping that once you see how beautiful it is here, I can convince you to take her place at the restaurant. It will be a new start for all of us.

Gin had read that section of Sara's letter so many times it had become etched in her memory. A place to live. The chance to work in the kind of restaurant Gin had dreamed of owning someday.

"I'm sure you'll have a wonderful time," Liz said.

Evie was looking at Cody, trying to gauge his reaction to the news, but Gin couldn't look at Dan at all.

"Should we clear some of these extra dishes away?" Lisa reached for an empty bowl, but Gin beat her to it.

"I'll do it." Gin pinned on her waitress smile. "I'm the professional." She avoided eye contact with Angela Moretti as she collected the disposable plates and located the oversize trash can posted outside the kitchen door.

"From the things you said at my parents' house, I didn't get the impression you and your half sister were close."

Gin suppressed a shiver as Dan came to stand beside her. "We aren't. Sara and Raine have written back and forth over the years, but I didn't know Raine had told Sara she was pregnant until last night."

"A lot happened last night," Dan muttered.

"Maybe this is an answer to prayer." Gin wanted him to know that she understood its power now.

"Or maybe you're running away again."

The word landed like a slap. "I'm not running away from anything." She just knew her heart wouldn't hold up under the strain of watching Dan watch Evie.

"The airline tickets you're going to buy. One-way or round trip?"

Gin remained silent but her heart thumped out a silent SOS.

This is too hard, Jesus.

But like Raine, she had to do the right thing.

"Never mind," Dan muttered. "I guess I know the answer."

"I don't know why you're surprised." She forced herself to look Dan in the eyes. "I never planned to stay."

And to prove it, Gin walked away.

Chapter 59

Wait.

It had become a familiar refrain over the past few weeks.

Every time Dan drove past the diner, every time he picked up his cell phone, every time he brought Ginevieve's name to the throne of heaven, he'd heard the word.

Dan didn't like it. Because every time the command—it was too loud to be a suggestion—popped up in his head, it brought him one step closer to the day Ginevieve would leave Banister Falls.

Staying had never been part of her plan; Ginevieve had been honest about that from the very beginning. But until Raine had announced they were going to visit her aunt, Dan hadn't realized how much he'd hoped Ginevieve would change her mind. What was even more difficult was accepting that he'd probably been a factor in her decision.

He shouldn't have kissed her.

He'd let his own selfish desires take control instead of thinking about what was best for Ginevieve. But the worst part? He wanted to kiss her again.

No wonder God was telling him to wait.

"Hey, Captain." Hopper jogged up to Dan as he was closing his locker. "We're going out for breakfast. Want to come along?"

"I thought I'd head to the gym for a while."

"Are you sure? It's Kitchen Sink Day. A three-egg omelet with everything in it—that's the kitchen sink part—if you order one between eight and ten. Free coffee too."

"Sounds good." Dan fished for his keys. "When did Marie change the menu?" The bistro owner leaned toward scones and spinach soufflés and cups of coffee that cost as much as a gallon of fuel for his pickup.

"Not Marie's." Hopper's freckles began to glow. "My Place."

Dan stared at him. "When did you start going there?"

"Food's pretty good, and someone spruced the place up with a coat of paint." Hopper shrugged. "If you sign up to play in the cribbage tournament on Thursday afternoon, you get a free piece of pie. Are you sure you don't want to come with us?"

In his mind's eye Dan saw Ginevieve, her braid swinging between her shoulder blades as she emerged from the kitchen. Saw the smile that had the power to strip the air from his lungs.

Wait.

This time, Dan heard the answer before he'd asked the question.

"I can't." He slammed the door of his locker a little harder than necessary.

"Okay." Hopper backed away. "Well, see you in a couple of days, Cap'n."

Dan slung his gym bag over his shoulder and stalked away before he said something he'd regret. To a member of his crew and to his Lord.

Kitchen Sink Day. Cribbage tournaments. Somehow, Dan couldn't picture Sue Granger implementing those kinds of changes.

But Ginevieve would.

He hadn't missed the way her eyes glowed when she'd told him about the restaurant in St. Louis. Ginevieve was a great waitress, balancing the right amount of sass with exceptional service, but she dreamed of doing more. Dan had no doubt Ginevieve could work her way up to manager status—if she stayed in one place long enough.

Maybe she'll stay in Maine.

The thought dogged Dan's heels as he left the station. The bright May sunshine failed to penetrate the dark cloud hanging over his head as he crossed the parking lot to the gym.

Dan heard the muffled thump of a basketball on the other side of the door, and the corresponding surge of irritation it created proved he wasn't fit for company. While he was debating whether to hit the court anyway or run off his bad mood on the open road, the door opened.

"I thought that was you." Cody, flushed and grinning, yanked Dan inside the gym.

"What are you doing here? Don't you have class today?"

"Seniors have the rest of the week off." Cody twirled the basketball on the tip of his index finger. "Mom is running some errands, so I asked her to drop me off at the gym."

Guilt chewed at the edges of Dan's conscience. He'd barely spoken to Evie since the Easter breakfast. Between her office hours at the church and planning Cody's graduation party, she was probably swamped.

"Does she need any help?"

"Mom's pretty organized, but you can ask her." Cody bumped him toward the center line. "I've got time for a game of HORSE."

"You're on." No way was Dan going to strip the hopeful sparkle from Cody's eyes. "I think my muscles are healed up from the last time."

A tide of red washed over Cody's jaw. "Sorry about that."

Dan bumped him back. "I was teasing." Kind of.

Dan won the first game and lost the second. Cody performed an impromptu victory dance when Dan missed from the three-point line.

He glanced at his watch. "Your mom isn't back yet. Do you want a ride home?"

"I'll stick around for a while. There's commencement practice at the high school tonight, and until then I don't have anything else to do." The gleam in Cody's eyes faded, and Dan had a pretty good idea what had caused it.

"How are you holding up?"

"Okay." Cody didn't pretend to misunderstand. "Raine and I see each other a few times a week as friends." Cody put air quotes around the last word. "She can be stubborn."

"She got that from her mother," Dan muttered, trying not to hold it against Cody that God hadn't told *him* to wait.

"Raine got upset when she found out about the scholarship, but the only reason I didn't mention it was because I didn't plan on *taking* it." Frustration leaked into Cody's voice. "I think she's using it as an excuse."

"Sometimes," Dan said carefully, "people pick the path that's easier."

"Easier on who?" Cody tipped his head back and stared at the ceiling. "Raine knows I want to be a firefighter, but I know *her*. For some crazy reason, she thinks she's holding me back. That I'll be better off without her. She's trying to make things easier on *me*."

Dan fell back, pinned to the concrete wall by the memory of the last words Ginevieve had said.

This is what I do . . .

For eighteen years Ginevieve had made sacrifices for Raine. Put her needs first. Her *dreams* first. That's what she'd taught her daughter. And it explained why Raine had sobbed in Dan's arms. She hadn't broken up with Cody, she'd let him go.

He released a careful breath. "I think you're right."

"I know Raine loves me," Cody whispered. "All I have to do is convince her that I'm better *with* her. How do I do that?"

Dan wished he had an answer, but all he could see was Ginevieve walking away from him. And all he could tell Cody was the truth.

"I have no idea."

Chapter 60

The flowers arrived on Saturday morning.

Gin was staring at her reflection in the mirror, applying a coat of concealer to remove the shadows under her eyes, when she heard a knock on the door.

"Mom? Someone's here!" Raine shouted through the wall. "I just painted my toenails."

But apparently it was all right for Gin to answer the door with her wet hair rolled in a turban and wearing the crumpled cotton shorts and T-shirt she'd slept in the night before.

Gin peeked out the window and jumped a little when a smiling teenage boy wearing a ball cap peeked back. She opened the door a crack. "Can I help you?"

"Delivery from Sweet Blossoms." He glanced down at his clipboard and chuckled. "Raine Lightly? Is that a real name?"

"They're for me?" Raine waddled to the door, a cotton ball tucked between each toe, and reached for the long white box. "And yes, it's my real name."

The boy turned as red as the roses painted on the side of the delivery truck, mumbled something unintelligible, and made a hasty getaway.

Gin watched Raine wrestle with the yellow ribbon tied around the box and had a flashback of her daughter opening up birthday gifts when she was young. All tug and twist, no patience. The top of the box came off, and Raine peeled back the layers of tissue paper.

"Roses!" Raine lifted the bouquet from the box and draped them over one arm, Miss America style. Two dozen pink roses, their petals just beginning to unfurl. "Can you open the card?"

Gin slit open the ivory envelope with her thumbnail and read aloud. "Congratulations, Raine! I wish I could be there today to celebrate your graduation, but we'll have a special dinner when you get here on Monday! Love, Sara."

Monday.

A month ago, it had seemed like forever. Now it was approaching like a runaway train. The last few weeks had flown by.

Sue hadn't bounced back from the surgery as quickly as they'd hoped, forcing Gin to work more hours at the diner. Her boss's record keeping was a mess, so Gin divided her time between the kitchen and the office. The first thing she'd done was give Wendell and the waitresses a raise.

She'd taught Wendell how to balance the books, trusting he wouldn't balance them in his favor. Denise had quit, leaving them shorthanded, but Nicki was turning out to be a great waitress, and two high school girls looking for ways to earn some spending money over the summer had filled out applications.

Sue had given her an inch, but Gin had taken the proverbial mile. After closing, she and Wendell rolled a fresh coat of paint on the walls and replaced a broken light fixture. Gin came up with some ideas to draw customers in during the slow times and was surprised when they worked. The guys from the fire department came in regularly—without their captain.

"Mom?" Raine's voice tugged at Gin. "Do we have a vase?"

"I'll take care of it—you finish getting ready so I can have five minutes in the bathroom before we leave."

"Okay!"

Youth was wasted on the young, and apparently so was sarcasm.

Gin couldn't find a vase, but a wide-mouth Mason jar made a decent stand-in. She dashed down the hall to her bedroom, where the green dress she'd bought on clearance at Macy's last spring was waiting for its debut. Shoes were another matter. Why hadn't she thought about shoes?

Because Dan Moretti still took up way too much space in her thoughts, crowding everything else out, that's why. The long hours at the diner, the last minute flurry of activities at the high school—they hadn't pushed him from her mind. Or her heart.

Gin slipped the dress over her head and adjusted the hem.

Raine yanked the door open and peeked in. Her eyes went wide. "You look great, Mom."

Gin turned sideways and pressed her hand against her stomach. Now she remembered why she'd bought the dress. The ruching at the waist covered flaws and provided a little give. The perfect dress for dinner *and* dessert.

"Are you almost ready?" Raine danced away. "I don't want to be late."

"Two minutes." Gin glanced in the mirror. She'd have to leave her hair down . . .

Her heart buckled as another memory washed over her. Dan tugging the elastic band from her ponytail. The warmth of his hands. The satin touch of his lips against hers.

Stop. Thinking. About. Him.

"What are you going to wear for shoes?" Raine was frowning at Gin's bare feet.

"I have to wear shoes?"

Raine grinned. "I'm pretty sure it's in the student handbook under Appropriate Clothing."

"Well, I hope cowboy boots are on that list." Gin, who'd taken a silent inventory of her closet, wasn't joking.

"Because that won't draw any attention." The sparkle died in Raine's eyes, and Gin knew what she was thinking. No matter what they wore, no matter what they did, people would be staring at them.

"This is your day, remember?" Gin pulled Raine in for a hug.

"What about tomorrow?"

Gin pressed a kiss against Raine's temple. "We'll figure that out when it gets here."

Chapter 61

Remember when we were standing in that hallway?"

"I remember we had to talk Max out of swiping the mascot suit from the coach's office and wearing it for the processional."

Dan realized his attempt to coax a smile from Evie had backfired when her eyebrows dipped together. "I forgot about that."

"Well, don't worry." He tried again. "It wouldn't cross Cody's mind to give his valedictorian speech dressed like a bobcat."

Evie didn't answer.

"Eves? Everything okay?"

"Fine." She stared at the stage. "Just feeling a little sentimental today, I guess. The last time Cody wore a cap and gown, he was graduating from kindergarten."

Dan had been in the bleachers that day too.

Someone clapped him on the shoulder. "Thanks for pulling some strings and getting us tickets to this shindig!"

Dan couldn't believe it when Sid and the other guys on Dan's crew claimed the row behind him. The limited space in the gymnasium meant each graduate was only given six tickets to distribute among family and friends.

"As much as I'd like to take the credit, I didn't pull any strings." Dan looked at Evie, who shook her head.

"I gave our extra tickets to your family."

"Well, four of them magically appeared at the station yesterday," Jerry said cheerfully. "Kind of like those cinnamon rolls."

Hopper pulled at his tie. "Can't miss The Codiator's big speech."

Dan smiled at the nickname, given to Cody by the firefighters when he was still in diapers.

"Sorry we're late!" Carissa plunked down beside Dan, and Emily crawled into his lap. He'd expected his parents to attend the commencement ceremony, but not his siblings and their families.

"What did you do?" Dan shifted on the bleacher to make room for his twin sisters. "Tear the tickets in half?"

"Your mother sent an SOS to everyone she knew, begging for leftover tickets." His dad winked at Evie as he sat down.

"And she didn't get one?"

"She's trying to convince Ginevieve to join us," Liz said.

Dan's head turned so fast he almost gave himself a case of whiplash. Ginevieve, stunning in a figure-hugging green dress, her cowboy boots glowing like a freshly waxed floor, stood just inside the doors, talking to his mother.

"You look like you could use a little oxygen, Captain," Jerry whispered in his ear.

Ginevieve's eyes met his across the gymnasium. By the time Dan worked up a smile, she'd looked away.

Dan's mom made her way to the third row—alone.

Ginevieve felt Dan's gaze as she claimed an empty seat near the front of the stage. The principal and several members of the school board were already seated behind a long table on the stage, and a hush fell over the gymnasium as the band began to play the opening notes of the processional.

Gin had graduated from high school, but she'd been six months pregnant with Raine and hadn't been allowed to join her classmates in the commencement ceremony. Her diploma had arrived in the mail a few weeks later without any pomp and circumstance.

She glanced over her shoulder, careful not to make eye contact with Dan as the graduates in their caps and gowns began to file in.

Angela had looked disappointed when Gin turned down her invitation to join the Moretti family, but Gin's emotions simmered close to the surface anyway. Being close to Dan, she ran the risk of having everything she felt for him bubble over, right out there for everyone to see.

Gin was where she belonged—and so was he.

Raine walked past, her gold tassel swaying with each measured step. When she was even with Ginevieve's row, Raine broke protocol and winked at her.

Gin winked back.

The district superintendent congratulated the seniors before turning the microphone over to Mr. Stewart, the tall, gangly principal who reminded Gin of a smooth-shaven Abraham Lincoln.

He beamed down at the graduates. "Before we begin our program today, I would like to introduce this year's valedictorian, Cody Bennett. If you could join me at the podium, Cody?"

The applause was drowned out by the hoots and hollers in section three. Some of Cody's classmates stomped their feet and whistled encouragement. People in the crowd smiled indulgently as Cody, trying to mask his confusion with a smile, joined the principal onstage and shook his hand.

"Every year I have the honor of presenting scholarships awarded to deserving seniors." Mr. Stewart retrieved an envelope from the podium and turned back to Cody. "Banister Falls High School hasn't had a graduating senior receive this particular scholarship until today, which makes the accomplishment even more noteworthy."

Gin sucked in a breath and held it. Had Raine been right? Had Cody changed his mind and accepted the Mansfield Merit Scholarship now that he knew she was leaving?

"Thirteen years ago, the Maxwell Bennett Memorial Scholarship Fund was established to help any senior who chose to pursue a career as a firefighter. This year"—the principal paused to clear his throat—"it is my privilege to present it to Cody Maxwell Bennett."

"Thank you." Cody looked dazed as he accepted the envelope. "I-I know I have some pretty big shoes to fill, but I'm looking forward to the challenge."

Gin blinked back the tears that sprang to her eyes. Because Cody was looking at Dan when he said it.

Dan lost sight of Ginevieve and Raine in the crush when the ceremony ended. "I'll be back in a few minutes," he told his sisters.

"The class is meeting outside for a group photo," Evie told him. "I'd like to take a few pictures too."

"Should I meet you over there?"

Evie looked surprised he'd asked. So maybe she wasn't as furious with him as he thought.

The Maxwell Bennett Memorial Scholarship. You'd think the captain of the city fire department would have known that Cody was a nominee.

"Dan?" His mom snagged his elbow as he sidled past the rest of his family.

"I left something in the truck." On purpose.

"I baked a cake for Cody, and I thought you might like to invite Ginevieve and Raine over for the afternoon."

"Raine and Cody broke up, Mom."

"I know . . . but Evie told me they still spend time together."

Angela held his gaze. "Seems to me those two teenagers have more sense than a lot of adults I know."

Dan wasn't going to touch that one. "I'll ask her, but don't count on it."

The mayor stopped Dan as he made his way back to the courtyard. "Looks like you're going to have someone vying for your job in a few years!"

"Looks that way." Dan spotted Raine and Ginevieve, standing at the edge of the cobblestone courtyard while families posed for pictures in front of the gazebo.

The sunlight picked out shiny threads of copper in Ginevieve's hair, and she was smiling at something Raine had said.

Raine saw him first. "Dan!"

"Congratulations." Dan wrapped the girl in a hug.

"Thanks." Raine laughed. "I think Mom was more nervous than I was."

Dan battened down his emotional hatches and looked at Gin. "How is Sue doing?"

"Bossy. Complaining about everything."

"So back to normal, huh?"

Gin's husky laugh pushed Dan's heart into overdrive. "Exactly."

"Will you take our picture, Dan?" Raine held out her camera.

"Sure." Dan welcomed the interruption. He was frustrated by the small talk even as he hung on every word Gin said. He missed her honesty. Missed the impatient tap of her cowboy boot. Missed *her.*

"Come on, Mom." Raine grabbed Gin's arm and towed her toward the gazebo.

Dan looked through the lens; it provided the perfect excuse to stare at Ginevieve without getting himself in trouble.

He snapped several pictures and handed the camera to Raine. "Mom is having everyone over for cake and ice cream this afternoon. You're welcome to join us."

Raine's smile faded as she glanced at her mom.

"We better not." Ginevieve tucked the camera in her purse. "We have some last-minute packing."

Dan had anticipated her answer, but that didn't stop disappointment from leaving a bitter taste in his mouth. "When are you leaving?"

"Monday morning."

"Do you need a ride to the airport?" Dan heard himself say.

"Nicki is going to take us. Her ex-boyfriend is holding her car hostage to get her to come back to him, so I told her she could use mine."

She'd turned Jasmine's keys over to Nicki.

"Okay." *Okay.*

"Tell your mom and dad thank you." Gin was already backing away from him.

"I will."

She didn't say good-bye, but Dan's hope slipped another notch.

Because he saw it in her eyes.

Chapter 62

The rising sun cast a pink glow in the sky as Dan hopped out of his truck.

Dozens of tiny flags and crosses made up of red, white, and blue flowers dotted the gravesites, but no one other than the grounds-keeper had ventured out this early. Dan had picked this hour of the day on purpose.

He knew Max wasn't here. People referred to the cemetery as a person's final resting place, but his buddy was in heaven, not locked in a grave. Still, the marble headstone gave Dan something solid to lean against when the memories became more fragile with the passing of time.

He took a shortcut to the massive sugar maple at the base of the hill and saw a flash of blue.

Evie sat on the ground, her back propped against Max's head-stone and a bouquet of daisies across her lap.

Dan hesitated, not sure if he should interrupt her solitude. He knew she visited Max's grave on Memorial Day weekend, but they'd never run into each other before. Before he could retreat, Evie spotted him. She lifted one hand and beckoned him over.

"I didn't realize you'd be here this early." Dan closed the distance between them and ignored the dew sparkling in the grass as he sat down beside her.

"I couldn't sleep."

Dan had a pretty good idea why. He and Evie hadn't had an opportunity to talk about Cody's announcement all weekend. There were too many people at his parents' house to broach the subject on Saturday. On Sunday, Dan had volunteered to fill in for one of the firefighters who'd been called away for a family emergency.

He released a slow breath. "I didn't have anything to do with that scholarship. I was as shocked as you were."

"I wasn't shocked, Danny."

"You weren't?" Because he'd almost fallen off the bleachers when the principal made the announcement.

"I was the one who called Chief Larson last Friday and put in Cody's name for the scholarship," Evie admitted. "He met all the criteria. The chief must have contacted Mr. Stewart before the ceremony."

Dan felt his jaw come unhinged. "You're okay with Cody staying in Banister Falls? Becoming a firefighter?"

"He is an adult, something he reminded me of last night. As you know, Cody can be pretty persuasive."

Dan heard a strange inflection in Evie's voice and felt a stab of alarm. "What?"

"He's proposing to Raine this morning."

Dan felt the ground shift underneath him. *"Proposing?"*

"Probably as we speak." Evie looked down at her hand. Her *bare* hand. A thin white line marked the spot where her wedding ring had been. "I married Max when I was eighteen, and Cody was born eleven months later. Which, I might add, he also pointed out last night."

"You gave him your ring."

"And my blessing."

That must have been some conversation.

"I know, I was kind of shocked too." Evie read his mind. "But life has been full of surprises lately."

"I'm sorry." Dan knew she thrived on routine.

"Me too. For a lot of things." Her gaze dropped to the daisies in her lap. "After Max died, you know our family and most of our friends assumed we'd eventually get married."

"I know." There was no point in denying it, but Dan wondered where she was going with this.

"I thought about it," Evie went on candidly. "You and I, we grew up together. Max was your best friend, and you loved Cody like he was your own son. Everyone would have understood, but it wouldn't have been fair."

"Because you felt like you were betraying Max."

"Because my heart . . . it just kind of froze up after Max died. You deserved so much more than what I could give you." Evie's cheeks turned pink. "When I invited you over for dinner. When I tried to—"

"Eves." Dan cut her off in an attempt to spare them both the awkward memories of that night. "We don't have to go there."

"I think we do." Evie didn't back down. "I've been so confused and angry about everything that's happened over the past few months. I guess I wanted to make sure there was something I could still count on."

"You can count on me. I've always been there for you and I always will be. Not because of Max . . . because you gave me your favorite pink shovel when mine broke in the sandbox."

Dan's miserable attempt to inject a little humor didn't lighten the serious look in Evie's eyes. Or reroute the conversation onto safer, more comfortable ground.

"But you didn't kiss me. Why?"

Dan plucked at a blade of grass while he searched for an explanation that wouldn't hurt her feelings.

"Fine." Evie's lips turned up at the corners. "I'll tell you why. It didn't feel right, did it?"

"No," he said quietly.

The smile moved to her eyes. "When *did* it feel right?"

When he'd kissed Ginevieve. Dan couldn't have stopped himself from reaching out to her, from drawing her into his arms, any more than he could have stopped his heart midbeat.

Now *he* was blushing.

"That's why it wouldn't have been fair to you," Evie said softly. "We're friends, good friends, and we love each other. But it isn't the kind of love I felt for Max. And . . ." Evie's gaze held his. "I don't think it's the kind you feel for Ginevieve, either."

Dan groaned. "Is it that obvious?"

"When I saw the way you two looked at each other, I knew."

Looked at each other?

"Ginevieve doesn't feel the same way about me."

Evie's mouth dropped open. "What makes you say that?"

"Um . . . the fact she's leaving in about two hours?"

"Have you asked her to stay?"

"I—it's not that simple. *Ginevieve* isn't simple."

"So you're going to give up without a fight?" Evie demanded. "Cody isn't sure what Raine's answer is going to be, but he's proposing because he wants her to know how he feels."

"He's afraid she won't come back," Dan muttered. "Cody thinks Raine is operating under the misguided notion that he's better off without her."

"Did it ever occur to you that Ginevieve feels the same way? About you?"

No, it hadn't. Not until now.

"She loves you, Danny."

"She doesn't trust me. You don't know what she's been through. Ginevieve . . . she's been hurt by the people who should have protected her."

"Then maybe she doesn't trust herself."

Evie's words sparked a warmth that radiated through Dan's chest.

Is she right, God? Is it time to tell Ginevieve how I feel about her?

Dan closed his eyes, half afraid he would hear that familiar command to wait.

"Do you know what else I think?" It was Evie again.

"What?"

"I think that two eighteen-year-old kids have more faith, more courage, than we do."

Dan rose to his feet and smiled down at her. "We can't have that, can we?"

Evie pointed a finger at the hill. "Go."

Go.

Dan didn't have to be told three times. He sprinted toward his truck.

Chapter 63

Raine lay on the floor of the tree house, staring up at the odd-shaped pieces of sky framed in the rafters while her heart framed the memory.

Her mom would want to kill her when she woke up and realized Raine was gone, but she'd left a note on the kitchen table promising to be back in an hour. Their flight was scheduled to leave at eleven, but Raine had to come up here one more time. Alone.

The baby stirred, a flutter as soft as the breeze that trickled through the piece of canvas over the door.

"Hello," she whispered.

"Hello."

Raine shrieked and rolled onto her knees as Cody crawled inside the tree house.

"You're a little jumpy today." He flopped down beside her.

Raine scooted away from him. "I said I didn't want you to go to the airport with me!"

"This isn't the airport."

"What are you doing here? We said good-bye yesterday."

"I don't want to say good-bye."

Raine braided her fingers together so she wouldn't reach for him. "Going to Maine is the right thing to do. We both need some time to think."

"I already did." Cody's fingers unfurled, revealing a diamond ring cradled in the palm of his hand. "Marry me, Wats."

Raine couldn't breathe.

"I can't." Why was he making this so difficult? "You'd be giving up your life."

"What if this is the life I'm supposed to have?"

"You don't have to do this." Tears clogged Raine's nose and throat and began to leak out her eyes. "Even if I stay in Maine, we'll work something out. I-I know you want to watch our baby grow up."

"Yeah." Cody brushed away one of the tears that rolled down her cheek. Smiled that lopsided smile. "But I want to watch you grow up too."

Chapter 64

Come on, Raine. We're going to miss our flight.

Gin stowed her carry-on in the backseat because the latch on the trunk was being persnickety again. Right before she closed the door, she heard her cell phone ringing in the depths of her purse.

Raine's name and number came up on the screen, and Gin didn't bother with pleasantries. "Where are you?"

"Mom . . ." Raine's voice was shaky, and suddenly Gin was too. "I'm with Cody."

Gin closed her eyes. "Are you okay?"

"Better than okay . . ." A sniffle. Yup, that was convincing. "Cody, he . . . he proposed, Mom. We're going to get married."

"Married." Gin sagged against Jasmine's rusty bumper. "Yesterday you weren't even dating!"

"I know." Gin heard the smile break through. "But we'll get things right from now on . . . here. Cody wants to talk to you."

Sirens began to wail in the distance. Ambulance? Police? Fire? Gin couldn't tell one from the other. She tried to see through the barricade of trees between Fifth Avenue and Birch Street and saw a flash of red and blue lights. Squad car. In spite of the bomb Raine had just dropped, Gin felt a little better.

"Hi, Mom." Cody's cheerful voice came on the line.

Oh, he wasn't going to get off that easy. "You're eighteen years old."

"Eighteen and ten months, actually."

No wonder Raine had accepted his proposal. How could anyone resist that wholesome blend of sweet and sincere? "Where are you planning to live after you're married?"

"I'm going to ask Mr. and Mrs. Moretti if we can rent the house next door. I'm sure he'll give us a break in the rent if I help him fix it up on the weekends."

Gin felt something welling up inside her. Laughter? Tears? She wasn't sure which it would be.

"Does your mom know?"

"I told her last night. She said I couldn't propose without a ring." Cody cleared his throat. "She gave me the diamond Dad gave to her."

Tears. Definitely tears.

Gin dragged the back of her hand across her face. "You know this isn't going to be easy."

"It doesn't have to be easy to be good," Cody said. "I love Raine . . . and I'll be a good dad."

He would—because Dan had shown him how.

Dan.

Did he know yet?

"Mom?" It was Raine again. "What time does our plane leave again?"

"My plane leaves at eleven. Your plane leaves after you and Cody have had a chance to talk some more."

"Really?" Raine's piercing squeal almost put a hole through Gin's eardrum. "You don't mind if I change my flight?"

"You and Cody have a lot to talk about, and so do Sara and I. It might be good to have a few days together, just the two of us."

"Thankyouthankyouthankyou."

In the background, Gin heard Cody saying something.

"Cody wants to know if you're sure you don't mind going alone."

Gin felt the spring breeze caress her cheek and lifted her face to the sun. "I'm not."

"Love you, Mom," Raine whispered.

"Love you too." *To the moon and back.*

Gin locked the trailer, called Nicki to tell her there'd been a change in plans, and took a cab to the airport. She stared out the window, letting the breeze sift through the window and untangle her thoughts, one at a time.

Raine, getting married. Raine, staying in Banister Falls.

Could she move two thousand miles away from her daughter? Her first grandchild? Could she be so close to Dan and pretend she wasn't crazy in love with him? Because that was the only way to describe it. Crazy.

Gin wheeled the carry-on into the small terminal and tightened her hold on the orchid Dan's father had given to her. The flower caused a delay in security and a chorus of sighs from the people in line behind her, but there was no way she was leaving it behind.

Her conversation with Raine had eaten away most of the time, so the passengers with priority boarding were already standing at the gate when Gin reached it.

She bought an overpriced bottle of water from the vending machine and got in line.

God . . . Gin paused, glad He was patient with the frequent starts and stops of her prayers . . . *I'm glad You're here. I can't do this without You.*

Some men, when trying to convince a woman they loved her, made a grand gesture. This was an act of desperation.

The call had come in when Dan was leaving the cemetery. A

two-vehicle accident at an intersection ordinarily wouldn't involve the fire department, but when one of the vehicles happened to be a propane truck, no one was going to take any chances. The firefighter Dan had filled in for the day before hadn't returned to work, so they were short one crew member.

Dan banged his forehead against the steering wheel before he turned his truck around and headed to the station.

The crew remained at the scene until they were sure the propane truck wasn't in any danger of exploding, but the delay had brought him dangerously close to Ginevieve's departure time.

Dan had tried to reach her on her cell, but it went right to voicemail. A quick call to Cody confirmed that Ginevieve's plans to fly to Maine hadn't changed.

Was she on the plane already?

He'd called in a rare favor—it helped to be on a first-name basis with the people who worked airport security—and been granted permission to park the fire truck next to the small terminal, but the ground crew was already loading luggage into the cargo hold of the plane. He couldn't get any closer, and he'd never be allowed to get through security without a ticket. Dan didn't even have time to *purchase* a ticket.

A feeling of helplessness, one Dan hadn't felt since he'd realized Max was trapped in a burning house, washed over him.

What do I do now, God?

When Dan opened his eyes, he saw a preschool boy framed in the window, staring down at him. A wide grin split the kid's face, and he began to pound on the glass.

Dan was attracting attention, all right, but not exactly the kind he'd had in mind.

But it did give him an idea.

He found a piece of cardboard in the back of the truck and continued to pray as he scrawled one word on it.

A little boy's cry of glee drowned out the music filtering from the speaker system. "Fire truck!"

Gin glanced over and saw a harried young mother try to shush him. The boy slapped his hands against the window instead, earning a dozen disgruntled looks from the people seated around them.

"Check this out!" A young woman wearing a UW-Madison hoodie lifted her cell phone and snapped a picture of something on the tarmac.

"Section C may begin boarding at this time."

The line moved, and Gin glanced at her seat number on the boarding pass. A small crowd had started to gather at the window.

"Hey, is there anyone here named Ginevieve?"

Gin turned toward the voice.

It was the girl with the cell phone. "Are you Ginevieve?"

Now everyone was looking at her.

"Yes, but—"

"Next in line, please."

Gin realized the attendant was waiting for her. She gave the woman her boarding pass and an apologetic smile.

"Come here!" The mother of the little boy was waving her over. "You have to see this!"

"You're all set, ma'am." The attendant smiled back at Gin, oblivious to the commotion going on around them. "Enjoy your—"

"Excuse me for a second."

The hammer of Gin's heart drowned out the laughter from the people who stepped aside to make room for her.

Gin's hand covered her mouth as she looked down and saw the fire truck parked below the window. Dan stood in front of it, still wearing his turnout gear.

Her gaze snagged with his for a split second before dropping to the cardboard sign he held: *Ginevieve.*

She had no idea what Dan wanted. If he'd come to say good-bye, why hadn't he written the word on the sign instead of her *name*?

What was she supposed to do with that?

The man who'd been behind Gin in line called to her. "Make a decision, lady. Are you getting on the plane or what?"

Make a decision.

Gin clutched the orchid against her chest as fear and hope battled for control. She'd done the fear thing all her life, letting it push her from place to place. But hope, the thing Gin had always thought so fragile, suddenly felt strong enough to . . . to *hold.*

And gave her the courage to choose the "or what."

The crowd at the window fell back, and Dan's heart dropped to the toes of his boots. They must be boarding . . .

But suddenly, there she was, looking down at him.

Looking at him like he'd totally lost his mind.

Ginevieve didn't move. Didn't smile. And then she . . . she disappeared.

A guy in a business suit peered out and gave Dan a thumbs-up. It was all he needed.

The automatic doors slid open and Dan jogged through them, startling everyone in his path along with the ticket agents stationed behind the counter.

Dan cringed. Oh. Right. A firefighter running into an airport. Probably not a good idea.

"Everything is fine." Dan cast a reassuring smile at a young family and nodded at the burly TSA agent as he made his way to the escalator.

Ginevieve had chosen the stairs instead, taking them two at a time, her ponytail swinging at her shoulder.

Dan was *really* looking forward to taking that little elastic thing out again.

She stopped a foot away from him, using the orchid his dad had given her as a shield.

"What. Are you. Doing?" Green eyes roamed over Dan's face, his body. Making sure he was okay. He felt every single glance like a physical touch.

Dan pulled her into his arms, suitcase and orchid and all, and kissed her as the loudspeaker crackled to life above their heads.

"This is the final boarding call for Flight 1284 to Chicago O'Hare," a voice droned.

Dan lifted his head and smiled when Ginevieve clung to him. Maybe it was a little pirate-like to take advantage of the dazed look in her eyes, but in this situation, Dan figured Mrs. Bardowski would understand.

"I'll follow you to Maine. I'll be waiting right here when you come home." Dan couldn't resist kissing the freckle on her cheekbone again. "Just tell me what I have to do to convince you that I love you."

The suitcase hit the floor. "You just did."

"The following you part or the waiting right here part?"

"The home part," Ginevieve whispered.

"Would Ginevieve Lightly please come to Gate B4?" the voice persisted.

"Ginevieve Lightly." Ginevieve tipped her head back and addressed the ceiling. "Has other plans."

"Care to share those plans?" Dan teased.

A smile that bordered on shy touched the corners of Ginevieve's lips. "To love you back."

Forget following or waiting. Dan wasn't going to let her out of his sight.

He dipped his head and nuzzled Ginevieve's ear. "I have some plans of my own, you know."

"What?" She sounded a little breathless, and Dan smiled.

"You'll just have to trust me."

Ginevieve melted against him, her eyes shining with a light Dan had never seen before.

"I'm looking forward to it."

Discussion Questions

1. Ginevieve Lightly ended up in Banister Falls when she and her daughter, Raine, were on their way to Minneapolis. Have you ever experienced an unexpected "detour" in your personal journey that had you questioning God's plans and purposes? What were the circumstances? The outcome?
2. In what ways did Dan and Evie's friendship help the healing process after Max died? In what ways did it hinder it?
3. Gin told Dan that she and Evie were "apples and oranges" even though they were both single moms. What impact do you think their different backgrounds and experiences had on the two women? How were they alike?
4. What was the turning point in Gin and Dan's relationship? Why do you think Dan was able to share on a deeper level with Gin than he could with Evie, his childhood friend?
5. From the time Gin was a child, no one really looked out for her best interests. Who are some of the people in your life who cared about you? Protected you? What are some of the barriers people use to protect themselves from being hurt?
6. Discuss how each of these characters viewed God. Raine. Cody. Ginevieve. Evie. Dan. Does their perception change over the course of the book? In what way?

7. Which character could you relate to the most? Why?
8. Evie tells Dan that she thinks "two eighteen-year-old kids have more faith, more courage, than we do". What do you think she meant? Do you agree?
9. How did you feel about Cody's proposal? What do you think Cody and Raine's greatest challenge will be?
10. "You do whatever you have to do so they know you love them." Share a situation where this became true in your own life.

Acknowledgments

The writing life is strange . . . sometimes I tell people that I spend most of the day alone in a room, listening to the "voices" in my head—but that isn't completely true! I might be putting the words on paper, but you are holding this book in your hands because an amazing group of people loved these characters as much as I do.

A heartfelt THANK YOU to Daisy Hutton, who leads the talented, creative team at HarperCollins Christian Publishing and gave me the opportunity to tell Dan and Gin's story. My editor, Becky Monds, for your insight, enthusiasm, and encouragement along the way. And to LB Norton—you can deny it all you want to, but you still make me look good!

I couldn't do any of this without the love and support of my family and friends. Thank you for praying for me, laughing with me, and answering the phone even when you KNOW I'm going to sniffle and whine because I fell into a plot hole or wrote myself into a corner. I owe you chocolate. Lots of chocolate. And especially to my Mom . . . my first reader, faithful prayer warrior, and number one cheerleader. You aren't afraid to ask the tough questions (or use your red pen!) and both push me toward excellence.

Thank you to Lt. Randy Pecard at the Marinette Fire

Department for taking me on a tour of the station and patiently answering my questions—and letting me sit in the fire truck! It helped bring Dan and his crew at the Second Street Station to life. Any mistakes are mine.

And, always, to Pete, my very own hero, champion, and best friend. If you hadn't given me the freedom to pursue my dream, well, you probably wouldn't be eating take-out as often! Looking forward to our next chapter. ☺

About the Author

Kathryn Springer is a *USA Today* bestselling author. She grew up in northern Wisconsin, where her parents published a weekly newspaper. As a child she spent many hours sitting at her mother's typewriter, plunking out stories, and credits her parents for instilling in her a love of books—which eventually turned into a desire to tell stories of her own. Kathryn has written nineteen books with close to two million copies sold. She lives with her husband and three children in Marinette, Wisconsin. Facebook: Kathrynspringerauthor

You are cordially invited to a September Wedding . . .

A September Bride

A Year of Weddings Novella